They all cried, his mummy screamed with pain,
appeared to have been struck down, the blood had drained
from his face, he had become an old man in minutes.
Michael held tightly to his father's neck, he joined in the
crying game and sobbed 'sorry' in his father's ear.

"There, there!" his father had comforted, "no one will take
you away from us." He squeezed his son and sobbed, "Oh
my darling boy, how could we have been so...so stupid as to
let you both alone by the pond? It was only a minute." His
tears ran down his face and washed away his son's fear.

There was the ambulance that came and went; then a police
man. Michael could hear his daddy talking through the
study door. Then his daddy held his hand and they sat down
in the wood lined, leather bound study.

"What did you see, in the garden?" Asked the police man.

Michael sank his head into his father's chest. He clenched
his eyes shut.

"Did you see Emma when you were in the garden?" The
policeman asked again, very quietly.

"Is Emma dead?" asked Michael.

"Yes" replied his dad, "We've lost our little Emma."

They all burst into loud wailing, the police man shifted in the
chair. He coughed, and asked Michael once more, "Did you
see Emma near the pond Michael?"

Michael just held his daddy tight.

"For God's sake man, leave the child alone, can't you see he's traumatised, we're all traumatised, leave him alone, I told you I found him in the greenhouse.... just leave him alone."

With that the policeman stood, shook hands with Robbie, muttered his sympathies, muttered about the Coroner's Officer and made his way out.

There followed in the Johnson household the rituals of grief, death, social ceremony and a darkness that enveloped them all.

Michael knew that he could be the light to awaken his parents love and then they would be alright again. They seemed to know that too.

From that day on Michael reigned supreme as the apple of his parents' eye, he was the centre of their lives and the focus of their undivided love.

There had been talk of another little brother or sister for Michael, but it had never come to pass. As time passed so Michael was nurtured and developed as his parents had planned; the very best prep school, then to Dad's old school in Wiltshire.

The Poisoned Banquet

Anthony James

ACKNOWLEDGMENTS

To the distinguished Psychiatrist
James J Cockburn MA FRCPI FRCPsych
my thanks for his detailed support and research papers on
morbid jealousy, without which this novel would be much
less insightful in painting portraits of victims and
perpetrators of domestic violence.
The Management of The Royal Albert Hall for giving me
access to roam in the dressing rooms and the stage as well
as allowing me to play the piano in the green room. My
thanks to my good friend Martin Gain who labored long
and hard, editing.
To my wife Dawn for all her love that sustains me.

Chapter 1

He watched as the black and white petticoat, that looked for all the world like the tail of a diving duck, twitch and then float still. The sun sparkled through the willow tree, it was an idyllic day; the mallards scattered, startled, as eight year old Michael Johnson peeped from the grasses that lined the pond.

Then he ran, as fast as his little legs would carry him to the far end of the garden, down to the old greenhouse and started to line up the empty pots. He concentrated hard, trying to clear his mind, counting the green pots and the brown pots and putting them into strict lines graduated in size. He knew he mustn't cry, after all it was Emma who wanted to play near the pond. When he had finished lining up the pots, which took quite a while, he felt grandpa would be pleased with him.

And then the screams began, but Michael shut his ears, and counted the pots one more time, indeed he had hardly finished when his father crashed through the door, and seized him up in a wild embrace.

"Mikey, Mikey, your sister, you were to look after little Emma, it was only a minute." The tears poured down Robbie Johnson's face; his son so innocent, so bemused. He clung to his little Michael and swept him back to the house – it was chaos.

His infancy wrought in the nightmares of Emma's death. Night after night he would wake screaming, always to be comforted in the arms of his beloved mother. Despite this he was a strong boy, aware that he was secure in his parents' love, the sole recipient of their devotion. He grew into an even stronger young man who excelled at sport and was no slouch at his school work. He was a leader who looked after his friends and colleagues, they willingly followed him, he was kind and considerate to those less gifted than himself, and in so doing built a fiercely loyal group of followers. But woe betide those who were outside his clan, with them he was ruthless; if these outsiders dared to compete, then Michael would mobilise his followers and the results were inevitably in Michael's favour. He was earmarked for Cambridge after becoming Head Boy and Captain of the school's renowned rugby team.

At school it was said of him; "He has the makings of a fine citizen, and the leadership skills to become an important influence in any field he chooses to pursue."

His House Master, Tim Walker, though, saw that beside the charm there was in Michael Johnson a ruthlessness; a determination, an ambition that transcended the ordinary. Even Walker had to admit that his suspicions could not be corroborated. Perhaps, he was subliminally jealous of this almost perfect student who seemed to sweep all before him.

Michael had grown to be fine looking young man, reminiscent of his father Robbie, with an athletic gait and handsome face. His humour too was engaging, though he was always self effacing and if you watched carefully, he was a stealthy observer of his peers.

Despite Michael's apparent serene progress, his nightmares came – always the same –night after night, year after year; Emma's contorted face staring up at him from the dark pond.

Michael's mother Tania adored him, and his relationships with women developed slowly but surely. His awkward teens saw him throw much of his energy into excelling at sport. He was sixteen when one day he happened on his parents in one of their more intimate moments, in an instant he had hated his father. In the maelstrom of his hormones he was jealous and angry. The boy started his journey to manhood, confused and jealous and it was not until he met Elizabeth that he quenched the fire that burned within him.
At seventeen Michael had lost his virginity in a startling and awakening episode with his second cousin Elizabeth, who was seven years his senior, from that day on the conquering of the opposite sex became one of Michael's measures of success.

Elizabeth had given and Elizabeth had taken away, it took Michael months to 'get over' her. When he went to her wedding, two and a bit years later, he had winked at her as she walked down the aisle of the Church. Later she had taken him aside and slapped his face and told him in no uncertain terms that their dalliance had been a mistake and she loathed the very idea of that shameful adventure. Michael had raged; raged within himself. He vowed that no women would demean him ever again. Oh Emma, had she not paid for all the girls and women who had taken away his rightful gifts!

From that day on Michael continued his conquest of the opposite sex with obsessive dedication, planning how to make them love him. He believed, however ephemerally, that he loved them too but there was always the steely determination to love them and leave them, always on his own terms. Many of the girls adored him; he was witty, handsome and generous. The list grew ever longer.

Michael knew his obligations to his mother and father; he knew what they expected, and each day, ever since that day in his grandfather's garden, he determined he would make them proud. He was aware of his gifts; he found school work if not easy then certainly engaging, team games came easily and he wanted so much to please Robbie, his dad, and go on to Cambridge and get a 'Blue'.

Despite his social graces, only a few, including his parents knew of his darker moods. Michael could be obstinate and determined; he even manipulated his mother and father, doing it so instinctively, so cleverly, that they hardly knew that on occasions he set them against each other.

Robbie, Michael's father, loved his boy, but from time to time he saw in him a glimpse of cockiness that he found distasteful. He wished some times that Michael would be less assured, less accomplished, but there was much to make him a proud father.

His mother Tania though, worshipped the ground that Michael trod, her faith and love were unshakeable.

Michael duly arrived at Cambridge, in the same College where his father had studied before him. He thrived both academically and on the sports field, it seemed that nothing was going to prevent Michaels' ascent, as his school teachers had foretold.

The first time Michael set eyes on Rachel George, was at University. In the clubhouse, the university sports bar pub was crowded and his old friend John Parry was drinking at the bar. At John's side stood the ravishing Rachel; Michael could hardly take his eyes from her, she was beautiful, poised and sexy despite the fact she was wrapped up in a winter leather jacket and green wellington boots.

For once Michael lost a little of his assurance, he felt as if his breath came in short rasps, he slipped from his usual assured opening line. She was so lovely; her golden blonde hair framed her lovely face, as perfect as porcelain yet as delicious as a pin up. She stood five foot something, graceful, feminine but sturdy. Briefly he saw in her the beauty that was one with his mother Tania. This girl was for him, it was love at first sight.

"My word Rachel, you have made a hit. Can I introduce Michael Johnson? "

"Hello Michael, I'm just glad to be in the warm, on this raw winter day." Her smile was enigmatic, just a hint of welcome or was it disdain? She extended her hand.

Michael took it and felt the cool, smooth and gentle but firm handshake, "Don't listen to John, I'm just one of the boys." Once more he was lost for words.

"Rachel is a budding concert pianist, just up with me at Kings for a couple of days. Music, you know Michael, tunes, organs and pianos and things." He turned to Rachel, "Michael is probably the most unmusical man I've ever met, absolutely bloody tone deaf. Go on old boy, have a pint."

"I'm afraid he's right," said Michael rather sheepishly, "I couldn't pretend otherwise, you'd find me out in a minute.... I hope you'll give me chance to make up for it ... my musical .....or non musical self."

"Michael, don't fret there are days when I think I'm not so musical too."

And so they drifted into an easier conversation, the three of them. John Parry sizing up the obvious attraction between the other two, drank his beer, and made a tactical retreat despite Rachel's irresolute objections.

So began the courtship between the two. Michael for once was unable to bed his quarry, though perhaps this lovely girl was not so much his quarry but his lifetime goal. She was, he thought, so comfortable to be with, 'her smile makes me smile, I want to laugh when I hear her voice.' Yet a year passed, and despite Michael's consistent and concentrated efforts Rachel had kept him at bay. Yes, it was true that Michael saw other girls, but for him it was not the same thing at all. These other girls were part of the game of being up at Cambridge. Rachel who was studying at the Royal College of Music in London was an icon of desire that never left him; even now he was nervous when he phoned her. He found it hard to gloss over his lies, and little by little Michael Johnson became a true lover, with no other girls at all.

Another year passed, Michael worked hard toward his finals, he worked and played hard and it was all ultimately in pursuit of Rachel. He would do anything to please her. He listened to hours of classical music; he made weekend visits and hung out with her zany musical chums.

He visited with her parents and that turned out to be quite an event; Rachel's father, Sir Lewis George, was a well connected business man with a hatful of international interests. He was not that old, or so Michael thought, Sir Lewis was handsome but what some might call a little brash. He delighted in Michael when they first met and rejoiced in taking Michael into his study and plying the young man with strong drink.

Rachel's mother was the beautiful but stately Margaret, who was charm personified and who watched Michael like a hawk. Rachel was the only daughter and Margaret lived for her daughter's success and happiness, though she often confused the two.

Amongst Rachel's friends they were, at least to Michael, a bunch of curiosities, her coterie of chums was exclusively drawn from musical circles. How different they were from his colleagues at Cambridge. The most obvious difference was their apparent lack of ambition as he understood it; they were all obsessed with music, their ability to play it, write it or even write about it. Their idea of success had nothing to do with material rewards, city jobs and million dollar bonuses. They hardly expressed interest in sport, it was all so bemusing; politics and philosophy seemed the only common grounds for conversation.

Rachel's girl friends may not have been from his university girl friends, but they were none the less attracted to Michael. Josie Fellowes a voluptuous clarinetist and friend of Rachel's for many years, for one, made no secret of her lust for the gorgeous hunk that was Michael. Annoyingly Rachel just laughed her advances off as being "Just Josie."

That response was typical of Rachel; she was sweet and kind without a nasty thought in her head. She had spent her young life devoted to music since the age of five; and still she worked and worked at her pianistic skills. Music to her was a calling, since her earliest memories music had been her constant focus, the joys and fascination of it; above all, the rhythm of it. Her life was at one with music, her ears aware of the beat of life, she heard music in everything.

 She practised five hours a day and there were very few exceptions. Apart from her mother her closest friend in the world was her personal teacher and guide Eva, an Austrian Jewish lady of some venerable age. Eva had nurtured Rachel's prodigious talent from the outset; Eva was as constant as the northern star, ever present when Rachel was not in College or the Conservatoire, Eva was Rachel's musical anchor the mother of her musical dreams.

Rachel though only twenty one, was something of a seasoned campaigner having figured in, though not been an outright winner of, a number of international piano competitions since she was twelve years old. She was already respected internationally as a classical pianist of the baroque and pre-classical periods.

Perhaps her greatest achievement had been her runner up prize in the Leipzig Bach competition when she was not yet twenty. Despite her success she was liked by all her friends because she was always ready to help other musicians either with individual sessions at the key board, or simply discussing ways forward in their studies. She was the sweet heart of many but the lover of no one. Popular, kind, loved by the girls and sought after by many of the opposite sex.

Boys of course had been a preoccupation she could not entirely avoid; they had been pestering her since she was very young. Her mother, though had been a Rottweiler of a sexual guardian, and Rachel had been brought up to be wary of the opposite sex. At home she had seen the unmistakable signs of her mother's anguish, as her father the jovial Sir Lewis had been a serial adulterer. Somehow all this had been kept as a subliminal undertone, swept under the carpet by her mother. The beautiful Margaret had seemed to settle for wealth and comfort; the price, a faithless husband, a price worth paying.

Of late the matter of her parents' union had become more vexed and when at home she could not help but sense the deepening of the angst between her mother and father. At long last there emerged one lover too many; Jacqui Boswell it seemed would succeed where many had failed; divorce was at hand. This hurt Rachel, it hurt her a lot, and to salve her injuries she turned more to Eva and less to her mother and away from her father, not that he seemed to mind.

Rachel's view of the ardent Michael was ambivalent; yes he was handsome, yes he was charming, he was smart and academically gifted, he was from a good family and no doubt destined for a great career, but he was a man, and her father's betrayal had shaken her faith in all men. She wanted Michael to be the man of her dreams, but her reticence to commit to a relationship dogged her, almost against her own will.

Chapter 2

Throughout his last year at Cambridge, Michael's world was a confused blend of ambition, frustration and exhaustion. His obsession with the apparently unattainable Rachel ate into his heart, he was in love and despite his best efforts to fall out of love and follow his former rakish ways, he failed utterly.

He visited her as often as he could, he was solicitous and restrained; he sensed that if he pushed too hard then she would fly away forever. Sexually she drove him crazy; she was at once sensual but always controlled, so far and no further. Her self-discipline was unfathomable.

There were times when Michael would teeter on the edge of rage, but Rachel would assuage him with what she called her compromise treats. Michael wondered sometimes whether she had other male friends, and when they were apart his jealousy was inflamed by the spectres of his imagination. His desire to have her and hold her was all consuming; it drove his vigour and shored up his resolve.

Michael did all he could to make Rachel love his loveable parents, Tania and Robbie. The parents in turn joined his not so secret conspiracy to make Rachel a member of the family. Robbie adored Rachel from the moment he first saw her and Tania had to admit that this was a fitting partner for her only son.

During the year Michael graduated; just missing a 'First', not that it mattered much, except to his ego, he walked into a job at LONY, a large Merchant Bank in the city.

Rachel was signed up by Music International, one of the largest agencies especially for the classical music scene. In addition to Eva there now stepped into her life, Max Luberoff, the agency's handler manager. Max was in his late fifties, he was of Estonian origin, was markedly eccentric both to look at and in his life style. Rachel got on with him immediately, and so did Eva. Now Rachel's musical future was enclosed by not one but two guardians, three if you included Margaret.

Michael seethed that he was even more of an outsider from her world of music, but his endeavour remained undiminished, his pursuit of Rachel remained his driving raison d'être. He turned up often unannounced where ever she happened to be, after concerts, over in Paris where she spent much of her time continuing her studies.

Rachel was charmed but sometimes unnerved by the unscheduled appearances of her man. There was an element of being stalked that she found mildly threatening. But Michael, always so generous, affectionate, kind and reliable, so persuaded her, that her worries began to ebb away, until they faded almost entirely. His dogged pursuit of her was at once a huge compliment, and eventually she began to trust him, he was such a protecting angel.

The year was an eventful one in many ways; Sir Lewis and Margaret George divorced, the new wife of Sir Lewis was already ensconced. She was the former Jacqui Boswell, some fifteen years younger than Margaret, who now lived with her new husband, Sir Lewis, in a Knightsbridge apartment. Margaret was of course left well accoutred and comfortable in the former marital home. She confessed to Rachel that she was relieved at no longer having to live with lies and deceit.

Despite her mother's divorce, Rachel at last made her mind up, Michael would be the one for her. She would admit him to herself, along with J.S.Bach, Eva, and Becky her piano, her world would become complete.

And so they married with great pomp and ceremony as befits the son and daughter of two wealthy London families. As the daughter of a knight of the realm they married in St Paul's. Everything was perfect.

The service ended with the mighty Cathedral organ thundering the Widor toccata, Michael with his lovely wife were invincible; Michael, already on the Mergers and Acquisition team at the Bank and Rachel, devoted to her burgeoning international career. 'Hello' magazine had done a deal that would swell the pages of their prurient publication and the pictures of the fairy tale couple, would be gobbled up by a million readers.

There had been just one area of contention surrounding the wedding; Rachel's maiden name George would be retained post wedding on the insistence of her Agent, Max Luberoff.

Eva of course had agreed with this initiative; Eva, who had taken Rachel under her wing when she was tiny child, had ensured she was accepted into the Menuhin School, to the Royal College in London and later to the Paris Conservatoire where she continued her studies. For years Eva had defined Rachel's life, what she did and when she did it. That is until Michael had been let in to her consciousness.

At the reception a quartet of Rachel's friends from the Conservatoire played a jaunty and mischievous 'Here comes the bride' out of key, as a welcome for the bride and groom.

There followed a line of the most glamorous and wealthy of London and musical society. Max Luberoff dallied too long, drooling over his client bride and aggravating Michael; who could never fathom this Svengali-like relationship between the odious Max and Rachel.

"She must have somewhere to practise, perhaps not four hours but at least two; remember we have some important engagements for my Rachel when you return"

"Firstly Max, she's my Rachel, and Rachel will decide where, when and if she wants to practise" The sudden sting of possessiveness cut the atmosphere like a knife.

"Of course Max, you needn't worry I'll be a good girl."

"I hope not too good" Michael laughed, the tension banished. Max moved reluctantly on.

"Darling, you mustn't mind Max, he's very important to me and he's a wonderful man, more of an uncle really."

"A lecherous old uncle, I wouldn't wonder" Michael snarled through his reception - line fixed smile.

"Don't be a bastard Michael," she ventriloquized back, "Max is Max and he'll only ever love music and little boys."

After the wedding they stayed at a London hotel quite close by. There they stayed not overly drunken or even sumptuously fed, just in love. Rachel undressed and wanted very much to be held and loved, but Michael held her at bay,

"Let me look at you, you take my breath away" – "You're so beautiful, and you're mine." He sang this last phrase and laughed. He took her in his arms and buried his love, contained his lust and consummated a union he was sure, was made in heaven. They loved one another with all the excitement of brand new lovers, yet with the patience and the kindness implicit in their new union. Their lovemaking, from this tender start, gathered a frenzied momentum, as they moved from tenderness, to indulgence, to the fringes of selfishness.

Rachel responded drinking in the passion urging him to deeper intimacy, and throughout a night of tumultuous physical passion gave everything she had. She gave without reserve; yet she gave not only as a commitment; but as a token of an unbreakable bond; that this man would be hers forever.

The following morning the young lovers Mr. and Mrs. Michael George Johnson rather tired but relaxed after their night of carnal bliss made their way from London to Venice. Was there a more romantic spot in the world?

Michael ruminated about music, could he compete with her love of music? Would he, could he share this wife, this love; with her teachers, her agents and her adoring fans? True there were few just now, but it was obvious that once she'd had the break and got that recording contract, the record company would push not only her musical talent but also her sex appeal.

In Venice, over her glass, she saw her husband with his dark brown eyes his almost jet black hair, his crooked nose. They could stare into each other's eyes with complete comfort, just dreaming of tomorrow together. Sometimes she found the intensity of his love for her daunting. He was so strong and yet so gentle with her. He was strong physically, he weighed some 190 pounds and none of it was spare.

Since they decided to marry, Michael, his first goal achieved, had worked with a passion and had become nakedly ambitious. She worried that perhaps one day he would challenge her musical world and all its ferocious demands. But all that was for the future.

It was on their second evening of their honeymoon that the first sign of conflict surfaced; Rachel waited until Michael had downed his nightcap, before she mentioned her arrangement.

"What do you think if we have a relaxed day tomorrow, I thought I might have a few minutes practice, won't be long say half an hour?" She resumed playing with her goblet.

"I'm all for relaxing sweet heart," his face was neutral. "But must you practise tomorrow we've hardly got away from all that, and you won't be able to practise on the yacht"

"Just so my darling," she smiled her sweetest smile, "I'd better do some when I can".

He poured another Cognac. That night, like the last, was a delight of mingling intimacy, another lesson in the road to oneness, but just the hint of selfish urgency from Michael. They slept longer and deeper. They awoke refreshed and after a light breakfast Rachel strolled to the empty bar and found the piano.

Rachel sat there alone closed her eyes and immediately made contact with the other love of her life, Johann Sebastian Bach. When she stopped she found that the terrace outside the bar was jam packed and the corridor also full of guests and staff. There was a spontaneous round of applause, much shouting and even cries of encore. She blushed. The Duty Manager rushed in with an iced glass of water that he placed near at hand with an extravagant bow.

She gathered herself and launched into a Vivaldi sonata that once more brought the house down. This time, as she finished, Michael was standing there, smiling a curious smile that she had not seen before; there seemed a sour edge to it.

"That's enough now darling, I've arranged a gondola ride and then lunch"

Uncertain she rose, pecked him on the cheek, muttered that she would only be a moment and made her way through the crowd of her delighted impromptu audience.

He followed her up to the suite; "How is the piano?"

"Better than I expected, really rather good, I bet it's delicious for swing and standard jazz. Tonight why don't we listen to the resident cocktail pianist, they say he's good."

"You can't be serious darling; you can't listen to some hack….."

"Michael don't be such a snob, there are thousands of pianists as good as me, many better playing in places like this. I like to hear other people make music, their way... that's what music is about, people doing it their way"

"All right Maestro I don't want a haranguing thank you."

They set off to see the sights with just a hint of coolness between them.

Their stay in Venice was punctuated by Rachel's morning concerts and the attendants fuss that so aggravated Michael. However by their fourth day he seemed reconciled to the celebrity status of his wife. Their fellow guests now jockeyed for position each day at ten o'clock anticipating Rachel's practice session. The couple were closely watched at breakfast to ensure that their fellow guests did not miss out on this splendid but free musical treat. The front desk Manager had even arranged seats on the terrace and had left the bar terrace windows ajar so that the audience got the best possible sound.

Rachel, for her part, took it in good humour and despite her best intentions she deviated from her normal practice routine and couldn't help but show off a bit.

Their last morning they left early by launch down to the Lido where they joined the Sea Witch; a 22 metre Scorpio 72 Clipper. She was beautiful, long and sleek with three masts a teak deck and spacious sunken cockpit. The yacht belonged to an associate of Rachel's father, though the boat was registered in Bahrain, the Skipper was English. Bob Carey greeted the couple with a charm that brought together deference and a quiet authority. He was about forty five with bright blue eyes and greying dark hair. He wore immaculate white trousers and short-sleeved shirt and a traditional marine peaked hat.

He struck Rachel as an attractive, competent and thoroughly trustworthy seaman. Michael also took an immediate liking to this mariner with a Cornish burr and a ready smile. There were two other crew members; the cook, the very attractive and tanned Olga Carey the skipper's wife and a shy young mate called Lavro. Lavro was Croatian and had been on the Sea Witch for just a few weeks. The boat that normally carried six guests was at the disposal of the honeymooners. They had planned to sail across the Adriatic to the Dalmatian coast then down to Dubrovnik and then back to the Italian coast ending their cruise in Syracuse.

"There's a package for Mrs. George-Johnson, it's quite large so I've put it in the stateroom."

"Mrs. George-Johnson, it's that bloody Max"

And sure enough they found on unwrapping, a silent keyboard so that even on the yacht Rachel had no escape from practice.

"Oh, dear Max, he thinks of everything." she was already playing silently on her new toy.

"Breakfast served" came the relieving cry from Olga. They sat in the open cabin and enjoyed a sumptuous breakfast.

Soon the Sea Witch set out towards the open sea under the power of her motors, and the low coastline of the Venetian Riviera melted behind them. An hour later the sails were set and the yacht made smooth progress in a good sailing breeze. The amazing thing was that the crew seemed to have disappeared. Michael and Rachel spread themselves out on the deck and bathed each other with sunscreen and then dozed; caressed by the Adriatic breeze and rhythmic slapping of the water against the bow.

Captain Carey outlined the plans for the cruise ahead, it sounded divine.

"We'll make Brioni by about six thirty, please let Olga know if you want to dine on board; the menus are in your cabin. Don't forget we're here for you, so if you want to change anything or want anything at all, just call, and Olga will provide if it's at all possible."

There followed a short safety and evacuation briefing, it was more fun than a serious issue or so the honeymooners thought. Their cabin was aft; they got there through the galley. The room was spacious with a lovely Queen Size bed, wardrobes, shower and vanity unit as well as a head. There was a bottle of chilled Krug set up on the bedside table and the menus discreetly by its side.

Michael lounged on the bed, poured two glasses of the champagne; "Come here my little piano player" he said removing his shorts. "I think Cap'n Morgan the Cornish pirate fancies you"

"Don't be silly, come to think of it I've seen you cast a roving eye at Olga the delicious kitchen Queen." She looked down at him, "As long as that eye points this way I'm happy"

"Who the hell is Mr. Khouri?"

"He's Daddy's partner in Bahrain, I think this boat's his."

"Cheers to Mr. Khouri, come here……………

They went to play with each other as the Sea Witch began to roll a little and as they picked up speed towards the end of the first day of their voyage. The next days of their idyll were filled with sun, breeze, loving and spending heavenly moments on deserted islands, skinny dipping or eating wonderful fresh fish cooked over open fires on the white beaches. Olga and Skipper Corey seemed almost genie like, in that they appeared and disappeared, prepared beach parties for two, and reappeared, always just at the right time.

Their cabin was cleaned and linen changed without ever once interrupting the honeymoon pair. Rachel clad in her bikini spent an hour each day thundering away on her silent key board. She would try to lock Michael out who otherwise would interrupt her in the nicest and most irresistible ways. After Brioni they had hardly seen another soul, just the occasional passing yacht or ferry.

Chapter 3

On the fourth night they anchored in the pretty harbour of
Hvar. John Corey and Lavro manoeuvered the Sea Witch
skilfully into the crowded harbour and tied up alongside
another yacht of similar size. She flew the Tricolours of
France.

Rachel and Michael walked around the harbour past the
Palace Hotel and round to the little Church that stood alone
on the port promontory of the harbour inlet. Here they
heard a choir practising in a style or idiom strange to them
both. It was a wonderful sound, bold, discordant almost,
with crude but the vibrant harmony of Croatian folk music.
They sat for perhaps half an hour in the back of the Church
listening in stillness.

They emerged into darkness, and then to a harbour and the
little town lit by a thousand lights, not the lights of London
or New York but the lights of this tiny ancient place, the spell
was magical. They walked among the cafes and the bars; the
quay was busy with tourists, traders and artists. The
painters all painted much the same scene; the impossibly
photogenic harbour, the bobbing boats, illuminated yachts
and the crowded quay front. Others displayed their wares of
still life, grotesque modernity, and kitsch scenes from other
tourist spots. They stopped at an inviting restaurant and sat
at a pavement table, they ordered wine and a delicious local
lobster. There was much confusion about the size and price
of the lobster but Michael didn't really mind. Even the
coarse Croatian wine tasted delicious; gritty and cool on the
palate.

"Uugh!" grimaced Rachel, "The wine doesn't live up to the surroundings." She laughed and took another swig, "Not so bad I suppose" Then another great swallow, "Rather nice actually" They both laughed as Michael replenished the glasses.

Then a crowd of eight tourists crowded onto the pavement re-organizing the tables and being as Michael put it; "A bloody nuisance."

"They're off that French yacht moored next to us," Rachel whispered, "they're from Marseilles. Whoops, he sounds like a banker, Sh Sh Sh," She listened intently to the French conversation, and then leaned forward and took Michael's hand, "That distinguished looking one with the moustache is the president of some outfit in Marseilles; he's entertaining the rest by the sound of it"

"Darling I couldn't care less, I just wish they made less of a racket, I was enjoying this spot."

With that the waiter emerged with a huge lobster of at least five pounds. The French contingent Ooh'd and Ah'd and Zut Alors! Other comments were offered and in a trice Rachel was in a conversation with the French man who though in his fifties was at least elegant and even handsome. Despite his very poor French compared with that of his wife Michael was reluctantly drawn into the general hubbub.

They were indeed the guests from the neighbouring yacht, Monsieur Allain introduced his guests all a little older than the Johnsons but not as old as their host M. Allain. Soon it emerged that the French were clients of the private bank where M. Allain presided. The men were by and large in their late thirties, early forties and all their ladies including Madame Allain were considerably younger. Michael addressed Madame Allain only to receive a quick kick from Rachel: He was confused.

Rachel excused themselves whilst she and Michael attacked the humungous lobster that was surprisingly tender and delicious with a spectacular salad. Their wine glasses were filled whether they liked it or not, as M. Allain and co pressed them with hospitality. The French ladies, all of whom looked like movie starlets, seemed jolly and relaxed.

"Michael," she half whispered, "I don't think that's Madame Allain, nor Madame anyone else, except organized by a Madame"

Michael was confused, "Say that again, Oh! Bless my soul do you think so... Ah ha, so that's how the banks work in France, I should get a transfer"

Michael however was now even less at ease, mainly because the conversation was almost entirely in French and colloquial French at that. Rachel of course was quite at home having become fluent in the language during her time at the Conservatoire.

The group drank heavily and by ten o clock they rolled back towards their respective yachts. Inevitably Michael and Rachel were invited aboard the French vessel for a nightcap.

They all made it safely across the gangplank and spread themselves around the Salon and cockpit. Ten was quite a crowd. Champagne was liberally served, music played. Michael was invited to dance with one of the 'ladies' on the tiniest space in the cockpit as a Monsieur Barre danced with the tipsy Rachel. The party went on for two more hours and eventually the love birds were helped back on board the Sea Witch by the ever-watchful Captain Corey.

In the Cabin they undressed chaotically Michael falling out of his trousers and collapsing back onto the bed. Rachel, one shoe on and one shoe off collided with the shower cabinet and sprawled in ungainly fashion on the floor.

"Mrs Johnson, you're pissed," Michael laughed.

"Mr. Johnson you're absolutely pissed yourself. You ought to be ashamed of yourself dancing with French tarts." She regained her feet and tumbled onto the bed alongside him. They kissed; he turned her onto her back.

"Did that fucking Frenchman feel you up, did he?"

"Only a bit," she giggled, "He was very nice actually" she giggled some more.

His hands tightened round her wrists, "You're a tart, you're my tart, now let's see you make me come."

"You're hurting me Michael, how can I be a tart without hands." An ominous shadow made her suddenly sober up.

"Come on you tart, if you can make up to that French bastard you can service me now."

He forced her, she wasn't sure if she helped but he forced her to do things she would have gladly done. The fun, the warmth, was all banished by this sudden emergence of this hideous jealous drunk. Was this her Michael, she sobbed and did what he wanted as quickly as she could. In a minute he was asleep. She drank some water, and then lay quietly beside him, afraid that he might wake. Then she dismissed this act of personal vandalism as a one off foible, a product of too much Postup, Cognac and Champagne. She rose again quietly and vomited in the head, she was afraid, but again he did not stir. For the first time in her married life Rachel George Johnson cried herself to sleep.

She was awoken by the sound of the throbbing engine as the Sea Witch manoeuvred out of Hvar. It was hardly light; Michael snored as he lay in the heap of alcoholic coma... He'd barely moved all night. She slid from the bed, threw on some pants and a sweatshirt and entered the Galley where Olga was preparing coffee and breakfast for John and Lavro. As ever Olga worked with precision and uncanny quiet. Rachel accepted a mug of steaming coffee but refused food. Olga assumed she'd wait 'til later and join Michael as usual.

She followed Olga to the wheel house above the cockpit where Captain Corey with the ease of a practised mariner guided them safely through the harbour entrance and into the open sea. The grey dawn rose behind the profile of the enchanting town and soon the town and island shrank away in the white light of early day. The Skipper then pressed a series of switches and Lavro scampered about on deck responding as the electric winches pulled up the sails. Lavro secured the sheets when John Corey bade him and with the boat now trimmed, the engines died and they set off for Korcula just two hours or so South West. The Island of Viz appeared on the starboard bow and though still very early in the day the water already had a translucent greenness that began to lighten as the sun peaked over the main land; its beams, like crystals of light spearing their way into the deep. Rachel sat alone on the deck trying to forget the dark night and let in the light of day into her aching emptiness. She argued with herself that what had happened had been a misjudgement by her; perhaps she had imagined it all. She had after all been very tipsy, even drunk... Then Lavro came from nowhere and pointed excitedly out to the starboard lea.

"There, look, there" he danced with delight, "Madame, dolphins!"

Then she saw them, perhaps ten or twelve animals, jumping and playing not more than a hundred yards away. Their grace and speed were miracles of nature. To see them was a thrill that Rachel had not ever imagined.

She laughed as the tears poured down her cheeks. It was a sign, everything would be well; last night was but a small and cruel illusion. And then the sun appeared in its fullness and as the dolphins leapt and dived and swooped, so the sun picked up their iridescent shining bodies. God in heaven these were beautiful and so was life. As quickly as they had arrived the dolphins disappeared, Rachel skipped back to the galley collected another mug of coffee and went back to their cabin where she caressed her husband awake, mopped his throbbing brow and smothered his whiskery face with kisses.

"The dolphins, come and see the dolphins"

Michael was dragged unwillingly from his bed to search in vain for the dolphins that were her sure sign that Michael would love tenderly forever.

Dubrovnik; they'd come down from Korcula in tightest trim, that is to say that Corey with their permission had driven the Sea Witch in her tightest sail trim to make the journey, averaging some thirteen knots as opposed to her cruising trim of nearer nine. It had been exciting; they had been confined to the cockpit but were invited to the wheel house where each in turn had tried their hand at steering the Sea Witch. Under these conditions the boat was permanently inclined at what seemed to Rachel as a dangerously steep angle. John Corey assured her that she could go even faster and in racing trim the water would permanently wash over the gunnels. The journey of some eighty eight nautical miles was covered in seven hours and they heaved to into the Dubrovnik area sometime after seven.

John Corey was apologetic, "I'm afraid we can't get a berth in the old port. The marina is around six kilometres out and very big and touristy, so I've arranged to put into the port at Lokrum, and you can commute with the dingy, only about ten minutes. The good news is that Lokrum is beautiful and quiet"

Both the lovers were already lost in the wonder that is Dubrovnik. Bernard Shaw it was, who had said; "Those who seek paradise on earth should visit here" As the Sea Witch nosed her elegant way close to the coast and as the old city came into sight, they could well believe it. As the sun set it blazed a light upon the old ramparts and lit the hills behind with a gossamer haze, they stood arm in arm.

"Oh Michael, I don't want this ever to come to an end."

"It never will; this loveliness will be part of us forever. Where ever we go there will be nowhere more beautiful."

Tears rolled gently down her lovely face, and they kissed a sweet kiss, so tender yet so deep. Bernard Shaw had been right. This was Paradise.

Michael declared a vacation for the crew and invited everyone to dinner as his guest. Corey and Olga accepted, but Lavro, would of necessity have to remain on board. Despite Michael's protestations the Skipper would not be moved. Someone had to remain on watch, even in the quiet of Lokrum harbour.

This place too, was beautiful; you could hear the white murmur of the whispers of all the lovers who had gazed at the stars from this very spot. You could hear the rustling of silks and the beating of wings, the sound of poems and the muttering of Latin prayers as if you were not in the harbour but in the cloisters of the nearby Benedictine Abbey. It seemed that Lokrum was under an eternal spell.

The Sea Witch was secured in this delightful place; they changed and the four of them clambered into the dingy and they sped across the channel into the old Port of Dubrovnik. The port nestled under the massive city walls, that welcomed rather than threatened; there was an air of festivity as if the history of medieval power had somehow dissolved into a timeless past that had just left this legacy of pure beauty. It was breathtaking! They entered the old city through the Ploce Gate, wonder piled upon wonder. Here was a medieval gem, a perfect fairy tale walled city, it was almost too much to take in. They dined again in the open air in a wonderful restaurant. They drank more of the very decent local wine and retired, scooting back to Lokrum across the moonlit sea. They were all very tired after a long day at sea, but had there ever been a more perfect day?

Back in their cabin Rachel lay in his arms, "Are you all right, my darling?"

"Yes, of course, why do you ask?"

"No reason, no reason at all, it's been an exhausting day, that's all."

"Yes, it has," she kissed him sweetly, rolled over, "Goodnight my love."

"G'night." He was asleep.

She lay there seeing her dolphins and listening to the gentle snoring of her husband, she was sure now, and soon she was asleep.

They marvelled at the beauties of the old City. Each one a revelation; each revelation, a facet of the gem that is Dubrovnik. They loved every moment; they walked every inch of the old City, examined every corner, rested in most of the little bars, and not only experienced the City, but also themselves in this magic place. It was as if they were enchanted and alone amongst the thousands of tourists. Here Michael was as she had known he would always be, gentle, amusing and attentive. That night, though exhausted from their day of tramping around the City, they dined on board, retired early and made the consummate love that banished all memories of the horrors of that night in Hvar.

They stayed another day; spending most of it on Lokrum, which in its way was every bit as enchanting as its famous neighbour. They swam in the bright blue sea, dined at the beachside and spent the afternoon in the delicious botanical gardens.

That night John Corey agreed that they were to start their journey across the Adriatic to the shores of Calabria. They would set out the following dawn. It would be a twenty hour journey; some at tight trim, some at cruise trim, they would not go too hard since the honeymooners were not a professional crew, nor were they fit enough to spend the whole journey on watch.

They retired to bed early, Michael pleasantly tipsy after yet another delicious dinner from Olga's five star galley. Rachel after a silent rendition of the two part inventions tip-toed onto the deck for a last look at the jeweled sky and to scent the night perfumes of Lokrum. She walked quietly to the bow where she heard the unmistakable sound of John and Olga Corey making lusty love. The scents, the sounds, were a heady mix and she made her way back to Michael with an animal intent. He was asleep, she woke him and took command, Michael responded at first with a languid sleepy stir, but then her desire awoke his most intense passion. This time she did not defer, she would demand and be satisfied. He would not dominate, it was she who would drive onto him and he would be her server. She climaxed, but wanted more, she climaxed again, but wanted more. He was satiated, but was prisoner to her needs. At last she fell on him soaked in sweat. Never would he dominate her in bed again, she would disarm his sexual power with a power of her own.

Their journey across the Adriatic was for Michael enjoyable and great sport. He took what duties he could, or was allowed by the Skipper. There was something macho and brave about setting out on a real voyage, out of sight of land, just driven by the power of the wind.

Rachel, after bidding the Dubrovnik archipelago farewell, was content to put in a long silent practice on her keyboard.

Michael marveled at her concentration, he could never share her passion or her communion with music, which enabled her to play piano concerti in her head, or sonatas on a sideboard. Here was a domain he could never enter, he had neither the skill nor the knowledge, and worse, he knew he never would. Now they were together, alone except of course, there was her silent keyboard. At least there was no Max or that crone Eva. They were the constant reminder of that other world, a world where Michael was excluded.

Rachel by contrast found the day a bore. For the first time, the constant buffeting of the sea, the roar of the wind, and the persistent swell were a chore. She made a few excursions to the wheel house, but apart from half shouted conversations it was boring; it was uncomfortable and too cold even to sunbathe, so she spent much of the journey with her silent friend that she played despite the constant list, for hours on end. For the first time she felt a little sea sick, she longed for her piano, a steady floor and a comfortable stool.

It was not to be.

She lay down in their cabin later that morning. She thought of her sex and how it had transformed from the demure half-light to stark need in these recent days. It had been that awful experience of Michael almost raping her that had borne in her a belligerence and self assertion that would change her forever. Last night had been the proof. She had felt desire before, but never had she felt the need to satisfy herself without reserve. She was responding to selfishness with selfishness. Something had been lost, her innocence had been defiled, and she was part of the process. Where did all the tenderness and giving disappear. Already the beauty of the dolphins and the peace of forgiveness had disappeared. She felt ashamed, bewildered and cried in the pitching bed as the Sea Witch skimmed the waves toward Italy.

Michael spent the whole day in the wheelhouse, enjoying the thrill of sailing in open waters. The wind varied from bracing to brisk, but there was not a moment when his boyish enthusiasm was abated. They saw few other vessels until the evening when they came across an Italian navy patrol boat. They were asked to heave to, Corey obeyed immediately and the Italians sent a dingy alongside in the heaving swell. Two seamen scrambled aboard, one of them an officer. The Officer saluted and began to address Corey in very quickly delivered Italian. Corey had trouble following and after some minutes appealed for an English interpretation.

"Si Capitan, my English is not too good" came the heavily accented reply, "I traaee."

"Very good," replied Corey smiling, "It's a lot better than my Italian"

They shook hands and the Lieutenant laboriously explained the reason for the challenge and asked permission to look round the Sea Witch. Michael stood awkwardly to one side mildly alarmed at the drama unfolding on the high seas. The patrol boats were pursuing two objectives, firstly to prevent the landing of any further Albanian refugees, and secondly to stop and search vessels as part of the drug prevention program.

First the Italian asked to see the boat's papers, log and registration documents. He was surprised, perhaps suspicious that there were only two passengers. Rachel sensing the change in the motion of the boat arrived bleary eyed on deck. She took her husband's arm and whispered her alarm. The Lieutenant was taken on a tour of the boat, Corey having first asked the passengers' permission to visit their cabin. They followed the visitor below and waited apprehensively in the Salon.

Not ten minutes had passed and the young Italian Officer seemed satisfied that all was correct. He apologized to the Johnsons. Rachel, who had scrambled from her drowsy bed, was clad in shorts and cotton blouse and nothing else. This did not escape the attention of the young Italian. He took her hand; bowed deeply, kissing it with an old world flourish, staring fixedly at her breasts that stood proudly behind their gossamer cotton screen. He then bowed to Michael and departed. Soon the sails were raised and they continued their journey into a glorious sunset.

In their cabin, Michael was aroused and anxious. He took Rachel in his arms,

"God, you look sexy, that bloody Italian couldn't take his eyes off you." He kissed her urgently, but she did not respond. She pushed him away

"Not now darling, let's have some supper and a drink and watch the sunset."

He pulled at her shirt and it fell open, "God they're... you're gorgeous, I can see why that Italian couldn't take his eyes off you" He pulled her back, she resisted, closing her arms in front of her Still he tried to embrace her and his hands thrust her defending arms apart. She felt that urgent dread return; was he going to force her again. Suddenly he stepped back.

He laughed, "OK, my love, no conjugal rights before dinner, but early to bed, I'm hungry for it. You drive me mad" He danced around the cabin, "You beeautifool laidy" he parodied the Italian.

She laughed, kissed his cheek "I'm going to put something decent on for supper."

"Yes you do that in case I have to eat you for my supper, you beeatifool laidy."

He left the room, she sighed with relief. 'It's a matter of degree she thought, I'm glad he's jealous, it means he loves me.' She put on her underwear and dressed for supper.

Eating supper under sail was not quite the stately affair that they'd experienced in port. For one thing the boat listed under sail so that the formal dinner layout was impossible. Olga delivered a finger buffet that would have done credit to Claridges, so they sat together their feet acting as a brace against the sloping deck as they enjoyed the lavish supper. It was fun; they giggled and enjoyed the messy bits of food not quite delivered to their mouths in the swaying cabin. They laughed and touched affectionately, both relaxed and for the first time in days; free from the sexual tension of their mutual stalking.

Michael, when supper was done, decided to return to the wheelhouse and Rachel chatted with Olga, who working with her miraculous efficiency, restored the salon to its pristine state in a flash.

Olga was about forty, very attractive with auburn hair and an athletic but feminine frame. She accepted a drink from Rachel; they sat out on the cockpit that now was cool but bracing in the early night air. Olga sat immediately into an easy gait, whilst Rachel found it difficult to be comfortable.

"How long have you and John been living like this, it's exciting, but I imagine you get pretty fed up with looking after a succession of guests?"

"Oh no, I don't, really I don't, we seldom carry more than four guests, and John so loves sailing, it's all he ever wants to do. Tell me, have you enjoyed it so far? It's important to us that you do."

"Olga, it's been fabulous, the most romantic interlude, we've both loved it. I hope Michael hasn't fallen in love with sailing like John," she laughed "I've been a sailing widow all day."

"John mentioned you had a silent piano, I didn't really understand, but now it makes sense, I believe you're a pianist. You're going to be famous, how wonderful, I don't know much about music, I just like to hear it." She smiled, "I must go to bed, the life of a sailor's wife is nothing if not demanding, breakfast at five for John, we make land early and he has to clear with Italian immigration and customs, hopefully you won't be disturbed, Goodnight Mrs Johnson."

"Rachel, please. Good night Olga."

They slept soundly after their day at sea, despite the listing of their bed. Michael crept in late and exhausted; content that he had learned and practised a good deal of seamanship during his long day in the wheelhouse.

They were awakened by the changing sounds, the throb of the huge engine and the sudden rightness of the boat. The sun once more streamed in through the portholes, and the noise of scampering feet on deck. It was nearly seven o' clock and the Sea Witch had arrived in Tropea, a little port whose ancient village tumbled down steeply from the hillside to a cobalt blue sea. The houses were closely packed together, their red tiled roofs reflecting off the water; now mirror calm. Gulls cried overhead, and the clear chatter of Italian fishermen echoed off the water as they landed their catches, and tended their nets and little fishing boats.

It was another post card perfect day in a picture post card place; they snacked on Olga's usual and wonderful breakfast, declining the cooked options. Carey explained that all the formalities had been completed. They would spend the next few days trundling down the Capo Vaticana before the short cruise to Syracuse.

They passed the days in a delightful lazy heady perfume of bliss. They swam and snorkeled, dined and visited the most delightful places. Ancient Churches, Roman temples, street cafes, bars and country walks. They were once more at peace, the troubles of the past seemed unreal to Rachel. Michael was once more the gentle, funny man she'd always known.

The romance of it all did not lessen when they travelled from Scilla to Syracuse. This City was a bustling place, from the harbour port packed with yachts and the buzz of traffic from the busy city. Michael could hardly hide his sadness that the sea odyssey had come to an end. Once more he invited John and Olga to dine with them, but they declined, they had to dash back to Monte Carlo. They bade their fond farewells at the dock as the couple's luggage was loaded into the waiting limousine.

They drove through the city to the outskirts of the town to their villa for their last three days. On arrival at the discreetly walled villa with its fragrant garden, and horizon pool that looked down to the sea, they were excited, but at the same time disappointed to find a small mountain of mail, faxes and a computer with a list of e-mails a mile long.

His was about the current deals at the bank, and his next month's schedules; hers about concert and ensemble bookings over the coming months. There was a long message from Max about repertoire he felt she should be working on, and another from Eva urging her to spend more of her time with this or that teacher.

Suddenly they were both exhausted and the following days they only made brief excursions away from the Villa. On their last night, they chose to dine in the town at a much vaunted seafood restaurant near the Port in the City.

The Italian men devoured Rachel with their eyes, but at least this time there were no approaches, and the dinner was all that they expected. Over coffee a dapper ancient gentleman, his cotton suit almost as venerable as himself, wobbled over to them, staggering, he relied heavily on his elegant Malacca cane. He sported an open necked shirt, a slightly crooked panama hat and a scarlet kerchief flared from his jacket breast pocket.

"My darlings" he began, in an absurdly theatrical twang, "may I join you?" He bowed a little unsteadily.

"We're just off I'm afraid" Michael signaled impatiently for the bill.

"How sad," muttered the old boy, "You see, I'd love to have a chat about home.... I'm stuck here in this God forsaken hole." He pulled his red kerchief like a matador wielding his cape; he mopped his sweaty brow, and sat.

Rachel raised an eyebrow, Michael shuffled but their new companion ordered three grappas in Italian and the three drinks arrived uncharacteristically quickly, before the bill.

"Please drink this with me, do an old man a small favour…….
I really don't want to be a nuisance you see, I shall go quietly I promise" He waved the approaching waiter away, Michael waved the waiter back; but it seemed that the old man had the greater influence.

Rachel uncertain, but keen to avoid unpleasantness, picked up the drink in front of her, "Thank you, but there was no need"

"My dear young lady, the pleasure is all mine, do tell me about yourselves, have you been here long?"

"Just a couple of days..., you?"

"Oh, me, just a bit longer, thirty eight years actually"

"You must love it here" Rachel smiled, eying Michael who appeared to be fuming, his grappa untouched.

"No, I'm fed up with the place; its only virtue as far as I'm concerned is the climate. Since my wife died I've fallen out of love with Italy, when my Cara was alive, then I belonged you see, but now she's gone, I'm marooned."

"I'm sorry about your wife." His eyes were far away, his fingers tapped uncertainly at the base of his glass. He was sad, a sad little man. "Why don't you go home? I assume England is your home?"

"Yes ...yes. I suppose so, but you don't know the intricacies of Italian family law. It was hard to marry Cara, but it is impossible now to divest my home or even cease to make oil and wine... impossible for you to understand."

Michael who had still not uttered a word, sat morosely at the table, "I'm sorry we have to go." He paid the bill. "Come on darling we have to go."

"Well good bye," she extended her hand, the old man took it and kissed it "It has been a pleasure my dear."

Michael took her elbow and led her emphatically from the restaurant.

In the car, Michael still fumed, "Why do we have to put up with people like that, what makes that old fart think that he can go round feeding off tourists?"

"I don't now, he was a sad old dear, I'm sure he'd have been quite interesting really. Didn't you feel a bit for him cast adrift in Sicily, how old?"

"I don't know, nor do I care"

"Don't be such a shit my darling," she nuzzled up to him, "Anyway thank you for a lovely evening and perhaps the most wonderful honeymoon anyone has ever had, I love you even if you don't like sweet old gentlemen." She kissed him deeply, "Our last night; promise you'll be good and we'll give each other a star finale"

Chapter 4

London; they returned to a damp late September day. Their new home, not really new, but quite new, that was now bursting with wedding presents. The house itself was a mews property in a most fashionable area of the West End; it had belonged to Robbie's father but now was in trust for them. Sir Lewis and Robbie had jointly lavished money on the mews house and they had converted the former garage into a music studio. Michael had merely complained that car parking would be inconvenient.

Rachel could hardly wait to get back to her friend 'Becky'. 'Becky' lived alongside a harpsichord, a vario system and various electronic gadgets. 'Becky' had been her eighteenth birthday present from daddy. She was a Bechstein Grand; beautiful to look at in her pyramid mahogany veneer, and beautiful to listen to with her wonderful cello like resonance and the colour of her tones.

They dined out in the little pub in the corner of the Mews called "The British Grenadier," the beer was good, the food indifferent. Rachel having resisted playing 'Becky' for at least four hours darted back to the studio while Michael retired to his study to pick up the threads of his work. It was after midnight when she felt his gentle hand on her shoulder,

"Enough now my sweet, we both have a busy day tomorrow"

Tomorrow was another day. Michael left the house at seven fifteen; no lavish breakfast just coffee and toast. The cleaning lady, Jennie, arrived at eight thirty and by nine Rachel was back in her studio. Her practice was not always the same, depending on her forthcoming schedule, but she was always tempted by JS; as she called Bach. This morning was no exception. First the beloved Well Tempered Clavier, then the six partitas; then Max.

"Ah, JS again, you're a naughty girl, I hope that my silent keyboard blazed with the sound of Bella Bartok, or Stravinsky. I will never know." He held her at arms length, "My God, you look wonderful, I hope that husband of yours has been looking after you"

"Oh Max, it's been wonderful, I can't begin to tell you, it's been perfect."

"Well my dear I'm glad for you, you know I love you, but today I'm afraid I've invited someone else to come and see you, and you look absolutely perfect. We want some shots for the new tour advance and for Concordia."

"Concordia! Max have you got me a recording contract with Concordia?

"Who else would get it if it wasn't me? eh!"

Max was in his mid fifties, overweight, luxuriantly bearded and gray haired, with uneven teeth. His face was florid so that sometimes he gave the air of someone who was not altogether sane. His eyes, edged with bloodshot, constantly darted about, never still. His nose showed signs of alcoholic abuse. But his one saving and all embracing grace was that he was always jolly, friendly and positive.

"Oh Max my hair's a shambles, I can't have a photo session, I'll look a mess"

"My darling," his Estonian accent now thickening, as if it added charm, "you can never look a mess. Go along now make yourself as beautiful as you can and put on a nice concert frock for Uncle Max…. One that shows how beautiful you are." He tittered.

"Max this is not a Playboy calendar; I want them to hear my music not look at my tits"

He howled with laughter, "Just a little look, my darling, just a little look."

She swept upstairs to get ready for the photo shoot. She heard Max playing Handel on the harpsichord. God, it needed tuning. She spent the best part of an hour doing her hair and make-up, then selecting a dress that would be both demure yet revealing, showing the artist in her and yet satisfying Max's demand for a glimpse, or more than a glimpse, of cleavage.

She chose a long black gown that was one of her favourites, selected a bra a little on the small side, plumped up her boobs and returned downstairs to the music studio.

Max was no longer alone; a young photographer and his girl Friday stood there with lights, reflectors and other paraphernalia of their trade They had already lit the room and Rachel's entrance raised "My darling, absolutely ravishing," He almost driveled the last word sending a shiver through Rachel.

She sat at the piano and obeyed the young photographer's instructions. Head up, head down, please play, please stop, please stand by the piano, and please sit again. Max minced around in the background whispering from time to time in the photographer's ear.   Rachel did her best but she was conscious of Max's almost salacious direction of the camera, happily the young photographer seemed to be his own man, and paid only cursory attention to the drooling Max.

It was over in a matter of an hour and soon Rachel was changed again and sat with Max spilling his plans and documents over the piano lid. He had plans for recitals in England, Northern France, Scotland and ensemble engagements in London and Germany.

He had a list of competitions over the next two years where he thought she could enter and do well.

"Oh Max you know I loathe competitions, I've never really recovered from that performance at the 'Busoni' last year. No more please"

"Dearest Rachel, have you forgotten how close you came in Leipzig or the teaching scholarship from Gothenburg. You are immeasurably better because you have been tempered in these competitions. There are many opportunities for you and I'm sure these prospects will hold a win for us. A win my darling," he drooled sucking in his excess spittle, " you know means just about everything, and you are so close, so close my dear, and still so young and so beautiful."

Rachel flashed back to her eighteenth birthday when she had nearly done enough to win the J.S.Bach International Competition in Leipzig. Of course she had played Harpsichord then, but she thought she had won. Indeed ever since that remarkable night she had dreamed of playing the Goldberg Variations so perfectly again. It had been a fleeting moment when everything had come together. Perfect recollection, relaxed dexterity, and a oneness with the music that so seldom happened. She felt then as the judges handed her down third place, (incidentally they did not award a first place), that a moment of sublime accomplishment had been passed by. Although she was outwardly thrilled to congratulate the young Canadian winner (second prize winner), in reality her heart sank into a profound and black void of disappointment. It had never entirely left her. She had then decided to leave the harpsichord behind her and to devote the rest of her musical life to the piano. Despite that, her love of Bach could not be banished and she'd felt somehow trapped on the wrong instrument with the right composer, or was it the other way around?

There was a knock; it was Eva, the perfect partner for Max. Together they would have made a fine waxwork for any chamber of horrors. Max; his fat corporation, his wild hairy head and Eva; skinny and tall with the most garish taste in couture. Her long face with a most exaggerated proboscis was surrounded by a witch-like mop of unruly gray hair that always gave the appearance of having been shaped by a combine harvester.

Weinstein and Luberoff, they could have been a vaudeville act.

There was much kissing and greeting as first Eva embraced Rachel, then Max though with considerably less enthusiasm. Eva always smelt of moth balls, as if her velvet Victorian clothes were horded in some camphor filled vault. However, even at seventy something or was it eighty something, her energy was formidable. Whist Max's accent was a tinge Estonian, Eva sounded as though she'd come hot foot from her very first English lesson. She had in fact been living in London for at least fifty years.

"Mein liebe, how are you, my little Rachel, I hope your experience wiz this Michael are got, jah?"

"My experience with my wonderful husband was just that …. Wonderful, thank you Eva, and what have you been scheming with Max since I've been gallivanting in the Dalmatians?"

Max laughed and chewed one of his disgusting but at least unlit cigars.

"Repertoire, darling, repertoire."

"Oh shut up Max, I want to hear from Eva."

"Tchroo, liebe, tchroo, hrepertoire, you know eet. Ghromantic hrepertoire ies what you must expand, expression rhgomance, you know ziss now you are a married woman, no? and Lizt, Bghrahms, and ghromance and so on, and so on, my deear, ziss is the vay to more concerti and to fulfilment no?"

"I hate to sound too much of a money grabber; but Rachel, you know she's right. We need to get you into more concerti work, broaden your appeal from your baroque recitals. We love you, we love the way you play, but we both feel that you have so much more to give."

"You want me to give up my harpsichord and all its associations, I've come a long way since Leipzig, Max, I'm happy at my piano and in the ensemble."

The ensemble known as the Rive Gauche Quartet met occasionally, they'd all been together as post graduates in Paris and every now and then they'd get together particularly at Les Printemps Festival and in Lyons each year. That aside; it was true. Rachel could not shake off her habitual love of Bach, Scarlatti and a multitude of baroque composers. It was as if in her early years, when Eva was her principal teacher, when those first mathematically perfect excursions in to this sublime music had driven a fascination and obsession so deep, that it had almost become a reflex, as if there was no other. Each morning as she extended her fingers over the keyboard she led into Bach without so much as a thought.

She knew they were right. She had a prodigious memory for music; she had after all learned all the Mozart piano sonatas by the time she was fourteen, and she still remembered every one. Her sight reading was unusually quick, even of contemporary works, it was just that she didn't feel motivated somehow to stray from her obsession...
If anything, she found in Bella Bartok and Stravinsky a link back to the beloved master that she enjoyed, but most of the romantics did little more than amuse her as exhibitionist exercises. It had been a long time since, as a child, she wept to the strains of Mendelssohn or Chopin. Now, alas, the main stream romantic repertoire held little fascination for her, they were always a chore.

"Grieg, my dear, I can get you an engagement to do the Grieg, with the Liverpool Philharmonic. Please do it for me, you did it last time so beautifully, may be a touch here and there....." he trailed off.

"We can verk my dear together OK, no?

"No Eva, I don't want do the Grieg, I want to do the Goldberg for Concordia."

There was a silence. Then Max, hands thrust deeply into his immaculate suit pockets, waddled to the piano, "I'm afraid that may not be possible, my dear, if Concordia take you on board they'll want you to complement their existing offerings and whilst they know of your Bach reputation they want more from you, they want at least a small variety and that includes some of the romantics." He shrugged, "Darling we're all selling something, they feel that right now JS is very well catered for by God knows how many. Strangely Rachmaninov too, so if we are to create a long term deal and that's the only one Concordia are interested in, then we'll have to turn your beautiful hand to a range that you must learn to love, it's not as if you're turning your back on the baroque, it's more like growing into an additional range. So Brahms, Grieg, Bella Bartok, to name but three will have to be part of your repertoire, if we are to do this deal. Now be a good girl and start work with Eva."

"Why Grieg, I've hardly touched his work since Gothenburg, that's what? ...Five years?"

"That my dear, is the point; remember how well you played the Grieg sonata, it got you the prize and that's what Concordia have turned up, a hole in their catalogue and a young but rising star with some track record. Money, filthy lucre, my darling, that's what makes the world go round."

Eva waving her talon like hands beamed her sweetest grotesque smile, Lieben, you vill do, because Max and I are alvays gright for you, no? So we start tomorrow, on zee Grieg no."

"What else have we on the schedule, aren't I in the West Country next week? Plymouth, Camborne and somewhere else, I've forgotten"

"Yes, quite so", Max bustled forward to give Rachel a hug, and so close the agreement.

"Penzance, my dear, Land's End, but soon, The Carnegie Hall." He giggled, his frantic eyes darting wildly between Rachel and Eva. Rachel remembered the Grieg sonatas; she'd quite enjoyed them insofar as one can enjoy anything in the sweatshop atmosphere of International competition. She had been nineteen then, and although she did not win a major prize, she had received an academic bursary award that had helped both with her expenses and her entry into the post graduate year in Paris. She recognised that she would have to follow Max's course if she was to rise from the interminable round of minor venue recitals. The West country trip was typical of her existence; sometimes in UK, sometimes outside, but the routine was always the same, travel, practice in the auditorium that varied from Churches to cinemas and even Town Halls, the performance usually entirely ignored by press of any note, and then on to the next venue.

Far from being glamorous, it was tedious and trying. She knew that if she didn't break into the next level soon, she would give it all up and simply teach a range of varied and often unwilling students in her new London home. This idea was attractive some of the time; at others it was too scary to be true. Perhaps Max was right.

Eva, coiling herself in one of her more bizarre scarves, uncoiled herself, embraced her pupil, and exited. As always theatrical, she trumpeted "Grieg, zen who knows, romantic perhaps romantic!" She was gone.

"Well Max, after the West Country what have we got?"

"In October we have an important engagement for you in Bristol, a BBC recital from St Mary Radcliff. Then another Bach recital in St David's Hall in Cardiff, you'll enjoy that, the Hall is beautiful darling, perfect for recitals. Then I'm afraid it's back on the road, up North to Carlisle, then Newcastle and York, all recitals. Then my darling comes our big chance, Grieg with the Royal Liverpool Philharmonic and a young guest conductor with an impossible Scandinavian name. He is something of a Grieg aficionado I believe. That's on the nineteenth of November. Not broadcast but recorded for Radio three. I have the details of your conductor here in this package. If it goes well he may invite you back to Scandinavia, Gothenburg again, you'll enjoy that."

"Phhhh, sounds dull, Max stop telling me what I will enjoy....but at least I'm busyish. Max are you sure we're doing the right thing, you know how I love JS and co.?"

"Unless you want to spend your life trying to be another Hewitt, I think you must have a broader repertoire. Darling you may have a lot more to discover not only about life but about music as well"

She sighed, pecked Max on the cheek, "Off you go Max, I'll be good, and do as you tell me, I hope you're right."

She sat in silence and after a minute or so placed her hands over the keys and the ringing of The Well Tempered Clavier filled the room. Then as if someone had slammed down the piano lid she stopped and after a moment she closed her eyes and played Grieg. For the first time for as long as she could remember, she was unable to recall the score after the first passage. She stared at the ceiling, wiped the tears from her eyes, 'I wonder what time Michael will be home from the bank?'

Michael's return was later than she had expected; he was tired but upbeat. She sat and listened as he prattled on about this and that and how he hoped to be on the team for a big acquisition for a big American client. Not once did he enquire about her day.

Over supper in the kitchen, it was already late, she mentioned the Royal Liverpool engagement; he merely said 'good show' but was clearly uninterested. They went to bed, Rachel wanted to be held and cuddled and loved, but it was not to be, Michael slept as soon as his head hit the pillow. Was this how life was to be? She lay awake listening to his gentle snore.

Marriage, honeymoons and being married, she'd experienced them all in three weeks and being married was the one she liked least. She eventually slept having remembered the whole of the Grieg sonata. She played it again and then Michael stirred her; kissed her gently and was gone for another day at the Office.

The days that followed were different. Rachel worked hard at being there for Michael, no matter how hard the days of practice, the travels, she wanted Michael to be excited just by being with her.

Every time she was away she rang him before and after every recital, sometimes of course he wasn't there at all, out to dinner, down in The Rugby Club, away on business. Every home coming was as good as she could make it. If he was tired she would relax him, if he was randy she would please him, if he was hungry she always knew of a good place to eat. Cook, she was not.

In a trice it was November and the Liverpool concert was only days away. She'd returned from the three concerts in the North of England that had included a Sunday recital, so a whole weekend with Michael had been lost. It was Monday and she waited anxiously to greet Michael from work. She waited and waited but by seven o clock there was still no sign. She rang his office; he was still there.

"What time will you be home? I'm missing you terribly."

"I'm in the middle of a thing," his reply was tart.... then a silence, then "Sorry I may be late and I'm afraid I'll be off to Chicago in the morning. Look, I know it's not what we wanted but I promise I'll get home as soon as I can; look, get something to eat."

"I don't want anything to eat, I want you Michael, please come home I've not seen you since Wednesday... I miss you."

He became tetchy again; "Sorry darling got to go" The phone went dead.

She sat there empty and sad, she ached for his company. She had never felt so lonely, so disappointed, and so black inside.

The door bell rang, Rachel's heart skipped a beat, perhaps it was him, but how could it be? It might be? It wasn't. It was Jacqui Boswell, step mother; the now Lady George. Jacqui was forty and looked about thirty two, they could have been sisters.

"Hello, Jacqui, I didn't expect you."

Her stepmother stood, hand on hip; dressed expensively and glamorously as ever. She glowed like a mannequin on heat.

"You've been crying, is Michael a bastard already? She swept past into the house. "What? All alone. Where's lover boy?"

"He's at work; won't be home for a while." Rachel felt downtrodden and hopeless.

"Oh good, come on, we'll go out and have some supper and some girl talk."

"No thank you Jacqui, I'd rather stay here and wait, he may be earlier than I think."

"Won't hear of it, now powder your nose, and I'll order us a table at the Capitol, run along."

Rachel did as she was told.

Since Daddy had married Jacqui Boswell, Rachel had never quite come to terms with the whole concept. Daddy as a philanderer, a cheat who'd treated her mother appallingly. The whole thing was unpalatable. She'd tried to be civil but she found it difficult, she didn't like Jacqui. She was a silly self-centred bitch. She could see that she was beautiful, but she was nothing more than a decorous tart, as her mother never tired of reminding her. She had never spent any time with Jacqui, nor did she wish to, but now she'd been caught in a vulnerable low; and company, any company was better than none.

Lady George demanded and got a table at the Capitol Hotel restaurant, a feat in itself formidable enough. She greeted the Maitre d' like an old friend and they were shown their table. She ordered a bottle of Champagne.

"Rachel, cheer up, all men are bastards some of the time, my sweet, it's only a matter of proportion."

"Oh it's not that, it's just that Michael and I seem to find it so hard to have time together, I'm working or he's working," she drank a healthy draft of the Krug. "That's a bit of a nice change, thank you Jacqui."

"Don't put up with it, they're just out there playing their silly games pretending that everything they do is so bloody important, I bet he thinks that your piano playing is just a hobby"

"Well he may be right; I'm still finding it hard to make any real sort of breakthrough, it's been my hobby since I was seven for God's sake, you'd think I could have got somewhere by now."

"Rachel, don't be such a silly child, you've accomplished more than most of us will ever dream of. You can't believe how much I admire what you do, so does your father and your mother."

Rachel was taken aback; this was the first kind word that she'd ever heard from daddy's tart. She was beautiful, groomed to perfection, her makeup precise but not over stated, her hair as always immaculate, her jewellery obviously expensive but not too glitzy. She reeked of style; she was perhaps too perfect; she was to Rachel, a symbol of superficial vanity. Jacqui spent nearly as much time making up as Rachel spent practising the piano. But here was this statement of support, even friendly admiration.

Rachel did not know how to reply; she drank more Champagne, and just murmured a demure, "Thank you."

Her long day without much food, eased the way for the Champagne to do its work, Rachel brightened and listened to Jacqui's quick but often course humour. It made her laugh, and as they ate and drank more she began to enjoy the evening. One thing she found admirable that whilst Jacqui would condemn men in general, she was careful never to refer to daddy, other than to intimate her real love for the man whom she called Lew...

As they drained the last glass of red wine, "Don't let the bastards get you down Rachel, you have done something none of them can, you've used your God given talent and got out there, and not been afraid. You've done it on your own. Oh I know you've got that crazy teacher, and that mad Agent guy, but you play the damn piano, you face your audience, you do it because you've got talent and you've got guts." She drained the last from her glass, "Come on I shall be accused of perverting youth, let's get you home."

In the taxi, Jacqui continued her unexpected home spun advice, "Now's the time Rachel, now when you're starting out. Love that dishy man of yours but keep some love for yourself as well.

Don't let the sod walk all over you, believe me you'll be better equipped to be a good partner if you stand up and be a partner, not a sleeping partner." She laughed, "I hope you're enjoying that end of the business," she laughed salaciously again "at least have your share of the fun."

The taxi pulled up outside the house, just behind another. Michael emerged from the first; Rachel stumbled from the second followed by a guardedly steady Jacqui.

"Hello darling," Rachel embraced him; causing him to drop his brief case, he was obviously surprised. He did not return the hug.

"Hello Michael, I'm afraid I've been using Rachel as a sounding board; it was so sweet of her to keep me company over dinner"

Michael still covered in confusion, picked up his briefcase, kneeling as was Rachel; now hindering rather than helping in the recovery of his case and papers.

"Oh, good to see you," he said His manner denying the compliment, as he shuffled towards the door, "well thank you Jacqui; I don't suppose you want to let your taxi go."

"No, you're right, Good night Rachel." She jumped back into her taxi and was gone.

"Keeping company with daddy's tart are we?" He snarled, as he fumbled for his keys.

"She just called out of the blue, any way some company's better than none"

"What's that supposed to mean?" They were in the hall.

"It means I was lonely waiting 'til God knows what time for you to come home, for God's sake Michael we've not seen each other for a week."

"What was she doing recruiting you into tarthood."

"Don't be such an idiot, I just think she wanted a bit of company, Daddy had to go to some business thing at the last minute."

"You said you were going to wait for me, you know I was at the Bank working. You just forgot all about me and went out with that tart,"

"Michael, it's twenty past eleven, I spoke to you around seven, are you seriously suggesting I sit on my hands and spend my time waiting…. Waiting for my Lord and Master to come home?"

"That's not it, you know I've been working, damn it… it's for us you know."

"No I don't bloody well know… what about my work, you don't give a damn." She began to cry, "you don't give a damn,"

"Oh Rachel I do, I do, but everything seems to demand so much from each of us, I'm afraid that we won't have time for each other." He held her tightly.

"Let me go you, you, chauvinist prat; I'm not going to spend my life hanging around waiting for you to come home, when it suits you, or the bloody bank. I'm your wife for Christ's sake, you're meant to be interested in us, not in you. Your career is not what we're about; it's about us, you and me.... Don't you understand?" She backed off, racked with sobs, "Jacqui's not the point is she? You just want me for you, anybody, just anybody else is a threat, Max, Eva, anybody. Well Michael, we're going to have to face up to the fact that I do, and will continue, to have a life; that you can be in or out of it, it's up to you..... But I will not just lie down and let you do what the hell you like, I have a life, and I will live it. It's predominantly for you, with you and through you, but by God, it's not by your leave."

She turned and faced the wall, her shoulders heaving with her sobbing. Her chest hurt, her heart she felt was close to breaking. She was afraid that she had said too much, would he react with spite or would he listen and hear how much she wanted to love him.

He put his arms around her, and although she could not see his face she knew instantly that the tenderness she so cherished had returned. She turned and they kissed deeply, the yearning for each other enveloped them and he carried her to bed. They made love as they used to, slowly, carefully and easily. Each pleased the other. When it was over they lapsed into a deep and peaceful sleep. Rachel had returned to the warmth of her belonging, secure in the love that only Michael could give.

In the morning they made their clinging farewells, he off to Chicago, she ready with her final days of practice before Liverpool and the Grieg.

"Take care my darling, don't work too hard and keep those American girls at bay." She clung to him for one more moment

"I'll ring you and I'll be back for Liverpool." He turned and rushed down the stairs his rain coat billowing behind him. It was seven-o-clock on a dull November morning and she felt suddenly alone, but for all the emptiness of her house she was happy. She made her way straight to the studio and to 'Becky' and she started her day, after a moment's hesitation, with Grieg's Lyric pieces. 'Edward Grieg you're a lovely man, I shall grow to love you.'

At eleven she still sat at her piano, having spent the last hour on the Concerto, she was happier now in that she felt she knew what she wanted to say in her performance. She then packed up her music score and made her way to Kensington for another hour on the same work with her old College Professor.

She had a wonderful couple of hours; not only was Sally Nye, her favourite Professor, able to spend the whole time with her, they were joined for half an hour by the mesmerising Barry Douglas; Prince Consort professor and one of the finest living virtuosos. They all listened and then proposed this and that, but by and large the session was one of friends sharing. Sally and Rachel had lunch together.

"You know Rachel we've all felt that your Baroque obsession wasn't right for you, not exclusively anyway, this work you've done just proves it"

"Yes I've enjoyed Grieg and Schumann and Bela Bartok, maybe I needed the baroque years after Leipzig, we came so close then to what I thought at the time, was all I ever wanted. Maybe it's since my wedding that things have changed, I don't know"

"Well whatever, I was quite taken with how you've moved on this morning, Barry was very complimentary by the way, and he's not a man who casts compliments around with abandon."

"Do you really think I can make a go of it? I have moments of panic sometimes; I have this nightmare that I won't remember a note."

"You'll be fine, I've never been surer of anything" They drank their water. "Here's my last piece of advice, and I urge you to take it, you've done enough on the Grieg Concerto, relax over the next few days, don't spend all your time on it, there's danger of losing your clarity that is clearly there right now, so no more than say forty five minutes a day." They got up to leave, "One last thing Rachel don't let the conductor, Jadesjo, push you around, your vision of this is lovely, make sure it remains your performance and not some safe rendering of an old warhorse. The audience will love it, but only you will know if you've spoken from your own point of view. Never give that up." They kissed and Rachel made her way happily home.

There remained but four days to the Liverpool concert, the house was a lonely place, she worked as Sally Nye had proposed, and fought with Eva, who as always insisted she knew better.

Mummy came round for supper and announced that she and three friends were all going up to Liverpool. Rachel's heart sank, not so much at the thought of the support in the audience, but with the prospect of looking after everyone after the performance.

She knew her mother could not resist showing off her daughter, to people who knew nothing of music other than that a 'concert pianist' was someone it was good to know, a subject for dinner conversation 'I was with my friend Rachel George, a well known concert pianist, we were back stage...' It was well meant of Mummy but nevertheless a tiresome duty.

Her mother Margaret without variation started her conversations with Rachel: "I still love him you know, but he wrecked my life not because he didn't love me, he did, but he was always looking for a new sexual adventure, God knows why, I gave him whatever he asked for, any way we won't go into that. It was just that his obsessive womanizing took him out of my bedroom and that was the beginning of the end."

Rachel never quite came to terms with her mother's tale of the marriage breakdown, but then there was Jacqui, Lady George, a young trophy wife if ever there was one. Margaret loathed Jacqui with a passion, but since their dinner the other night Rachel had a sneaking regard for her stepmother.

"Mother, please understand that I'll be thrilled that you, Janet and whatshername are coming, but after the concert if all goes well, I have to meet someone from Concordia Records and so I won't be able to have our usual chat"

"Oh we'll quite understand, we won't be a bother at all"

Rachel didn't believe a word.

Each night Michael rang, just before bedtime, they billed and cooed for half an hour if Michael had the time. He may be delayed by one day, but for sure he'd be home in time for Liverpool; each night he wanted to know everything, where she'd been, who had she seen; Rachel, so excited about her next few days was delighted to account for each moment sure in the knowledge that this was sharing life.

Max visited on the Monday with last minute details of the arrangements; they were to leave by train on Tuesday evening, they would stay at a place some way out of Liverpool where they would spend a quiet evening On Wednesday morning they were to be at the Philharmonic Hall at eleven for rehearsals that were limited to two hours. The concert would begin at seven thirty and the Grieg would be presented at around eight ten. They should be at the Hall from seven when she would have the opportunity to warm up on a piano in the artist's room. Harold Gingrich, European Vice President of Concordia would join them for a post concert supper. Max seemed put out that Michael was going to be on the scene at all. Eva had been banned from approaching within thirty miles of Liverpool, she was deeply hurt but Max had insisted, and in the last analysis Max's word was law.

Their journey to Liverpool was uneventful; they were driven from the city centre for around forty minutes 'til they arrived at a delightful Country House. There, they were greeted by the owner, who was an ancient but charming gentleman who put them at their ease. Rachel's room was huge, a double, with an ancient but supremely comfortable, bed. It was dark but there were no lights to be seen through her windows, they were deep in the coastal countryside.

Dinner alone with Max was a bit strained. Max was trying too hard to be nonchalant, but was clearly as nervous as Rachel. She didn't sleep very well, this was usual before recitals and concerts, she never did. She was up early and walked in the windswept gardens with the stark beautiful views of the rolling land that lead to the sea. Breakfast was an enormous buffet with all the traditional trimmings. They ignored it all and drank coffee, orange juice and ate a little toast. It was still only nine-o-clock, so Rachel amused herself playing on an upright piano in the large lounge. She played the Grieg piano sonata in E that she'd played in Gothenburg so long ago. Max sat quietly by.

"Today will be the beginning, my darling, I can tell, today you will arrive."

Soon it was time to go and the long drive seemed interminable to Rachel, they soon left the countryside and drove through the dreary suburbs of the City. They arrived at The Philharmonic Hall a little early, the foyer that was a remarkable place in itself. They found themselves in Egyptian fantasy, a mock Tutankhamen tomb. Rachel could hardly contain her light headed mirth.

An attendant approached, "Sorry Box Office closed till eleven." he said; he was almost unintelligible. He spat and choked out the words in a violent Liverpool twang.

Max waved an imperious arm, "My man this is tonight's soloist Ms Rachel George-Johnson, I am her Manager; now please show us to the auditorium."

As soon as the doors opened they heard the lush sound of the orchestra playing Neilson's fifth symphony. They stood there taking in the delightful hall, the sights and sounds of the rehearsal. The conductor looked almost dwarf like on the podium... He directed the Orchestra with the minimum of movement. The Orchestra stopped abruptly, the little man who was as broad as he was tall spoke quietly, took up his baton and the orchestra responded.

A tall silhouette made a swift way up through the stalls to where Max and Rachel were sitting, "Can I help, oh Ms George, and Mr. Luberoff; I'm George Plackett the General Manger, you're both most welcome."

They spoke in a low key as the orchestra continued with the rehearsal. At ten to eleven precisely the orchestra stopped, the conductor addressed the players briefly and they took a break. Plackett lead Rachel to the platform;

" Jamo, may I introduce Ms Rachel George. Ms George, Jamo Jadesjo"

He bowed, so that she could see the top of his enormous auburn haired head. When he straightened she saw that he was no taller than her. He had a wide, open face with bright brown lively eyes. His mouth was broad and his face freckled. His luxuriant hair was neatly cut; everything about him was neat. His hands were broad, his fingers short and beautifully manicured. She liked him instantly.

"It's a delight," he beamed, "I've heard so much about you, not only of your performance in Gothenburg but also of your wonderful baroque repertoire. I've been looking forward very much to today, now then; would you like to meet the Leader? A tall, rather diffident man moved hesitantly to Jadesjo's side. He shook hands; his hands were warm but dry, testimony to the work already done that morning.

Rachel refused the opportunity to get to know the piano, she sat and just warmed up without self consciousness. The hubbub subsided as the Orchestra reassembled in the appropriate formation of seventeen wind, tympani and the string sections.

"Quiet every one," the orchestra settled in an instant, "It is my honour to introduce Miss George, Miss Rachel George," There was a tapping of bows and polite applause; "Miss George is a soloist who knows Grieg, indeed has an international reputation, made in Gothenburg," he turned and grinned at her, "so let's listen to what she has to say on the piano."

He half turned to Rachel, "I'll take it from the top and we'll go straight through, is that OK?"

Rachel nodded, the orchestra tuned. Then they were silent. Jamo raised his baton and they were off. Rachel just didn't catch her breath, she played as she wanted to play, only in one short period in the first movement did she feel the slightest uncertainty, she seemed just an eighth of a beat away, in an instant they were in perfect time. The little conductor seemed to be listening so intently but at the same time translating and directing the orchestra. He made little, almost comic signs, his eyes flashed from Rachel to the orchestra in nano-seconds. She felt that he was holding her hands as she played. The last movement was on her in no time. The wonderful climax cascaded over them and then it was over.

There was a silence that echoed through the hall, and then a clacking of the bows and a tapping on the other instruments. Jadesjo stood, his arms raised, his face wreathed in smiles.

"Oh, wonderful, just a few things I think..." He smiled. "You must tell me how these hacks cramped your style. It is important that you let me listen to you some more, your ideas and tempi are so bright and refreshing," He blew her a kiss; "tell me Miss George what shall we do?"

Rachel still dazed from the immediacy of it all, almost overcome, found it hard to say anything, and then she remembered the few times of uncertainty. They played through these sections again but by twelve thirty they were finished.

The party had lunch together, Jamo and Rachel immediate friends. Max his eyes darting if anything more maniacally than usual, whilst Placket sat quietly by, reminding everyone of the time and making sure that details such as Rachel's clothes, warm up requirements and other issues were covered.

They decided to return to the Hotel for a rest and Rachel retired and lay on her bed more excited now than nervous. Of course she was nervous but the little Swedish Conductor with the big heart had so boosted her confidence that she felt nothing could go badly wrong. She got a message that Michael was on his way, he wished her luck and looked forward to seeing her after the concert. Flowers arrived at the Hotel from her mother; God knew how she knew their whereabouts. Max was heard playing the piano down stairs, he played quite well really; he was a frustrated pianist himself. Rachel had never learned about Max's past. She pottered in her room, the strains of his playing rising up the stairs. Dear Max, such a close friend, yet so distant.........

At six they left for the City, Max dressed in one of his extravagant bow ties and a really beautiful suit that shouted ££££. His perfume had been so liberally applied that Rachel could hardly resist opening the limousine window. However her hair had been styled for the occasion, though not the sort of thing that Rachel usually worried about, but tonight she was conscious of everything, everything had to be right.

This time they were dropped off at the artists' entrance, they went to her dressing room, they opened the door and the scent of the banks of flowers almost floored them. They were all gorgeous; even if some clashed. There in the middle was a huge array of white roses, she knew from Michael. The card read, 'I know they'll love you, but you'll always be mine, all my love, be a smash! Michael'. There was another huge arrangement of roses, clearly expensive and obviously from her daddy, the card said 'Good Luck, Love daddy.' There were messages of good luck from Sue Nye, Eva and a very formal note from Cy Allman, President of Concordia USA who was also in town with Gingrich, wishing her well. She changed into her favourite black dress, Max oohed and ahhed, drooled and cooed.

"You're delicious, if only I liked women, I'd not keep my hands from you."

They both laughed. The clock ticked slowly, she moved to the Essex upright and started her exercises, and then she moved to the Lyric pieces. She relaxed and didn't even hear the door open. Jamo stood beside her silent and it was a while before she noticed him.

"Rachel, that's just wonderful, would you mind if I talk to Max about a trip for you back to Gothenburg."

"Oh Jamo, of course not, but we haven't got through tonight yet"

"You'll carry us through Rachel; even if the orchestra has a bad night and I make a mess, you will carry us through."

"Oh Jamo don't be silly I'm so excited about working with you tonight, I just hope I'm good enough."

"I've never been surer of anything in my life," he pecked her cheek, shook both her hands in his and turned to leave. She noticed that he was not wearing tails but a short black evening jacket cut rather like a jacket worn by a bull-fighter. She thought he looked wonderful.

She went back to the piano, and fiddled about, as Eva would have said. She just wanted time to pass. Max eventually came up to her quietly, "My darling, you'll be a smash, would you like me to stay or shall I go and listen to you from the stalls?"

"It's all right Max I'll be fine."

She was alone, her heart pounded as she heard the orchestra play the opening work, she fiddled some more, quietly now as she was conscious of the musical vibrations, she was afraid of being heard. She had to go to the toilet and then was overcome with panic that she would have no time. But time was not that merciful; she sat at last in silence and concentrated as she had been taught. The tumult of the first movement; the sparkling opening, the descending minor seconds and the major thirds. She closed her eyes and tried to live the music.

Then she heard it, the building spoke, the applause thundered quietly through the walls, her time had come. There was a tap on her door, she looked in the mirror, moistened her lips, straightened her gait, "I'm coming"

She followed the floor manager to the stage wing where Jamo and the Leader were waiting. The tall leader rather self consciously bade her good luck, he smiled, adjusted his spectacles and walked on stage to the polite applause.

Jamo looked at her, "OK, you'll be great ...ready?"

She could hardly speak, her heart thumped like a rank of tympani, "Yes" she stammered.

Jamo's gentle hand steered her in to the concert hall, she found her way to the piano, Jamo came up beside as the applause rang out. She blinked into the sea of faces in the semi darkness beyond, comprehending nothing.

Jamo took his place on the podium; Rachel sat, felt an urgent need to adjust her stool, then decided against it. She closed her eyes, 'Music where are you?" She took a deep breath and looked up, Jamo stood poised; she raised her hands over the keys, nodded; they were off.

The first movement, the longest, went with the energy and tumbling spring that Grieg had magically created; the thirteen minutes disappeared in a trice. She had not imagined that she could be part of such a glorious song, she was part of something so much bigger than even this great Steinway, it was a hymn of praise and she was lost in the glory of it. The second movement is a relaxation that set the musicians in a sweet harmony, there was no uncertainty here, the adagio flowed delightfully in a sweet unison between piano and orchestra. Then, the dances of the third movement and then the end, so complete, so perfect, so sure.

Then a fleeting moment of stillness,... a brief eternity, then the roar of the audience crescendoed to the roof tops. Her eyes were filled with tears, her breath came in gasps. Her hands lay on her thighs, her head down, the tears began to flood. The noise, the shouts, the bow tapping, the 'bravos' rang out, and she embraced Jamo who now stood beside her, he stepped back, she shook hands with the grinning Leader, the clapping, the clapping, the clapping. Jamo again gently pushed her to the front; she stood quite lost for a moment and then bowed. She turned and was pushed gently back again, the clapping, the clapping, her breath came back and she bowed a little bow, then she grabbed Jamo lest he should escape, and hoisted his hand with hers. The clapping, the clapping; the roars and the stamping.

Jamo bowed deferentially and they walked off the platform, but the stamping and clapping resonated even louder. They stood together in the wings, he offered his handkerchief, and then once more he gently touched her towards the platform, she set out towards this thunderous applause. 'Thank you; you wonderful people of Liverpool, oh thank you.' She then discovered she was alone, the orchestra still tapped their instruments; the audience stood and roared, the tears welled up once more. Then from stage left came a gentleman with a huge bouquet of flowers that she received to more applause. She turned and left the platform once more. Still they clapped,

" Jamo please,"

"After you"

"Promise"

"Promise"

This time the applause renewed with seemingly endless vigour. Rachel turned to the Leader and beckoned to the orchestra to rise. They sat steadfastly in their seats. Jamo though asked the orchestra to rise and they did. Once more the applause thundered out, again she followed the gentle direction of Jamo and they left the platform for the last time.

One more hug from her conductor, and she followed Plackett to her dressing room. "I shall see you're not disturbed, I'm sure you're exhausted, performances of that calibre always take so much out you artists."

The door closed and she was alone, suddenly the euphoria had subsided. The sense of anticlimax was overwhelming. She undressed and showered, God, she'd perspired buckets. As the water washed over her she felt the relaxation through her body and her focus returned. Soon she'd be with Michael and that would wash away all her fatigue.

The interval was over and the Nielson symphony resonated like a shadow of sound through her lonely vigil. She did her hair, made up and then just sat and waited, rested. It wasn't rest, it was an anxious prowling, she hated to admit to herself that she craved not only Michael's company but Max's and for that matter anybody else's, she wanted to be complimented, she wanted to be the centre again. This was always the same after recitals and perhaps more so tonight; first the desire to be alone; then a compulsive desire for company. Once more the echo of applause, then the first visitor, the delightful Jamo Jadesjo,

"Rachel I can't wait to show you off in Gothenburg, you were born for Grieg, who ever made this happen is a genius."

Then as if by magic, the genius himself, Max his eyes darting, his beard bristling, his bow tie at a crazy angle.

"Darling, fantastic"

He spread his arms and she collapsed into his arms, then as she looked over his shoulder, there was Michael,

"Does hubby get a cuddle?"

She whooped with delight and rushed to him planting a long unselfconscious kiss of epic proportions. The door was flooded, there was Mummy and her silly friends, a tall dark and it had to be said handsome stranger, who recognised Max and engaged him immediately. The room was a hubbub of noise and laughter, Rachel unashamedly basked in the lime light that she adored.

Cy Allman was the tall dark and handsome stranger. He was six foot four with a long chiseled face, eyes that were steely blue and with dark, just ash-graying hair. He looked around fifty.

"Darling, I want you to meet Cy Allman, and of course" turning to Allman "Michael Johnson; Rachel's husband." Max made the introduction in his inimitable startled way; introducing Michael was a necessary and obvious abstraction.

Allman though took it all in his charming stride, "Wonderful to meet you both, but I'm confused, George or Johnson?"

"Rachel and Michael will do" shot back Rachel, holding Michael's hand close to her side. She was always aware of the discomfort that Michael felt, he was in her territory and he didn't much care for the subsidiary role.

"Cy, Cy Allman," he extended his elegant hands first to Rachel then to Michael. At each hand shake he looked directly into their eyes. Rachel was disconcerted, Michael held his gaze.

"Excuse me Mr. Allman I have to get rid of mother and her cohorts, I won't be long." She sidled off to a great cacophonous greeting from her Mother's chums. Rachel knew to keep the meeting short would need all her skill.

"Well Michael," began Allman, "it must be pretty exciting being married to someone as talented as your wife"

"Yes, it is, but we're first and foremost a couple; we have a lovely home in London, the trick is to spend time in it together."

The small talk continued, Jamo returned, now dressed in a very ordinary woolly jacket; he greeted Allman, but obviously knew him well. He was effusive to Michael about Rachel. Michael was comfortable with the little conductor; he was an easy man to like.

Allman hosted supper in his suite at the Adelphi Hotel. The talk was of music, praise for Rachel and there were even hints as to the potential that lay ahead. Jamo it turned out was on contract to Concordia for a series of CD's to be recorded in Gothenburg. The recordings were to be a Scandinavian Series covering works as diverse as Sibelius and Nielson.

Rachel, ever conscious of her husband's discomfort, watched him closely, he was obviously tired after tramping across the Atlantic overnight, and although he was doing his best to appear interested he was finding it hard to stay with it.

Much to Max's discomfort Rachel made her excuses, bade a fond farewell especially to her new friend Jamo. She hoped, much like a small child wishes for a Christmas present, that they would work together again. Nothing had been decided; at least not formally, and she knew that the machinations of the music business were tortuous and fickle.

She hugged the little man, "Gothenburg", he said, "soon." He waved and they hurried into the cold damp night for the ride to their country retreat.

Michael could hardly think, he was so tired, Max babbled on in the car, why didn't he shut up? He was pleased that it had all gone well; Rachel he knew would be more relaxed now that this particular engagement had been completed. To go by the audience reaction then she had really done well. But who knew? Provincial audiences loved the old war-horses. He enjoyed it, he was proud, but he was also just another punter. What made the difference between Barry Douglas, or John Lille and any number of pianists was a mystery to him. Max, what a pain; Michael dozed to incessant chatter of the Russian émigré, any way Russia or somewhere, possibly an illegal immigrant.

He smiled to himself as he imagined Max being dragged away by a posse of police. Rachel, my Rachel she makes me want her all the time, I can't bear it when we waste time apart. Tonight on stage she looked so gorgeous. Down at the rugby club he could hear them shouting lewd remarks.

His Rachel; the wife who had surprised him on honeymoon; God she liked sex, that night she'd worn him out she was so keen. He wondered if the demure and beautiful girl he'd met in Cambridge was the same girl who was now his wife. She'd been so demure and chaste, it had taken God knows how long to get her into bed. Since their honeymoon she'd changed, she was more moody, more assertive, and much more assured between the sheets.

"Wake up Michael, darling we're here"

They staggered into the house, where Max insisted they had a large cognac before they retired. Max bade them good night, and they went to their room.

Michael wanted Rachel, she was, he knew, the object of many men's desire. That bastard Cy Allman, he'd spotted him right away. Smarmy American with the power to influence her career, he'd have to watch him. Rachel undressed; he felt the shortness of breath, the surge of his desire. She seemed so happy, so open to him, had she been excited by all that attention from Allman? Despite his fatigue he wanted her, now.

Their coupling lost the restraint and care that should have come from her contentment. Michael could not resist mumbling remarks about her other admirers. He became hard and excessively dominant, she fought back matching his raw desire with her own. He seemed to go beyond even that and the shadow of the night in Hvar returned.

Michael slept in the leaden arms of Orpheus, exhausted by the rigors of his lovemaking and the jet lag. He had rid himself of his awful fantasies. Tomorrow would be another day they would spend together. He looked forward to going home.

The journey back to London was mercifully without Max who shuffled off to more meetings in Liverpool and Manchester. Mr. and Mrs. Johnson spent a pleasant day together travelling on a train that rattled through the dull November countryside, with little else to do but to search through the papers scouring them for reviews of Rachel's last night performance. There was a nice piece in the Guardian which described Rachel's performance as fresh, of her as a star in the making. The local Liverpool paper said much the same, but Rachel felt that the correspondent had not been at the concert at all. The remarks she said; smacked of plagiarized notes of a record sleeve.

Back at home and Michael was soon back to work calling the bank, his colleagues in the United States. His trip to Liverpool had been something of a chore for him, although he'd never let Rachel know that. The deal in the States was going well and he was due to return to Chicago the following Sunday.

Chapter 5

Michael loved his job at the bank. From the first day when he'd been very nervous, he'd known that this was the place where he wanted to be. The City excited him; the power here was immeasurable, the opportunities endless, the people, his sort. He belonged here.

He knew with a certainty that he was more able than most, he was sharp, and he had charm. He'd made a lot of connections at Cambridge, and his father Robbie, an Alderman of the City, could be relied upon to point him in the right direction. The bank, was small by international standards; LONY Capital was the result of a merger in the distant seventies of two banking dynasties in London and New York, hence LONY. The bank had three divisions and Michael had spent his first year learning the different aspects of each one.

Michael was immediately at home in LONY because it seemed to be populated entirely by ageless wiz-kids, virtually all graduates of Oxbridge or the Ivy League. He'd made friends easily and at the end of his first year he'd been snapped up by the PEP Funds Division. This Division invested in primarily European or US up and coming private corporations. The investment was always a sharply drawn issue, with defined goals and within selected market segments. Michael had spent the last year working in the healthcare sector.

His present project was the merger of two Bio technology companies, one in Chicago and one in Cambridge, England. The job straddled the PEP and Venture Capital Divisions, so that Michael's role was highly visible both in New York and London and to key department heads. His boss Alistair Bingham, a forty year old vice-president of the bank, seemed absolutely at ease with Michael's role and his responsibilities. This was by far the biggest job he'd undertaken, but Alistair gave little advice unless he was asked, and seemed content to be debriefed on his fortnightly meetings with Michael.

Michael had made errors; he had not ensured the US due diligence was completed in synch with the UK operation; he had underestimated the resistance of both companies to the planned merger. Since LONY held large slices of equity in each, of course they had little choice, but the Americans in particular were dragging their feet.

Just as Rachel slogged away at her piano practice, so Michael immersed himself in patents, intellectual property rights, asset valuations, and equity splits, the massaging of egos and international marketing plans. Added to this there was the constant to-ing and fro-ing across to Chicago, New York, London and Cambridge. Alistair reckoned that the combined operation would increase their equity stake value at least five fold in two years after completion. Maybe if both corporations pulled off their present research projects it could be as much as twenty times.

The stakes for Michael were high; a success would net him between a half million to three million pounds in bonuses, depending on the performance of the merged businesses; a failure would see him possibly jobless, at best transferred to another division and a restart at the bottom.

Michael's life style could be summed up as: work hard, play hard. Money was not a problem; he had a handsome salary and almost limitless expenses. He worked from seven am when in the office, and spent his time travelling in the most effective way, travelling outside working hours mainly overnight and at weekends. When in the States he worked alongside two like minded colleagues in Ricardo Brevi, an Italian American whose main out of work hobbies were booze and women. So far Michael had joined in the booze part of his friend's hobbies but had remained strictly faithful to his delicious Rachel.

Hugo Love, his other main US friend was quite different; he was an older hand than either Michael or Ricardo. At the age of thirty two he'd already been married twice and gone through innumerable 'live in' relationships. He now vowed that he was giving up trying to find the right girl and would live on TV dinners and casual sex for the rest of his life.

Hugo in some ways reminded Michael of Bertie Frobisher, utterly reliable but accident prone, at least in his private life. On the whole he preferred the company of Hugo to Ricardo. Ricardo was too brash, too brazen, and almost vulgar. Hugo was much more, well European, even Anglo Saxon.

Hugo also had an incredible talent; he could remember any numeric relationship in absolute detail. He had the kind of talent for remembering a fantastic amount of detail, yet he would often forget to take lunch, and follow up by forgetting dinner as well. In some ways Michael liked to look after Hugo, he was vulnerable despite his great talent.

Life in America for Michael consisted of fourteen-hour days in the office followed by four hours of drinking and watching out for Hugo. Hugo would fall for any girl that even so much as smiled at him, hooker or policewoman it made no difference. Michael guided him out of the Manhattan or downtown Chicago bars into Steak joints or Chinese restaurants since these were open all night and besides that's all that Hugo would eat.

A week with his American colleagues, not surprisingly, exhausted Michael who returned to London and Rachel; worn out, exhausted but always a step nearer his big pay day. Rachel he knew was the most beautiful girl in the world, but it became increasingly difficult to sustain their once, head over heels relationship. It annoyed him that she was so often away when he came home. Her piano became a symbol of her unfaithfulness. The damned piano got more attention than he did. So did that crazy Max and the crone Eva.

After the Liverpool concert, Rachel's workload increased dramatically, she seemed more distant, more concentrated than ever with new projects, attending lessons at huge cost with this Master and that. Her stays away were longer and further away; no longer recitals in the village halls, but concerts and broadcasts from foreign cities. Her diary of engagements went impossibly far ahead. In London at social gatherings he was often unescorted. The other wives, never failing to remark; that 'poor Michael was on his own again'.

Worst of all when they were home together, their combined exhaustion often cramped their affection, dampened their ardour and stole their precious time together like a thief in the night. At every parting there was a sense of an opportunity lost, time gone forever, minutes that should have been treasured cast away on the cold breeze of fatigue.

Sometimes, despite their best efforts, they even passed each other over mid Atlantic bound in opposite directions. It was absurd, but such were the demands of each one's professional life there was little or no choice.

Michael sometimes spent time in London down at the rugby club. He still enjoyed a game for the London Banks. But there was no denying that his fitness was in decline and he found it harder and harder to keep in trim. Still he enjoyed the bon-homie and company of the 'boys'. Bertie also played for the lawyers and sometimes they got together and usually drank themselves into oblivion.

At the Bank in London, he had a few friends with whom he'd occasionally have lunch. Richard Hayter he'd known from Cambridge days, and Ben Flowers an Oxford man with a keen sense of humour. They were both married so that they saw little of each other outside work, there was a sense of rivalry between them; each acutely aware of the other's projects, status and ranking. Hayter was a big strong fine figure of a man, though he was of all the London people, the quietest. The only hobby that Michael knew he was interested in was horse racing. Incongruously on his desk among all the paraphernalia of reports, the Financial Times there was always the Racing Post Hayter was something of an expert on European stocks and his specialty was European fund management.

Michael's US project demanded more and more time in New York, Chicago and Cambridge, they were now preparing the prospectus for the shortly to be merged companies. The protagonists, although now having accepted the merger and their roles in the new entity, remained prickly, uncomfortable and downright difficult.

Hugo Love; Dr. Hugo Love to give him his proper title, now had the key role of analyzing the research of both arms and arbitrating the best way forward including the division of future research and associated facilities. He was a brilliant scientist who'd studied for his PhD in the joint venture Harvard-M.I.T. Division of Health Sciences and Technology.

There was literally hell to play about the distribution of resources of the new company and an equally unseemly row between the two great seats of learning in Cambridge England and Cambridge Massachusetts about associated research support.

All this placed a huge burden of pressure on the merger team. The time table for the completion of the merger slipped by; and they all knew that LONY's aspirations were unreal. Michael could not judge whether any blame had been placed at his feet with Bingham remaining supportive. In the US though, he felt that William Ross, the urbane but brilliant Vice- President had cooled to him. In meetings Ross frequently referred to planning errors and missed deadlines, he constantly referred to Ricardo Brevi for advice in preference to Michael. The whole team, except Hugo was under enormous strain.

Hayter was assigned to the team principally because of his European experience and he would complement Brevi with his wide USA experience, and despite his quiet help Michael felt irked by his presence on the team. This aggravation became more acute when on a visit to Chicago; Hayter seemed to strike up a firm friendship with the dreadful Brevi who it transpired was a gambler and horse racing buff as well as lecher and drunk.

Suddenly there seemed two teams, Michael and Hugo versus Hayter and Brevi. Hayter though late on the scene was very bright and was adept at listening and making very good points from other people's data.

He never made the running but could be counted on to score points in project meetings when either Bingham or Ross was present. Brevi was decidedly anti Michael and appeared to have made up his mind that he could take over the project if Michael's position could be exposed as lacking control. Ross seemed to feed on this, and often stoked the rivalry.

After fifteen months of furious work, innumerable transatlantic flights, and a multitude of false dawns, Michael was exhausted, frustrated and for the first time a little uncertain.

Bingham seemed as cool as ever and took everything in his stride. He never queried progress but always debriefed Michael with patience and incisive interrogation. The aquiline Alistair Bingham was supportive only in his constancy; Michael never really felt he could relax with his London Chief. It was as if Bingham was like an imperious vulture that sat on a very high mountaintop and observed his mortal prey beneath. The only comfort he ever gave Michael were the odd derogatory remarks about "our Colonial cousins" in the States.

Michael's rock was Hugo. Hugo was far from the best business brain but he was miles better equipped than anyone to talk to the company founders, the research fellows in the universities and was the only one, perhaps even better than the partners themselves, who understood the science and the creative challenge that lay ahead for the merged company.

Hugo was one of those rare beings who could understand the most complex scientific issues and imagine the future potential. However Hugo was very bad at projecting his ideas. This was Michael's strength and together they made a great team.

Hugo was a tall and ungainly fellow with a shock of untidy dark hair; his attire was expensive but could have been dirt cheap for he always looked a shambles. His shirt collars though clean were always crumpled, his suit wrinkled and his ties half way round his neck. He needed tidying up and to some extent this was why the ladies felt they could mother him. Of course in practice those who tried, failed and soon got fed up with living with a man who constantly forgot what time it was or even what day it was. His eyes reminded Michael of Luberoff in that they never seemed to point in the same direction simultaneously. His mouth was wide and slanting, and above his high coloured cheek he sported a very pronounced mole under his left eye. Once met, he was hard to forget. By far his most engaging attribute as far as Michael was concerned was Hugo's absolute reliability and honesty. Hugo would always be on top of his job even if he had no idea what day it was. Michael felt he was Hugo's organiser, guardian and mouthpiece. They had become firm friends and enjoyed above all things to share a joke and to relax together with a beer; Hugo making squinting eyes at passing females and Michael making sure that they ate at least one meal a day.

As the pressure grew with time, Hugo frequently confirmed his trust in Michael, and also their partnership; how Michael need never fear Hugo. In their partnership was an implicit pact that was based on nothing other than good old friendship, a simple but abiding affection. Apart from his closeness to the shambling scientist, Michael could never be certain of anyone else. Michael knew that this was the jungle and Hugo was the only thing between him and the unholy alliance of Ross, Hayter and Brevi.

Hugo, though, was in many ways, so weak. His behaviour with women was positively adolescent. He was attracted to the opposite sex without any reserve whatever. Whores, some of them certainly were, and any woman that would give him the slightest sexual comfort was elevated to the status of delivering angel in an instant.

There had been a number of instances when Hugo had tried to introduce Michael to assorted female company. Michael had been steadfastly aloof. He saw these women for what they were; sluts and tarts. Women who preyed on men; who used their sex to get favours.

They were not like his Rachel of course, though sometimes in the half slumber of his jet lagged existence he dreamed of her, and that evil green-eyed God had scratched insidiously on the walls of his soul. After all; these musical types were a strange lot, arty crafty, half of them queer in one way or another.

What Michael resented so much about these musicians was their separation, their aloofness. He could never get close to Rachel's inner being; all those bloody musical notes. Yes she was a wonderful musician but was she so different that he didn't know her? After all he remembered her performance on honeymoon, how she'd taken her pleasure, yes, it was her pleasure; she'd dominated him. At least she'd tried to, but since then he'd been the master. Or had he?

As time went on, the fatigue got to everyone on the 'team'; Michael had at last agreed a deadline for the launch of the prospectus with the senior echelons of LONY on both sides of the pond. Hayter and Brevi had committed to delivering the investor pool and the PR and supporting hype was set in motion. The bank's army of lawyers, auditors, accountants, publicists, and regulatory advisors were mobilized. From this day on there would be no respite and no excuses.

Ross and Bingham seemed to change gear and both became decidedly closer to the action. Far from the detached and almost isolated responsibility, now they crowded in on him. There was hardly a moment there was not a query from one of the team, the prospective shareholders, the publicity people. The Principals seemed to have settled as they now worked flat out together to finalize the prospectus and to begin the integration process.

The animosity that had existed between former rivals had dissolved between them, as they worked frantically; orchestrated by Hugo, now trusted by everyone in both camps. Michael began to feel the sense of accomplishment; at last things were coming together. The insecurity of the last few months began to disappear.

Even Ross seemed more comfortable and much friendlier. He still praised the efforts of Brevi and Hayter but then the US side of LONY drove the investor group. There were still problems to be dealt with, the British Government's Department of Trade and Industry wanted details of the technology exchange implications and the US Government agencies also sought assurances about the eventual control over huge medical and bio-tech potential... Lobbyists on both sides of the Atlantic worked at fever pitch.
  Both Hugo and Michael were intimately involved with the politics of the issue albeit behind the scenes as Bingham and Ross brought their connections into play.

Chief among the UK lobbying team was Sir Bradley Walmer, a former Government Minister. He was an unpleasant fellow or so thought Michael as he and Hugo dined in the Bank. The luncheon had been arranged so that Walmer could be appraised of the key issues before he used his influence to 'persuade' the DTI of the efficacy of the proposed merger.

Bingham was his usual courteous self, except that he was more deferential to Walmer than Michael had expected. Walmer was supercilious in the extreme and treated Michael and Hugo as if they were not there, or worse as if they were office boys. Nevertheless they both behaved impeccably and spoke only when spoken to.

"I understand your wife is a very successful pianist." The sun glinted off Sir Bradley's bald pate.

Michael, rather taken by surprise, responded: "Yes, yes Sir; she's doing very well."

"Well you're a lucky man, Jennifer, that's my wife, says she's splendid, and we'd both like to see you at the Mansion House dinner, I'll arrange it."

"That's very kind of you Sir, I'd be honoured to come, but my wife's calendar is often booked up, however I'll do my best to drag her off stage for the event."

Bingham looked pleased; personally he wouldn't dream of inviting such junior members of the firm to the Lord Mayor's banquet, but good for young Michael. Bradley Walmer was a man of mixed reputation; a defrocked politician and now a mover and shaker in the City. However he was a man who no one really trusted, though no one dare exclude him either. His connection to 10 Downing Street was a reality; no one understood why the Prime Minister leant his ear to this rather unpleasant fellow. It was common belief that Walmer 'had something on the P.M.'; there could be no other explanation.

As the merger came closer to completion things became much less stressful in their way, success seemed to lead to success. Now that people could see that the merger was on track, everyone both at the bank and at the operating companies became as helpful as could be. Even Brevi and Hayter seemed to read the signs and resigned themselves to roles of supporters in a winning team.

Ross in particular transformed from the aloof overseer in the US, to avuncular advisor, a facilitator who now brought all manner of support that in fact would have been such a boon in the earlier stages of the deal. Alistair Bingham remained aloof with his British smugness absolutely intact. He assumed an air of satisfaction and even on one occasion went as far as patting Michael on the back.

"Always knew that you were the man for this my boy; Yanks don't have the finesse d'you see, well done."

As the last lap of the project loomed just the permission of the Department of Trade and Industry stood in the way. When patience was all but exhausted, another luncheon with Sir Bradley Walmer yielded up the news that all was well and that the Government would announce the all clear. This they duly did two days later, Sir Bradley Walmer had delivered his promise and no doubt picked up his reward, what that was, Michael had no idea.

In the event the whole launch of the new joint venture company was a huge success. The new shares were greatly oversubscribed and the opening price was above LONY's wildest dreams.

Michael, not yet thirty one years old, was feted on both sides of the Atlantic, it seemed that he could choose what his next assignment would be, he was unassailable; the enfant terrible of the LONY Bank. His share options in the Bank were considerable and his bonus huge, he was already a wealthy man who seemed destined to become wealthier.

"I'll miss you pal", mumbled Hugo, as they celebrated the completion of their partnership aboard yet another flight from Chicago to London, "Jeeze man, I'll be working with I don't know who, maybe that shit Brevi, who cares, could I have some more Champagne please?"

"We'll stick together Hugo, never fear, I know you're the hot shot bio sciences guy, but I reckon there are a bundle of deals out there in your field, I'll try and get into the same field, then we can stick together…. Any way you're the bright bastard, not me; it's just that we'll keep it a secret." They laughed and drank more fizz.

Next Monday would be the first time for twenty-eight months when Michael would not worry about Scicom and Cambridge Bionics.

Scicom Bionics was now a reality and Michael was at least a million pounds richer. This weekend he'd relax with his old friends, maybe watch some rugby and have a drink or two with Bertie. Bertie and Hugo would be a great pair. It was a pity that Rachel was away again, in Austria, playing her bloody piano, but then; who cared?

Well, he did for one, he missed her terribly. The London home however comfortable stank of emptiness when she wasn't there. The quietness hung loudly blotting out the sounds of life; he listened in vain for the echoes of the piano from the studio. He missed her by his side at night; he missed her body and her loving in their bed. How he hated those nights alone.

When he was away from home he always looked forward to the telephone calls, they were always brief but somehow reassuring. When he was the one at home he was eager to hear her voice but the silence when the phone call was over was terrible, it echoed through his head. And then those dreams of her with other men in other countries and faraway places, they shared her company, the smell of her. Then those dreams, those awful dreams of her feeding the lust of others, drove him into himself, a bitter sweet voyeur in the agony of his dreams.

Chapter 6

In their frantic lives, the waste ate into their relationship like a cancer. They became separate, not separated, just two more and more independent people. Yes they cared for each other, yes they loved each other, but more by rote than by will. Then there was Michael's fits of jealousy that so frightened Rachel but after each episode Michael seemed able to ignore the whole thing. Rachel persuaded herself each time that this was the last; this was just a hiccup, in their frantic but ordinary love affair.

There were the wonderful exceptions, like the trip to Paris where Michael had brought both Hugo and his boss William Ross to hear Rachel play the Schumann. Ross a very cultured and charming individual; was an important man in LONY. Ross had been charm itself, Rachel for once had met someone from Michael's world who seemed genuinely interested in her music and who saw in her, not just a beautiful woman, but a musician to whom he could relate. They had dined, the four of them, at 'Les Tois des Passi'. The food and ambience was wonderful; the men were all charming. Michael basked in his wife's glory. Hugo was, as he always was, instantly and hopelessly infatuated with Rachel, who responded by treating him as a silly but nice schoolboy. This worked well, for Michael obviously felt safe and in control. He was able to enjoy the improbable flirting of Hugo and the banter balanced by the gravitas and charm of the urbane Ross.

That night it was as if they were back in their Cambridge days. They were at ease, Michael comfortable and proud. Rachel in love and focused on her husband as if the entire world was no more and that only the two of them existed.

These idyllic nights were becoming the exception rather than the rule. At the Mansion House dinner where they were guests of Sir Bradley Walmer, the glitter, the pomp was a thrill for them both; they were able to talk to the great and the good. They were seated with Rachel between Lord Worcester, and Sir Bradley Walmer and Michael between their Ladies.

The night started well being the only plain Mr& Mrs on the table they were warmly welcomed in to the august company. Wine was taken in abundance; the speeches were received with solemnity. The men dominated the conversation, mainly about the City and its dealings. Rachel was charmed by Lord Worcester whose old world charm was a delight. Jennifer Walmer made a fuss of Rachel, surprising her with her knowledge of Rachel's career and indeed about music in general.

Sir Bradley Walmer though was a different cup of tea. She felt or thought she felt his knees touching hers several times throughout the evening. She recoiled sharply on the number of occasions that this happened but the lanky banker simply grinned at her and continued his conversation with the gentlemen as if nothing had happened.

She suppressed her discomfort and merely smiled at one of the ladies, to all and sundry nothing was array. Michael later accepted the Walmer's invitation to after dinner drinks back at the City quarters of his Office. Rachel felt some foreboding, but she said nothing; this was Michael's night and she would do all she could to make it a success.

There assembled a gathering in the splendid offices of the most venerable banking institutions in London, at least fifty other guests, Champagne being dispensed without reserve. Sir Bradley Walmer looked down on the assembled company, his bald head shining like a drum major's mace above the crowd, with his polished cheeks and his luminous pale blue eyes.

The Prime Minister looking exhausted and haunted as he always did, stood quietly in a corner of the sumptuous room with his more glamorous wife like a peacock beside him. Walmer sought out his young guests and lugubriously attached himself to Rachel's side. He led them to the PM who was visibly relieved to see people present who were less than sixty years old! He smiled wanly, shook hands firmly, the conversation was stilted and awkward. Rachel became uncomfortable, Sir Bradley crowded her space. She felt herself stiffen as this predatory lanky old man closed in. Michael who was drinking at a frantic pace was clearly delighted to be mixing at these ethereal heights. The euphoria and the champagne made him voluble and excited. Rachel wished that he would shut up. The peacock gave Rachel a strange knowing look, smiled and took her to one side.

"My dear, I've heard you play, and I must say you're as beautiful close up as you are on the platform"

"That's sweet of you, but I'd prefer to be known for my playing than my looks, thank you all the same."

"I know Jennifer is something of a music buff, and quite one of the City hostesses, but my dear take a tip, Bradley is something else, take care my dear.'

With that she turned back into the small crowd that had gathered round the PM leaving Rachel detached on the fringe. Jennifer Walmer the perfect hostess, cruised around the company occasionally stopping to chat with her husband. On cue she whisked Rachel away to meet some 'feminine company rather than these boring City men'

The ladies, all twenty years her senior, were charming and pleasant. Several were obviously drunk but in the best possible taste. Rachel enjoyed being the centre of attention and relaxed, as the dowagers seemed content to engage in entirely undemanding but pleasant conversation. She looked around and was relieved to see there was no piano, and so relaxing, took more of the excellent Champagne.

"I can help your husband you know," he whispered sloppily into Rachel's ear. She recoiled from his rancid alcoholic breath as a spray of spittle landed on her bare shoulder. His arm slipped round her waist, "more Champagne my dear?"

"You've been a lovely host Sir Bradley, but thank you, no more. I have a busy day tomorrow." She looked around frantically for Michael who she could see watching but at the same time apparently flirting with some mature dowager at the other side of the room.

She cast an eye around for some form of rescue, but all Michael seemed to do was leer from the other side of the room. The whole thing was becoming a nightmare. Jennifer Walmer at least twenty years younger than the balding Bradley cruised by and Rachel swore she saw Jennifer wink at her husband.

Rachel had now edged along the room and found herself near the open balcony windows. Sir Bradley then with an almost brutal push tried to manoeuvre her out onto the cold balcony. She was able to side step towards a passing waiter and grabbed another glass of Champagne she didn't want. Sir Bradley persisted and took her elbow once more. Again he tried to lead to the balcony, again she resisted. Throughout the last fifteen minutes or so of this boorish behaviour she had done her best to be charming and polite, but now her temper was rising, not only because of the rampant Knight, but also because Michael appeared to have deliberately abandoned her.

Jennifer Walmer arrived just as Rachel was summoning the courage to throw her Champagne over this lecherous idiot.

"Come along Bradley, you're monopolising our glamorous guest, I must take her away to meet some others. You mustn't mind Bradley; Rachel he's just a silly boy really………… refuses to grow up."

She led Rachel to meet a range of City people that meant nothing to her. Duty, duty; she knew that this was her duty to support Michael. She spent the next hour talking to a variety of Lords, Ladies and other assorted persons of importance. They were rich, some were famous, but they were all old. She felt like a museum piece being examined by a group from another planet; a planet where rich old human reptiles fed with their great jaws full of money.

 They were happy and kind enough but they were a world apart, was this what Michael would become; an old rich reptile, feeding in the city where the only values were of avarice and self importance? She wished that a friendly and familiar face like Robbie would appear to lighten her night out that had now become a miserable early morning. Michael had now rejoined her and positively bristled with enthusiasm, fuelled by a surfeit of Champagne.

Rachel dragged him away at close to three am. He suddenly appeared quite drunk, as if he'd come off duty and relaxed. He teased her on the short journey home about the attentions of Walmer. She angrily enquired why he'd not come to her rescue but it was a hopeless conversation, he was drunk.

At home they drank coffee and made their way to bed. Michael became amorous, and at first Rachel was pleased, but the stink of stale Champagne on his breath reminded her at once of the disgusting Bradley Walmer.

She also knew that to change course now would be difficult, Michael's ardour was clearly seen and felt, her own appetite, though dampened, was still warm. She hoped that they could consummate their desire with the minimum of fuss and in the shortest possible time. His drunkenness would surely lead to his early sleep.

She took control doing all the things she knew he liked best. She steered clear of having to kiss him on the mouth, the avoidance of the alcoholic stink became a paramount strategy. She led him to the shower and took him in the ways he could never resist. He showed no signs of fatigue, but drove hard holding her hair and pulling her head viciously on to him.

It had started again, her sinews stiffened; her alertness sprang up, as his verbal abuse and fantasies of her infidelities filled the shower cubicle. Rachel tried to assuage his torrent of abuse by denial but it did no good.

"Bradley Walmer, I saw the bastard and you go out on the balcony, did he feel your tits did he? Did he finger fuck you?"

"Is that what you want is it, for other men to have me?"

"I've seen them; they all want to fuck you." He pounded
into her; her head crashed into the shower door.

"Michael stop, for God's sake." He pounded on, she felt the
blood run down her face as her drunken husband drove into
her. She put her arms to protect herself as her head crashed
repeatedly into the shower door. It was useless to stop him;
he was screwing her, fucking her like an animal. There was
no love, no care. Just carnal lust fuelled by his crazy
jealousy. 'God please get it over with'.

After what seemed an age, Michael came in a huge rush. As
soon as his climax had abated so did his sneering abuse. He
simply withdrew, slapped Rachel on the behind, towelled
down and went to bed. Rachel remained in the shower. She
knew the sound of the water would blot out her crying; not
that she cared. She wanted to scrub herself clean, she
wanted to stay in the safety of the cubicle, she curled up and
sat, her knees drawn to her chest as the tears poured down
her face, the water flooded down on her, but it could not
wash away the bitterness... Where had it all gone wrong,
where did this monster come from. Where was Michael,
that lovely tender man who had so loved her? Where was
all the tenderness and the giving?

At a quarter to five she slipped into bed beside the unconscious Michael. He looked so sweet and vulnerable; it was only his putrid breath that remained from that hideous episode. It had been more than two years since that night in Hvar, and yet no matter how she tried to blot them out, these episodes returned time and time again. Booze was certainly a part of it, but how could she stop these outbursts of insane and lecherous jealousy? The sun shone through the window as she drifted off into an uneasy sleep.

Chapter 7

They said her playing both in concert and recital had a depth and maturity beyond her years. In the last two and a half years since her marriage her studies had all but consumed her; she had discovered anew all those things and composers she had believed were not for her. JS and Co were always there, but now as friendly comforters, often used as recital encores, easy and familiar. They remained her musical spiritual core or bedrock but her new adventures into romanticism and modernism drove her on as if her desire was to know all music. She had now set out on this impossible road without end. There was always a hill to climb, a road to cross, a corner to turn. It was a journey that Michael could not follow. Now it was Max who was restraining her, and Eva shouting;

"Zees is too much, you must do more focus, you must rest with Liszt, you must do more work on Bella Bartok No 3." She was right, Rachel rolled on like a great intellectual juggernaut consuming a wider and wider repertoire, discarding some on her way and knowing sometimes that she should dwell with this or that composer, but she was driven by her consuming musical appetite and curiosity. Since the deal with Concordia Records she had gone on to work with Jamo Jadesjo in Gothenburg, they had recorded several concerti together and the Schumann was tipped for a Grammy. Her Bella Bartok was acclaimed in Hungary, and tours were planned to Australia and the United States.

MIL and Concordia were delighted, they encouraged her and exploited her work ethic; her future with their support was assured. The musical world was at her feet. The one thing that was missing was a companion, a husband who would woo her, welcome her home and love her and her music. The endless travel, the hotels no matter how luxurious or quirky became a bore. She longed for time alone with 'Becky' and new adventures without outside interference.

Max was as close a friend as she had, she always whined when he or at least another representative from MIL were unable to escort her. She became demanding of her concert managers. She expected things to be on the spot, rehearsals on time. She began to pick and choose as to whether she would sit into sponsors' after-concert dinners. She grumbled about the concert instruments, she judged everyone against her favourites and was seldom pleased. Despite all this, her constancy was in her performances. In recital, there was for her no audience, just her dialogue with the composer through the piano. Her degree of concentration and commitment were unfailingly of the highest quality. She was driven into isolation, an icy cage of loneliness and obsession with her music. She asked no quarter from her managers or recording company, she would do as they asked; in fact the more work the better. Her work became her life and her life was fast becoming her work. Michael was an anchor, a man she could say she loved. Was he a man she could live for?

On those innumerable nights alone she dreamt of their honeymoon, of the dinners and thrills of their life together, but there always loomed those terrible episodes of his angry and jealous intimacy. Was she to blame? She liked sex, very much indeed, but sex for her was now either alone, masturbating in solitude with her dreams of sweet coupling, or warily wanting Michael, more and more afraid that their loving would turn to his morbid jealousy.

Was she to blame? Other men certainly made it plain that they wanted sex with her, except dear Max; he was her guardian. That was why she wanted him near her, he was a rock albeit a peculiar one. Michael hated Max for the wrong reasons; Max wasn't a danger to Rachel, nor was she in any sexual way attracted to him; Max was as homosexual as it was possible to be. She had seen him make eyes and liaisons with a hundred men, most young and attractive, from Maestros to Mail men.

She'd been tempted, a number of times. Cy Allman had come closest to seducing her. He was an attractive man, big, powerful, but at the same time contemplative and gentle. He was of course deeply into music and had charm aplenty.

It was in Baltimore, he had turned up quite unexpectedly at the concert venue and had been invited to the Sponsor's after-concert supper. She had played the first Chopin Concerto as ever with bravura and precision. Her reception had been ecstatic. Had Cy not turned up she would have cried off the supper, but he needed to discuss her next recording cycle.

The supper was the usual sort of affair, about a hundred or so of the Baltimore culture vultures and the corporate sponsor and his guests sat down to a splendid meal. The principals of the orchestra were seeded around the ten or so tables, the conductor, a young up and coming American, and Rachel made a late entrance to applause from the gathered party.

All in all it had been a hard tour with six recitals and four concerts in two weeks, now she had a short break before she continued south; it was to end in Dallas; three recitals, three more concerts and ten days later.

Despite her protests Cy insisted on escorting her back to their hotel, where on arrival Rachel made her excuses and went to her suite and as usual rang Michael in London. Not unusually there was only the answering machine to talk to.

When Rachel answered the tap on the door she knew it would be Cy Allman, and despite herself she invited him in. Was it just the disappointment of the absence of Michael that made her she feel the need for company? Her pulse raced a little though she told herself this was just some company and anyway they had things to talk about.

Allman smiled above her, "I thought perhaps you would like a little company?"

"Why not," she held the door open and Allman stepped into the suite and stood hand in pocket looking round.

"Just like mine" he smiled. "Have you got a cognac or perhaps a Scotch?"

"I'm not sure," Rachel didn't know where to look, a solitary drinker was what she was not.

"Try the cabinet"

Rachel took down two cognac glasses and put the bottle of Cognac on the coffee table, "Help yourself, just a small one for me, excuse me I must just powder my nose."

In the bathroom she looked at herself in the mirror, she was shaking, she knew this was a mistake. What to do? She had no idea; instinctively she tidied her already tidy hair, applied refresher to her lipstick, sat on the loo and thought about what to do next. When she returned Cy was sitting, sprawling almost in the armchair, his drink hardly touched. He smiled, then stood up, "No please, sit down." She sat as far away as she could, bolt upright her legs tucked primly under her chair.

"You were wonderful tonight, I didn't dream that you could have played the Chopin so... so well.... so elegantly."

"Thank you kind Sir," she sipped her brandy.

"Really Rachel you've come on so far in such a short time, we've really got high hopes for you, if I can persuade Max and MIL we'll see a lot more of you in America and I hope we can move you on from the Gothenburg partnership."

"You don't have to," she stared into her glass, "Really I have such a good relationship with Jamo and the orchestra, I'd like to do as much as we can together."

"Of course, I think the Scandinavian series will be big, but not as big as you with the Chicago playing Chopin, Rachmaninoff and Brahms."

The idea was breathtaking, Chicago, Berlin, Vienna these were the orchestras that she had dreamt of playing with throughout her life. Recording with them almost guaranteed a series of concerts and a relationship that would put her on the musical map for life.

"Really, do you think we can get a date with the Chicago and who would conduct ? Barenboim?"

"Maybe, it's early yet, but I promise we'll do all we can to make this a realty. But what about you Rachel are you happy?"

"Of course I'm happy, I've got everything I ever wanted, and more, these last years since Liverpool and the Gothenburg recordings have been more than I ever imagined. I owe so much to you for having the faith in me."

"No I don't mean your career, Rachel you are a beautiful woman yet you spend so much time alone, that can't be right. You know that I admire your musicianship but you are the loveliest woman and it seems to me that you're missing out. You can't be in love with a piano, or can you?" He smiled, but his approach was as open as it could be, there was no room for doubt here.

"Cy, you're quite wrong, I am in love with my piano." She looked away, "Yes sometimes I'm lonely, but I know I can't have everything. I love Michael but he's never going to give up his wonderful career to follow me around the concert circuit, so ..." she suddenly felt miserable, "I can't have everything, I'm grateful and happy with what I've got." She drank a little more brandy.

"Wouldn't you like someone to hold you sometimes when you're tired, when you're fed up or blue, wouldn't you like to sleep with a man who values you and enjoy each other?" He was standing now only feet away from her, she stared down at her drink. "Rachel I want to hold you and I want to make love to you.... now,... right here and now, no one will ever know, you need to be loved, and you deserve to be loved,... right here and now."

"Cy, you're close to the truth but it's not all the truth, not nearly all, if I go to bed with you now ..... I just couldn't look Michael in the face ever again..... don't be cross, I didn't mean anything by letting you in, ...yes....I did, but I was wrong."

He put out his long arms and picked her out of her chair and folded his arms around her and kissed her deeply, for a moment she responded. Then she was overtaken by the weight of it all, she let him kiss her and she felt his arms, his chest and his thighs thrust towards her. They were strong and urgent but at the same time tentative and sensitive. In a moment the mood had changed and now she felt swallowed in the heat of her own desire. His hands stroked her throat and slid down the shoulder of her gown, his tongue probed urgently into her lips and mouth, his hand cupped her breast and his other hand pulled at her bottom urging her to his thrusting groin. He smelt wonderfully masculine but slightly scented like pine needles on an autumn night. They moved towards the bedroom, when the brr...brrr....brrr of the phone rang. Cy led her insistently towards the bedroom, Rachel struggled free. She stood, her gown undone, her breasts exposed, she caught sight of her disarray in the mirror. It was somehow shocking.

She picked up the phone, "Hello...." Her voice shook.

"Hello darling, I'm sorry I was out when you phoned, I hope I didn't wake you, were you asleep?"

"Just dozing off,"

Cy came up behind her and started kissing her neck and his arms reached round and fumbled through her gathered gown. She struggled from his embrace, "Michael darling hang on a minute I have to put the light on and get myself together."

She put down the telephone, pulled up her dress, walked to the door and opened it, Cy pulled on his jacket and tip toed passed her stopping to kiss her on the cheek. "Another time" he whispered and was gone.

"There, that's better", she relaxed, but still confused and for the first time conscious of the drinks. "Where were you? You old drunkard, when I phoned earlier?"

"Just late at work,"........... and so the empty conversation went,

"Love you, I miss you, ring me from Tennessee."

"Love you, Good night."

She put down the phone quietly and lay back and cried a deep cry that echoed all her pain. She loved Michael, but she would have gone to bed with Cy Allman. What sort of a bitch was she? They'd pilloried Jacqui her step mother but she was no better, God what a farce, what was she thinking about even letting Allman into her suite; it was madness, now how was she to face him tomorrow? This man was just about the most influential person in her world. He must think I'm a trollop, he must be full of hope, what was it that he said, ...'Til the next time .... Another time?' There would be no next time.

As she tried to sleep, the feeling of him returned and she caressed herself, then the tension was gone, the cognac did its thing and she slept.

The next morning she took breakfast in her suite and then moved out of her hotel, there was no sign of Cy Allman. She was relieved, and got on with the grind of her tour that took her to Richmond, Virginia where she gave a recital of her old favourites, then on to Charlestown for another recital, then to Nashville where she repeated the Chopin with the Baltimore Orchestra and the delicious Paul Carr, then to Atlanta and finally to Dallas.

Here she was welcomed by a delegation of Texan ladies, who swept her to a splendid hotel, The Adolphus, where her several thousand dollar a day suite was everything she could have expected including a fine grand piano; a Yamaha. The leader of her reception party Mrs. Louis B Ferrier the Third explained that the only way to give Rachel any peace and to save war breaking out amongst the Symphony patrons was not to invite her home as a personal guest. However, apart from the rehearsal time she would have the full attention of the patrons' committee. Rachel had a whole afternoon that she'd planned to use as rest, but it was not to be. Her MIL representative advised that she should follow the patrons' wishes as far as she could since they boasted between them a sum in the arts patronage about the size of Mexico's GDP. The day was a flurry of limousines, mansions and receptions, ending in the mansion of one of Texas' greatest oil magnates.

It was to be an informal supper party, Rachel was promised that she would be back in her hotel by nine o clock at the latest. The limousine would pick her up from the Adolphus at five-thirty; this gave Rachel time to change but little more. She was tired and her humour was tetchy, the Texan charm was almost too generous, she needed time alone, she longed to get on that flight back to England. The concert with the Dallas Symphony was to be her first concert performance of Rachmaninov's Rhapsody on a theme of Paganini. She wasn't nervous about the performance, but she was nervous about the rehearsal time available. The Conductor, Andrew Litton, would be a new relationship and this she knew was the most vital issue that could make a huge difference to the quality of the performance. Nevertheless she had to face an evening with Mrs Louis B Ferrier the Third and her assembled cronies.

Rachel was born into a very comfortable life style, back in England people would say that she came from a rich family, indeed that was true. However nothing could have prepared her for the sumptuous riches of the household of Mr. Louis B Ferrier the Third. The gates and the approach were impressive, but the mansion could only be described as fabulous. Her limousine drew up in the coach house entrance, where Lu' and Nancy Ferrier greeted their guest. "Just a few cocktails and meet some friends," said Mrs. Ferrier (call me Nancy). Louis Ferrier the Third (call me Lu) was tall, maybe six two, had a fine athletic figure, his sunburned face sported gray moustache surmounted by a full head of silver gray hair. He bowed his blue eyes twinkling with southern charm, "We are honoured to have such a beautiful and talented guest, Miss George."

The entrance was large enough to be a sumptuous hotel foyer; it ran straight through the house to a fully glazed wall that showed off the splendid gardens beyond. Her hosts led Rachel through the atrium hall to a reception room where there were at least eighty guests.

"Come on Rachel," crooned Nancy, "come and meet some of the guests, "Andrew this is Rachel."

Andrew Litton was charm itself, a fellow musician with whom she struck an immediate rapport.

" I'm looking forward very much to working together tomorrow, I've heard so much about you and I believe your tour has been a huge success."

"You're very kind, it's been hard work, tomorrow is the biggest concert by far, so I, like you, look forward to it, I hope I'll be up to the job."

"I have no doubt, Cy Allman tells me you have talent and stage presence to spare."

She felt herself blush, she swallowed from her Champagne glass, almost gagging. She gathered herself. "You know Mr Allman?"

"Oh yes, of course, everyone in the business here knows him, in fact he's in town, I expect he'll be right here pretty soon." He craned his neck.

"Andrew, you're going to have Rachel all to yourself tomorrow, I'm going to drag her away now to meet some other folk." "Are you all right my dear, you look a little …. how can I say… taken aback?"

"No I'm fine, thank you Nancy." They pressed on through the group, then she saw the two things that she had hoped not to see, the full concert grand and the unmistakable back of Cy Allman, clad in an impeccable suit talking avidly to a group of Texan gentlemen.

The next hour was spent talking to the delightful group all of whom seemed to be entirely at home in these Versailles type surroundings. All the men seemed to be in Oil or politics, all the women did nothing except work on their charities. It was as if each of the ladies was the patron of a different charity and they spent their time supporting each other's causes. This, as far as Rachel could work out, meant an eternal round of fund raising and cocktail parties. Nancy Ferrier was a key patron of the Dallas Symphony; her husband's oil company was definitely a key patron of Mrs. Ferrier's pet projects.

Inevitably the confrontation with Cy Allman. "Rachel, how lovely you look, well I guess I always say that." He laughed and Nancy tittered, Lu muttered "pretty as a picture."

"Have you been busy since I saw you in Baltimore, Mr Allman?"

"Oh please call me Cy.. I may be your recording company President, but I hope we're friends Rachel" His smile was fixed. She looked straight into his eyes. She could not hold his gaze, she looked away. "As you may know Nancy, we at Concordia have a great deal of faith in Rachel's future as a recording artist; we've got a lot of plans for Rachel over the next two years."

"Will you play a little for us Rachel?" Nancy asked quietly.

"Of course Nancy, it would be a pleasure, anything you particularly like?"

She looked up at Allman, turned with some relief and walked to the piano. After Nancy had made a brief speech of welcome and introduction, she cautioned the guests that Rachel would play for just a few minutes. There fell a hush and Rachel thought a moment and then played Art Tatum's salute to Bach, this brought the house down. She followed this with a selection from George Gershwin . Despite the cheers and real enthusiasm she declined to play anymore.

The guests surrounded her anxious to say 'thank you', or just 'well done' and to wish her well for the following evening. It was already nine o clock .

 Andrew Litton made his way through the throng, "tomorrow is going to be a fun day."

"I look forward to it Andrew, how much rehearsal time will we have?"

"As much as you need, which I don't expect will be much, sleep well, I look forward to tomorrow."

Nancy and Lu ushered Rachel to her waiting limousine, they were very sweet and Rachel felt warmed by their generosity. Just as the limo pulled up, Cy Allman appeared;

"The Adolphus, could I beg a lift?"

She was stunned, there was nothing she could do, but smile thinly and mutter "sure"

In the car they were silent until they had cleared the Ferriers' estate.

"About the night in Baltimore..... I'm sorry if I gave the impression that...."

"I'm not a bit sorry," he reached for her hand, but she withdrew it, and looked out the window into the drizzle that had begun to fall. "Look Rachel you know I find you irresistible, I'm never going to be able to feel any other way, and I'm not sorry. You're the most beautiful...no, desirable woman I've ever met, and I just want you."

Rachel continued to stare out of the window into the dark drizzling rain, what did Cy want? To get her into bed and perhaps use her when he chose, after all he knew where her tour took her, he could even influence Max and MIL as to where and when she travelled.

What did she feel? Firstly strangely miserable, there was no doubt she found Cy attractive, she could still evoke his smell, she could still feel his silky firm hands on her. Michael, my Michael, I love you don't I? Yes I do. I do! She stirred from her reverie, disturbed by Cy's tiny but definite move along the seat toward her.

"Cy, you're a very attractive and charming man, God knows you have the influence of life or death over my career, but despite all that I'm twenty something going on fifty, and I love Michael. I will always love him,.... Sometimes this is lonely, desperately lonely, but I'll live with it, for Michael and for my Music."

"Then there's no chance for me then?"

"No Cy, no chance at all,... I'm sorry it was foolish of me to invite you into my suite the other night, I knew what you wanted, ...I was stupid. Can't we forget about it?"

"You mean like it never happened?"

"Yes, like it never happened."

"No, but I'll try."

"Thank you, Cy."

There had been no call from Michael and there was no answer at home. She bathed and climbed into her sensationally comfortable bed. It was difficult to sleep; Michael where are you my love? Andrew can I do this Rachmaninov, Cy will you leave me alone, Oh Cy, Oh Cy. She fought the idea but she wanted him, she hated herself but she imagined him in her arms and in her bed and inside her.

The next morning was much the usual except Rachel was more than usually apprehensive about the rehearsal. Suzy Lamb the local MIL representative picked her up for the short journey to the Meyerson Symphony Center.

There followed all the usual business; of entrances and practice room, dressing room, dresser help if need be, refused, and then the introduction to the Orchestra. Andrew was as charming as he had been last night. As usual they took it from the top, though unusually there seemed considerable differences between pianist and conductor. Rachel was uncomfortable, she missed a number of entries and she and Andrew had seemingly endless differences over the Dies Irae particularly in the seventh and tenth variations. In consequence the first so called walk through was anything but, and although the total work should only last some around thirty five minutes the whole of the morning was taken up from nine thirty to twelve fifteen. Even then Rachel remained unconvinced that she and her partner, the maestro, had a discernable unity. Andrew Litton was calmer, he felt he'd got to know his soloist, though he had reservations about some of her tempi, he knew that on the night they would be fine.

The afternoon, as with all of her bigger days, dragged. She mooched about the hotel, had a light lunch with Suzy Lamb and retired for a nap. It was an hour later that the phone rang and it was Max.

"Max, Oh Max where are you?"

"Down stairs darling, just can't wait to see you, can I come up."

"Right now? Yes of course." Max was one man in the world she would receive without her make up and her hair in a mess, in fact the hairdresser was due at five. Max his eyes flashing in their eccentric circles arrived dishevelled despite his thousand dollar suit. It was lovely to see him.. She gave him a big hug.

"Oh Max, how lovely to see you, I'm at the end of my tether, I'll be glad to get on that plane tomorrow; anyway Max, what brings my gallant Manager to my side so far from home?

"Darling I'm here to listen to you, but I'm off with Cy Allman to Chicago tomorrow, to see what we can fix for next year, if not Chicago maybe Montreal or Los Angeles. Concordia feel you've got to make a connection with an American partner."

Cy Allman, the name made her catch her breath. They chatted, took tea, and it was time to get ready. First her hair, then the dress from the valet, and then another read of the score. Then it was time to go. There were flowers from the Ferriers, a bouquet as always from Max and a short note from Andrew; it read; 'Where you want to go, I'll be there with you, Good luck Andrew.' It was reassuring and very kind, the note helped a lot to settle her nerves. She warmed up in the practice room then waited in the eerie silence of her dressing room. Then the tap on the door; "Miss George", the stage Manager led to the entry wing.

They came to the variation seven in seamless unity, then the spell broke; for an instant she felt confusion, her tempo slipped from confidence to hesitance. She looked to Andrew whose hand came back toward her in a most relaxed but definite tempo, she took his lead and the crisis was passed. At variation ten again a slight uncertainty, again Litton showed the way with uncanny subtlety. Then the cadenza that went really well. From then on she relaxed and they moved easily through the minuet and scherzo of the middle variations to the great romantic rhapsody of eighteen and to the rousing finale.

It was done. Rachel sat quite still on her stool despite the loud, even rapturous applause; she stood and said to Andrew, as they hugged,

"Thank you Andrew, you showed me the way."

"Listen Rachel, it's for you." The applause thundered on.

"No Andrew it's for us, and for you", as she shook hands with the leader.

They took several curtain calls, she received her bouquet and she walked back to her room absolutely drained. There in the stillness she went through the usual anticlimax, she closed her eyes and half lay, half sat on the chaise longue and dozed.. The building was not the place where you could hear or sense every change, perhaps it was the modern engineering of the place. It was eerily quiet. As she got ready to shower and change for the Patrons' supper, she noticed a note by the telephone. Just another well wisher, she disregarded it and stripped for her shower where she lingered in the relaxing warmth of the water. She came out, rearranged her hair, made up, dressed and idly picked up the telephone message. It was from Robbie.

It read: 'Please ring me as soon as possible at home, no matter what the time. Love Robbie.'

She rang immediately. It was three forty a.m. London time, what could it be? The phone at the other end was picked up instantly. A shiver ran down Rachel's spine.

"Hello, Robbie, it's me Rachel."

"Hello, Rachel darling, how are you,..... look I'm sorry to be the bearer of bad news, but Michael has had an accident" He spilled it out, in an uncontrolled deluge of information,

"The bloody fool went and played rugby with Bertie, anyway he received a bump to his head , I'm afraid it's a bad one, he's still unconscious. He's in King's College Hospital, the doctors don't know quite what's up yet but they may want to operate to relieve pressure on his brain…. They don't know too much yet, but I'm afraid that it's serious….." there was a silence…., Rachel could hardly take it in. "I thought I ought to let you know… Tania is at the hospital"

"What shall I do?" she began to cry, she looked around the empty but lush dressing room, where was she? God, Michael please be better.

"When are you due home?"

"I'm due to fly tomorrow night, maybe I can get out now, I'll check, …. Robbie how is he really?" She was crying now uncontrollably.

"Well it's not good, I really don't know but Tania rang an hour ago and said he was going into surgery about now. Darling that's all I know, just come home as soon as you can."

"I'll ring you as soon as I can, will you be there?"

"Probably but here's my mobile; in case."

She put down the phone and slumped into the chair. Her shoulders heaved as the pain for her beloved Michael racked her body, the tears flooded down her face and the fatigue overwhelmed her. She was lonely and helpless. She didn't hear the knock on her door but it opened anyway and Max led a group of admirers joyfully into the room. Max stopped;

"Darling, what is it?" He turned immediately and shooed the crowd away but Nancy and Lu were not to be denied. She flung herself into Max's arms, her sobbing enveloping her and alarming Max.

"Sh.. Sh.. my darling, tell Max what is the matter."

It was a good ten minutes before Max and the Ferriers understood the issues. Lu without a word left the room, made a quiet announcement to those gathered outside. Max, as soon as he was able, rang the airlines but to no avail, the next aircraft to London was not due to leave for another seventeen hours. Rachel was swept back to her hotel where Nancy and Suzy Lamb kept her company and generally tried to comfort her. At eleven thirty Lu arrived.

"OK young lady, get packed, you'll come over to our place, my aircraft will fly you to Kennedy as soon as is possible and we have you booked on Concorde at eight forty five am tomorrow, you'll be home around six pm tomorrow, I guess it's the best we can do."

The relief, like a shaft of light, raised her spirit. Lu, the southern gentleman, had made the impossible, possible. Where there had been the black despair of hopeless separation there was now the hope of early reunion. Where there had been the clawing mists of empty time there was now the urgent way to touching her darling Michael. For in that touch she knew there would be salvation, not just for him but for them both.

Suddenly where there had been despair now there was hope and Suzy and Nancy gathered up her belongings and prepared for the journey back to London and to her man. At that moment despite her anxieties and her fears she felt enormous affection for the Ferriers and Suzy Lamb, for they had given of themselves without a second's thought, they had gathered round like the family so far away and in an instant had blessed her with their care and love. They fortified her and made her strong; in their organizing they gave her purpose, a context that contained her panic. They gave her a steadiness that could so easily have dissolved into self-centred hysteria. Now she knew that she had to get to Michael's side to make him whole again, that was her purpose plain and simple.

Chapter 8

The journey, despite the private jet and Concorde passed in a blur; there was just the engulfing and exhausting impatience to get to Michael's side. She arrived at King's College Hospital some seventeen hours after hearing from Robbie.

Since arriving in London Rachel had been in touch with Robbie constantly. There had been little change in Michael's condition, he was still unconscious. There had been little or no discernable change since the operation, despite the pressure that had been relieved round his brain.

Rachel knew that all this would change. She would touch him and he would know, he would come to her from where ever he was; love would bring him out like Lazarus from the tomb. She was so sure she was almost relaxed, the power of their love knew no bounds, she would hold his hand, kiss his face, speak his name and all would be well.

On the long journey from Texas she had thought just this one thought, it would be all right: Doctors didn't matter, nor drugs, nor operations, just love. The car pulled into the car park of Kings College Hospital in Denmark Hill, south east London. It was a typical wet gray English day.

The Victorian Buildings slumped miserably in the grayness of the drizzle, the lights shone dimly through the murky windows, people scurried huddled under their umbrellas, nurses and visitors alike; the grieving, the uplifted, the forlorn, the desperate and the condemned.

Rachel however, though she saw the miserable scene was obdurately optimistic.

Down the long corridors the smells of hospital, the disinfectant, the steamed food, the polish and the pain, the hope of life beginning and the despair of life ending; but for Rachel a journey to renewal, she was sure all would be well.

 Robbie and Tania, seated, both silent in their own worlds, staring at their different horizons, Robbie's eyes fixed close at hand, on the floor, Tania's further away through the mural painted wall. Robbie sprang to embrace her.

"Oh my sweet girl, you look so tired." He held her at arm's length; the hollowness of his eyes betrayed the depth of his grief.

"Is he all right? Where's Michael, I want to see him." She pulled away. Tania entangled her in a three people embrace but she wanted an instant freedom to see her darling husband.

"The doctor's with him now, you can see him in a minute. Shhhhhh now, it won't be long."

"How is he? Is he better, has he come round?"

"No, my dear, he's ugh, still in a coma, the doctor says he could be like this for a while."

Hope did not vanish but it melted into the background, all the hope that had sustained her through the long miles from Dallas was suddenly shaken. Panic fought its way, empty and bitter, crowding out hope and drowning her with despair. 'Michael, oh Michael I love you so', it hurt to think about him locked away in unconsciousness.

She stopped her struggle and collapsed into Robbie's arms, her sob became a moan of agony as she sank into the blackness of despair. It was disorientation, her energy and her heart deserted her. Here at the end of her journey was emptiness, no sudden miracle. The disinfectant, the nursing staff, the harsh white light, the numb people waiting just like them came into focus. 'Michael, my Michael you shouldn't be here', her sobs came from the pit of her being, for the first time she faced the fact that she might lose him forever.....her wail screamed her fear and her loneliness. Tears flooded her face, she buried her head into Robbie's chest whilst Tania gently stroked her back.
"Shhhhh.....Shhhhh.' There wasn't much more to be said.

She learned that it had been a freak accident, Michael had been swung from a tackle into the knee of a very large forward. The blow had been just above his right temple towards the front of his head. He had been unconscious from that moment.

It had taken more than an hour to get him to hospital, first at Mitcham, and then he had been transferred to the head and cerebral injury unit at Kings. He had then undergone surgery to lessen the pressure on his brain that had been caused by severe bruising of his brain lining, a subdural hematoma or some such. The doctors were pleased that the reduction in pressure had been seen to improve Michael's condition. However he remained in an induced coma and the doctor would watch and wait.

Rachel sat slumped on the waiting room chair and tried to take it all in. She was overwhelmed with fatigue, it seemed that time had stopped, she was in a perpetual moment, suspended forever, exhausted, lost, and horribly alone. Despite the proximity of Robbie and Tania, she was hopelessly detached; it was a cold place, bleaker than anywhere she had ever been. She did not know if she wanted to see Michael, not unless she could make a difference, there echoed somewhere that hope of miraculous recovery, a whisper of his name, a calling him back from beyond. She couldn't breathe, the tears and her nose ran like rivers, rivers of despair.

She looked up and she saw him for the first time, his white coat, almost sun bright, his round ruddy face and his crystal glasses over his fat nose. His eyes were blue, his hair fair going grey at the temples, but none of this mattered. Professor Anthony Shepherd exuded hope and competence. His gaze was one that had been in this situation many times, he would know what to do. Instantly she put her trust in him, even before he opened his mouth.

"Mrs. Johnson, - I expect you'll want to see your husband, and we'll go in, in a moment, but first I expect you'd like to know how he is." He smiled, just a reassuring flicker.

She blew her nose and responded with a sniffle that meant yes.

"Michael is quite ill, but the good news is he is stable. We have been consistently measuring his responses and so far they have been poor, but he has had a very nasty crack on his head. His skull has been fractured and there was some internal bleeding. We believe that has now stopped and that the pressure or swelling around his brain has stabilized and even begun to improve. As you know, we had to do some surgery to help this process and it went well."

"Will he be alright, I mean will he be well again?"

"He may well recover entirely, though such a recovery will take time, and then again he may recover to some degree, I'm afraid that right now we must take one step at a time, and you must help us by being patient. If there's anything you want to know or if you want to bring in anyone to give another opinion please do so, but I believe he is in the best hands possible here."

Rachel didn't say a word, the Professor took her arm, "Come along we'll go and see Michael and I'll explain some more."

She was not prepared, there was Michael but it was not Michael. It was a man swathed in bandages and with tubes and wires protruding into a myriad of machines and monitors. What she could see of his face below his head dressing was a greyness and hollowness that just was not him. She stood and stared, the professor at her elbow, and the overwhelming fear and sadness returned. Her shoulders heaved once more and tears ran down her tired cheeks. She wanted to hold him but she was afraid, not of him, but the mass of wires and tubes. She could not move.

Then there was an arm round her, it was the IC sister, "Come on love, come and talk to Michael, come and hold his hand, he'll like that." Rachel was led as a child is led and his cool hand was put into hers, she held it tight in both her hands.

"Michael look who's here", cooed the Sister, "now she's come home it's time for you to get better." She pulled a seat up and there Rachel sat, awkwardly at first but then she held his hand with purpose, talking and breathing through them, prepared to stay forever.

"Can he hear me?"

"Maybe, maybe not, but if you like to talk to him that will be nice, there's no telling what stimuli he'll respond to."

"We're looking for eye movement and then verbal response; we can monitor all these no matter how slight, so gentle comfortable stimulus is good."

"Hold hands, talk away, we want to bring him back as soon as we can, you can help, you can stay here as long as you like, we'll make a cot up for you if you want to sleep over."

Again she chattered through her tear filled face, "Oh Michael, Michael I'm here, I'm here, I'll always be here" But soon she could speak no more and pressed his cool hand and bathed it with her tears.

The Professor patted her shoulder, "You must look after yourself, and there may be a long way to go here." He spoke softly, his Scottish burr softening the grimness of his message.

"In Intensive Care we have medical and nursing staff here at all times, so there'll be not a second that Michael is not monitored, so if you need to rest, you must. I'm happy that he's stable now and my registrar will call me if there's any change, so I'll slip away and have a wee rest." He shook her hand and then held both in his and said, "Keep hold of his hand if you like, and chatter away if you can, and if you like, share a prayer or two, I'll see you later, but don't forget to look after yourself. Sister Warren will look after you both."

His white coat slipped out of the room unnoticed as Rachel dried her eyes and recounted to Michael her adventures in America, though she did not mention Cy Allman.

The sister rubbed her back and cooed some more, "We'll get you a cup of tea."

She saw for the first time the blue bruise that shadowed his forehead, and realised that all this paraphernalia of pipes and tubes and wires was keeping her Michael alive. She stroked his hand and promised they would spend more time together, why they could retire right now. She would keep him forever no matter how ill he was, he would be cuddled, loved and coddled forever. She whispered at first, but then, with the encouragement of the nurses, she began to chat away. Soon it became an obligation to keep up the one way talk, perhaps he was listening - perhaps he was not. She was afraid to stop, he may slip away, and this endless chatter was his lifeline, their only chance.

She played music with her fingers onto his hand; maybe he could sense the rhythm.

A minute, an hour, an eternity; her eyelids drooped she had difficulty staying awake, but she must, she must.

"Come on my dear, you must get some rest." It was Tania and the Ward Sister. "Come and rest, we'll let you know as soon as anything changes. "Robbie will run you home, it's only twenty minutes."

"I want to stay, I'm all right, I really am." She sat determinedly in the chair but she knew she needed to sleep, to rest. It had been a day and a half since she had last slept; she had given a concert, travelled four thousand miles and cried an ocean. She was without energy, and without energy there was only despair.

The house was cold and dark, it was full of emptiness, there was a chill of loneliness that made her cold. Robbie carried her overnight bag, put on the coffee and fussed to no particular avail. They talked about what might happen, but it did not help. They were helpless.

It was two o'clock in the morning; she curled up in her lonely bed, cold and broken. Sleep came, but not for long.

As the drizzled light of dawn crept into her kitchen window she had already phoned the hospital – no change. She was listening to the answering machine, to Bertie who wept his guilt, he would be with her soon, he promised.

There were concerned messages from the Bank – anything, anything, they would do all they could, chauffeurs, limos, independent medical opinions, anything.

There was a message from Max, he would be arriving at Heathrow about now and would catch up as soon as was possible. Dear Max!

Jacqui Boswell had phoned with some advice, "Look after yourself first so that you have strength to look after others."

By eight thirty she was back at the intensive care unit, Professor Shepherd was already there. He smiled when he saw her.

"There's a definite improvement, modest but a definite improvement – still a long way to go but in the nature of things the improvements tended to be – not always of course – but usually progressive…, "

"Is he awake?"

"No, but his eye responses are definitely better, he was scanned earlier and the brain inflammation is settling… settling very well."

"When will he be awake? When will he be able to see me? Can he see me now?"

"I'm afraid not yet, but we must be patient, just be aware that he is better than he was. We cannot rush his healing; we can only assist it. You see his brain has been insulted – received a trauma, it's a very sophisticated organ and it will, as it were, heal itself. There are signs that this is happening but the extent and speed of recovery is impossible to predict. So as I said to you last night, you must be patient."

"Thank you, Doctor," her voice reflected the down she felt, all the more steep because of the moment of hope.

"Mrs. Johnson, please, I beg you to be patient, if Michael is to get well, you're part of the team that's going to make him well. So hang in with us …." He trailed off, his dilemma between kindness and brutal probability stuck in his throat.

And so another bleak morning stole into her life, and minute by minute it ticked relentlessly on, punctuated by the encouragement of the wonderful staff and a series of tepid cups of tea.

Tania, despite having spent the night at the hospital, spent time throughout the day together with Rachel on their watch of their beloved Michael. They were shooed away each hour as Michael's equipment and comforts were seen to. The Professor appeared frequently, he peered in Michael's eyes, read the various print outs, adjusted the various feeds and drugs and scurried off to his next patient.

Then there was a sudden urgency in the next station. There were buzzers and running, the peaceful air of efficiency was shattered as nurses and doctors including Shepherd ran to the patient. The visitors, a gaunt middle aged couple retreated, the lady shrieking her distress, the man cajoling her to leave the scene, his arms wrapped around her, sheltering her and at the same time shepherding her away.

Rachel watched fascinated as the fight for the young girl's life was fought and eventually lost. It took perhaps a half hour, then there was a standing down, a switching off, a walking away, a feeling of life itself tip toeing out of the intensive care section. She saw in Shepherd a slumping of his shoulders, he had lost a patient and he had lost something of himself. He paused only for a moment, his hands deep in his pockets, then, he brought himself up and walked out of the ward. Rachel wanted to run after him, hold him and bring him back to Michael.

Then she cried and grieved for the patient she had not met or did not know, she wept for Shepherd and all that painful giving, day in day out. Quite involuntarily she prayed for him and all his people.

"His eyes, Rachel look at his eyes."

Yes his eyes were flickering, his eyelids whilst not opening, looked as if they might, they twitched. They rang the buzzer as if there were a need, but the station nurse was already there.

"Good, good, signs," she said monitoring all the instruments, "I'll get the doctor."

Michael became conscious that evening at around six o'clock. He became aware of his wife, mother and father nearby; although it was not clear that he recognised them. His hands responded to squeezing but only very weakly. There was hope, lots of hope.

Chapter 9

Life was different; although Michael had recovered well, he was not the same. He had recovered slowly over the three months that led to Christmas. The progress had been slow, at least for Rachel who could not wait to see her husband dashing, articulate and charming as she knew he could be. Now, although his speech was almost perfect, just a slight hesitation where there had been none, he seemed much less confident. Although he confessed to looking forward to returning to work, she knew he was afraid.

She had cancelled all her overseas work during the last quarter and it had been a strain fighting with Max and Eva who would brook no interruption to their student's career. She would refuse any engagements that kept her away overnight, though Tania had offered to either have Michael at home, or come and stay herself.

Bertie had become a constant visitor, three or more times a week he would call and take a good deal of abuse from Michael, ostensively light hearted, though Rachel sometimes winced at Michael's cruel barbs. Bertie though never seemed to mind. They had been out on a number of occasions to Dulwich Village and Bertie had managed to curtail their beer drinking to the reasonable.

Drink, Doctor McMaster, Michael's new physician, had warned, should be avoided, certainly to any excess. Michael still found it difficult to concentrate, particularly on the written word.

He laboured long and hard over Bank LONY reports but he was clearly exhausted by the time he finished even the shorter papers. Then he was given to bouts of foul temper. He would insist on interrupting her practice and would barge into the music room and demand that Rachel do this or that, there and then.

In company though, with the exception of Max, he was polite and good humoured in the extreme. He always told Tania how much he relied on Rachel but he screamed at her about her lack of care as soon as his mother had left. He was becoming more and more a Jekyll and Hyde character. By and large his good side was for the world, his bad side for Rachel and sometimes dear Max. When he first came home he had been affectionate and very dependent on her, as time had gone on that dependency had become a clawing demanding insistence that she look after him and exclusively him.

Prior to his release from Kings College Hospital, Rachel had been advised to consult a clinical psychiatrist, a Doctor Rodney Lucas. He had warned her that just as Michael's injuries had generated some physical symptoms there could well be psychiatric symptoms that would arise. It was essential that Rachel relate any behavioural changes to him or McMaster. She had tried to broach the subject but on each occasion Michael had been present and she had funked the report and dwelt instead on issues such as fatigue and some reading difficulties. Michael had roundly denied that he had any reading problems and put down his fatigue to mastering the complexities of his homework.

Intimacy had all but dissolved, their sexual unions had been infrequent and empty of either tenderness or passion. Michael talked in ways about these matters that were crude and unsettling. Rachel remembered Professor Shepherd, she must be patient, he would continue to get better.

They had arranged to spend Christmas at Michael's parents' home. They arrived on Christmas Eve that was a typical damp English day. Tania as ever greeted both as her own, Robbie in his usual avuncular, welcoming way. Robbie had suffered enormously during Michael's illness and recovery, he had aged over those few weeks and the strain seemed destined never to leave him. He'd lost weight, his hair seemed whiter, his mouth tighter, his eyes; those merry eyes had lost some of their sparkle. Rachel tried to deny it, but in her heart she knew it, they shared a secret, a dark and awful secret that neither would readily admit. They knew, in their heart of hearts, that their darling Michael would never be the same ever again. Tania, did she know too? It was harder to say, she was determinedly loving and supportive as a mother can be, but more, she seemed to have faith that her beloved son would return in his fullness, another day, another month, she would never lose faith. Robbie looked at the facts, Tania looked through them.

These facts, what were they? Robbie, not yet sixty, saw in the eyes of his daughter in law that her spirit was dimmed, her adoration of Michael somehow sadder than joyous. Nothing had been said, they'd held each other tight through those first days when Michael was so ill.

They'd rejoiced together when he started to recover, they'd even laughed together to dispel their doubts. But since Michael had been home he'd seen the erosion of Rachel's devotion, there was something that distanced the two of them. Rachel was attentive and caring, and when he visited they seemed as devoted as ever, but on that one morning as he left them he caught a snippet from behind the music room door that had shocked him. That Michael could say anything so cruel or foul was too shocking, he'd almost staggered with the shock, he'd almost fallen over, collapsed as the words so obscene that had struck his ears. From that moment he had watched his lovely daughter in law with care and concern, but he could not bring himself to approach her, or in any way concede that he'd heard his son's outburst. It would be too humiliating for them both.

Tania was not without her own doubts, but she put them aside, after all it takes time to get over these things and Michael was practically his old self. True he wasn't quite as articulate as he used to be, but no one would notice that except of course his mother. Rachel was a lovely child and Michael was well wedded and bedded, but Rachel had her career. She worried sometimes that Rachel didn't put Michael first, of course they were young and had a long way to go but sometimes she worried that maybe there was something in Rachel's genes that came from Sir Lewis. She was a go ahead girl alright, somewhere there was a thought that perhaps Rachel was happy when things were going well and she was free to junket round the world. She never seemed to think about children.

Tania couldn't wait for her first grandchild. It aggravated her that Robbie wouldn't speak to Michael about it. It was Rachel's wretched piano that made the difference; sometimes she felt that Rachel loved the piano more than she did Michael. But how would she be now that things were less certain? Anyway, things were already so much better, Michael was to start work again in the New Year and everyone at LONY was looking forward to getting him back into the fold. That would cheer Michael up and they'd all be back to normal.

This Christmas Tania was determined to wipe away the fears of the last three months and she'd conspired with Rachel to make this a Christmas that Michael would never forget. With the help and connivance of the Bank they'd ensured that Hugo Love would be in England over Christmas so he was invited along with Bertie Frobisher, two of Michael's best friends. Rachel had invited Josie Fallows in the hope of putting together two lost souls; she'd certainly educate Bertie into the ways of the world in no time at all. Other houseguests included Uncle Harry, now widowed, as well as two couples who were close friends of the family.

On the drive down to the Johnson country retreat, Michael and Rachel bickered their way down the turgid M25 and then down the Sussex main roads that eventually gave way to a more rural setting.

The cause of their mutual displeasure was Max.

"How could you be so rude to Max, you behaved like a pig, Michael, how could you call him a pimp?"

"Well isn't he? He arranges for you to sell your wears to the highest bidder, he walks into and out of our house as if he owns it... owns you. He's a slimy, cockeyed pervert, and you can't expect me to like him."

"I don't expect you to like him, you've made that obvious since you first met him, however I do expect you to be civil... how would you like it if I called Alistair a supercilious prick, which is what I think he is by the way?"

"At least he doesn't procure young women for his clients."

"Look, if you think you're going to bully me into giving up my career Michael you can think about something else, I am not going to pack up my music for you or anyone else."

"What about me, thought we promised to stick together... what was it, through sickness and health, richer, poorer etcetera... or have you forgotten that?"

"What about you Michael, you tell me you're cured, better, recovered whatever, and recovered from what?...... some bloody lunatic outing with 'the boys', lots of bravado that nearly got yourself killed. Michael you can't have the penny and the bun, you are better and you have to get back to work and I have to get back to my career. ......so please try and show some respect for my colleagues."

"Colleagues, Max bloody pimp, has he got anyone into bed with you yet?"

"Michael if you say that once again I'll swear I'll....I'll.... Shut up!"

"Can I stop the car and grope my wife? You look sexy when you're mad."

"Michael shut up and drive, we're late already."

The rest of the journey was spent in a cold silence, as they drove to of the Johnson country house.

"Happy Christmas, happy fucking families."

"Michael, behave!"

The help, Raymond and Joan, sallied forth as if by magic to welcome Mr Michael and his bride with proper deference. They were taken to their bedroom, one of eight at Haver Hall.

"Michael, Michael darling is that you, Rachel are you alright? Is everything OK? Got everything?"

"Yes, mother don't fret we'll be down in a minute.' Michael called to his distant mother poised but excited at the bottom of the stairs. "Oh God, mother's in a state; house parties were always a bit fraught even when I was a lad. I do hope she's not going to fuss all the time."

"Tania's gone to a lot of trouble to make us at home, there're some surprise guests, who you will like, so be a good boy and show how pleased you are to be here."

"Can we stay here and make love, please, pretty please?" he began to fondle her as she continued to unpack.

"Michael, stop it …… stop it, now go and see your mother, I'll be down in a minute."

The house was large though not old, perhaps one hundred and fifty years. It had high ceilings and large fireplaces, a huge kitchen and it was beautifully furnished throughout. Despite its size, Haver Hall was the essence of comfort, the fires were all burning, the carpets were thick and the furniture luxuriant. There was room to get lost, to be on one's own; in the Conservatory, the garden room, the study, the games room or the field room, not to mention the dining room and the huge drawing room. In addition to the massive kitchen and pantry there were several outbuildings that included stables, garages, servants' apartments and tool sheds. It was, in short, a Victorian Manse of some substance.

As Rachel was coming down the stairs she heard the front door open and a whooping and hollering as Hugo and Michael hugged.

"You crazy English bastard, playing football without a helmet – shit let me look at you, Man you look great."

"Hugo what the hell are you doing here on Christmas Eve far away from all your New York floosies?"

Rachel raced down to be with them, "You're our Christmas present to Michael, he needs some male boy company after all the nursing, your Tania's idea and I'm so glad you could come."

She launched into Hugo's bear hug, it was wonderful to see this shambling bear of a man again.

Tania appeared from her Christmas tree decorating in the drawing room, "Raymond, take Mr. Love's things to the daffodil room would you." She embraced Hugo warmly.

"We're so pleased you can be with us this Christmas. You're most welcome, please be at home, anything you want just ask."

"Mrs. Johnson," Hugo wrung his gloves anxiously, "You can't know what this means to me I'm...well you're so kind."

"Nonsense, you'll have to excuse me I've got things to do."

"Me too" Rachel turned and joined Tania at the Christmas tree.

"Do you think it's a good idea Rachel?"

"What Tania.... what's a good idea?"

"Getting Hugo and Bertie here."

"Michael looked thrilled to bits, we'll just have to watch the drinking. You know Michael still has to go steadily."

"But he's so much better isn't he?"

"Yes…..yes he is." Rachel passed a crimson Christmas ball to her mother in law. 'I hope he is, I pray he is.' She bit her lip.

Bishop Harold, late of the diocese of Chichester was the next to arrive. He'd aged since the wedding, now he was eighty something, and he looked it. He had lost weight, his hair was thinner and his shoulders stooped. His formerly round and cherubic face was gaunt and surmounted by a meanly aquiline nose. His eyes were greyish, greenish blue, transparent with just a hint of the sparkle of old. Retirement had denuded him of purpose, and his loneliness had been multiplied by the death of his only love, other than the mother Church, his wife of nigh on forty years, Mary.

Rachel thought he smelt like Eva, of mothballs, as she hugged the old man in welcome, and he immediately seemed to cheer up as his favourite niece gave him a hug. Uncle Harry had been a constant strength during Michael's recovery, especially in the early darker days. When Rachel had settled into the ghastly days of waiting for Michael to emerge from his seemingly unending coma, Uncle Harry came when he could; he made the long journey from Chichester in his ancient Daimler car. He had waited patiently by, always offering a prayer before he left, often late in the evening.

He never pressed his beliefs or his religion; he merely offered himself and his prayers to the family, quietly and generously. He came and slipped away each day, he never preached, though he inspired hope, he never demanded but he frequently comforted, he never ostentatiously prayed but he often held the hands of his sister or his niece and they joined him in his supplication and they received a peace and reassurance from him. Rachel loved him as a pastor and friend who, though much older, had wisdom and a generosity of spirit like no one else she had ever met.

Whereas Robbie was kind, loving and humorous, there was always a reserve that had a sexual nuance. In Uncle Harry's arms there was succor and warmth, in Robbie's there was a self-consciousness as between man and woman. She was never his daughter, always his son's wife, and that reserve never changed not even in their days of despair and mutual support.

Uncle Harry was Tania's elder brother, nearly twenty-five years her senior and now her only surviving sibling. She treated him more like a father or even teacher, they had not been close as their age difference was so unusually wide. Tania had seen little of Harry during his Church ministry, first in London and later as he graduated into the inner circles of the Established Church.

They had been brought together at the deaths of her sisters and parents, and they had only really become close over the last five or so years. Harry for his part had been increasingly reliant on his younger sister as he grieved for the passing of his beloved wife and shortly after, as he grieved for the passing of his role as the seventy fifth Bishop of Chichester and the one hundred and first Bishop of Selsey.

Josie Fallowes' entry was always a loud affair, she was as effervescent as ever, eccentric, crackers, wild or unusual; it depended on your point of view. Josie had spent her years since the Academy in a whirl of sexual affairs, and an almost complete obliteration of a promising career as a clarinettist. In the years since the wedding of Rachel and Michael she'd had at least three live-in lovers and several other 'relationships'. These were from anything from a one-night stand to a weekend party at Longchamps. Josie had kept in touch with Rachel, though they had spent little time together over the last few years, there had been regular phone calls and a few letters. They always made Rachel laugh or cry, there seemed little that was normal or ordinary in the life of Josie Fallowes. She had accepted the invitation to come to Haver Hall, rather she had begged for an invitation since her latest Beau had deserted her for whatever reason. A desertion at Christmas time Josie considered inconvenient and piggish behavior in the extreme, even from a Henry Dingamans, a womanizer and gambler of ghastly reputation.

Rachel wondered why Josie, a beautiful and attractive woman had let her life become such a shambles. Josie seemed to have a self-destruct button that she pressed almost daily. It was an enigma, to which there seemed no rational answer.

Bertie Frobisher arrived having forgotten half his luggage, his dinner jacket had no trousers nor did he have his evening shoes. They laughed it all off and soon Bertie and the Bishop were sharing a scotch or two before dinner.

It was a custom at Haver Hall that on Christmas Eve every one under the roof was expected to join in the Christmas Eve Feast that was always the same. Everyone included the domestic staff. Raymond was something between Butler and Estate Manager; he was a widower and had been with Robbie since they first moved to Haver Hall some twenty years ago. Joan Hambling the cook housekeeper, had been with them around ten years, she was married to a ne'er-do well salesman who had deserted her some five years earlier, much to the relief of the Johnsons.

Not only was the occasion unchanging, so was the menu, great food and excellent wine from the house's massive cellar. Tania worked with Joan on this feast from start to finish, they occasionally drank too much sherry in the kitchen before dinner and one year Tania had slipped whilst transferring the gargantuan joint of beef from oven to serving trolley. She had sat on the kitchen floor, the joint between her knees, laughing and crying simultaneously, that was three years ago. From that date Robbie had instituted the custom of wheeling in the beef.

Dinner was always at seven sharp, and this was inevitably followed by the visit of the village Church choir who would sing Carols in the Garden room at nine. At eleven, those who wanted, would troupe to Church where Bishop Harold would conduct the Christmas Eve Midnight service. Since his retirement no one wanted to change the system and Uncle Harry enjoyed the occasion enormously.

At dinner Rachel sat between Hugo and Bertie. Hugo was overwhelmed by the Englishness of it all and was subdued almost to the point of dumbness. Rachel did her best to 'bring him out' but it was not easy. The beef was served from the trolley and guests were invited to carve their own. It was all very carnivorous with Michael leading the fray, carving mountains of rare beef for himself and encouraging Bertie to compete.

"Michael behave, that's far too much, you won't sleep."

"Darling don't worry, you'll go to Church with Uncle Harry and no doubt do your penance, in the meantime we boys will sink some of Robbie's splendid Claret."

"Michael, you're drinking your inheritance," Robbie laughed, he loved parties and it was so good to see Michael in good form.

"Well Hugo what do you think of our English Christmas?" asked Tania, ever the conscious hostess.

"Ma'am it's wonderful, I can't believe I'm here really, and it's so kind of you to have me with your family."

"Oh shut up Hugo, we're pals and my pals are always welcome, you too Bertie."

"Quite so," interceded Uncle Harry, "The spirit of Christmas is primarily to love our friends and family. Hugo why don't you come to Church later? You'll see the real community celebrate." He looked round the table, "I don't want to push, you know I don't, but it would be nice if we all went."

"I'd love to come." Bertie as always wanted to please.

"Me too." said Hugo.

"What about you my dear?" The Bishop peered at Josie over his glass.

"Gracious Bishop I haven't been to Church for years, I'll skip if you don't mind."

"Well that's a pretty good party Harry, anyway let's get the Carols and the choir visit over first," said Michael.

Raymond got up to leave the table. "Where are you going Raymond?" asked Tania

"I thought I'd be sure the Garden room was ready for the Carol singers."

"Do sit down and relax Raymond, we've been doing this for God knows how long and you still can't relax."

"That's it, relax Raymond, do as mother tells you." Michael smirked.

There was a short but clear silence.

"Rachel, are you going to play for the Choir?"

"I expect they'll have their own Choir Master who'll want to do all that."

"Bloody think so too." Michael's mood was suddenly sour.

"Michael don't be rude," snapped Tania.

"For heaven's sake Mother, I'm not a school boy."

"Then don't behave like one."

"Well Rachel, I expect you'll be glad to get back to normal when Michael goes back to work... anything exciting coming up?" Robbie smiled, his smile nervous, his intervention a non-sequitur.

"Scandinavia again, not so clever in the winter, although I love the music and the people, but I won't be away long, maybe ten days." She added the latter nervously watching Michael, but he seemed to take no notice: Again a silence.

At nine precisely, the Church Choir consisting of fourteen children and nine adults and Mr. Pedigrew, the Choir Master, entered the Garden room.   Mr. Pedigrew was a man of sixty plus, wrapped in a woollen scarf and unfashionable gabardine rain coat, and a dew drop hung precariously at the end of his nose. He had been Choir Master at St Augustine's since his early twenties and he considered the visits to Haver Hall the zenith of his calendar. This was particularly so since the Bishop was present.

"My Lord Bishop," He wheezed, "How delightful to see you looking so well. We have, Sir," he bowed slightly, "missed your Ministry over this last year or two."

"Bunkum," replied Uncle Harry, "Bishop John is a wonderful man; smarter, holier and altogether a better man that I could ever be, so don't talk nonsense... what are you going to sing for us?"

Mr. Pedigrew, much chastened by the Bishop's rebuke, hastily turned to arrange his Choir round the piano. They were good; not a Cathedral choir, but good for a small village Church Choir. And whatever one thought of Pedigrew, his efforts were strenuous, constant, musical and deeply traditional.

It was a delightful hour, the Choir sang those familiar Carols that everyone, even Hugo, could hum along to. Uncle Harry sat with his umpteenth glass of claret and it was not apparent whether he was sleeping or deeply wrapped in the music.

Robbie and Tania stood on either side of the fire place patiently listening – Robbie was entirely tone deaf - but he liked the idea whatever it was, he enjoyed being the Country Squire.

Hugo tried to hide his tears, Bertie was already quite drunk, whilst Raymond and the Housekeeper sat bolt upright on the settee. Josie straddled the arm of the big armchair where Michael lounged, his arm lolled with intent behind Josie's delectable bottom. Rachel sat primly on her own enjoying the music making. This music like any other she absorbed without criticism, it was beautiful and she accepted it with delight.

The Choir adults were served with hot toddy or anything else they fancied and the children were given toffee apples and soft drinks. Before they left the whole party conducted by the humble Mr. Pedigrew joined in "Oh Come, all ye faithful." Robbie presented his annual cheque for a hundred pounds for the choir fund. This magnanimity guaranteed that next year the choir would reappear.

Just before eleven they all piled into the cars to go to St Augustine's for midnight service, Bishop Harry carrying his vestment bag on his lap and causing a furore when he jammed his crosier into Robbie's leather upholstery.

It was in Church that Rachel first noticed that Michael had not come, everyone else except Josie was there. She turned her mind to 'Once in Royal David's City', but she could not help but wonder what Josie would do to get her hands on Michael. The children were singing 'Away in a manger'.

In Haver Hall Michael had difficulty in getting his trousers down as he and Josie wrestled with their lust in the guest room known as the Bluebell room. By the time the Church party returned Michael was slumped in the same chair, this time though he was finishing a bottle of Krug, Josie was nowhere to be seen.

"Michael, why didn't you come to Church, darling?"

"I didn't want to leave Josie all alone." He leered at her, almost begging her to ask something more.

Instead she turned to Uncle Harry, "That really was a lovely service Uncle Harry. Old Pedigrew does a good job, I must say, it was quite lovely."

"A night cap anyone?" Robbie invited the assembled company, but there was not an enthusiastic response.

Hugo excused himself, kissed Tania gallantly on her hand issued more effusive thanks and retired. Bertie swallowed a large scotch in about a millisecond and was gone and Uncle Harry crept quietly away.

"Where's Josie?"

"Went up a while ago." slurred Michael.

"Come on sweetheart let's get you to bed." Rachel put on her best loving wife demeanour, but as soon as she went to help him out of the chair she smelt the unmistakable stink of Josie's violent perfume. Her heart sank, a leaden sickening feeling, it even weighed down her limbs. She knew in an instant that the spell was broken. Michael had been unfaithful. As the pit of her stomach rose with bile, anger and confusion, her breath came in stunted heaves, her eyes misted with tears that could not be allowed to flood in front of Robbie. She turned her back to him taking Michael's arm and leading him out.

On the stairs she struggled with Michael who was drunk and uncoordinated. The scream of pain within her urged an escape, a scream, a flailing of Michael, to tear his beautiful face off his skull, to wipe away the anger – anything, she could kill him.

'Oh Michael, you have thrown everything we had away, you've taken all the magic and the wonder, the trust and the reliance we had one for another, and you've trampled it in the dust of a moment of lechery.' The tears now streamed down her face as they got to the bedroom. Michael still oblivious to her pain, struggled out of his clothes and shambled to the bathroom. Rachel sat on the bed staring at nothing, hoping that she would wake up, that this was a mistake, but that in its way made her agony worse, because she knew that this was real, in her face. Things would never be the same again.

Not tonight, not in a minute, not in an eternity. They undressed and climbed into the luxuriant bed, still she said nothing. Michael snored and was asleep in a trice. Rachel lay there, her anger sublimated by her empty sadness. Sleep stayed stubbornly away, she felt shrivelled and dry, old before her time and all the while Michael's snoring droned on minute by minute.

At the dead of night, she could stand it no more, she crept from her bed and put on her robe and made her way downstairs to the kitchen. There she made tea and sat on a kitchen stool staring at the wall, within her lonely miserable self.

"Hi Rachel," it shook her from her reverie, "Can't sleep eh! Neither can I."

Josie looked a wreck; not the siren of earlier, just a girl like Rachel, strangely vulnerable, hopelessly unstable, emotionally bereft. Rachel looked back at her friend and said nothing. What could she say, 'I hate you, you bitch, you filthy tart, you nymphomaniac …. What could she say?'

"Hi Josie," Rachel stared unseeing, until she noticed the bruising on Josie's wrists. At first there was a shock, then the realization that the coupling of Michael and Josie had been something she would have recognised; the brutality, the one sidedness, the bestial taking of poor Josie.

Without understanding, she felt a surge of sadness for Josie, lost and forlorn in her constant search for love, or at least warmth, but finding nothing but a series of empty physical dalliances that counted for nothing, except the erosion of Josie's soul. "Hey, have a cup of tea, I shan't be long, I've just not slept well....worrying about Michael I suppose." She held her breath, she had not meant to say anything of the kind.

"Oh Michael seems fine, I guess, but I don't suppose I know him as well as you." She poured her tea.

"Josie, you're a silly bitch...... just leave Michael alone." She spoke quietly, as a matter of fact; then she walked up to Josie and gave her a tender hug. "Josie your perfume is shit." She made her way slowly to bed. Michael was still fast asleep.

Christmas day was altogether brighter, the drizzle had lifted and the December sun shone on the dew mantled lawns, the trees largely without foliage reflected the sunlight from a million water droplets, it was altogether a brighter day.

Routine at Haver Hall was as scheduled as a well oiled clock. Breakfast was at nine thirty, those who wished went to Church, only Hugo volunteered to accompany Uncle Harry. Lunchtime cocktails were served at midday, sundry visitors were expected, then after a buffet snack a walk in the grounds till four, weather permitting. Rest, then dress for dinner (black tie), presents distributed from under the tree, then dinner sharp at eight.

Rachel's agony of the night previous had become altogether more cerebral, none the less painful for that. She found herself absolutely lost. She had no idea what response to make or how to make it. Apart from her chiding of Josie in the early hours of the morning she had spoken to no one. She had greeted Michael coldly, but he seemed indifferent. She could hardly talk to anyone except Josie, but that would surely bring about a showdown, she couldn't under any circumstance have all this come out at the Christmas gathering.

Then there was the ridiculous idea that had seemed fun in the planning. Josie and Rachel had planned to give a short fun recital after dinner. It was to be one of their favourites from College, The Poulenc clarinet sonata, and then ad lib some Cole Porter and some standards for Christmas. They'd agreed yesterday that they would get together to rehearse the Poulenc whilst the family troop was out walking. Now it seemed an impossible idea; making music with her husband's lover or was it to be with her husband's victim?

And what of Michael in all of this? Josie was a harlot and a tramp; she'd been waiting years to get Michael into bed. They were left alone and no doubt Josie who was still a very attractive female would have encouraged his advances, she may well have taken the lead.... Anyway, what man wouldn't have succumbed? Daddy, bloody Daddy would. Robbie? Maybe. Uncle Harry was the only man she could definitely rule out and maybe that was only because of his age. Men were all the same, led by their penises.

Michael had been strongly sexed she knew, until now she'd believed that he'd been faithful. Had he? Was Josie the first; was she the twenty first, one hundred and first? It was all a muddle. Muddles are vexing because she had no idea what to do, or what to say. She was locked in a prison with no prospect of escape; she had no idea where to go or what to do. After avoiding company all morning she knew only one thing, she could play the piano.

The house was quiet after the chaos of Christmas morning. The guests had been force-marched on their obligatory afternoon walk by Squire Robbie. Rachel sat at the piano playing some sad but salving tunes for their promised Christmas soiree-Rachmaninoff. She knew that Josie had to join her soon to practise. She still felt the misery of Michael's unfaithfulness burn in her tummy, she didn't know whether to spit at Josie or hug her in her miserable loneliness; confusion fused with the bitter sweet lament of the music.

"Where shall we start?" Josie, clarinet in hand dumped her music on the piano.

"Anything Goes?" Rachmaninov drifted into the past.

"OK, the Cole Porter numbers."

"Did he hurt you?"

The clarinet wailed and whistled.

"Look I'm sorry, Christ I can't believe what I did, Rachel, what have I done?" More wailing, a whistle and a rush of tears. Josie her hair dishevelled, held her clarinet as if to play, but stood and cried, and cried.

"Come on Josie the show must go on." Rachel resolute on her piano stool declined to get up and comfort her old friend. Josie was the bitch who had seduced Michael. She saw the welts on Josie's wrists. "Did he hurt you?"

"Let's play the Poulenc. It was the best thing we ever did together at school."

"How about the Romanza, 'Tres Calme' before the 'Allegro con fucko'"

"You mean 'fuocco'"

"Do I?"

They played the bitter sweet lament. They played it as if they had rehearsed forever. At the end, there was a silence; both women stared at their music. Josie looked down and trembled both for her lost art and most of all for her lost friendship.

Rachel, after staring at her still hands for a moment, spoke:

"Josie you silly bitch, why don't you work at music, you're so bloody good at it. Just stop fucking every man who passes you…. and love your clarinet, you can at least trust your music and your talent……" The silence hung like a thick veil…. "OK the Poulenc is just as it should be let's hope we don't get them all weeping and wailing." Despite herself she laughed. "Anything Goes! Take it away."

They practised and romped through a selection of Cole Porter. They heard the family arrive in the boot room.

"Do you want me to go? I mean first thing in the morning, or now, if you like, I can easily make an excuse."

"No Josie I don't want you to go, I want Michael to come back."

They packed their music hurriedly before they were faced with the family throng. The boys gathered boisterously around the drinks cabinet, Tania dashed to the kitchen to harass the cooks.

"Come on Ladies," Robbie called, "some Champagne or hot toddy."

"Sure that would be nice, my mouth's very dry after all this music making." Josie, her composure returned, strode purposefully to the male throng.

Rachel packed her music and went quietly to her room. There she sat on the bed and stared listlessly into the darkening evening light, trying as hard as she could to find her feelings. Only numbness remained, even the anger was gone. Certainly she felt no angst against Josie, she was a rather pathetic lonely soul. Nor did she feel anger about Michael, just an ache and a fear that something irreplaceable was lost forever. It wasn't that he'd had sex with Josie, it was the betrayal of their relationship that till now had been inviolate despite its problems. Her wonderful caring husband, her beautiful mate, her hard working workaholic jealous selfish sometimes shit of a husband, was not that any more. Not hers, not exclusively, lovingly, solely, only, hers. She lay back on her lonely bed and heard the faint noises of the Christmas revellers downstairs, the tears rolled down her face and she tasted their lonely bitterness.

She was awakened by Michael; again obviously drunk.

"Come on Rachel let's get a move on. You know Robbie wants his Christmas dinner to be on time."

He walked straight passed her and into the bathroom, "we need to be down at seven sharp" He called with a lilt in his voice obviously pleased with himself and oblivious to Rachel's misery. She responded in kind.

"I'll put out your dinner jacket, which cuff links do you want, the 'Cambridge' or the 'City'?"

"Don't mind, but could you take a spare to Hugo, he's had to borrow one of dad's jackets and I don't think he'll have cufflinks or a tie – do I have a spare black tie? Take him one if we have one."

She gathered the things as she was told and tapped on Hugo's door. Hugo answered attired in a dressing gown, his hair in customary disarray and wearing his confused 'please help me' look.

"Hello, uh... Rachel what can I do for you?"

"Don't panic Hugo I've come to help, I've brought some cufflinks and a black tie, do you have everything else you need?"

"I guess so, but....." He gazed at the black tie. "How does this thing work?"

"Hugo no problem come along to us when you're dressed and Michael will tie it for you, we're just along the hall.....OK."

She turned to leave when she sensed that all was not well with Hugo, she turned once more, Hugo stood awkwardly in his door way.

"What's the problem Hugo, can I help?"

Hugo shook his head, "I'm not sure, it's this jacket, it's kind of... you know   kinda small I guess."

"Let me see, let's see what we can do." She entered his room already a shambles after just a day's residence.

Hugo slipped out of his dressing gown and stood in an uncomfortably tight pair of Robbie's trousers, and evening shirt at least two sizes too small. He squeezed into the dinner jacket that seemed very tight, but the thing that reduced Rachel to a broad smile was that the arms were at least three inches short.

"Whadya think?"

"Well it is fashionable to show a bit of cuff," She avoided laughing, but only just.

"You're laughing at me."

"Sorry Hugo darling but you are all tucked up a bit. But you'll be fine"

She returned to their room, Michael emerged from the bathroom towelling his hair.

"Hugo's in a mess, Michael you have to find him another dinner jacket and shirt, about the only things he's got that fit are your cufflinks and a black tie, and by the way he can't tie that. He looks more trussed up than the turkey; you have to do something even if all the men change back to lounge suits."

There followed a speedy but discrete search for the appropriate clothes for Hugo, and soon after Rachel emerged from her shower the problem had been solved. Tania had prevailed on Raymond the House Manager to hand over his dinner jacket, he would wait on table in formal uniform.

The diversion over, Rachel sat at the dressing table putting on her beautiful diamond teardrop ear rings and single diamond pendant necklace that had been Michael's Christmas present. Probably twenty thousand pounds worth of jewellery, but what did it mean if her husband was humping Josie whilst the present nestled under the Christmas tree. She, with the assistance of Robbie, had bought Michael a fine set of golf clubs, indeed all the guests and family in this rich household exchanged gifts of outrageous material worth.

Of all the gifts that Rachel received by far the most touching and generous was from Bishop Uncle Harry. He had presented her with an early bound collection of 'Byrd' masses for organ. They had bought Josie a fine leather music attaché case. Hugo had received a set of City of London Cufflinks. (He had broken down and wept). Bertie received an antique Tantalus from the family for his rescue of Michael during that fateful day on the rugby field. Tania had received a complete new kitchen for the London home. All in all fortunes had been spent on last minute extravagances that meant little, except perhaps to Hugo, who found the whole English Christmas scene overwhelmingly warm and generous.

Christmas dinner at Haver Hall never varied. It was traditional, extravagant and tended to be drunken; Joan supervised an army of temporary serving staff, all drawn from the village. Robbie exulted in his squire's role and Tania fussed for no reason at all.

Rachel, still numb and lost, sat between Uncle Harry and Michael; she could not but help feel the warmth of his delightful Uncle. She did her best to entertain him and be civil to Michael who still seemed oblivious to the situation. Perhaps he felt he had remained undiscovered or perhaps he didn't care.

 Hugo who sat opposite mooned over her, hopelessly infatuated as always, Josie sat beside him, but for all her whiles could not compete with Rachel, for Rachel was Hugo's all time calamitous infatuation, Hugo's mooning adoration; an unqualified compliment. Hugo was the sweetest, most innocent, hapless man she had ever met, she could quite see the attraction of taking him in her arms, and taking him to a motherly bed. Sweet kind Hugo, even now in his borrowed dinner jacket, his ill fitting shirt with crookedly tied tie, his eyes swiveling slightly reminiscent of Max, ugly but cuddly, chaotic but comfortable, shambling as ever absolutely reliable.

He was the man that Josie needed; she knew it. They were the two misfits who could make a match, two lost souls who could find each other. Why she should consider Josie in any charitable light defeated her logic. She ought to have hated the bitch but she didn't. She hated herself more, Michael had strayed and he'd strayed because she could not offer him what he wanted. She seemed to float outside herself viewing the Christmas dinner from some ethereal corner. She was detached, in shock still, lost and bemused. It was hard to stay polite at the family Christmas, everyone was so jolly, including Michael who seemed still to be oblivious to her suffering. She felt the detachment chill her soul, she felt herself as a snail withdrawing into her shell, and no one would hurt her again. Michael was her perfect man, now imperfect, deceitful, irresponsible and possessive. Already the light that made her love him in so unqualified a way was going out, the sadness made her tears flow, her shoulders shake. She excused herself and ran to the ladies room.

When she emerged, Uncle Harry and Tania waited for her away from the dining room.

"My dear, what's wrong, something is I can tell." Uncle Harry put out his arms and she reluctantly kept him at bay.

"It's nothing; really I've just been out of sorts, that's all."

"Darling are you sure? Every thing's all right between you and Michael, please tell me dear, I only want to help, you know Robbie and I adore you and well... I know it's been a strain since Michael's accident.... I mean is everything all right?"

"Yes, we'll be fine Tania….. really…. I'm being silly, come on let's go into dinner I'm sure everyone is wondering where we are." She took both their arms and led them back to the table.

The light hearted musical offerings went down well, Josie was terrific in the jazzy Cole Porter offerings. She murdered the Poulenc probably because she was up to her ears in Champagne. No one seemed to notice as the majority shared her degree of inebriation.

They sang songs round the piano, the Bishop doing a more than passable impression of Old Blue Eyes.

Eventually it was inevitably time for bed, Hugo and Josie seemed to be getting amorous, Bertie was positively blotto, Michael full of charm and reeking of too much cognac and sexual desire. Rachel, despite her own deliberate toping, felt a welling up of loathing and fear as she and Michael made their way to bed.

Once in the bedroom, Michael started to make up to her, he tried to bind her in his drink stinking embrace. She pulled away.

"What's the matter my pretty wife, no Christmas spirit?"

"Michael, if you are in any doubt, I know that you went to bed with Josie last night, yes I know… you bastard… she told me so don't bother denying it."

"Darling, you know Josie's a tramp she's been trying to get into my trousers since we were first introduced... she came on to me.... You know, it wasn't anything just a romp that's all... I was a bit pissed...Oh shit what can I say."

"Don't say anything, just shut up and get to bed, and you so much as lay a hand on me and God help me I'll kill you. Now shut up and get into bed."

Much to her relief Michael responded meekly rather like a school boy who'd been told off. He curled up with his back to her. She lay there rigid, still fearing that he would change and advance on her again. After about ten long minutes, he muttered, as he slid into an alcoholic sleep.

"I down know wha yurr thinking, your screwing all those musical types Cy what'isname........zzzzzz." He was asleep.

She lay awake with her pain, it was everywhere in her heart, her stomach and her head. The bleak cold of loneliness made worse in a way by being in the midst of all this Christmas spirit and apparent family bliss. A paralysis beset her mind; she could not look forward, but only back, bemoaning the perfection that he had thrown away. Had he thrown it away, or had they thrown it away? She couldn't think clearly, one thing she knew, things could never be the same again.

Chapter 10

They returned to London, and the remainder of the holiday visiting was soon over, New Years Eve was another one of Michael's City cronies' affairs. It was typically expensive, a lot of material junkies displaying their incongruous wealth. Many of the men were younger than Rachel, the new breed or generation of dealers and slickers who though hardly out of university made huge piles of money. They brought their groupie girls whose dresses vied for the most indecent revelations. The whole thing was leant an air of respectability because it was a Charity Ball held in one of London's premier hotels on Park Lane.

The tickets at two hundred guineas a piece, were given out by the city merchant houses to their young Turks; some of the older guard were there too. Much to Rachel's delight Hugo was there now resplendent in a made to measure Tux, Bertie had on his arm a plain young lady named Thelma, she seemed to be more used to horses rather than this sort of jamboree but the great thing was Thelma didn't seem to mind. Josie Fellowes was Hugo's escort and she was attired, even for Josie, in the most outrageous dress. It was held together by gold safety pins and her ample bosoms were hardly confined. All in all it made her look, or so Rachel thought, a bigger tramp than she already was. Hugo in his uncomplicated way though seemed pleased and remained studiously engrossed into Josie's ample charms. The arrival of Rachel disconcerted him for a while but Josie brought him to heel with a judicious stroke of his arm with her left breast. The girls exchanged smiles.

Michael was all charm and engaged the younger men as someone with a track record and the reputation of a rising city star. He looked the part; strikingly handsome, in some ways the ravages of his injuries had added a wrinkle or a grey hair or two. It had removed the vestiges of youth and conferred upon him a maturity and ruggedness that was new. He was, as Rachel looked at him, changed in appearance and in nature. Michael was different.

Jennifer Walmer appeared from the throng and insisted that Rachel circulate with her to meet the Charity committee including the Duchess who despite her continental roots spoke with an impeccable English accent. She looked down her nose at Rachel.

"Jennifer, who is this lovely girl?" Her hand was extended limply and gloved. She shook hands as if to hold any tighter might cause her become infected by some disease that was widely prevalent outside royal circles.

"Ma'am, this is Rachel Johnson the pianist."

"How lovely" the duchess crooned, "Isn't this the young beauty you were telling me about?" She transferred the royal gaze to Rachel, "Yes you are lovely and so young, has Jennifer asked you yet?"

"Not yet." Jennifer responded, "but I'm sure Ma'am, that she'll be a great asset on the committee."

Rachel was at a loss, what were they talking about.

"Come along" whinnied the Duchess, "Come along and meet some people."

They turned and Rachel was introduced to a variety of Royal hangers-on and minor celebrities, Lords and Ladies in Waiting, none of whom made any impression on Rachel who remained bemused and curious about what committee had been talked about.

The rest of the night was engaging in its way, Hugo and Josie seemed locked in embrace most of the time. Rachel couldn't make up her mind whether this was a display for her benefit, to assure her that the Michael thing was over.

Michael was charm itself, he enjoyed meeting his city chums and was flattered by the good will and apparently genuine welcome back to the fold. All night Rachel expected the dreaded Bradley Walmer to reappear but happily there was no sign of him.

Michael, her Michael, so handsome still; she watched him fascinated by his physique and the way he moved. He was still, as far as Rachel was concerned, the most beautiful man in the world. She mused that perhaps her greatest passion was after all physical. Why not? It seemed that was what made the men's world go around. Were women different? Was she any different? It was time to go, two thirty a.m. Quite late enough, Michael was to return to work tomorrow - a New Year; what would it bring? She hoped she could forgive and start again.

In the taxi on the short ride to the house, Michael was blessedly sober, contrite and romantic. It was easy for her to forgive at least for that moment. It was then she decided that they would start anew. Tonight they would be together; she would blot out the memory of Josie, of jealousy, and just work hard at being in love again. And yes she would make love; she needed to, to feel him close to her and inside her and to be re-assured that her Michael was who she wanted him to be.

The New Year from those first moments was a new beginning.

Michael set off to work at 7:15, and by 8:00 Rachel was with Becky. What would the year bring her musically? Already there was a crowded calendar of engagements, Concordia wanted her to concentrate on her concerti repertoire but Rachel felt that the fulfillment she initially felt in the spectacular musical arenas was superficial. Since Grieg, she'd expanded her concert repertoire extensively, it had been a hard road. Concordia constantly pushed for popular romantic performances, but the physical demands of some of this were very heavy indeed. They wanted her to record the second and third Rachmaninov concerti, but she felt they were just too masculine in their demands; the spreads were often too wide, too big for her hands. Sometimes during practice and in lessons, her hands and shoulders ached. These monumental works with all their majesty, their tunes, their spectacular appeal, they were just too physical.

There was always the call of the recital hall and her freedom there to express the works she loved as she saw them. These works were like friends who matured with knowing. She felt them change from within herself, each time she played the Beethoven's middle sonatas she learned more and they became a different experience each time she played them. The audiences, that only a year or two ago were her adrenalin pump, were still important but not as important. There were so many things she wanted to do and play, but there was always pressure from MIL and Concordia to do this or that.

The push for recording the so called great concerti and the draw of the great orchestras however remained the course by which the record buying public judge and that in turn generated demand for appearances and engagements. To some extent this was a treadmill she had determinedly set to labour on, and there would be no turning back. The demands were almost overwhelming, and that January morning she knew that someday soon she may have to face a choice. A choice between a career, largely set in Northern Europe as a recitalist of middle rank, or to turn the treadmill slope up and continue to aspire to truly international celebrity.

When Michael had been ill at the start she had quite decided that she would devote herself to the former, but as the struggle to restore him to health had unfolded and the changes in him had been manifested so her resolve lessened, and her dreams of her musical youth returned. The Carnegie Hall still beckoned.

At 11:30 she had an appointment in Covent Garden with 'Hands' her physiotherapists who as their name implied specialized in looking after musicians. Of course they just didn't treat hands but the whole anatomy that contributed to a healthy and vigorous lifestyle. Repetitive Strain Syndrome is common amongst musicians and a number have to retire early with chronic problems. Rachel kept up a regular regime of physiotherapy with Betty Grimshawe, a large and jolly lady from Manchester. Betty had looked after Rachel for at least five years and they had become firm friends. Their sessions were a thoroughly relaxing therapy for Rachel both for the physical treatment as well as the gossip.

"How's your husband?"

"Much better, Betty, he's back at work today… I suppose it will take him a while to settle…. But he'll be happier with 'the boys' and playing the great commercial hunter."

"My old man is still on holiday – lucky bugger."

"How's that Betty?"

"He's not back at school yet, he teaches… but you know that don't you."

"Yes I do, but with all my trouble with Michael I've forgotten such a lot; like you and how much good you do me."

"Very pleased I'm sure." Betty mock curtsied, "your wrists are a bit stiff if I might say, are you working too hard?"

"Bloody Rachmaninov, he's wonderful but I think he wrote for men, it's awfully tough though…. "Rachel dozed under Betty's soothing massage.

"Your Michael, it is Michael isn't it?"

"Yes."

"He's a banker isn't he…. in the city?"

"Yes. I'm not sure I'd call him a banker, he always seems to be doing deals that I never associated with banking… he's a sort of wheeler dealer really… anyway he loves it… sometimes I think he loves his job more than me."

"They're all the same dear, my Eric, you'd think the whole education of the nation rested on his shoulders, he flaps and worries about his students and their University entrance and every summer I may as well be somewhere else for all the notice he takes of me."

There was another lapse as Betty transferred the muscle relaxing TENS from one arm to the other. "Mind you in the holiday when he's not fussing about some new syllabus, he's forever expecting me to drop everything and look after him; it's as if my job is of no importance."

"I know what you mean, and he's jealous too…. I can't think why, he knew I was going to travel a lot when we married."

"Rachel love, I can see why he'd be jealous of you my dear, you are a bit special, not only beautiful but.... I don't know.... so clear and confident about yourself."

"Oh I wish I was, Betty.... I wish I was."

After therapy, there was a meeting with Max and Harold Gingrich, Max's immediate Boss. She never really liked Gingrich; he bored her, always talking schedules and fees. He seemed disinterested in the music, Rachel was to him just an income stream to be exploited.

The Restaurant was full but the Maitre d' whisked her to an upstairs room where Max and Gingrich sat, already well on their way to finishing a bottle of wine. Max as always gave her a hug and his effusive best wishes for the New Year. Gingrich simply shook hands and mumbled his greeting.

"Darling we have to catch up," Max was his hyper self," I have arranged to recover some of your lost engagements – now my love you'll have to work just a bit harder to get yourself back on the map."

"Max you're very sweet, but can I have a drink first please?'

"What am I thinking about, a little Volnay perhaps?"

"No thanks Max just water please. And how are you Harold?"

"Well, thank you," Gingrich looked startled that Rachel had addressed him at all.

"Darling it's our New Year's first working day for goodness sake, have a drink, this Burgundy is really delicious, please for Max's sake."

"All right, but a glass of water too please."

Max liberally sloshed the fine wine into her goblet, at the same time launching into enthusiastic and over the top compliments about how divine she looked.

"Don't you ever shut up Max, I'm in jeans and tee shirt for God's sake, I've just had a divine hour with Betty at 'Hands'. I look a wreck but at least I'm a relaxed wreck, so Max cut out the nonsense ...Darling." She mimicked the last word.

"Well now that darling Michael is quite recovered we can get back to a full calendar, so we've got what we can for you Darling and some of the later year stuff is going to blow your mind; you're going to love your Max even more than you do now." Max flapped his wrist in the most effeminate way, "Rachel, Jamo wants you to do the Proms with them."

The waiter approached, "Are you ready lady and Gentlemen?"

"The Proms....when, what are we to play?"

"September 5th darling; the Gothenburg are doing two nights and on the second they want you to do the Grieg."

They ordered their lunches, Max as ever enthusing like the obsessive foodie he was.

"I'm talking Proms here, Grieg for goodness sake." Max's eyes whizzed in concentric circles, "The Proms and that's not all, maybe Chicago, Barenboim, maybe too, we must celebrate."

Rachel couldn't bear to keep up her composure; she leapt round the table and gave him a spectacular hug, planting a great lipstick kiss on his cheek.

"With Jamo at the Proms that's special Max, you are my favourite man, at least over lunch, forgive me Harold."

"The Prom appearance will do no harm to sales, particularly your Grieg; that has done quite well already."

"I'm so glad about that." Her sarcasm was lost on Harold.

Max guzzled the rest of the wine. He ordered liver but was more interested in the urgent delivery of the second bottle of wine.

Despite herself, Rachel was persuaded to take a further two glasses of the red wine, though she resisted calls for Champagne from Max. She left the restaurant feeling euphoric and almost skipped to the taxi rank.

It seemed ages before Michael arrived home from work, she buzzed around the house, she played a little in the studio, strictly against Betty's instructions. She rang her mother and shared the news about the Prom engagement. She couldn't wait to tell Michael.

As soon as he came into the kitchen she knew something was wrong, Michael wore the expression of a thunderous cloud. He threw his briefcase into the corner and walked straight for the whisky decanter.

She felt his entrance like a blow to her stomach, in a second all her euphoria evaporated.

"Not a good day, come and give me a hug – I've got some good news that will cheer us up." She extended her arms and Michael paused and moved stiffly into her embrace.

"I can't fucking believe it, they've got me working for…. for… Derek Hayter…. Jesus, do they have any idea what a prick that guy is, I've got to run around at his beck and call." He squeezed her.

"Never mind darling, it's your first day back I expect they are running you in gently." She released him, "come on let's sit down…. drink your scotch, then we'll go out for a bit of supper." She knew then this was not the time to mention her news. Her success was the last thing she would talk about. He needed coddling and she would wrap him up in love and salve his wounds.

Throughout their evening things did not improve, Michael was deeply wounded by whatever had happened at work, he drank furiously, ate little and swore a lot. Rachel for her part tried to encourage and make light of his problem; this was a mistake, and eventually just had to listen to an outpouring of abuse about the bank and Hayter in particular. As far as Rachel could gather, Michael had been asked to work with Hayter on the analysis of a new Bio-tech project, this time based in Italy.

During the tirade against Hayter she remembered the warnings of Lucas the Psychiatrist, 'Watch for any signs of exaggerated behavior; any over the top reactions to setbacks, any wild responses,' and to let him know. She didn't like Dr Rodney Lucas; their visits to him after Michael's release from Hospital were always strained. He'd been professional in the extreme, but he seemed always to be watching, asking, sucking in information and seldom giving anything back to Michael or indeed to her. Lucas had measured Michael's healing in terms of improving cognitive and responsive behaviour. He had, after two months, announced that Michael would return to near pre trauma fitness. He had taken Rachel aside and told her in an almost impossibly obscure way that Michael was likely to recover entirely and then again he may not. It was in that session he had warned her to expect some behaviour changes. He was specific about the possibility of mood changes and what he called exaggerated behaviour patterns or rather changes of patterns or the breaking of patterns. Was this such an example? Rachel felt confused and uneasy as she escorted her inebriated husband on the short walk home.

At home she plied Michael with coffee that he eventually threw partly into the sink and partly on the floor. As he undressed he started ranting:

"I suppose your day was perfect my gorgeous pianist wife, out with that pervert Max.... fucking pervert." He mumbled and stumbled into the shower.

Rachel said nothing, she undressed, quickly put on her robe and waited quietly as she felt her fear rise. She closed her eyes and gathered herself for the storm that surely must come. How she wished she was as drunk as Michael.

As Michael lumbered back into the bedroom the telephone rang, Rachel answered, it was Robbie. "Hello Robbie............. yes of course." "Darling it's your father he just wants to know how things went at the Bank today."

Michael took the phone, "Hello dad, yes everything was fine, I think they're molly coddling me a bit to start........... yes it's good to be back at work...... fine Dad, fine good night thanks for ringing.... yes she's fine.... good night ....love to Mum... good night." He put the phone down, "Good of Robbie to ring."

All his anger had evaporated as if by magic; they climbed into bed, he reached for her tenderly, they cuddled gently, she told him about the prom. He seemed sleepily pleased. Rachel listened to him drift into his reassuring regular snore; he was asleep. She stayed rigidly awake, wondering if she should talk to Dr Lucas. It had been a tough day for Michael, she knew; she would wait and see.

The following days were practice and more practice; she worked with Sally Nye and with Eva. Rachel was astonished to find that Eva despite her age and arthritis could pour such light upon the problems posed by the Rachmaninov. They sat for hours in the studio while Eva coached and coached almost as if they were back in their early days at The Menuhin School. After three days of almost continuous practice Eva announced that she was satisfied.

"No more, is all, no more.... meine liebe no more, you are more than your Teacher........ you are grown up now... do zis Rachmaninov now and zen no more...... I sink you can do this.... ut you are right it is too physical you will hurt yourghzelf if too much....yah!"

"Eva, thank you; you've helped so much, I think now maybe I can do these concerti because of you and Sally" She hugged her old teacher and breathed in the musty camphor. How old Eva felt; dry, and gray and spent, her bony frame so frail under the velvets and the taffetas of her eccentric bundled clothing. In her embrace she felt the loneliness of a teacher who had always sat alone and watched her students reap the rewards of her selflessness. She had not loved Eva, who had loved Rachel without reserve or any expectation of reward. Eva had been excluded from all the glory; she was not even allowed to come to that night, now so far away, in Liverpool. Yet here was Eva who for the umpteenth time had turned the key, had opened the way.

"Eva, if Chicago comes off, I'd like you to come and hear me play, will you do that.... Please for me?"

"Meine Liebe, you do not have to …. You know you have repaid me so many times, after I am gone you will repay me still, not many can say zat; imagine in thirty years your talent will still be grhrowing….no, zat will be pay for me still,… yah." She wrapped herself in her improbable camphor cloaks and left, but her step was not as steady as Rachel had remembered.

Rachmaninov had almost broken her; the demands both physical and mental were close to overwhelming. Eva's advice was priceless and to the point, 'Do this now and don't repeat, too often, it was just too difficult a challenge. Her time at Hands and the ministrations of Betty Grimshawe became a thrice weekly therapy.

Michael for his part settled to the old routine of long days and frequent trips. He was quieter; less voluble when at home, he seemed more introvert, noticeably less enthusiastic about his job. He seldom mentioned his projects or prospects, even Hayter the object of so much abuse seemed to have faded from his horizons. He appeared quite unexpectedly at home when Rachel was sure he said he was going to be away. She saw him in Covent Garden quite by chance as she came out of 'Hands' just before she was due to fly to Cologne to perform a recital, it was a crisp sunny Thursday morning;

"Michael" she called, he saw her and seemed confused, first he looked away then he turned away, thought better of it and eventually waved back.

"Hello darling fancy bumping into you; thought you were off to Cologne."

"Just on my way to the City airport actually – come on, come and see me off."

In the taxi Michael explained he'd just been to see a customer or somebody in the Strand. Rachel thought nothing of it. He was keen to know how her hands were and what went on at "Hands."

"Why don't you get an appointment? It's not just for musicians and freaks you know, it's one of the best Physio practices in London and they just don't do 'hands' and pianists, they have a whole raft of physio experts. It would be good for you Michael; I'll make an appointment for you just to relax awhile. After all since your accident you've done hardly any exercise."

She hugged him. She explained the issues about her tendonitis that had flared up after the stresses of the Rachmaninov. They had a cup of coffee and a sandwich at the Airport terminal; kissed goodbye and Rachel flew off for her one night recital engagement.

Rachel's programme of work began to settle into a busy rhythm; once the Rachmaninov 2 and 3 were recorded she played them live three times in England and continental Europe. The CD was well received and it was rumoured that it might be up for a Classical Brit award and possibly a Grammy.

Max remained as enthusiastic as ever and worked assiduously stretching her engagement book well ahead, as well as grabbing any stand-in work that was of the right calibre and prestige. For the first time in her career Rachel really felt the pace of her workload and felt the attendant fatigue.

It was at a very longstanding engagement in Newcastle on Tyne that she first felt she couldn't perform; she really did not want to go to the recital. She sat in her hotel room and felt the mixture of self doubt, sheer tiredness and the beginnings of another attack of tendonitis. Here she was barely twenty eight years old and she felt burned out and old. Not only old, but lonely and old. It was a difficult programme of Beethoven including the Opus 110. She went and performed, but she knew it was poor, even if the audience seemed satisfied. For the first time in her career she felt drained, not from the outpouring of wonder but from a labour that contained little more than physical exertion. She excused herself from the post recital gathering and drank a large amount of Cognac and cried herself to sleep.

On her return to London she found an invitation from the Duchess to attend with her spouse, a dinner party at the royal country retreat. She put it to one side in the kitchen and rang Max's office. Max was not there and she left an urgent message for him to ring her back.

She told the secretary that it was very urgent in that she was going to cancel a number of engagements because she was not well. The message had the desired result since Max was on the phone within minutes. She was not to do anything; Max would be round in a brace of shakes.

Max arrived at around two o'clock. He was all concern and kindness but urged Rachel to think carefully before cancelling any engagements unless it was absolutely necessary.

"Darling we all love you, but that's the problem, everybody wants you and now is not the time to take time out, the Prom is only a few months away - we know you must be fresh for that, but darling we have so many engagements, all of them are vital in one way or another. I beg you Darling think before we do anything we will regret."

"Max I know I had a break when Michael was ill but these two last months have been like hell; I really feel washed out. My problems with tendonitis don't seem to want to go away; it's that bloody Rach two and three, they've ruined me."

"That is the point we had to cancel a number of things because of Michael and we don't want to cancel any more, darling we don't want you to have a reputation as unreliable, do we? You can do that maybe one day when we're big enough but not now Darling, not now."

He was right and she knew it, it had only been three or four months since they had rebuilt her engagement book after all the cancellations following the US tour, any further cancellations now would be disastrous.

Max fidgeted about, Rachel wept intermittently aware that what she wanted was impossible, but reluctant to admit it. She made tea, they did not even venture into the studio; that made the meeting so strange, away from music, they seemed different people; Max somehow more manipulative; she more counter-dependant.

"Max I need a rest, I don't care how long but we have to do something, I'm absolutely worn out."

Max fished in his pocket and whisked his diary out rather like a conjurer, "Darling there are difficulties, but Max will do what he can, but I beg you, let's not throw away all your hard work, we don't want the boot on the other foot do we? I mean our recitals cancelled by promoters, but if we get the label….. 'known to be unreliable', Darling what can I do?"

"Max I don't know, it has been nine months now since we got back to normal, whatever normal is? It's not been that busy except the Rach works, it's just I'm so tired."

"Darling it's probably a reaction, now that Michael is well again you will be well again, anyway let's see what we can do." He thumbed through his diary, "Ireland we can drop, that's next week, we have Uretsky who can stand in, that will be a help darling, I'll see what I can do to cut down in May, we have to do Scandinavia and we have to do the BBC, I'll see what I can do about Munich. There darling, that will lighten your load."

"Oh Max you are sweet but can't I have this Bristol engagement cancelled, I can't really do it, Schumann, Max please... Please...?

"Darling it's too short notice, it's Friday, the day after tomorrow, it's out of the question, be a brave girl for Max, then you can rest... please for Max."

It was hopeless; she knew that she would have to go to the Coulston Hall and do the Schumann, there was no way to get out of it.

"All right Max but please let's spend more time planning and less time filling in, no stand-ins .... please."

They embraced, neither quite sure of the other. They knew that they needed each other. Without Max, Rachel would be lost, she knew it. For Max, Rachel was still the one in his stable who could be the one; she could be up there with Martha Argerich, or Jennifer Hewitt.

Rachel George could be up there alongside the greats, Carnegie Hall, Boston, Paris, Berlin and New York they were all just around the corner. She was precious to MIL, to Concordia and Max had to admit to himself, she was the nearest thing he had to family.

Despite the earliness of the hour, four o'clock in the afternoon, the front door burst open and in thundered Michael. He was drunk. He staggered into the kitchen slinging his brief case into the hall before bursting into the kitchen where Max and Rachel sat at the breakfast bar.

"Well whadowehave'ere then, Max you old bastard, what are you up to eh? An my lille Rachel aren't you at your piano….tinkle tinkle. Whadoyahavetodo in the kitchen….?" he slipped and nearly fell headlong. Rachel rushed and helped stop his fall. Michael pushed her aside.

"Eh Max you bloody creep, wh'isit eh?"

Max, his eyes now circling concentrically, made to get up to leave.

"Sidown, don't mind me I'm only the husband, the whimp."

"Michael sit down and behave, I'm sorry Max," Rachel moved between the two men.

"Michael. I'll make you some coffee. Now please sit down."

Michael slumped into the chair vacated by Rachel. His head bowed into his hands. He reeked of beer and whisky.

Max got up, "I think I should leave."

"Yes that's right, piss off!" Michael sat up, looking unsteady but belligerent.

"Perhaps that would be better Max, I'm really sorry, let me see you out." She hustled Max out past the half supine Michael, making his getaway with speed. Rachel returned to the kitchen where Michael was standing with a tumbler in one hand and a bottle of scotch in the other. He stood stubbornly swaying from side to side.

"Michael, for God's sake what's got into you? You're drunk as a lord for Christ's sake; it's only four o'clock in the afternoon. Now put that whisky down and go and have a shower."

"Shouldn't be home yet eh, disturbing you and your pimp planning some more adventures eh?'

"Michael shut up and don't be so bloody stupid."

"Stupid; you think I'm stupid, everybody thinks I'm stupid... Do you know where I've been, do you know? Do you want to know ....I don't suppose you give a damn, I've been on the piss with my redundancy money; yes those bastards have thrown me out. Those smarmy lying bastards at LONY have thrown me out...that bastard Hayter, he had me thrown out.... because he knew, I knew, he's a looser.

"What do you mean you've been thrown out? The Bank can't do that."

"Can't do that, whatdoyathink they are? A bunch of piano players? Of course they can do that, they've done just that. Two hundred thousand pounds, allowance to hold onto venture share preferences, and bugger off... Not up to the mark old booy.... too many mistakes old boy, now fuck off, now.... clear your desk, get out, go away." Michael dumped himself back in to the chair, throwing another whisky down his throat as he sat. He stared at Rachel.

"What about Alistair Bingham, surely he wouldn't stand for this..?

"Oh sweetheart how innocent you are, it was Alistair Bingham who told me to get out.... he didn't say get out, who cares what he said, what he meant was, get out, fuck off, never darken our doors again."

"But why? Why you've only been back at work twelve weeks, before that you were the man on the way to the top .... why?

"Don't know.... face didn't fit, Hayter absolutely shat on me, that's what did it."

God how life could change so much in two days, her own career in doubt, Michael without a job, but why?

The silence was shattered by the phone ringing.... it was Robbie; "Hello Rachel look I've just heard that Michael's finished at the bank, did you know?"

"Yes, he's here, do you want to talk to him?"

"Yes.... no, I don't know Rachel, are you all right?"

"Michael it's your father, he wants to talk to you."

Michael stared blankly back, picked up his jacket, waved a flapping hand and lurched into the bedroom.

"I'm sorry Robbie, Michael's upset he doesn't want to talk to anyone."

"Are you alright my dear?'

"Yes, thank you of course, what happened Robbie?"

"I don't know, but I think Michael's done something foolish, or, I don't know, anyway Bingham's boss phoned me to say that they were sorry but there's no way back for Michael.... that's all they're going to say, I'm sorry I have nothing else.... look, I think it would be good if I came over and took you two out for dinner – perhaps we can work something out."

"Robbie that would be lovely except I don't know how Michael is going to be.... naturally he's deeply upset.... and a little drunk I'm afraid."

"Silly young bugger; look I'll come over about half past seven any way and we'll see how he is – look Tania's out of town so it'll be just me."

"Thanks Robbie, we'll see you later."

She put down the phone and with some foreboding followed Michael into the bedroom, he was in the shower, she went inside the bathroom, "That was Robbie, he's coming over later." The shower stopped running and through the frosted screen she could see him, his back was towards her. His shoulders shuddered, he was crying. Rachel whipped the screen open and thrust her arms about him,

"My beautiful boy, what have they done to you?"

 He shuddered close to her, soaking her with his wet body, no longer the threat but the pathetic Michael, lost, alone and without a shred of defiance. Rachel took him from the shower and wrapped him in a towel and led him still weeping to the bed. There she lay him down, and cradled him in her arms, and enjoined her tears to his, then she kissed him and stroked him and loved him.

"Yes," she whispered, "yes, you are the most beautiful man in my world." In their lovemaking there was solace and there was hope, if they had each other they had the world.

Chapter 11

The dinner with Robbie was an unusual affair. Robbie was gentle and probing, trying as best he could to find out what had caused Michael to be expelled so summarily from the bank. Michael was at times evasive, sometimes petulant, but cunning in the way that he spoke of complicated and apparently rational matters. All these fantastic coincidences he would have them believe had conspired to his demise at LONY.

Rachel watched Robbie who despite his sensitive and indulgent listening obviously did not believe a word. She too felt the undercurrent of lies and half-truths, some of Michael's remarks were too fanciful, too fantastic to countenance. She watched Robbie who in turn watched Rachel. They both made excuses and supported the more improbable claims that Michael made. He was their boy; they loved him, father and wife. In their hearts though, they shared a foreboding that there was something horribly wrong.

Despite Rachel's best efforts, Michael had drunk at least a whole bottle of claret on his own, and whatever else he had consumed earlier in the day conspired to induce obvious signs of drunkenness. Robbie helped Rachel, much against her protests, to put Michael to bed. It was only nine-thirty.

"Will you have a night cap Robbie?"

"Yes please, my dear, a small brandy would be fine, some black coffee too if you don't mind...I say my dear, I'm very sorry about this. I don't know what to say.... I spoke to Bingham but he was bloody evasive.... I don't think we'll ever know the reason."

"So you don't believe him either? All this stuff about Derek Hayter and these Italians.... whatever else he said.... I couldn't follow half of it."

"Is he alright? You know he's been back to work such a short time after the accident, do you think he went back to work too early?....Look Rachel are you OK, I mean all right.... you know, are you two getting on alright?...." He tailed off embarrassed, for Robbie to be so direct was just not done.

Rachel took his arm in hers, "Robbie he'll be alright, I'm sure this was a one-off thing.... I know Michael and so do you.... he'll be fine." She poured the coffee wondering if she believed what she had said. Dear Robbie he was so kind and he loved Michael. Was she shielding him or herself? Did she believe in Michael's recovery? She did not. But it wouldn't help sharing these doubts with Robbie. Michael was going to need all the help he could get.

"Well," said Robbie, "whatever's happened we must look to the future, I know money's not the worry for now but things move on, I'll do what I can to.... well you know oil the wheels to see what's up.... Look Rachel you keep up your work; Tania and I know how important it is to you, so we'll all pull together, eh! So don't be shy, he's our son and we love him and you of course.... So don't be afraid to ask us for anything.... anything my dear, do you understand?" He kissed her gently on her forehead, drank the remainder of his brandy and left.

After Robbie had left, Rachel sat in the kitchen and tried to work out where she stood. She knew that Robbie knew that Michael was not.... well, normal. He wanted to protect his son; she wanted to protect her husband. Was telling each other half-truths and downright lies the way to help? She doubted it, but for the life of her she had no idea what else to do. Schumann was her next project and despite the lateness of the hour she went down to Becky and they worked on the Schumann into the early morning. It seemed that her husband's pain had taken the place of her tendonitis.

She crept to bed, fearful and weary. Tomorrow, or was it today, she would have to travel to Bristol and rehearse and perform and return to London the same night. How would Michael be? Who would look after him? Should she try and see Alistair Bingham or perhaps Dr Lucas? She practised the opening of the Schumann in her mind as she often did, until the curtain of sleep enveloped her exhausted soul.

Michael showering awakened her; she looked at the clock, it was only six thirty.

"Michael darling why are you up so early?" She hesitated and bit her tongue.

"I'm not crackers if that's what you think, it's just that I'm used to getting up and I've got things to do, better start looking for a job."

"Darling why don't you take a few days off, there's no rush, come on, come back to bed."

"Thank you but no, you stay there and I'll bring you something up, juice and toast and coffee, what do you think?" With that he slipped on his dressing gown and went to the kitchen.

Had Michael done a handstand, she could not have been more surprised. Her first response was to rush after him, but she did not. She lay there and waited for this suddenly domesticated husband.

They had their curiously domestic breakfast together, Michael seemed bright and back to his old self. They parted at eight thirty, she to Bristol, he to somewhere in the city to some meeting or other.

Rachel's day was like so many others; travel, rehearsal, rest, performance and in this case more travel back to London. She arrived home at midnight surprised to find Michael waiting for her. His greeting was warm and welcoming, despite her tiredness she felt renewed in his arms.

"How was your day my darling, brilliantly tinkling the ivories as ever I suppose," He laughed knowing that his compliment was a challenge to the gravity of her calling. For once she didn't respond.

"My tinkling was fine thank you kind Sir, and how was your first day of freedom from the LONY Loons?"

Michael picked her up and spun her round, "Quite exciting actually, I've spoken to a few pals and I think we'll be back to work quite soon." He then rambled, or so it seemed to Rachel, about the opportunities that lay before him. Apparently there were numerous and prestigious competitors of LONY who were falling over themselves to get hold of him. When he got home after lunch with Bertie, he'd had at least a dozen phone calls. Michael shone with the confidence of old; it was as if the rigors of his injuries had fallen away and that his physical well-being was tied directly to his self confidence.

They drank a bottle of Champagne and toasted the future. They tumbled into bed and made love with that marriage of sweetness and desire that obliged them to fall in love all over again. For the first time in many days Rachel fell asleep without the shadow of Josie Fellowes, or the worries of Michael's inconsistencies.

Her diary was full; many of the engagements were in small towns and festivals, the relics of her earlier career. Her engagements were booked far ahead and it was Max's job to ensure that as time passed so her reputation grew. From Rotherham Town Hall to Carnegie Hall is a long journey but she was now well on her way. Her repertoire was assiduously widened with cajoling from Eva and advice from Sally Nye. The release of her recording of the Rachmaninov concerti 2 and 3 had been a success, not a smash for Concordia. Eva still fussed and behaved as a strict schoolteacher with an adolescent pupil. Eva agreed about the Rachmaninov problems and urged Max to plan a diary that played to Rachel's strengths that Eva saw as the early romantic and classical schools. The arguments between the three of them went on interminably, Max driven by MIL to get the more glitzy and prestigious engagements. Concordia insisted on works which they felt the market demanded, tempered by their own range of offerings from their other tied artists and orchestras. Occasionally Harold Gingrich would seek to review the 'appointment portfolio' and was always driven by the income potential for Concordia that could be spun off from Rachel's growing reputation and the reviews from her live performances.

The next two years were now almost entirely filled; the most important or exciting engagements for Rachel being the London Prom to be performed later that year, the tour of Scandinavia in the late autumn. There were interesting possibilities where she was sometimes spoiled for choice.

She wanted to accept an invitation to play in Salzburg; Mozart of course, but music for two pianos. Max was against the idea because the other pianist had not yet been identified, MIL's first choice was already engaged and fees were not what Max expected from such a prestigious outing. Still Rachel was keen; she remembered how she loved the Mozart music for two pianos at the Menuhin School. This matter was unresolved and it was agreed to wait to see if the second pianist was commercially and artistically acceptable. The promise of Chicago had still not been fulfilled but that was in Cy Allman's and MIL's USA Office territory.

Four weeks to the day after Michael had lost his job at LONY he started work again, this time, as a Vice President and section investment manager for 'First Mercantile,' an American Bank in London. His new salary was as generous as his old one and if anything he seemed to be better rewarded than before. Firstly his job entailed a month in New York getting to grips with his new environment and to try and get Hugo Love to join the Bank Headquarters in New York as Chief Technology Analyst. This was a task that Michael assumed would be a joy and one he could bring off with ease. He left for New York in good spirits, though Hugo had been strangely muted when Michael had spoken to him on the phone. Michael had not been specific, simply declaring that they should meet for old time's sake and have a couple of drinks and dinner.

Chapter 12

In the Parker Meridian Hotel in New York, Michael unpacked
and phoned Hugo; they arranged to meet the following
evening for dinner, Hugo was dissuaded from bringing along
his girlfriend, not a good idea as far as Michael was
concerned. Michael spent the next day with his new
employer, meeting his new colleagues at the Wall Street
Office. As befits a new Vice-President from the London
Office, Michael was treated with deference and style. The
Bank's President, Jonathan Haigh the Third, was a delightful
man, short on stature, but big on charm and humour.
Michael towered over the diminutive man with his polished
baldpate, bright eyes and brilliant white moustache.

They sat in his twentieth floor office with a spectacular view
down the legendary financial street.

"Michael I can't tell you how thrilled we are to have you join
us, we watched your work on the Scicom deal and it was
really impressive."

"Well, Sir."

"Heck Michael, don't call me Sir, no, for goodness sake,
Jonathan will be fine"

"Well Jonathan, you're very kind, it's a delight to be on
board, First Mercantile has a fabulous reputation and I'm
glad to be here."

"Fine, but some would say that LONY was also a fine outfit so we were surprised when you left them. Michael, I know we like to keep things confidential in the business and HR is happy enough but I'm intrigued that they let you go."

"After my injury, I felt that I was not put back in my rightful place, I felt I'd proved myself and perhaps I was a little impatient, but maybe it was a good time for a change any way."

Haigh's blue eyes bore into him. "Well young man we have plenty for you to do and we look forward to your contribution to our investment strategy. How about this guy Hugo Love; can you get him to come to us?"

"I believe so, Sir...sorry... Jonathan, but of course I can't guarantee it. But I think so."

"Anyway it's a good time to be with us, you can get to know your new colleagues and learn something of our Wall Street operations; I'll get Bill Wagner to show you around."

First Mercantile was much like LONY, same departments with slightly different names. Same sort of people; all competitive and rich. London was a relatively new venture for First Mercantile, they'd been there only ten years. They'd built up a strong merchant section with a good reputation particularly in aggressive acquisition battles.

The London Chief was a quiet but very astute first generation American, Igor Vlacic, who had been an outstanding student at Harvard and had come to London to do his Doctorate at LSE. He had remained in London ever since and had assumed his present role having been persuaded to join First Mercantile for an enormous golden handshake. Since his arrival two years ago, First Mercantile had pulled in some spectacular clients and fought two successful headlining takeover battles as well as engineered some wonderful mergers and acquisitions in the former Soviet dominated central Europe.

Haigh's guiding principal was to get the best in the business almost regardless of cost. Michael was another such acquisition though there remained a nagging doubt about Michael's departure from LONY.

Bill Wagner was a young WASP, charming and knowledgeable, prematurely balding, a Vice-President at only thirty-one. He treated Michael with quiet charm, listening and answering all his questions with an assured lucidity that Michael found reminiscent of Alistair Bingham. Michael considered the quality of those he had met so far, these people were good, there were no fools like Hayter here. He would have to be on his toes to compete, or even to survive.

Following the tour and endless introductions, Jonathan Haigh hosted a lunch for all the Board members with Michael as the principal guest. It was all very civilized, but Michael was conscious that every one there was listening to his every word, watching his every gesture and recording every response. These were the elite of First Mercantile, a family of like minded money makers with only one woman in their midst.

She was Marge Flynn, a red headed fiercely elegant lady in her late thirties. She specialized in Float valuations, and was internationally regarded as a powerful and astute economist who seldom misjudged the markets.

"Tell me Mr Johnson.... Michael, we are dying to know, why did you leave LONY, we all admired the work on Scicom, surely you must have been flying high?"

Her green eyes stared at him unblinking. There was an audible silence round the table.

"As I explained to Jonathan and Chester, you are aware that I had an accident last year that meant I had to be away from the office for three months – though it felt longer – when I returned things had moved on and I guess out of consideration.... or maybe other people had moved up, but anyway I wasn't put back as a project leader.... perhaps I was impatient... anyway here I am and I'm pleased to be here."

"There was no question of your fitness to resume then?" Marge Flynn looked him right in the eye.

"I'm sure Alistair.... Alistair Bingham that is, felt perhaps I ought to be eased back in; it wasn't that easy for anyone in retrospect.... you all know we have to maintain momentum.... I felt perhaps I had lost some.... in the sense that the plum project that I would have liked was to be led by someone else. Anyway, I decided four years at LONY was enough, proud of the work I did at LONY and equally happy to have moved on at this juncture."

Ms Flynn was not to be denied, "Are you saying that four years with a company that had treated you spectacularly well was a fair return to your employer?"

"No not at all, it's just that that's the way the cookie crumbled, of course I was sad to leave LONY, but we have to move on. Now I'm here I hope we'll be colleagues for a long time." Michael reached for his water glass; he wished fervently that this interfering woman would shut up. He felt the dampness under his arms, an agitation rise in his stomach. Bloody women, would they never leave him alone?.

"Jonathan assures us that LONY's loss is our gain, so we all look forward to working with you." She raised her water glass as did all the gathering, "Welcome Michael to First Mercantile." Her gaze had not left him, her green eyes smiled but behind the smile Michael sensed the steely coldness.

Despite numerous invitations to dinner, Michael made his excuses and set out to recruit Hugo Love as his first and very confidential task for Jonathan Haigh.

He had chosen to meet Hugo at a Russian Restaurant on the West side, it was a place where they'd spent time before, drinking vodka, getting drunk, and where Hugo ogled the beautiful women, many of them from the exotic East. The atmosphere was as ever decadent but to Michael strangely familiar and comforting; it was like old times. He settled down to a chilled shot of vodka infused with spicy cinnamon and ordered a caviar topped blini. He doubted if Hugo had changed his ways and would doubtless be starved of food.

Hugo as always was late, but not as untidy as ever. His dress, no longer eccentrically wrinkled, no longer confusing the casual observer to enquire whether he was a tramp or dramatically rich. He looked sharp and typical Wall Street. He was almost impossible to recognize.

They greeted each other with a hug.

"Jeeze, Hugo what happened to you, you look wonderful."

Hugo looked sheepish, "Do you like it?" He span around, "all new clothes, all new Hugo."

"Come on Hugo, you'll always be the same.... we'll always be the same.... let's have a shot or two." He gestured to the Barman who delivered a couple of large vodkas.

Their conversation was quick but at the same time reserved, they both skirted round Michael's recent departure from LONY. Hugo announced that his new love was The love, the only, the first, even if she was the twenty-fifth, because the others didn't matter. He was going to marry once more and Rachel and Michael were to be the people whose availability would determine the wedding date. And last but not least, Michael knew the bride to be, could he guess?

Michael took several efforts remembering all the ladies, secretaries, assistants and associates they had known at LONY and in Scicom on both sides of the Atlantic. Each time he drew a blank. By now Hugo was beginning to fly on the wings of his sixth vodka and laughed and giggled like the schoolboy he would always be. He stuck his arms out and flew around the lounge, squeaking, "You'll never guess, you'll never guess" then howling with laughter. He was deliriously happy and Michael could not help but enjoy the moment with his dear pal, how good it felt to be back in the old routine with Hugo.

"Hugo, never mind the women, how about you and me teaming up again, we were the best! The best, my friend, we could conquer the banking world."

"Team up, no my dear that's not for me, not that I don't love you and I love Rachel too", he swayed back on his heels, "Because Mikey, I am giving it all up, I am going back to school, to MIT to be precise.... whadya think about that?

"Bloody nonsense Hugo you'd be throwing away a fortune and not least the chance to work together again, don't be a bloody fool."

"A bloody fool as you Brits put it, is what I'm not, in fact I'm an American smart arse, I have accepted a new Chair in Global Resource Economics at MIT, so to you Mikey come and kiss the Professor's arse" He howled some more, "let's have another vodka,"

Suddenly Michael understood that Hugo was serious, he was going to go back to MIT. He also saw that this is where Hugo would be at his brilliant best, where he would be happy and fulfilled. Suddenly the happiness deserted him, what was this silly American bastard trying to do to him. For God's sake didn't Hugo realise that he was part of Michael's plan. Hugo, who Michael had brought from his petty academic cradle into the light of international commerce – how could he do this?

"For Christ's sake Hugo are you absolutely crazy, don't you want to work together anymore? No more Scicom's, no more beating the other guys to the punch. No more screwing the Derek Hayters of this world?" There was no jollity, just a sudden intense almost desperate appeal.

Hugo though was having none of it; he was having a great night. He was on top of his world. Michael's change of mood had gone unnoticed. Hugo waxed on about the new chair foundation, the involvement of the World Bank and the UN, the profile of his new appointment, but most of all about the good he could do in the world.

His enthusiasm was unbounded, he was alive with the excitement of it all, he was going to lead the research into the industrial harmonisation of global natural resources and so bring about the new revolution where the technologically advanced would work in partnership with the underdeveloped countries with mineral and other resources. He would harness the technologies of emerging economies and build an international team of technocrats who would prepare the way for change and mutual support between the advanced and the developing world. It would be his life's work.

Michael sat there in the decadent lounge; his mood darkening, he was not going to be able to deliver Hugo to First Mercantile and more particularly to Jonathan Haigh. Damn, Hugo, he was a fool who was easily led, no doubt on this occasion by his new girlfriend. Damn women they were always in the way. What the hell was he doing sitting here getting pissed with Hugo, Hugo wasn't worth a damn thing, God he was tired he wanted to get back to his Hotel.

"Look Hugo I have to go; I guess I'm still wrecked by the old jet lag."

"You can't go yet, have another vodka." It was whistled up as if by magic, "and besides you don't know who the future and rest of my life, Mrs Love is."

"One more drink and I'm out of here, OK who is the lucky girl?"

The vodka closed in, the chanteuse sang in a seductive voice as she suggestively stroked the microphone in her sinewy hands, her tits bulging sensually over the top of her dress. Michael was suddenly interested.

"Naughty boy," cried Hugo, "you're behaving like me and you have your lovely Rachel at home." Again, more schoolboy laughter.

Shit, Hugo could be tiresome, "I'm off Hugo, I really have to go."

"Its Josie, I'm going to marry Josie." Hugo beamed.

"That bitch, are you serious? she's a tramp."

It was too late he'd said it, he didn't care he'd said it, it was too late now. He just felt the pain as his nose exploded all over his face. Blood was everywhere, his head hurt where he hit the table. He just cleared his eyes to see Hugo in floods of tears as he stood over Michael, then he turned and was gone.

The Manager and the seductive chanteuse lifted him to his feet, they helped him steady himself, and then Elaina, the singer, sat down next to him, she cleaned the blood off his face, she smelt good, and they drank more vodka. Who the hell was Hugo anyway?

Elaina encouraged him with more vodka, the smoky night drifted and memories of Hugo and his trollop Josie began to fade. His anger though left a bitter ember that stirred his misery. Whilst Elaina was beautiful and he wanted her, there was something coarse about her which he found repulsive, it was a woman who wanted his money in exchange for sex, it was a woman who as always wanted something from him. Through the alluring fumes of the vodka, the charm and instant celebrity of Elaina's cabaret companion, Michael watched her willowy body and imagined the delights of her favours. He wanted to have her now, but no, she had to stay and complete her cabaret obligations, for God's sake did she not know it was almost six a.m. UK time. He was exhausted.

His nose throbbed, his throat was dry, and his body ached as the yellow cab took them back to his hotel, it was two a.m. New York time. He wanted to get this over, this? What was this? It was to satiate himself and to give this Elaina what she deserved – a good screwing – or whatever Michael deigned to give her.

There was a banging on his door.

"Is everything all right in there.... open up this is security."

Michael pulled her hair back with a jerk, "Shut up you bitch, now see what you've done."

Elaina was bent forward over the bed, her arms tied behind her with the silk drape tie, she was naked. Michael thrust once more into her, extricated himself, pushed her head down into the bed, untied the chord, put on a robe and went to the door.

"For Christ's sake shut your mouth"

Her scream became a whimper, Michael opened the door. There a burly security man stood, implacable, arms folded across his chest.

"Sir, you're making a racket.... I think the lady ought to leave." He peered over Michael's shoulder.

"Mind your fucking business." Michael tried to shut the door but the security man's size twelve boot was in the doorway.

"Ma'am are you alright?"

"I'm just leaving." Elaina bustled around getting her things together, she was zipping up her sleek gown, her make-up ran down her face, her wrists bore the welts of her restraint. She hastily gathered up her jewellery, with reflex skill she stuffed all the money from Michael's wallet into her handbag. Within seconds she was at Michael's shoulder.

"Thank you Michael, I think I should leave now."

There was a momentary stand-off, but Michael after a second of hesitation stood aside.

"Good night Sir, I hope if you're staying with us for any length of time, you have more restful evenings.... You get my drift." Said the security guard as Michael slammed the door.

It was almost five in the morning; he looked in the mirror,

'Jesus, what have you done?' He slumped onto the bed, but the image would not leave him, his swollen nose, the bruises spreading under his eyes, his dishevelled hair, he looked like a vagrant. What would Rachel think? He covered his eyes and cried himself into a shallow sleep. Despite the luxury price tag of his suite, he was awoken by the sound of the New York streets and the rattle of room service trolleys. It was still only six thirty. He shaved and showered, ordered breakfast and tried to plan how to talk his way out of the lurid black eyes and his swollen nose. What was he going to report to Jonathan Haigh? He decided to go with a mugging story; it would also cover his expenses with Elaina or whatever her name was.

At eight o clock sharp Michael reported for work and waited nervously for Bill Wagner to pick him up from the sumptuous Wall Street reception area. He had persuaded himself that his injuries were not that obvious and that they might go unnoticed.

"Good morning Michael, my goodness what happened to you?"

Michael's illusions were dispelled.

"Got mugged outside my hotel last night, this is not so bad really but the bastards got all my cash though, but that's all the damage."

"How awful, did you get the police or anything, gosh Michael that's just awful, are you sure you're OK?"

"Yes, I'm fine, a bit of a shocker but I'm OK now, no point in crying over spilt milk."

"What did the police say?"

"I just picked up my wallet, checked my cards and went for the cover of my room, didn't think there was any point in making a fuss and besides it was late.... you know fright, shaken up all that sort of thing.... anyway I'm fine, just a bit of my dignity out of joint, that's all."

At each introduction that morning everyone stared at Michael's nose, everyone asked what happened and Michael repeated the mugging scene so that by eleven o clock when he was due to meet with Jonathan Haigh the invention had taken on a reality of its own. The number of muggers? - Two, the attack? – Frontal and sudden, the grabbing of his wallet? The extracting of cash and his collection of the wallet and its scattered contents from the sidewalk. Finally his hasty retreat to his hotel room.

Jonathan Haigh showed no surprise when Michael was ushered into his office at the appointed hour.

"As an adopted New Yorker I'd like to apologise for the assault, I can't believe that this sort of thing can still go on in Manhattan, however Michael you seem to have survived with remarkable equanimity, British stiff upper lip I daresay, here let me look at you." He came round his desk and peered directly into Michael's face. "My God, that's a nasty bump, have you seen a doctor?"

"No I'm sure that's not necessary Jonathan."

Jonathan was already on the phone, "Tell Doc Andrews I want him up here right away." He turned to Michael, "We have to remember your recent injury my boy; this cannot help, we need to be sure you're OK and fit for duty."

Then as if none of this conversation had gone on at all, Jonathan Haigh launched into a disposition on his Bank's policy on investor relations, the sectors and types the bank felt most comfortable with, those sectors they were least comfortable with, the major portfolios, the big players. After some forty minutes of his tutorial there was a buzz and in walked Doctor Stewart Andrews, a jovial and well heeled medical man.

Michael was whisked away to the medical examination room in the basement and given a thorough examination by the jovial Doctor. He was returned to the dining room for lunch, where much to his consternation the other vice- presidents all looked aghast at his battered image and where Jonathan announced that on medical advice Michael would be resting that afternoon back at his hotel. Bill Wagner would have a quiet dinner with him and they would resume his induction programme the following morning. Michael protested but it was in vain.

Marge Flynn looked slightly amused, and allowed herself just one quiet remark;

"My, my, aren't you the one," she almost cooed over her fork of smoked salmon.

Despite his embarrassment Michael was relieved to return to his hotel. He was absolutely exhausted, and relieved that he wouldn't be gawped at by all the smart young bankers for the rest of the day. Apart from that, Jonathan had not raised the issue of Hugo. He needed time to see if there was a way back.

In the emptiness of his hotel suite Michael dozed fitfully, he dreamed of his beloved Rachel and fought the demons of last night. Elaina, or whatever her name was, was an affront to him. At one moment he saw that she got what she deserved, even if she did clear his wallet of six hundred dollars, at the next, he couldn't believe he'd done what he'd done. Rachel; was Rachel having affairs with her musical hangers on, they all must lust after her beautiful body, she was built for sex, she was the sexiest woman he had ever set eyes on. Every man in his right mind would want to have her.... and he knew how she loved sex, how she'd do anything except just the one thing, and she was so keen sometimes it made his balls ache just to think of her.

Was he sorry about the Russian tart? Yes he felt guilty, and although he loved Rachel, he knew, although he didn't want to know, that she was just as unfaithful as him. How could it be any other way?

He roused himself and dressed and walked absently with no aim in mind except maybe to look for a present for Rachel. He found his way to Broadway and walked to Times Square.

How tawdry it was; how unlike London. How many worlds away from Haver Hall? Sex was everywhere from grotty little cinemas advertising their X rated porn, to shops that sold every conceivable device for sexual deviance. The air was pungent with the fried onions and hot dogs mixed toxically with fumes of the honking traffic. Democracy and the worship of Mammon, here are your temples. Why couldn't this place be crammed with bookshops, musicians and places to meet. Because that's not what people want; the ideas of his Cambridge days and of Plato had been decimated into the lowest common denominator, this is what people wanted, grime, ease and sensuality. For that matter it's what he wanted much of the time, and as he strolled high and mighty, he recognised the tentacles of sensuality that rose from the drains and sucked him and Rachel into the abyss of his all consuming jealous love.

He stopped in a fashion emporium or was it sex shop, and bought some outrageous lingerie for his siren. She would be irresistible in these gossamer veils. Would she show herself to anyone else, it gave him a curious thrill to think of that. His head ached again; it was where he'd hit his head last night. With his purchases made he hailed a cab back to the shelter of his hotel.

In Jonathan Haigh's office the following morning Michael sat, his head still aching. Despite the solicitous enquiries from Jonathan, Michael protested that all was well. After some minutes on banking business Jonathan got to the matter of Hugo,

"How did it go with Hugo Love? I didn't want to press you yesterday."

Jonathan sat back, his eyes set kindly but expectant. He really did look like everyone's favourite uncle, yet he was renowned for his toughness and acuity.

"Not so good I'm afraid, Jonathan, he is going to pack it in with LONY but he's going to take up an academic post at MIT. I think it's all to do with his new girl friend. Hugo I must say has more girl friends, wives and peccadilloes than the rest of us put together, so he may well change his mind."

Jonathan leant forward on his sumptuous desk, "Is money an issue here?"

"Actually I don't think so, Hugo is a strange guy in many ways, not typical of our industry, he is at his core an academic, and I'm sure that this post in MIT is his ideal .... I don't know, his idea of the top of the world."

"No need to waste any further time on the man then?"

"I'll keep a watching brief; we're family friends so that'll be easy and a pleasure." The lie passed easily.

He spent the weekend with the Wagner family in their home in Connecticut; they were charming though Michael thought their children boorish and ill behaved. Ginney Wagner was a plain woman who held down a job with a fashion magazine in Manhattan, the kids were looked after by a nanny throughout the week and saw their parents only at breakfast, bedtimes and weekends.

They held a dinner party by way of compliment; their guests drawn from their peers. The caterers did a sublime job and Michael played his part as an English gentleman should. The other guests at dinner included a Lawyer and his wife, and the President of an executive jet leasing corporation and his extremely attractive wife. In some ways she reminded Michael of Marge Flynn, she had a voluptuous figure with a big-featured face with green eyes and red blonde hair. She had high cheekbones and a generous mouth; she smiled a lot. Her name was Margitte and she was originally of Norwegian stock but now without a trace of anything other than a cultured New England accent. Her husband Graham Speller was a handsome and charming fellow who exuded the assurance of a man who has, if not all, then pretty much everything.

As usual, Michael's American friends just loved his accent, and were almost painfully polite. There was a restrained generosity with the wines that Michael found mildly aggravating, and the conversation predictable. They discussed stock markets, interest rates, families, the businesses of the guests, much of which interested Michael not a jot. Except, that is, when it came to Margitte Speller, who it transpired was also in the fashion business, and a partner in a very up market fifth avenue boutique. Despite the pedestrian conversation, Michael felt his now permanent headache retreat and himself irresistibly drawn to the charms of Mrs. Speller. Their eye contact dwelt that extra second, a touch, albeit fleeting, of their legs under the table. Dare he dwell? Perhaps! He kept his eyes steady, daring her to return his gaze and perhaps move her lovely leg to touch his.

There it was an unmistakeable tarrying of limb on sensuous limb, the direct 'I dare you' stare. He held her gaze and smiled, she smiled back, the contract was all but made.

He was to be in New York for a further three weeks. Yes he would be lonely. Yes, he would miss his wife. Yes he would love to see his fellow guests again whilst in New York. Yes he'd love to receive messages at the bank or at his Hotel, his suite number was 1208 – 'Please note Mrs Speller' in silent parenthesis.

On the Sunday he walked down the leafy suburban roads with Bill Wagner, he had declined to join Ginney and the children to Church. Bill as always the perfect host had insisted on staying home and keeping Michael company. Michael was relieved to escape the screaming children and nurse his hangover in relative peace. It was a pleasant morning;

"Thank you both for being so kind and taking me in this weekend, there was no real need you know, although I do appreciate the comforts of home, you and Ginney must allow me to take you to dinner in town one evening, it'd be a small gesture."

"Michael don't think about it, we're thrilled to have you, we've really enjoyed you being with us. I know the kids are tickled pink to have a live Englishman in the house."

"Super dinner last night, really enjoyed the whole thing, lovely friends you have. Gorgeous girl, that Margitte and lovely man Graham, how'd you get to know them?"

"Customer of mine originally, we underwrote the flotation of Speller Aviation, that was five years ago, he's really taken off since, forgive the pun."

Michael gently probed for more information about the delectable Mrs Speller. Apparently she was also a successful businesswoman in her own right and her boutique marketed European labels as well as her own exclusive brand, Norgritte lingerie.

Soon the grind of familiarising himself with First Mercantile's operations was back in full swing, always punctuated with the daily Vice-Presidents' luncheon where Michael was interrogated with all the charm of the Spanish Inquisition. In fact he found it hard to take in all the information, all the names, all the figures, all the operational diversity. His head ached from morning to night. He was sleeping badly. Each night he had a duty dinner with one VP or department Head; there seemed no respite.   The memory of Mrs Speller began to fade.

He had to attend a black tie affair with Jonathan, Bill and Marge to hear the legendary Alan Greenspan speak at the Association of Merchant Bankers Annual dinner. Whilst the dinner reeked of money there was nothing of the style of the great London dinners, such as the Lord Mayors' banquet. Michael sat drinking steadily to contain his perennial headache. Marge sat next to him in a dashing gown that showed her to be all woman! Of course he knew already but he found it hard to concentrate on following Greenspan for all his worldly wisdom, when Marge's sensuous bosom rose and fell with majestic rhythm, perhaps excited by the economic prospects for the following year. Perhaps they heaved for him?

Despite the rigours of his work and the diversions of New York, he was constantly mindful of Rachel; he phoned each evening, and became upset when he was unable to have a daily chat. Despite his knowledge that she was away working at this recital or that concert, she was not at the end of a telephone and this irked him. He thought of her, his lovely Rachel being made up to by all sorts of disreputable musicians. These delusions became his dreams and his dreams became his insomnia, his headaches became his constant companion.

In his third week Marge commanded that he join her for dinner, he had been working in her department for three days, studying the formula and mechanisms that had been used in recent IPO's, public offerings and the mergers that had been masterminded at First Mercantile. The minions most of whom were brilliant young economists could never quite answer the finer question regarding the final valuations. Apparently the ultimate decision was always made by the Board who were always led in these matters by Marge Flynn, whose instinct was already a legend. Offerings by First Mercantile were always taken up, and always taken up by the right buyers. Flynn had a reputation of delivering value to the market and a realistic expectation to the client.

Everyone knew that Marge Flynn was well worth her several million dollar a year reward package. She was an icon in the bank, she was what all the young sparks desired to become. It was rumoured that she hooked up with juniors some times, the young men or women seldom survived for long after such couplings. Everyone knew of Marge's appetites but no one, not even Jonathan, talked about them.

They were to dine at the Balthazar; a restaurant to eat in, not to conspire in, or even to romance in, it is one of New York's temples devoted to culinary consumption. Michael was relieved when informed of the venue, his ambivalence toward Marge Flynn had disturbed him from the moment met her. On the one hand she was a beautiful woman, on the other she was shrewd, smart and a powerful adversary who had been the most sceptical of Michael's past. Her Irish eyes stared through him; they changed from seductive to penetrating in nanoseconds. Of all the women he'd ever met, she seemed impervious to his charm and indifferent to his physique. Her department was run with military precision, researchers delivered their findings on time. The bank's ability to find out everything about clients was legendary; many an offering had been delayed until client management responded to the findings of Marge's research team. Not only did they work efficiently, they worked secretly and Michael guessed that if anyone could find out why Michael had left LONY, it was Marge.

Marge was dressed in grey silk, perhaps nearer silver than grey, her shoulders were bare except for the delicate straps, her hair was different, Michael couldn't tell how, but it was different, showering down to her alabaster shoulders.

Around her neck she wore a necklace that was solid silver (or platinum) with a huge stone that was suspended at her throat. The whole effect was stunning. Whatever his thoughts before this moment they were redundant and confused. Marge had him on the back foot from the off.

"Well Michael isn't this nice, a chance to have a chat off site."

She waved him to a seat at the table for two. He could smell her perfume and at the same time feel her assurance; it was strange to be with this ravishing woman who was clearly in charge. Michael was unsure, disoriented, he found it hard for once, hard to begin.

"Yes, it is nice Marge," he replied lamely, his headache banged insistently. "I'm starving; this is one of my favourite places."

"We New Yorkers tend to forget you Brits have been here before, you're such an accomplished bastard Michael, we're still reeling with excitement that you joined us." She let the Sommelier pour the champagne. "Here's to you Michael, this beats the lunchtime water doesn't it?"

"Thanks, but you're hardly the one to get excited Marge, or at least I wouldn't have thought so, after all you're already a legend, a beautiful legend if I might say so."

"Michael, now then aren't you the charmer." She smiled; was it demurely or mockingly? Michael decided the latter. She swallowed a large gulp of the wine, "What do you think of First Mercantile Michael and do you know what we think of you?"

"You go first Marge, I think you have the advantage."

"No first tell me about Rachel, and home and what you think of Vlacic, what do you know of London's plan for the Central European strategies?"

The food platter was before them, and the next hour passed as Michael relaxed and talked of home and what he knew of the London end of the business. He was careful about his comments about Vlacic, he was after all another of the 'wunderkind' breed, Jonathan Haigh's disciple, the type of person that made First Mercantile. Beneath the bland conversation Michael was conscious of her ever-present acuity, her razor sharp responses and her constant evaluation of his every word. He was aware too that his command of the subjects was not as sharp as he would wish, this bloody headache got in the way.

Marge certainly knew how to put away the booze, Michael felt satiated with the splendid food and wine, so far things had gone moderately well and his wariness of her became more relaxed. In fact when you got to know her she was just another very attractive woman. Indeed she was attractive enough to get into bed, Michael's mind slid into his groin driven torpor. Yes he would have her, for all her airs and graces, he would show her what a good man could do.

The brandy balloons refracted the golden liquid and all was well with the world, soon he would round off a great evening with Marge, he would give her the best fuck she'd had, ever! His moment of consummation was not that far off, he'd better get set.

"Marge it's been a fabulous evening, I can't believe we should leave it here...." Over his brandy glass he smiled his most charming smile.

She took his hand and raised it to her lips; she licked his index finger and then took it sensuously into her mouth. She fixed him with her eyes, no longer boring inquisitively into him, more a laughing - dare you - invitation.

"Would you like to fuck me Michael?" Her voice dropped from its refined Boston clip to a contralto throaty rasp. There was something almost rapacious about her. Here thought Michael was a sexual adventure that would leave all the others as mere dross.

His groin stiffened at the prospect, he took her other hand and licked her palm, "Your place or mine?"

"Let's get out of here before I do something I shouldn't." Her hand quickly withdrew from his, she thrust under the table, she felt the profile of his erection; "Should be fun. Let's get a cab."

The cab ride was infinitely short or long, it was taken up with an intensity of every sexual exploration short of copulation. When they arrived at Marge's apartment block they were a bundle of entwined animals. They could hardly wait to get into the twenty-third floor apartment and their coupling was frantic, rushed and confused. Marge undressed herself, and Michael, with a practised ability that would have done credit to a magician. Their initial carnal desires were spent in minutes. She straddled him naked except for her hose, her hair now something of a mess but to Michael as he looked up past her milky white and rosy breasts, she looked wonderful. She pressed down on his chest with the heels of her palms, her Irish eyes drugged with the pleasure of it all.

"Well now Michael," she rotated her hips urging him to rise again, "That was good for starters, but the night is still young." She ground her hips again and played between their love- juiced bodies with fluttering fingers.

"Marge you're fantastic." he urged his body to renew its energy, but that bloody headache pounded, was it the booze or the pulses of the sex, it was getting worse. He could not hide his grimace, nor could he prevent his cock from shrinking, this headache was overpowering him.

"Marge I'm sorry, let me have a break I've got a bit of a headache," he tried to roll free. Marge was surprisingly strong.

"Now, now Michael, Marge'll make you hard again just be patient," she rolled her thighs again, she flexed her muscles, but she felt Michael slipping from her. Her look hardened, her legs relaxed and dismounted and disappeared to the bathroom.

Michael lay there, his head thumping, naked and unsure. Pathetic, that is how he felt; pathetic.

She returned in a silk gown that in no way diminished her desirability, she walked past the prone and flaccid Michael with hardly a look. "Get dressed Michael, it's getting late." She backhandedly threw his shirt to him.

He cleaned himself up and dressed in the isolation of the bedroom. When he arrived in the sumptuous living room, Marge was leaning on her kitchen bar drinking another brandy. She looked tired.

"Some kind of stud you turned out to be, a quickie and you're off, is that it?"

"No Marge that's not it, look I'm sorry but I really do have a humungous headache." He looked down embarrassed; this bloody woman had the upper hand again. "Have you got any you know…. aspirin or something?"

She laughed, "Are you serious? I've got some coke if that's any good? Michael you're the first man ever to turn me down with a headache, as hook-ups go Michael I have to say you've disappointed me." She poured another brandy, "Do you want one?"

"No thanks, I mean I don't do coke, and I won't have another brandy." He closed his eyes wincing with the pain as it hammered into his right temple. "Shit, I'm sorry but I think I'd better go; I feel awful."

"Michael if you can't perform there's no need to make a drama of it, don't think we don't know about you, my beautiful British boy, because we do. Don't you think we know why you left LONY? Do you think for one minute that I couldn't find out what you'd been up to? You couldn't cut it Michael, after your bump on the head, you couldn't cut it." She swaggered towards him, the brandy was beginning to unravel the beauty and the composure. "Do you believe for one minute that we couldn't find out every fucking detail of your miserable exit from LONY,do you think we took in all that crap about the poor Brit gets mugged?" She slumped onto an armchair. She turned her hair now shambling over her eyes so that he could not tell if she was looking at him or not. "Jonathan, who is our high and mighty bloody chief, said that you were worth the risk…. worth the risk? Michael you're not worth a damn…"

Michael felt the bile rise in him, this dreadful woman, this bloody tart; who the hell did she think she is,………… if it wasn't for this dreadful headache he'd have screwed her like she'd never been screwed before and now the bitch was laughing at him. He'd teach her, and before he knew it he hit her, he hit her hard so that she went spinning out of the chair onto the floor. The brandy glass flew across the room and splintered on the shining marble fire hearth.

"Fuck you Michael, get out….get out…." Her screams followed him into the hall; he made his way, feeling like a criminal to the cold refuge that was his hotel.

Chapter 13

The news that Michael was to return over a week early filled Rachel with delight. She found the brief message on the answer-phone on return from an overnight recital. Her darling was on his way home and would be on the 'daylight' from New York and would be in Heathrow at ten p.m..

She cancelled Eva's coaching session and gave the rest of her afternoon and evening to prepare herself for his homecoming. She travelled to Heathrow as a surprise to meet Michael off the BA flight from New York. It was a rather damp evening but nothing could dampen Rachel's delight, she dressed for him in the clothes that were his favourite, made up to look her best and set out in the hire car to meet her beloved Michael.

'Arrivals' at the airport was less like a bazaar at this time of night. Michael's plane was on time but she knew it often took an age to get through immigration, baggage reclaim, customs and all the rest. After an hour of waiting she became anxious, she'd already established that his flight was in and that people from it had come through some thirty minutes ago. Eventually after a further thirty minutes she instructed the limo driver to stay put while she went off to find a BA helper to find out what was going on.

Another hour elapsed before she was ushered into the office of a very helpful station officer who on enquiry established that Michael had indeed been on the flight but had been stretchered off and was now in Uxbridge Hospital. Details were sketchy but apparently Mr Johnson had been unwell, how unwell she couldn't say, the station officer seemed hopelessly and frustratingly unclear of the details.

It was nearly midnight, six hours since Rachel had set out on her journey of joy that she eventually found him in the neurological ward at Uxbridge. After yet further frustrating and infuriating delays Rachel was able to ring Anthony Shepherd's registrar at Kings College Hospital.

An hour later still, Shepherd got hold of the Team leader at Uxbridge, and things, albeit eight hours after Michael landed, the team set about relieving the pressure from an apparent haemorrhage from the old damage; it soon became apparent that there was additional damage from a more recent trauma. Rachel was unable to explain or throw any light on these unexplained new problems. Prof. Draper the head of neurology who had arrived at this ungodly hour opined that the damage was recent and probably exacerbated by flying.

The whole nightmare was repeating itself. Tania and Robbie arrived at about eight a.m. and they settled like practised mourners at a wake to wait and see what God and medical science could deliver.

Rachel, whose sweetest dress and best makeup had now degenerated into a set of dowdy wrinkles clung to her husband as she was allowed. Her hope was as implacable as ever. Her prayers a chattering insistence that God pay attention. She saw the dew clad morning draw on, but the relief that this time Michael was in apparently less danger was palpable, it gave way to euphoria almost joy. It turned out that by one o'clock the following afternoon Michael was awake and coherent. He was grateful, almost cheerful that his headache was much relieved. Just to see Michael sitting up and taking tea was more exhilarating than the applause from a packed hall. Once more life had a new beginning.

McMaster, as businesslike as ever, was insistent that Michael rested for at least four weeks.

Lucas, the psychiatrist, arrived on the second day at the clinic armed with his tests and the single minded arrogance that so distressed Rachel. He spent an hour with Michael and when he emerged from Michael's private room he asked Rachel to sit with him, Tania was put out that she was not included; she hung around outside the visitors' lounge looking haunted.

Lucas was a man who Rachel had always found profoundly unattractive; he smelt a bit like Eva, his clothes clearly meant nothing to him. His jacket was at least as old as Rachel. He beckoned her to sit down.

"Well here we are again," he smiled from behind his thick spectacles, his lizard type leer. "Singularly unfortunate that your husband has received another injury so close in time and proximity to the last one." He looked up expectantly.

Rachel looked back, what was she supposed to say? There was a silence.

"After the last episode, I assume since you had not been in touch that your husband had been quite well and normal?" He leaned forward twiddling his pencil.

"Oh yes, he was fine, a bit anxious I suppose and a lot of things happened, you know he changed his job...."

"Yes, why did he do that Mrs Johnson, any reason that surprised you?"

"Well I think the business wouldn't wait for him to have three months away without him having to prove himself again.... I don't think Michael felt that was right. Anyway he got another job with another bank amazingly quickly.... I don't know what's normal about merchant banking? .... anyway Michael seemed quite happy." Why did she feel it necessary to lie? Looking back under the gaze of this curious man was unnerving; she would not betray Michael's trust. It was between the two of them, they, would sort it out.

Lucas gnawed his pencil, "Did you notice any changes in his behaviour? I mean by that anything that seemed overstated, exaggerated, out of proportion?"

"No, I don't think so." She looked out of the window avoiding Lucas' curious refracted stare from behind his pebble like spectacles.

"Well then, let me say at once that we know your husband has received two injuries that were concussive and led to haemorrhaging in the region of middle frontal gyrus," He pointed to his own head just above his temple. The bleeding and inflammation have now been assuaged but we find it hard to say if there is any residual damage." He looked up from his note pad. "You follow?"

Rachel nodded.

"The scans reveal that there may be some scar tissue but very modest residual damage, the insult to the brain seems not to have left any great physical damage.... you follow?"

Rachel nodded, "That's good isn't it?"

"Oh yes, good, very good, however we cannot ignore any traumas as fierce as your husband has received and although he seems a tough man there may well be residual consequences that are not immediately recognisable."

"What does that mean?.... Do you mean Michael being not well mentally?"

"No of course not; we do not differentiate, dear lady, between not well physically, or not well mentally. No, on the contrary, the physiology of the brain is physiology after all, if you bang your arm it hurts and gets stiff as it recovers, the brain is no different.... perhaps there is more we should know...." He droned on, Rachel lost him after about a minute...."Do you follow?"

"Oh Yes.... But how is Michael?"

"Tell me Mrs Johnson, how well do you think he is?"

"I noticed has had difficulty in recalling where he is and what he's been doing…. I mean he knows where he's been, but he was vague about his work, I mean when I asked him if I should get in touch with his boss; but strangely, his new boss was vague about Michael, he's not been to see him, ….I don't know it's a bit surreal really…. otherwise Michael seems well enough, very tired but I suppose that's ….oh I don't know, he seems like a man who's had a second bang on his head in six months…. whatever that means."

"Mrs Johnson in many ways you are much better positioned to judge if Michael is well, or not well, you and the people close to Michael will see how he recovers. It is crucially important that you take note of anything that you think is different or even curious. Hopefully there will be little if any change in behaviour in the long term, but for now there may well be short term problems of response and memory that I'm sure will get better and I see no reason why Mr Johnson should not make a full recovery."

"Thank you Doctor Lucas, that's very reassuring."

"I'll be along again before Mr. Johnson leaves hospital, if all goes well he can go home to rest in a day or so, Mc Master will tell you that's not entirely my department." He swept his notes into his briefcase, shook Rachel damply by the hand and made his way out.

Nightmares and redemptions, they piled into Rachel's life one after another. Three days later Michael was transferred to a private West End clinic and his old medical team had been reinstated. Drs. McMaster the physician and Lucas the psychiatrist attended Michael's recovery.

It was in the clinic that Robbie and Tania insisted that Michael's recuperation continued at Haver Hall so that there would be no further interruption to Rachel's work.

Tania insisted, "Michael just needs time, we're all relieved that there's no more damage this time and I'd like nothing more than to have my boy at home. It'll be a load off your mind I know, so that's all there is to it." Tania as ever ignored all the drivel from doctors that implied her son could in any way, visible or invisible, be damaged. "Besides you'll want to see that there are no further disruptions to your engagements."

The inference was, that had not Rachel been so intent on her career, then none of these events would ever have taken place. Rachel clenched her fists, she hesitated but she knew Tania was right.

"You're so sweet, I know Michael will be so happy at Haver, but you know I'd do anything to stay with Michael if I could." It sounded hollow.

Robbie shuffled in the background. Obviously the mother love was not to be challenged. Rachel did her best to understand Tania's viewpoint but her mother-in-law's attitude irked her. Robbie she saw was weak in Tania's presence. A bond that she thought she had with him was, if not broken, compromised.

The problem that remained, the one that Robbie could not understand, was where was First Mercantile in all this. Michael is flown home ahead of schedule, there were these rumours of a mugging in New York and the responsible employer was nowhere to be seen. He discussed it with Rachel who appeared to be in the dark about it and they were keen not to tax Michael who was still very tired and slept a good deal of the time.

Eventually it was decided that Robbie would get hold of Vlacic, the London Chief of First Mercantile, and find out what was going on. Tania was not at all bothered and thought it improper to think of work in any way since what Michael really wanted was rest and recuperation at Haver Hall.

On the evening before Michael was to be released from the clinic, Tania was down in Haver preparing for the arrival of her son.

Robbie and Rachel bade Michael a restful night and made their way to dinner. Michael had been much more alert but still very tetchy about work and the whole business about the attack in New York. Bertie Frobisher who had visited several times in the last few days was quite adamant that First Mercantile were responsible and should be much more attentive. Robbie had blustered about it; Rachel had been bemused by all this, though her concern for Michael, his relocation and her next engagements rather pushed the First Mercantile issue into the background.

They sat in the Bar and had an aperitif, Robbie's a scotch and Rachel a Perrier water. Robbie talked about nothing in particular and Rachel felt that he was avoiding something, though she knew not what.

"Robbie, what is it? You're being evasive about something, is it about us coming down to Haver?"

"No. Good gracious, no, we're both looking forward to you coming, Tania's beside herself with delight, no, no, nothing could be further from the truth."

"Well then what is it? Come on Robbie – Father in Law dear, what is it?" She smiled and patted his hand.

"It's about Michael and all that business in New York, it's still a bit of a mystery but as far as I can gather, Michael's blotted his copybook again. I don't know how.... any way, he signed a settlement before he left New York and is no longer in their employ." He supped his scotch. "Not that it matters; he seems to be getting better, don't you think?"

There was a stunned silence. Rachel tried to take it in. Michael had lost another job? Her darling City star, lost two jobs in as many months, it was impossible.

"Robbie are you sure? Michael has been very evasive I know, but surely he would have said something, perhaps he can't remember, Oh God I can't believe it!."

"I can't either, I haven't told his mother yet. That's why I was so matter of fact with Bertie, I don't want him going off like a time bomb if Michael is in some sort of trouble with First Mercantile; I don't know what to think."

"What did Vlacic say? He seemed such a nice man to me, and what about Michael's head injury, surely they were his employer when he was injured, and surely they have some responsibility?"

"They seemed astonished that Michael was in hospital. Vlacic said he knew nothing whatever about it, he said he would get back to me but so far I've heard nothing."

"What are we going to do Robbie? I don't know if my husband's got a job, we don't know if there are going to be any ramifications from this episode, or who is responsible. What a mess, what are we going to do?"

The waiter showed them to their table. They sat and waited whilst the waiter stopped fussing, had taken their order, and left them in peace.

"Rachel the important thing is to get Michael well…. I wasn't going to raise this but you and I are the only ones who know…. aren't we? You know, about LONY."

"Yes we do, oh Robbie do you think that Michael is not well, did he do something awful to get fired? "

"As I said, we have to get Michael well, but in his own interest we have to find out what's what, and get to the bottom of the LONY thing and this latest thing with First

Mercantile…. bloody silly name isn't it First Mercantile; wretched Americans."

"How are we going to find out, do you think we ought to have it out with Michael?"

"Sorry my girl, but what do you think? Do you think Michael's up to it, and do you think we'll learn the truth if we ask him? I haven't asked you before, I suppose because I was afraid to, but has Michael been alright since the first accident, I don't mean physically, I mean moodwise?"

"Dear Robbie, are you asking if your son is changed? Well yes he is a bit, you know a bit more moody, but bearing in mind the LONY business you'd expect that wouldn't you?"

"Would you? I don't know …. look darling, in the privacy of your marriage to my son only you can tell if everything is …. normal or whatever…. you know what I mean?" Robbie was relieved to have to try the wine.

"What does Tania think?"

"I think you're avoiding my question; however as far as Tania is concerned if Michael was Pontius Pilate she would see no wrong, so I'm sure Tania thinks he's having a hard time and it's anybody's fault except Michael himself…. you still haven't answered my question…. tell me to shut up if you like."

"Does she think it's my fault?"

"She wants grandchildren, you know that, it's none of our business whether you want children or not, but Tania still wants grandchildren."

"Do you want grandchildren, Robbie?"

"I just want you and Michael to be happy; grandchildren would be a bonus."

They pushed their suppers around their plates in silence.

"What are we going to do then?" Rachel sat, her dinner untouched, her wine hardly supped.

"Aren't you going to eat that lovely fish?"

"Thank you but my mind's elsewhere, I repeat what are we going to do?"

"Bertie, we have to take Bertie into our confidence, that is, if you agree. Bertie will get to the bottom of all these issues and we trust him and so for that matter does Michael, if and when we have to discuss what comes out of all this. What do you think?"

"Dear Bertie, he always seems to get the dirty work, but you are right Bertie is as discreet a person as there is. Who'll talk to him, you or me?"

"Leave it to me Rachel, leave it all to me." He took her hand and squeezed it gently. "You and I and Bertie will help Michael through this, whatever this is. Don't worry."

They parted at the door; Rachel made her way home to her empty house and spent the rest of the evening with Becky. She played old JS and she felt better.

Chapter 14

Michael came out of hospital and was pampered at Haver Hall; Tania devoted all her waking hours to mollycoddling her son. Rachel went down every evening she could but Sussex was much less convenient than the West End house. Practising in the lounge at Haver was not the same as at home with Becky. As much as she tried to avoid it, she found herself spending nights alone at their West End home. Her schedule that coming summer was busy and the prom was not that far away. She concentrated on fewer concerti; the Grieg of course and Beethoven 4 in particular. Max announced that they would dash to Salzburg to meet with a prospective duet partner for the proposed Mozart two piano gig.

Michael seemed content at Haver Hall and as the weeks went by he seemed of equitable mood, though sometimes introverted and maudlin when alone with Rachel. Their sex life was as boisterous as ever. Michael's jealousy had transmogrified to fantasy sex that Rachel went along with and enjoyed, though the limits were sometimes beginning to frighten her. The blatantly sexy underwear that Michael had acquired in New York was much in evidence as were the devices that Rachel considered naughty but nice. Rachel tried always to love her man, sex was fine and sex was fun, but she always tried to bring him home. Home to her heart, and the real love, where sex was only a part, maybe the cementing part, but there were other things that wove their web of love. Michael's night games were all right as long as there was tenderness and a giving and taking; sometimes she found it hard to bring him back from his lonely self-gratification. She saw him drift away as his features hardened with a lust that belied their intellect and their caring one for the other. The nights when things got a little out of hand, or a little more physical than she would like, she put down to her 'man management' role, she believed she would always be able to control him.

Rachel was worried about Eva; she coughed and wheezed a lot more despite the onset of Summer. Her concentration seemed shorter and she was tetchier in lessons. Not that they were lessons,more a commentary on Rachel's rehearsals, still Rachel valued them and a modest stipend was paid each month to her lifelong tutor. Rachel and Michael were planning their return to the marital home, Michael seemed quite himself again and McMaster had given him a provisional clear bill of health. There were obvious provisos that he did nothing that could in any way risk further injury, even golf was ruled out for a further six months. He should not drive and always sit in the rear of any motor transport, and he would meet McMaster and Lucas once a month for the foreseeable future; well at least six months. Michael liked Lucas even less than Rachel and it was one of those situations where they conspired together, often laughing at the psychiatrist's mannerisms and the 'you follow' verbal suffix to practically every sentence.

So as Michael's health got better and Rachel began to relax so Eva's obvious decline came more to the fore. As the sun streamed through the transom of the studio window Rachel played an early Beethoven sonata. They were planning a new recital programme of early Beethoven, Haydn and

Mozart. It was to be themed not very originally; Rachel George-Johnson plays the Classics.

Eva had arrived late, she coughed and spluttered but had settled after a cup of strong tea. All had gone well and Eva was her usual self, wagging her finger at her pupil, urging speed here and subtlety there. Then quite suddenly she fell from her stool.

"Eva, are you all right, oh my God Eva," Eva had fainted and caught a heavy fall. Rachel did her best to help Eva get up but the studio had only one chair and that was a library chair on the other side of the piano. She made Eva as comfortable as she could and as she was about to bolt up the stairs to phone for an ambulance, Eva called from her chair.

"Meine Liebe," she swallowed with a great sucking noise, "Meine liebe, come help me up. Your Eva is a silly bitch, falling about like an old voman, eh?"

"Eva stay a moment, I'll get help."

"Help, vot help? I am old and silly, zer is no 'elp for old age, come girl help me up."

With a titanic struggle Rachel helped Eva back on to her music stool,"Now Eva, be a good girl and stay there, I'm going to get the doctor and then a cup of sweet tea"

"No do, for what we want a doctor, maybe the tea id goot jah!."

"OK," Rachel fled to the kitchen, Jennie her cleaner had gone, she put on the kettle, and rang the doctor, who was already involved in some other emergency, so the Practice advised Rachel to ring for an ambulance. She didn't know what to do. Laden with the tea she returned to the studio. There, Eva's shallow complexion had returned to a living grey, but she still looked dreadful.

"Eva I'm going to ring for an ambulance, you really can't go about fainting, you're not well."

"Rghediculous, I don't vant any such thing, I shall be goot now, in a minute, maybe I can use zee bathroom, jah?"

Rachel helped her shaky teacher up the stairs to the bathroom., Rachel still shook with fright, she was so afraid that Eva would collapse again; there was an awkward shimmying at the bathroom door, Eva wanted it closed and Rachel insisted it remained ajar.

Eventually when Eva was comfortably ensconced in a lounge armchair Eva was persuaded that Rachel could call Eva's doctor. She raised Doctor Rubin on the telephone who listened carefully to Rachel's description of events.

"Please, ask Eva, has she had food today?"

"Food, what for I vant food, maybe I have something when I go home."

"No doctor she has had no food."

"Send the silly woman home; I will call on her this afternoon at about two thirty. Tell Eva if there is no food in the house we will fight again, she knows what I mean."

Rachel relayed the message to Eva who grunted a non-committal response. She seemed her feisty self already. Thirty minutes later Rachel insisted that she help Eva from the taxi into her flat. It was a pleasant terrace ground floor flat that Rachel remembered from her school holidays. It looked much the same. Eva led the way in, into the front living room, full of bric-a-brac and too much furniture. Rachel tried to seat the agitated Eva, but it was as if Eva was afraid of what Rachel would find, she scurried ahead trying to shoo Rachel away, trying to get her to sit down. The phone rang it was Eva's doctor enquiring if all was well.

After a wasteful ten minutes or so, they both sat on the kitchen breakfast bar drinking more tea. Rachel had seen that there was little, if anything, in the fridge when Eva retrieved the milk. Rachel wrestled with her sensibilities, and then with a sharp intake of breath stood and announced she was going to see what shopping Eva needed. Without waiting for Eva to concur she made a brief but direct inspection

There was virtually no food there at all.

"Eva for goodness sake what do you have to eat?"

"I am about to shop, I shop every Zursday. Now if you let me go, I go, jah!"

"No Eva, not today, today is Tuesday and you're not to shop today, I will do a little shopping for you."

"Liebe, you cannot shop for me, I vant vat you don't know."

"Eva, darling Eva, you need a rest, just you sit and rest and I'll pop to the shops and get you a few things, what do you want except Battenburg cake?"

"Battenburg I like, you remember, yes please a nice cake."

Rachel had another more studied view of the sparse supplies; escorted Eva to her comfortable living room and went shopping.

Two days after Michael's return Rachel received a phone call from Jennifer Walmer reminding Rachel of the forthcoming meeting of the City Charity Group, the Duchess was so looking forward to meeting Rachel again. She offered a number of dates so that eventually Rachel could not refuse. And so it was arranged that Rachel would attend the meeting to be held at the Walmers' Oxfordshire retreat six weeks hence. Jennifer would be in touch with details nearer the date. Anything to do with the Walmers gave Rachel the creeps, she had taken an instant dislike to Sir Bradley, though she failed absolutely to understand Jennifer Walmer who was at once charming and at the same time curiously subservient to her unpleasant husband.

Michael was not as settled as Rachel first thought; out of the earshot of his mother he again became taciturn and moody. He complained bitterly about being forsaken by the City and he was extremely tetchy when Bertie called. Bertie's visits were just as friendly; he still held himself responsible for Michael's first accident and all the consequent misfortune that had since befallen his friend. Bertie had also taken up the issue of Michael's severance from First Mercantile;, he had discovered much of the truth about Hugo's assault on Michael, but he was still in the throes of getting to the bottom of it. His attempts to speak to Hugo had proved fruitless. However he was satisfied that Michael's severance terms were clear, fair and appropriate. As always it was impossible to find out the reason for the decision to split, but the contracts were clear and it was quite within the Bank's right to terminate Michael's contract during the early probationary period. The one hundred and twenty five thousand dollar settlement was generous and Michael had signed a confidentiality clause together with a 'hold harmless' guarantee to the Bank. It was watertight.

Bertie had considered whether there was any point in sueing Hugo for damages, but he could not get any sense out of Michael to support the action. Bertie, as always sensitive, recognised the intensely personal nature of the rift. Despite having been briefed by Robbie he had succumbed to Michael's demands that any information was filtered through him before it went to Robbie. He had strict instructions not to inform Rachel of the matters at all.

Michael otherwise spent a good deal of his time of his first week home, out and about, Rachel had no idea where. Michael's desire to be seen to be doing something important, something that was contributing to the family income was palpable; he talked of meetings and important people he had met. These commentaries Rachel knew to be complete nonsense or extreme exaggerations. It was a worry and over the first week she frequently contemplated ringing Dr Lucas. However such was her dislike for Lucas that she demurred, preferring instead to wait and see.

Max had arranged for her to fly to Salzburg to meet with the festival Management and to try out with her two pianos partner. She had never heard of Igor Franek, a seventeen-year-old Polish pianist, who had apparently emerged as a rising star from the conservatoire in St Petersburg. She was worried about leaving Michael on his own but he seemed almost pleased. On the morning of her departure, Michael had come into the bedroom as she packed.

"Aren't you taking your best undies?"

"Sweet heart, why would I do that? Don't be silly, you know I'll be with Max and some crusty old musicians."

"But you, my darling, always need to be happy and satisfied." He moved closer and pulled her to him, "you'll need your rations." He licked her neck.

"Stop it Michael, I have to go and stop being silly." She tried to push him away, but he would have none of it. He thrust his hands up her dress and tugged at her tights.

"Come on, let me see that you've had your share before you go."

"Michael, stop it, I'm late already, please stop it." She begged, but in an instant she knew it was no good. She yielded to him. If ever there was a wrong time to have sex, but worse to have sex accompanied by her husband's fantastic view of her sexual adventures, then this was it. Was it better to humour him or rebut him? His commentary became wild and foul, his lust again detached and introvert. She could have been anybody. She watched his contorted face as he bore into her, responding as she thought would get this thing over with. He came grunting like a crazed pig. The storm was over. Michael collapsed and his mood immediately turned to more gentle humour.

He got up, kissed her primly on her forehead. "There, that ought to keep you out of trouble for a day or two."

Though she didn't understand why, the loathing of two minutes ago had dissolved; he was just her vulnerable Michael.

She kissed back, just as primly. "I've got to shower again, now you've really made me late you horny beast; go away and leave me to finish and get ready." Like a lamb Michael went out of the bedroom.

Saltsburg was pleasant in the Summer sunshine. They met with the festival managers who exuded gravitas; they talked of dates and programmes over a boring but early dinner. Young Franek was not due to arrive at the rehearsal hall until later that evening or even the following morning. Rachel was bored and excused herself as soon as she could, to go and practise.

She sat at one of the two pianos in the studio and started to play an early Mozart sonata. Then she exercised with some Chopin etudes. She had been playing for around forty five minutes and then stopped for a moment's rest.

From the back of the auditorium came a solitary clapping, Rachel peered into the gloom and saw the tall figure walk toward her. As he emerged into the light she was taken aback, for Igor Franek was nothing like her expectation.

He was tall, and skinny, his pallor was of someone who had never seen the sun. His hair was dark and cropped square across his forehead, his brown eyes danced beneath his dark eyebrows that ran straight uninterrupted over both eyes. He was dressed in a suit that had been made in the middle Russian market, it had a high breast collar and was buttoned by three buttons; it was black. His shirt seemed three sizes too big and he wore a narrow tie that also seemed black.

His face was slightly spotty with the look of a young man who had recently started shaving. He had an awkward smile.

"Good evening, I am Igor Franek." He bowed and put out his long white hand. Rachel took it and was shocked how cold it was.

Rachel bowed back and took his cold hand. "How do you do, I am Rachel George-Johnson. It's very nice to meet you." She looked around but there didn't appear to be anyone else around. "Are you on your own?" She couldn't think of anything else to say.

"Of course, why not?" Franek replied in his clipped Silesian accent. "You are very beautiful." He smiled, embarrassed, shuffling from one foot to the other. "You are also beautiful as a pianist I think."

"Thank you, shall I call you Igor, would that be alright, please call me Rachel."

"Shall we play? I cannot wait to play with you, you will, I'm sure be beautiful, I will do my best."

Without further ado Igor sat at the facing piano and started playing, Rachel sat and joined in and without a further word they romped through the D major sonata for two pianos. Rachel was just amazed, the pins and needles, the hair stood up on the back of her neck. There was no applause at the end, just silence, but those first moments of silence were as thrilling as any ovation had ever been. Igor, this Igor was truly wonderful. They both sat for a moment, then Igor coughed shyly,

"That was not bad I think."

"Not bad at all." Replied Rachel, "Shall we play something else?"

"No, I don't think so. Sometimes not bad is pretty good. Come we must go to bed."

"I must find Mr. Luberroff my manager to see what our schedule is for tomorrow."

"Schedule, what schedule? I will play with you Rachel....is OK?"

"Yes, it's OK but perhaps we ought to go through the programme together tomorrow, I mean while we have the chance."

"OK, but I am OK I know these works so do you, but it's OK. Thank you, Rachel, did you know you are the most beautiful musician I have ever met, it is very pleasant for me to be with such a beautiful lady to play piano. It will be good."

Rachel couldn't help but laugh at this stumbling adolescent adulation, what a nice boy Igor was. "Thank you kind Sir, you're very kind but we must keep our minds on Mozart. We'll meet in the morning, Good night Igor."

"Good night Rachel." They went their separate ways at the Hotel entrance.

Rachel found Max in the cocktail bar; he was talking to a man that turned out to be Igor's minder, his father. Rachel could well have guessed it by the man's pallor that was so reminiscent of his son's. Mr. Franek senior was a Professor of Music from The Academy in Katowice; he was like his son in lots of other ways. Whilst Max tipped down vodka after vodka, Mr Franek drank little or nothing. He had the same naïve charm of his son, a directness probably the result of

English being very much their second or even third language after Polish and Russian.

Both men were delighted to hear Rachel express delight in Igor's pianistic skills and her obvious liking of the boy. Mr Franek senior excused himself and Max invited Rachel to have a nightcap which she accepted.

"Max, he's a delight, absolutely direct and the most wonderful technique, we played the sonata without hardly exchanging a word and it was fabulous, we really got on like four hands from the same soul."

"My word, darling you have been impressed, a musical Romeo has at last called at your balcony." Max whinnied at his own humour.

"Shut up Max, why must you reduce things to bedroom humour all the time? I tell you Max, that young Igor is a wonderful talent and I'm really excited about the idea of playing together with him. He's only a kid, looks a bit like his Dad actually, looks like they've been locked in a vault somewhere."

Tomorrow there was to be a kind of audition, the powers from the Festival committee would gather at nine thirty to listen to Rachel and Igor, whilst at the same time Igor and Rachel could practise. Max was vague as to how firm arrangements were.

"Max, is this an audition or not?"

"No it is not, but then again the Festival fathers are very particular, so yes it is, but then again of course not.'

"Thanks Max that's very helpful, I shall sleep well."

In her room Rachel rang Michael who was at home; that in itself surprised her. Their conversation was sweet and non consequential, until Michael said he was making progress in finding another job with a former contact and friend. He declined to disclose the identity of the prospective employer, since "Odds and ends need tying up tomorrow."

She wished him luck, he said he loved her, and Rachel went to bed content. Her thoughts soon turned to the magic of Igor Franek, his sensitivity and responsiveness at the keyboard were the things of dreams. Perhaps their first coming together so informally was a fluke, that tomorrow they would be altogether useless when under the gaze of the Festival fathers. No! That was too fanciful, such talent could not dissipate, surely tomorrow would be a delight.

At the auditorium, the Franeks were late, quite a lot late, Max was consequently very twitchy, the Festival managers were huffy and clearly concerned that this young Pole was not respectful of their manifest importance. Rachel was disappointed; she'd so looked forward to starting with the verve they'd enjoyed last night. She sat nervously at the piano to the right, last night she'd been at the other. She listened to Max and the gaggle of impresarios distractedly; she exercised on her keyboard getting nervous. 'Where the hell was Igor?'

At ten o clock Igor and Jan his father, arrived. Franek senior apologised to the Management group whilst Igor ignored them all and walked up to where Rachel sat and sat beside her, pushing her to one side with an angular hip.

"Duets are better, more intimate, what do you think Rachel?" He started to play a fragment from the duet in D. "Come on, you know it." He coaxed her. Reluctantly she joined in this time only vaguely aware of the score. "Come on," he cajoled, "You remember, from your school days."

Despite herself, Rachel laughed and did her unselfconscious best to go along with Igor, but it was hopeless. After about three minutes she quit. Igor stopped. It was then Rachel became aware of Max and co at the front of the auditorium. It must have sounded like a shambles. She nudged Igor in his ribs,

"I think we should be serious,"

"Music is many things; wonderful, tumultuous, melodic, sweet, sad, many many things Rachel, but it is seldom just serious."

He took his place at the other piano.

"The Fugue."

"The Fugue, on ....Two!"

Nothing had been lost from the magic of the evening before. They romped through the fugue, and romping was exactly what Rachel thought was the way to play the it. It was exuberant, it was fun, it was joy, being all too short. At the end there was a short silence before the applause from the select group in the stalls. Jan Franek shouted something in Russian or was it Polish, Igor shouted back and they were soon in a shouting match, Rachel had no idea what was going on.

Eventually Franek senior sat down, Igor shrugged. "He always thinks he can play better than me, he thinks we played too fast, he is a crazy man." Igor replayed some phrases from the fugue with heavy exaggerated rhythm, then looked up and laughed. His father shook his fist, but smiled at the same time.

They played the Sonata just like the previous night though perhaps with a tiny bit more discipline. Rachel thought it wasn't quite as good, Igor made a rude sign at the audience, "see what happens if we go to pieces in front of an audience." They laughed, and Rachel started the last movement again. Igor was with her immediately, this time it was going well when Igor started apparently losing his way. Rachel was quite disconcerted. She stopped playing; then she heard what he was doing. He was playing his right hand and her left hand part.

"Come on" he shouted, "see if you can?" She tried; it was not at all practical, nor indeed at all easy. No one else had any idea what they were doing. In parts it worked well, but for Rachel it was just too difficult, for Igor it was fun. Igor could envisage the four parts, read them and play first part first hand soprano and second part fourth hand base leaving

Rachel to work out second part third hand soprano with first second hand base. Although Rachel new both parts well it was extraordinarily difficult to play the wrong couplings together. Igor just hooted with laughter as Rachel made error after error.

They struggled to the end of the movement; there was a silence from the jury in the stalls. Franek senior suddenly roared with laughter, but he was alone, the other 'judges' clearly not comprehending what had happened in the last movement. Franek muttered to Max who in turn explained to the Saltsburg grandees what had happened. There was a palpable exhalation of relief.

Max rose to his feet, his eyes doing their Catherine wheel orbits;

"Please Rachel do that last movement again, and Darling no fooling around please ….please!"

They played it again with consummate ease; it was delicious. The applause this time was spontaneous and enthusiastic. The Managers had heard enough, they all retired to discuss concert details and timetables. The two pianists were left in the empty auditorium to do whatever they chose.

Despite his almost comic ugliness, Rachel found in Igor a musicianship and humour that was attractive. This young rather gormless young man was a pianist with the most incredible technique. The precision of his playing was to be compared with Kissin, and already at just under eighteen years old his expression and touch was as sensitive as hers.

She looked across the pianos and watched how different he was when he was at the keyboard. He came alive; gone was the stiff almost military formality, gone was the clipped expression. You could hear the music smile, you could hear it sigh. Young Mozart she was sure would be pleased to hear this true genius at the keyboard.

They practised the concerto without an orchestra; Igor hummed, grunted and waved his way through the unheard orchestral accompaniment, he took the first part on the first rehearsal and then insisted that Rachel took it on the second run through. There was a spontaneity and freshness that Rachel found inspiring, this boy really drew the best from her.

Just before they broke for lunch Igor came round the piano and bustled his way alongside Rachel on her stool. She felt his bony hip against her own. He insisted they play a duet; again Mozart. She could feel his energy and watched his skeletal hands become beautiful as they hammered or kissed the keys. When they finished, Igor leaned over and kissed her. She was touched, and leaned back and kissed him in return. The kiss was not a kiss on the lips; it was not a kiss as Rachel saw it, of passion, just a kiss of affection between musicians who shared a bond that would never be broken no matter what happened in the future. Their one day and a bit of music making had been a thrill and an experience close to ecstasy for her. There had been moments of hubris so complete, laughter and gentleness, excitement and adrenalin rushes; all that had been experienced through her fingers and through her ears. It was a world for which she was profoundly grateful, a world she reminded herself that was of priceless worth.

Back home, Michael was pleased to see her, all sweetness and smiles. He'd booked a table for dinner at one of their favourite restaurants and although Rachel was tired she looked forward to an evening out with her favourite man. She'd hoped for a shower, sex, and sleep. Putting off sleep for a few more hours wasn't difficult but she needed to make love, she wanted Michael, to be one, together again.

As they got ready to go out she joined him in the shower, soaped him down, played with him, kissed him, felt his muscles in her hands, stroked his manhood, kissed and sucked him until he was as hot as any pressure cooker. Then soaking wet he carried her to the bed and they made love in that old fashioned way, lots of stroking and lots of passion. She straddled him as they climaxed and she felt him fill her. It was wonderful and satisfying. They collapsed in a damp heap, she wanted desperately to sleep and dream of Igor and Mozart, but Michael would not allow it.

"Come on sleepy head, the table's booked for nine.".
Over a delicious dinner full of unhealthy delights, they ate ravenously, the sex having drained them of energy. The Italian wine was delicious and Rachel for once let herself go and indulged the hunger so keen after the rigours of Saltsburg and her homecoming.

"Well my darling piano player how was your beau in Saltsburg?"

"Very young, going on eighteen, not good looking, very strange," she took another mouthful of wine, "but absolutely ravishing talent. You'd call him a geek or some such, that's what I thought when I first saw him, but he's.... until he's at the piano.... and then.... well I don't know he just flowers.... his confidence and ability is stunning, he made me feel a bit of a has been."

"I think you protest too much,"

"Don't be silly Michael, let's not start all that nonsense again, my darling there's no one in the world who could do for me what we just experienced, you must know that?"

"But I don't play the piano"

"You can't lay eggs either, but that's not why I love you; let's eat up I want to shag you again as soon as possible."

"Sounds good to me.... let's go. You're very randy Rachel, what brought this on?"

"Mozart makes me randy," she laughed. "Why? Are you complaining?"

"Let's get that cab."

At home the wine did its work and they spent an hour of uninhibited indulgence. She posed and chassied and stripped, she treated him every way she knew how. Because of the alcohol she humoured him until it was too late. The mood shift was like a gathering thunderstorm, the sun of their love was darkened by his jealous rage. She sobered too late, but knew that the only way to peace was to make sure he came. At last it was over, her wrists were sore, her sex bruised, but there was no other damage apart from a slight swelling of her lip. Michael as always fell asleep almost immediately. Rachel went wearily to the shower.

'Oh Michael, so close to heaven, so close to hell, what are we to do with you my darling?' Was this thing getting worse? Was this jealousy, this cruelty a result of Michael's illness? Should she get hold of Lucas?

The next day Michael seemed oblivious that anything was amiss, over breakfast he commented on a 'delightful evening', oh! how she wished it had been, it was so nearly perfect. She bit her swollen lip, and failed to summon up the courage to speak. She could only muster a half cheery;

"You were a bit of a rough rider, my love." She said it shyly with a half smile. Michael tapped her affectionately on the hand.

"You'd make any man wild."

After he'd gone to the city still in search of a new job, Rachel got on with a normal day. First an hour and a half of practice, then she had her regular appointment at 'Hands,' and a chat with Betty that was always as therapeutic as the massage.

Betty noticed her bruises immediately.

"What have you been up to dear?"

"Oh you know, playing at this and that."

"Looks more like a bit of the other if you ask me."

"Oh, Betty can I tell you something …. in confidence that is."

"Of course you can dear your secret's safe with me dear."

"Well it's Michael, he likes …. you know…."

"He likes a bit of BDSM does he? I can tell dear, you've been restrained, your wrists are quite badly bruised…. look dear I don't have to tell you this is not a good idea, I don't mean what you get up to in the bedroom that's your affair, but you are a pianist dear and this is a dangerous thing to do….can't you use silk or velvet or something?'

"What do you mean, silk or velvet?"

"Well darling, if he wants to restrain you, get restrained in comfort, you can buy these things; it will probably turn him on and save you the business of him grabbing your wrists. I've noticed this before I never said anything, but think of your future darling…. that is if I'm not speaking out of turn, your other option is to kick him in the nuts dear, I'm sure that won't be popular."

They laughed. Then Rachel was silent as Betty worked on her shoulders and arms, then the heels and palms of her hands. It was an almost hypnotic delight. 'I suppose velvet hand restraints wouldn't be out of the way when she considered the rest of their toy collection.' There remained a nagging doubt that she may be sliding down a slippery slope. Michael, it was for Michael, and that made it all right.

As she stepped out into the sunshine, she felt better but still unsure. Betty was right she couldn't allow Michael to keep grabbing her wrists; she walked unsurely into the West End streets that abounded with shops that offered every sexual accessory from underwear to whips. She couldn't summon up the courage to go in any of them. Eventually as she stole a view of a large store that specialised in 'Love' products she saw a middle aged lady and her daughter emerge. At least it looked like a mother and daughter. They were both laughing. Through the door Rachel saw the staff were female, and what customers there were, were at least fifty per cent female albeit many with their male partners. She took a deep breath and walked smartly in.

"Yes Madame can I help you?"

It could have been in Harrods, the assistant was young smart and attractive. There was nothing vaguely disreputable about her. Rachel though still felt tongue tied, she didn't know whether to claim she was just browsing, that was absurd and the thought made her almost hysterical. Should she run for the door? She stood rooted to the spot.

"Well Madame I can see you've not been in before, now let's see if I can help?"

"Well, do you have …. or velvet …. uhmmm…. ties…. you know "

"Restraints, is it what Madame is looking for; hands and feet Madame?"

"I'm not sure." Rachel's mind was numb with embarrassment.

"Metal or leather are both in demand," she beckoned and Rachel followed meekly to a screened display counter where there was a bizarre selection of hand cuffs, whips and all manner of curiosities, some of which Rachel could not begin to guess their purpose.

"We have blind folds, some lovely leather cuffs and collars, some are decorated with diamonds, would Madame like to have a look?"

"No thank you," She spotted the velvet ties in a pack marked Submissive Bliss. She pointed dumbly at them.

"Oh yes Madame very popular, they're thirty two pounds, shall I wrap them?"

Rachel could not wait to get out of the shop. Her next nightmare was that she should be seen emerging from this decadent palace of erotica. She rushed out head bowed; she didn't look up for a whole block. When she got home she hid her parcel of contraband in her wardrobe, and spent the next hour fretting about how to introduce her…. what she'd decided were.... her wrist guards. What to do with the ankle guards was too horrendous even to contemplate.

Eva did not turn up for afternoon practice, so Rachel spent the afternoon in the studio alone with Becky. There was a phrase in a late Beethoven sonata that bothered her; she needed Eva. She rang Eva's number and was about to put the phone down when Eva answered. She was obviously very unwell; she could hardly make herself heard.

Rachel without further thought leapt into a cab and arrived at Eva's flat within minutes. She rang the bell but there was no reply. She tried the door but it was locked. She walked to the front bay window but there was no sign of Eva. It had only been a week since Eva had collapsed, what was she thinking of? She should have gone to see Eva immediately on her return from Saltsburg. Was she too late?

God, she'd been out buying sex toys when Eva could have been dying. She became more and more agitated. She rang the bell to the upstairs flat, another old lady appeared; she was blonde and rotund with florid features. She was also from Austria or some Eastern European country. She spoke with Eva's broad central European accent.

"Vat is't my dear?" She wheezed, "vat can I do for you?'

"It's Eva, I can't get a reply, she won't answer the door."

"Is she zer, maybe out?"

"No she's there I just phoned. Please can you help, do you have a key?'

"Vait." She croaked and waddled back up the stairs to her flat.

Rachel continued to wrap the door and scurry back and forth to the front window. There was still no sign of Eva. Eventually the neighbour huffed and wheezed her way back down stairs, she had a key.

"First, who are you, a student?"

"Yes I'm a student and a friend, please open the door."

They found her, by the telephone, she had not been dead long, but the absence of life was so emphatic as to be shocking. It was not Eva; it was a cadaver, a dead thing. Still wrapped in her velvet and taffeta, her stockings wrinkled, one slipper askew, her hands clawing at what had been life. There was an odour that was part Eva, part decay, it was a fetid reminder that death and age are not elegant companions.

Rachel stood quite still, unable to touch Eva's body. Seconds passed, the neighbour suddenly broke the silence with a guttural moan and foreign mutterings, she fell to her knees and took Eva's head to her lap and started to cry with a tragic wail. Who was she?

Rachel picked up the phone dialled 999 and called for an ambulance, she then called Eva's doctor who said he would be there right away. The rest was a blur, people came and went, Eva was taken away categorised as D.O.A.; dead on arrival at the hospital. The Summer day had deadened to a grey overcast evening as Rachel walked the long walk from Eva's place back home. Everything seemed the same; the traffic roared by, workers and shoppers made their way to tube stations and apartments, the lights came on in the shops, the evening newspapers were on sale. Eva was dead. Rachel was stunned, who would she turn to? Who would help with the Beethoven? Who would nag her to practise? Who would listen and show her the way with such kindly insights?

Grief was not something she had known; at first there was bewilderment and then in those standstill moments of realization came the certainty of loss. Her walls came tumbling down, there was nowhere to touch, nothing to hold, just the dreadful certainty that Eva was no more. The pain was unexpected, the ache and the gnawing emptiness was something she had never known. There was a vague familiarity with uncertainty, even pain when Mummy and Daddy had split, but it seemed unreal from her musical cocoon, she'd never known Daddy anyway. But Eva; Eva had been her daily guide, her talisman, her musical mentor for twenty years and more. Eva had been like the morning, she lightened every day, being so constant and caring in her old Viennese way.

Rachel could not see as she wandered down Kensington High Street as the tears poured uncontrollably. No one noticed, or if they did, they didn't care. She stumbled into 'The Columbian Coffee House' waited in the short queue ordered her black straight coffee and then realised she had no money to pay for it. The young man behind the counter looked as if he'd heard it all before:

"Look lady, don't waste my time, we don't do free here!" He snarled the last words. Rachel burst into tears, turned, but found herself restrained by a grip that was gentle but firm. She looked up and through her tear filled eyes made out a tall middle aged man with greying hair and kind grey eyes.

"It's alright, let me pay, take your coffee – it's fine."

Rachel snivelled her thanks and took her steaming cup to an empty table near the corner. She sat and stared into the steaming blackness of her coffee, at the same time wiping her eyes.

"Is there anything I can do to help?" It was the stranger.

"Oh no, it's very rude of me I meant to thank you ....I do apologise."

"Not a bit of it," he offered his hand, "I'm George Swift, please let me help if I can."

He stood there hovering over her, hesitant, "do you mind?"

"Oh please sit down." Rachel supped her coffee, escaping from conversation.

"And you are..?" enquired Swift.

"Rachel, Rachel George-Johnson."

"I hope whatever upset you is not too awful."

"Oh…." She sighed …"awful, yes awful." And she started to cry again.

"Look, can I get a taxi to take you home?

"No, I don't live far from here; the walk will do me good, no thanks I mean…… look you've been very kind but I better drink my coffee and be off, my husband will be expecting me." She had no idea why she said that bit about her husband, was it she was suspicious of this man who'd seemed so kind.

"Let me at least accompany you home, you seem so dreadfully upset."

Why not? He seemed nice enough. She smiled a wobbly smile, somewhere between a grimace and a sob. "Thank you."

They put down their coffees and walked into the dusk, shop-fronts lighting the pavements with pools of tepid light and made their way to the crescent mews.

On the way Swift seemed content to say nothing, he just enquired about their destination, nodded and walked protectively by her side. Rachel babbled first about how unnecessarily gallant he had been, and then spilled the details of her dreadful afternoon.

They stopped at the entrance to the mews. "This is it, you've been very kind." she offered her hand which he took, and dwelt with it.

"I can't say it's been a pleasure for that would be an offence, but it has been a pleasure to have been of service. Perhaps if you feel you would like to, I could buy you a coffee again. Please take my card"

"Thank you, but I don't think so…." She took his card with hardly a glance and put it in her pocket. "Good night and thank you again."

She opened the door and was immediately assailed by Michael who he took her in his arms and swept her round with her feet off the hall floor.

"Your clever man is back to work again, you're talking to the Vice-President of Walmer Holdings." He squeezed her tight.

Rachel, her thoughts confused, pushed him away, stared up at him, tried to smile but her jaw wavered and the tears came again, through them she could just mutter "Darling, well done." She ran into the kitchen and then sobbing started again. She turned away from him as he followed her.

"Aren't you pleased? I'll be back in business, now that I'm fit, a job in town and everything I've always wanted."

Rachel still with her back to him, poured herself some water, "That's terrific, I really am pleased, but Eva died today." Again a shudder of pain and tears.

Michael was quiet, he turned and left the kitchen, she heard him walk away to the sitting room. She mopped her eyes, blew her nose, and considered what to do next. She knew her grief had thrown a blanket of coldness over Michael's good news, his boyish enthusiasm. It was the kind of shock that sent him into moods, she knew it. Despite her own misery and gloom she'd have to pick herself up and join Michael in his moment of joy. She took a deep breath and followed her man to the sitting room.

He sat there, the Champagne in front of him, his head in his hands, he looked forlorn; she walked to him, took his head in her arms and cradled his head to her midriff.

"I'm sorry darling, to be so miserable, I am really happy for you, but losing Eva today was such a shock."

He pulled her down onto his lap offering her a glass and whispered "Tell me all about it."

She did, sipping her champagne she poured out all the extraordinary tale of her teacher's passing. Michael sat stroking her hair and not saying a word. They were interrupted by the phone; it was Doctor Rubin who explained to Rachel the details of the funeral which was to be held the next day according to Jewish custom.

No sooner had that conversation ended when the phone rang again; it was Max, he was obviously deeply upset and promised he would take Rachel to the ceremony. There were many other calls, all relating to Eva, it was as if the network of musicians all over the world had mobilised at the loss of one of their own.

At last as they made their way to bed, she was able to give time to listen to Michael's good news. He had indeed been appointed as vice- president of Walmer Holdings. The name sent a shudder through her and yes it did transpire that the Walmer in question was the dreaded Sir Bradley; lecher, man of mysterious influence and apparently untold wealth. Rachel held back the revulsion at the idea of Michael working with or for that odious man. He was obviously excited at his prospects though he admitted that the terms were more incentive driven than the fat salaries that he was used to in the city.

Eva Weinstein was interred in the Jewish cemetery in South London on a bright sunny day. The whole experience was a strange one for Rachel as she mixed with a large crowd of Eva's friends, relations, students, fellow teachers, and musicians famous and unknown.

She was amazed at the number of people who turned up, it was often said that if you go to an old person's funeral there would be only a few, but here there were at least one hundred and fifty and many of them musical "names". Even in the segregated male/ female arrangements, there was an obvious devotion from so many. Eva had given of herself for so many years and with so much quiet distinction, it was hard for Rachel to believe how privileged she had been. Eva had been more than her teacher she had been her guardian and musical mother. Rachel was acquainted with grief for the first time in her life and it hurt.

It transpired that Eva had willed to Rachel all manner of musical items, some original scores, including a Liszt manuscript, an antique metronome from Vienna, letters all in German, some to Schnabel and Giseking. In all, these musical memorabilia were worth a great deal of money. However despite Michael's cajoling they were all accommodated in her studio, the Liszt manuscript having been appropriately sealed and framed at Sotheby's.

Sally Nye had lined up a number of teachers who could spare the time to act as Rachel's alter ego, but none seemed to have the instinct of her beloved Eva. Sally gave what time she could but she was the only one who Rachel really felt at home with. There would be no one who would fill the breach; Rachel must come of age and find her way.

Despite the lack of Eva's counsel, she had matured; the recitals that immediately followed the death of her mentor were in their way more thoughtful, more emotionally balanced than ever before. Indeed she felt for the first time in her career that she was confident of her own musical judgements.

Through the immediate aftermath of Eva's demise Michael was patient, happy and supportive. After a two week stay in the London Office he had flown off to some obscure part of the former Soviet Union. On his return he was in high spirits, things were going well.

Michael was delighted to announce that they both would be at Deddington Hall; Rachel as a committee member of the Duchess's City Charity, and he to entertain some clients of Walmer Holdings. They would be staying the weekend as guests of the Walmers.

Rachel felt as a fly does, close to a spider's web. She slept that night, not at all.

Chapter 15

Rachel received from the Duchess's office the agenda and outline proposal for the next Charity event. It was to be a Gala evening of music and dance drawn from London's premiere artists, included was a list of those who had been invited to perform, those who had accepted, and those who had yet to reply. The Duchess would value Rachel's views on the form and programme as well as seek her help with closing in on her professional colleagues. She passed the whole thing over to Max who knew every manager and impresario in London. He returned with all things accomplished on the Thursday before they were to travel to Deddington Hall.

She journeyed separately by chauffeured car for her luncheon and afternoon gathering of HRH's committee. Jennifer Walmer greeted her like an old friend and even the Duchess was relaxed and charm itself. The house was a dramatic Tudor manor house that had been much extended during later centuries. The estate was well over a hundred acres of lovely north Cotswold rolling land. The gardens were immaculate with emerald lawns, lines of ancient yew trees stood soldier straight along the driveways, and flowerbeds almost unnatural in their tidiness. There was an overwhelming air of wealth and opulence, there was no place here for the second best.

The meeting was held after a divinely cooked but delicate light luncheon. The service was impeccable with a supervising butler and two footmen in attendance on the six ladies and one gentleman, the Duchess' secretary. The

Duchess drank copiously, and Rachel followed suit, just to assuage her nerves.

The meeting was businesslike and soon Rachel relaxed, it was obvious her views were listened to, and that Max's preparation impressed the gathered company. Quite without thought Rachel proposed that she and Igor Franek would feature the Mozart for two pianos, this she felt sure would fit into what was to be a Gala evening where this delightful music would add sparkle and delight. The more she thought about it the more she looked forward to it.

After the meeting was concluded the Duchess took Rachel aside, "You've been a great asset my dear, we'll keep in touch and I'm looking forward enormously to the Gala, I shall try to get the Palace to put it in the diary but they're not all that into music you know. Still I'll do my best, but the Prince is getting on a bit, so I won't promise."

Rachel didn't know what to say other than mumble, "That would be an honour for us ma'am."

"By the way is there anything more than piano playing with this mysterious Pole of yours.... Frankel or whatever his name is?" She smirked in a way that made Rachel feel uncomfortable. She blushed involuntarily; giving the Duchess she was sure, the impression that Igor was more than a fellow artist. 'Was he?'

"Oh No Ma'am, he's a young but very gifted pianist and I've spent only a day or so with him working. He's fantastic, but well ma'am if you saw him, he's just a gawky kid really but he plays like an angel." With that they said their goodbyes, the Duchess wishing everyone well and apologising for having to leave before the party.

She took afternoon tea with Jennifer who showed her round the sumptuous residence. They passed through the Ballroom where there were a number of people erecting a stage of some sort, probably for the band said Jennifer rather vaguely.

The dining room fit for a palace was beautifully laid for a party of thirty or so. Rachel was dying to ask who was coming to the dinner party but again Jennifer was evasive, 'business people'.

"We have one of these parties about once a month, Bradley likes to make sure that his clients are entertained.... appropriately, I'm sure you'll enjoy the evening, a lot of people from the near East and old Russia I think and I'm so looking forward to you helping keep the party going."

"I'll be delighted to help in any way I can, but I'm not at all sure what I can do." Hardly any point in offering to do the dishes she thought, suppressing a smile.

"Just be beautiful and charming which is easy to these Genghis Khan types, darling, I'm sure you'll be a hit."

The conversation meandered away as the afternoon turned golden in the lovely Cotswold sky. Rachel made her way to her room to wait for Michael and his guests. She still couldn't get Sir Bradley out of her mind, and despite the friendliness of it all there remained an apprehensive shadow that refused to give way to the light.

A discreet tap on her door and the luggage was delivered. She was disappointed to learn that Michael had been delayed but there was a note that Michael and Sir Bradley would be with them for cocktails at around seven.

She unpacked to find that Michael had changed all her clothes, instead of her black evening dress there was a scarlet silk number that was more appropriate for an intimate night at home. Gone was her sedate underwear and in its place the erotic ensemble Michael had brought back from New York. God! What was he thinking of now. She'd worn these things before and they'd always been a precursor of one of Michael's more extreme sexual rantings. All this, and Bradley Walmer in the wings, set her already nervous mood, into high apprehension.

She thought of ways to get round the issues, spill something onto the dress and beg another from Jennifer, though she was at least four sizes bigger. Refuse to wear the dress at all; Michael would be beside himself, if she did wear it, she'd look like a trollop.

There was no choice, she decided after half an hour of nervously pacing the grand room, she would have to wear it and try to carry it off, not as a strumpet, but as the deranged pianist that she surely must be. She laughed to herself as she popped the cork of a bottle of Champagne and slipped into the luxuriant bath. She dozed and relaxed in the silky bath, as the sun slipped below the horizon and the weather and the environs of Deddington Hall became cooler and dark.

She woke with a start, it was twenty to seven she must rush and dress and be ready to meet Michael and his new associates; Sir Bradley was put to the back of her mind. The red mid-thigh hose, the delicate silk panties and the skimpy bra, were despite their vulgarity, sensuous to touch and have next to her skin. She pulled on the dress and again there was no escaping the overtly sexy nature of her attire. In the mirror she had to admit she'd have made a wonderful tart. Another glass of champagne, a sharp intake of breath and she set off for the library to meet Michael, the newest Walmer acolyte. She was apprehensive but she could not help the excitement. She'd try and be what Michael wanted, an attractive and sexy woman who'd be a charming and relaxed hostess in these most splendid surroundings.

The one thing that irked her was these uncomfortable high heels; she seldom wore them and never when she was working which was most of the time. They were painful and she felt her gait was like that of a tight rope walker, how could that be attractive?

She entered the library and there was an audible gasp as she entered the room, all the men seemed to turn at once, and Rachel felt embarrassed but pleased. She stretched out and accelerated her walk, the eyes of all upon her till she embraced her handsome husband.

"Jesus, you look good enough to eat." He squeezed her.

"Down Boy, I've got a bone or two to pick with you about the luggage."

"Not now sweetie, come and meet some of our guests."

It was then she saw them; the women, the same sort of women from long ago in Hvar. All these men had a very attractive woman on their arm, so at last Michael had got his way; he was in banking just like that far off man from Marseilles.

Jennifer Walmer, as attractive and smart as ever, hugged her.

"Oh to be twenty something; you look stunning darling, all the other ladies are jealous as hell. Michael I'm going to drag Rachel away to meet some of the guests, come along my dear. First have a glass of bubbly.... is your room alright?"

"Mm yes please, the room's lovely."

"Listen dear these are the rules, we have to spend all the time buttering up the men, I'll point out the ones who need most care and attention. Apparently your Michael has brought two key players on this transcontinental pipe line deal, one from something Stahn, can never remember one from another, and another gentleman from Turkey who's a Minister of something or other, any way, these are they" she whispered from the side of her mouth.

Nikolai Mendova was large in every way, his head sat the size of a large pumpkin upon his equally massive but stilted frame, he was almost as wide as he was tall. Indeed Rachel in her impossibly high heels had to consciously give at the knees to ensure that they enjoyed the same eye level. His eyes were slightly oriental and the colour of his skin pale bronze, his eyes almost black. When he shook hands with her she felt the huge physical power despite the gentleness of his grip. He spoke with an accent that was strange to her ear, not Russian but more Iranian or Arab. Beneath the overly applied deodorant she took in his unequivocal masculinity. His gaze focused without any diffidence, he eyed her up and down dwelling on her cleavage. She felt suddenly threatened by Mendova's overt sexist arrogance. Yet she could not unlock the eye contact, nor had she a mind to. She would not be dominated by this man whoever he was.

Jennifer prattled on, enquiring about how many times Nikolai had visited England and what a marvellous linguist he was. Still Mendova never moved his focus, nor shifted his intense gaze, boring into Rachel. At last she gave up the struggle, extended to her full height and shifted her attention to the smoke laden companion. In contrast to Mendova, this man was a nobody. Rachel was relieved to smile at him and use his forgettable face to escape the intensity of Mendova, whose devouring eyes seemingly touched her physically. The more she tried the more she became self conscious and felt exposed in her provocative dress. 'God Michael had something to answer for.'

After what seemed an age, Jennifer took Rachel by the arm and led her off to meet Mehmet Bakirahn, Minister of regional development of Turkey. If Mendova was short,

Bakirahn was tall and lean. He was in his early fifties, dapper, moustached and luxuriant hair that was black speckled with grey. He took Rachel's hand and brought it to his lips in an old fashioned way that was gallant and charming, he was urbane and civilised. His conversation was engaging, he knew of Rachel's celebrity at the piano and he enquired about Rachel's views and ideas on the meeting of Indian, Arab and Western European musical cultures.

Michael arrived greeting 'Mehmet' as if he'd known him for ever, and it seemed that the two of them were at ease, but then if Michael turned on the charm who could resist him? Certainly not Rachel, to have him alongside her lifted all the stress of the Mendova encounter; she knew that with Michael she was safe.

That certainty was short lived as Bradley Walmer and Nikolai Mendova rejoined the group. More champagne was served and Rachel for want of anything to cover her nervousness took her fourth glass in less than two hours, she felt herself a little unsteady and flushed under Mendova's devouring attention. The announcement that dinner was served came as a great relief and Rachel excused herself to powder her nose. On the way back, she was assailed by another woman of about her age; she was pretty, her name was Anna.

"Honey where did you get that dress, it's a knock out, you must be on Sarah's top book, any way who's your target?"

"Target?"

"Yes, you know which guy is your hit? You look top table to me."

"I'm sorry I don't understand, I'm with my husband Michael Johnson."

"Oh, sorry," Anna moved swiftly away.

Michael met her at the door to the palatial dining room; there was one great dining table, laid out meticulously with thirty or so places, sixteen to each side and one at each end. They were seated offset and opposite the Walmers, next to Rachel and opposite Jennifer sat the inevitable Mendova. He bowed and helped her into her seat, holding her bare arm unnecessarily in his cool but massive hand. Michael helped the lady to his left. They sat and as they did so, an army of waiters swarmed from their invisible cover to spread napkins, pour wine and deliver a variety of breads.

At first Rachel was relieved to see that Mr Mendova was busily talking to his escort, a woman of about thirty who looked beautiful and poised.

"Who's the lady with Mr Mendova?" she enquired of Michael.

"I think she's his London interpreter or assistant, not sure actually, isn't the Sancerre beautiful, quite magnificent, I hope this lot appreciate it."

"And who's that gorgeous thing with Bakirahn; surely that's not his wife?"

"Darling, why don't you ask them after dinner, I've no idea, she's from the London office I think, I really don't know every one yet. Look my darling drink your wine enjoy your food and just relax."

The first course was at hand, exquisitely presented. Mendova devoured his in an instant. Rachel had hardly tasted her first nibble when Mendova turned to her:

"Mrs Johnson, may I call you Raquel? Michael has told you of our business? He was very welcome in Tashkent and we hope he will bring you next time he visits."

"Rachel…. its Rachel …. not Raquel, but yes," she bluffed, "Michael did say how much he'd enjoyed his visit, and I'm sure I'd love to visit Tashhhh", she slurred a little, "your lovely country."

She tried another mouthful of food,

"I shall be pleased to arrange everything for you; maybe even you could play the piano for us." Mendova, leaning conspiratorially toward her, "We shall send you Government aircraft, you will be V.I.P., when the deal is signed Michael must bring you for celebrations." He dabbed his broad mouth, "It is important we are close friends, I think." He patted her knee hardly heavier than a butterfly.

Sir Bradley, bald head shining, blue eyes like ice opals, grinned broadly, "I'm delighted Nicolai that you've had the chance to meet with Michael and his lovely wife, Rachel," he inclined his head, "they are of course like all my associates, part of the team, isn't that so?"

Rachel, now quite tipsy, looked back at Sir Bradley, paused, "What Michael strives to achieve, I always support." She remained unsure in her addled state if this was the right thing to say, but she just couldn't think of anything more appropriate.

"Quite so", he replied, "Michael is a key man, and we have a great opportunity to move forward on this pipeline issue, I'm sure Nicolai will agree." He nodded to Mendova, who immediately picked up his glass.

"A Toast to our venture, to you Sir Bradley and your team and the beautiful ladies, and of course our Turkish friends." He held his glass out toward Mehmet Bakirahn.

Rachel following Michael's example raised her glass and they drank.

Bakirahn, not to be out done, rose a little unsteadily, "We are all grateful to be here, in this lovely home, and to thank our English friends for bringing us neighbours together. I toast our hosts and especially Sir Bradley and Mr Johnson."

Everyone in the room rose; Rachel after a brief hesitation joined them, and felt quite proud of Michael, though she had no idea what it was he was supposed to have done.

"Darling, you must tell me all about the things you've done, you've only been with Bradley a month or so and you're a hero." She snuggled his arm, "I'm so glad I know this is what you want, I'll even be nice to Bradley." She giggled.

"That's my girl, you keep up the good work, Nicolai there is the man who can make us all rich, this deal is worth half a billion."

"Half a billion? How much is half a billion?"

"Five hundred million pounds, my darling, five hundred million pounds."

The main course arrived, as did the red wine, apparently one of the world's finest.. Michael swilled his glass, breathed in the gorgeous aroma, "This, my darling, is the sort of wine we can get used to if this deal comes off." His hand slid up her thigh, "God you look wonderful."

"Be a good boy, wait till I get you to bed, besides you never know who's looking."

"Darling everyone's looking at you, who else would they look at?"

"Lots of lovely ladies I must say," Rachel looked up and down the table and it occurred to her she'd never seen such a group of women, that with exception of Jennifer and her London associates, were all twenty five to thirty five, and all really pretty.

"Michael, who's Sarah?"

"Sarah, that's the lady with Nicolai, she fixes things for Bradley, looks after foreign visitors, that sort of thing."

"You mean she's a Madame! Don't you," she giggled conspiratorially, "Am I one of her girls?" She took another drink.

"Oh shhh! Don't be silly.'

Jennifer intervened and they were soon engaged in a conversation about the day's business with the Duchess' committee.

Nicolai Mendova seemed genuinely interested, though he clearly had no conception of the great and the good doing charitable works. Rachel found herself in a long conversation, explaining the concepts and ideas behind the work she'd been asked to do. Her dinner remained untouched, but her wine glass was refilled again. She felt more at ease now with Nicolai, true he still seemed transfixed by her body, but what the hell, Michael had set her up to look like a tart anyway. Mendova asked about her career and the disciplines of playing the piano, suddenly taking both her hands in his and tenderly traced down her fingers and across her palms with his. It was very intimate and immediately Rachel felt a sensuous reaction, withdrawing her hands quickly and took refuge holding her knife and fork.

Michael was engrossed in conversation with the lady, lady?, on his left. Rachel couldn't escape the polite ministrations of Nicolai. His intensity was in some ways alluring but at the same time unnerving. She knew he was flirting outrageously with her, and she had to admit he had charm, mysterious and masculine, masculine as in bull. He was, she reflected, a great bull of a man. She couldn't escape an inner curiosity that he would be tumultuous in bed.

Dinner came to an end and the guests were shepherded into the huge conservatory where a jazz trio played mainstream old time pops. She danced with Michael, comfortable in his arms.

"Are you enjoying yourself?" Michael asked.

"Um, yes I think I am; am I being good?"

"Darling you're the belle of the ball."

"Good, kiss me." They kissed and smooched some more. "I want to get to bed, I'm a bit tipsy and I want you."

"Just hang on darling, I'm dying to have you to myself, but we have to be hosts and hostesses – so be good a bit longer."

"Must I?"

"Yes you must, I see Nicolai is very taken with you, you seemed to get on like two love birds, I saw you holding hands."

"Don't be silly Michael, though he did try to flirt a bit," she ground her thighs into his, "but I was not to be taken in."

"Don't you fancy him a little bit?"

"Michael stop it, you'll be all excited and anxious again."

"You do, I can tell, and I don't mind.... you have to be nice to him anyway, so I don't mind."

In the warmth and safety of his arms she felt quite calm, sexy and protective. "You can't mean I should flirt back, do you, you'd be jealous and mad at me?"

"Darling I know you, and I don't mind if you flirt a bit."

"How much can I flirt?" She nipped his buttocks, "How much?" she ground her thighs into his and she felt his reaction surge back at her. They kissed again, Rachel was deeply aroused and the rest of the world was of no matter.

"Talk of the Devil," he broke off their smooch, "Nicolai, why don't you dance with Rachel."

"It would be my honour."

Rachel randy and tipsy, hardly saw the irony of what was going on as Nicolai Mendova took her into his huge arms and rather mechanically chassied into the dancing group.

"You are very beautiful, Mrs Johnson, may I call you Rachel."

"Please do....Nicolai."

His physic was nothing like any one she had ever known, he seemed to be a collection of ropes and muscles on an iron frame. She could feel the muscles on his shoulders, they were hard but supple.

"Weight lifting"

"What, what's that Nicolai?"

"I was a weight lifter, I got a silver medal in the Olympics, it was some time ago, but I have still the, how do you say the frame?"

"Yes, the frame.... I see." She was slightly embarrassed

"You have hands of a pianist, beautiful and strong and sensitive, I have muscles of a weight lifter, hard, ugly and demanding. If I stop training I shall just get extremely fat, it is the way I'm afraid, so I still train, just like you."

She said nothing. Rachel felt a sudden sympathy for him, she felt his arms pull her closer, she didn't resist. He felt his hands reach down her back then felt his manhood, Oh dear! She pulled out of her reverie, smiled, took his hand and raised it to her waist, and withdrew her head that had slumped onto his shoulder. She looked him in the eye, "I'm sure all those muscles are not ugly at all." She smiled; she meant it just as she said it.

He returned her gaze, "Perhaps, one day you will see."

She laughed, "Come now Nicolai, you're flirting with a married lady."

They broke off and she sought out Michael who was chatting to Sarah. "Michael, no more booze for me, I really ought to go to bed."

"Mrs Johnson, here take these, they'll help you last out the night, lessen the effects of the alcohol, really they're harmless, just like the things you buy over the counter at the chemist, honestly."

Sarah reminded Rachel of Jacqui George, beautiful, immaculately groomed but basically a tramp. Who the hell was she, to offer Rachel tablets? God they could be drugs.

"No thank you I'll just drink a lot of water, really that will be fine. Michael, be a darling and get me some water will you."

Michael went as instructed.

"Mrs Johnson,"

"Sarah, do call me Rachel, I'm afraid I've drunk too much, I'm not used to it."

"Oh I know the feeling well, I run a lot of parties for visiting delegations.... Government people and that sort of thing, so that's why I take these caffeine tablets some times, that's all they are, they keep me going till bed time and then I sleep like a log."

"What sort of parties do you.... um.... host?"

"Ones like this. I fix up partners some times, sometimes just the chefs or entertainment or whatever, I'm a night owl, I spend most of the daylight in bed, a sort of modern day vampire," she laughed, "no not really, it's a hard business and I can't afford to make mistakes, my next one is next week in Cannes. Big money but no room for error; anyway, that's enough about me."

Michael arrived back with the water, Rachel took the glass, "How many tablets should I take?"

"Just one, if you tire again you can always have another, absolutely harmless."

Rachel took the white capsule and swallowed it with water. "Oh here comes the wrestler Nicolai Mendova, bendover." she giggled. Sarah smiled and took Mendova's arm as they moved into the ballroom for the cabaret.

She took Michael's arm, and in so doing she felt her anxiety melt away, they walked slowly into the ballroom, that like all of Deddington Hall was sumptuous and luxuriantly comfortable. Whatever Sarah's tablets contained they seemed to work inordinately well, gone was her tiredness though she still felt light headed, Michael at her side radiated all the wonderful things she so believed in. He looked beautiful, he radiated charm; all those there seemed to hang on his every word. She had, Rachel decided, been too wrapped up in her own world. She should support him in his own environment, after all she had experienced a lovely day with the great and the good, perhaps she had misjudged everything because of the ghastly Bradley Walmer; had she misjudged him as well? He had given Michael a job and he seemed to trust Michael with whatever it was he did, by all accounts huge deals with these foreigners, strange people really, quite unlike any one she'd ever met before. Yes, for the first time she felt she was in a position to help and she'd do anything she could to advance his cause. She tucked his arm in close to her side, she was, she knew, the belle of the ball, and she loved it.

More Champagne was in evidence and it seemed natural to assuage her thirst, it was lovely bubbly. Jennifer Walmer came over and fussed. Everything was going so well, was Rachel enjoying herself? Indeed she was, as she downed another glass of champagne.

The room was laid out with settees surrounding the smallish stage; she barely noticed the farewells of a few of the vaguely familiar guests who were leaving the Walmers and the Johnsons to entertain the delegation and their ladies. Their ladies? The young hostesses were all attending to their men in a manner that Rachel thought if not exciting then at least interesting. The pretty girl she'd met earlier was sitting on the lap of her man, in what could only be described as a passionate embrace.

She nudged Michael, "The visitors' wives seem to be very cosy with their boys." She couldn't help but stare, at the same time feeling the desire rise in her.

Michael kissed her languidly looking around him, "well darling if we want the half billion, they have to have what they want," He squeezed her breast and put his arm round her pressing against her behind, "this darling is just another day at the office, Bradley calls it making friends for life, the life of the deal that is." He kissed her neck and she felt the delight of his conspiratorial lust.

They took their seats on a settee, next to Sarah and Nicolai. The gossamer curtain lifted and the most delicious woman sang a medley of love songs. The champagne flowed, Rachel was in a decadent heaven she smooched shamelessly with Michael and let the sensual music envelope her. Michael held her and kissed her and put his hands where they should only go in the privacy of their bedroom, but she wanted him and shameless though it was his hand between her legs was heaven and if anything she didn't want him to stop there.

Then much to the loving couples chagrin the singer stopped to modest applause. The sound of a dance band filled the room and she was in Michael's arms, she felt like a rampant school girl, she just wanted Michael to take her somewhere and do it, yes do it, make love to her right there. There was a tap on Michael's shoulder, Sarah, pecked him on the cheek, "Come on Mr Host, you can't keep Rachel all to yourself," and she moved smoothly into Michael's arms and they danced away.

Once more she was in Nicolai Mendova's enormous arms. First there was shock, then confusion, then 'duty calls,' I'm the hostess. Through all the multitude of emotions; the strangeness, the shock of all this blatant sexuality, there remained her own sexual charge. Michael winked at her from Sarah's clutches. She could not help but notice Sarah's hand massaging her husband's buttock. Nicolai's smell was overwhelming, underneath his perfume there was an odour of predatory maleness that she'd remembered from the first night she'd let Michael take her to bed all those years ago. She felt Mendova's rope like muscles in his shoulders and his firm but sensitive pressure of his hips against her. She could feel him rise against her. He kissed her neck and despite herself she put her arms around his neck and kissed him back, this time on his lips. His tongue melted and snaked with her own, and his enormous hands drew her pelvis into his.

In all this hedonistic lechery there remained in Rachel a primeval call, something was wrong, despite the excitement, the thrill, the adventure, this was not right. She struggled from Nicolai's grasp and returned to the settee. Mendova followed, hovering; worst of all, he said nothing. They stood there, Rachel now feeling quite dizzy, Mendova still trying to dominate with his eyes.

"I'm sorry Nicolai, that shouldn't have happened." For want of anything to do she quaffed her umpteenth glass of fizz.

"Rachel, may I still call you that, you are the most beautiful woman I have ever seen, and I know you are one of the.... how do you say.... passionate." He moved so close she could feel his breath on her face, "I want you, and I know you want that too."

Michael and Sarah returned and in a rush Sarah bade them all sit down for the last cabaret, it was already three in the morning. Rachel protested she wanted to go to bed, Sarah handed her another white capsule that she took with more champagne.

The lights went down and Rachel just wanted it to be over, to get to bed, she'd tried her best but the whole thing was out of hand and Michael seemed intent on flirting with Sarah. Once more the elixir of Rachel's magic capsules did their work and Rachel felt renewed, excited though light headed. She mused on the amount of champagne she'd downed in the course of the night; it would make an elephant tipsy. However she settled down only mildly alarmed that she was separated from Michael who was on the next settee.

The lights dimmed and the cabaret started, an acrobatic and statuesque black man danced onto the stage, dressed exotically as some sort of potentate from the Tales of a Thousand and One nights. He was followed by two gorgeous female dancers, presumably by their dress, from the males' harem. They danced before him seductively and wound a spell of heavy sensuality. Rachel was transfixed by the scenes not ten feet in front of her. As the scene unfolded it became more and more sexually charged until it was a ballet, but a pornographic one, that despite the skills of the participants, was a live sex show. In her daze Rachel didn't know whether to stare as her instincts told her, or get up and leave the room. The negro was splendid. Magnificent, muscled and oiled, his skin shone, his hips and thighs were a rippling mass of sensuality and there standing before her was the most magnificent penis she had ever seen. The sight of him in his nakedness took her breath away. The scenes of the two women and the black athlete varied into every sexual combination that was possible, it was hard to keep her emotions in check. There was part of her who wanted to get up and join in, even the girls were alluring, siren like and expert in their ministrations to themselves, their girl partner or to the phallic master. The extraordinary thing was the audience, at least those near seemed equally transfixed, there was an atmosphere of almost quiet reverence as the Caliph had his way. Inside, Rachel boiled with desire, never had she been remotely stimulated like this.

Nicolai's hands smoothed her thigh, she was frozen in this foreign land of public lust, lost but straining for release. She put her hand on his and after the mildest rebuttal, guided him towards her warmest place.

She looked around and saw that the elegant Turk, Bakirahn, was in the throes of orgasm with one of Sarah's 'Ladies'. She caught sight of the polished head of Bradley Walmer, his blue eyes leering from across the room. The very sight of him, jarred her from her sensuous reverie, but she found it hard to move, her head began to swim. Then there was Sarah:

"Come on Rachel, we must get you to bed."

Then Michael, "Come on my darling let's get Nicolai and Sarah to help you to bed."

Then dreams of what? Michael grinding into her, Sarah smoothing her, Nicolai, huge and broad, heavy on top of her, what were they doing, "yes, yes, Michael I want you.... no, that hurts, leave me alone.... I want to sleep...."

Chapter 16

Rachel awoke, came to, surfaced was more accurate. Her mouth was dry; she had a headache of enormous proportions. She was alone in the enormous bed, naked and sore. On her left wrist was, she was astonished to see, the velvet restraint that she'd bought those weeks ago in Soho. She staggered from the bed feeling nearer ninety two than twenty nine.

She stood in the bathroom, she examined herself in the mirror and saw herself, as though she had been in a fight, there were welts across her tummy and breasts, and light but unmistakeable bruises above her right knee and inside her left thigh. Her sex was sore, and her bottom was sore. She felt sick, and vomited into the lavatory. She ran a bath and slid gently into the salving waters.

What had happened, she remembered bits of last night, but they made no sense; the more she tried to remember the more confused she became. Too much champagne, she must have got hopelessly drunk. Oh dear, she hoped she'd been …, well been what, she remembered the cabaret, God it was disgusting, how could she face anybody this morning. Exploring her aching genitals she decided that Michael had once more been brutal, and she feared that in her state she may have been a willing participant.

She towelled down, she felt better though still groggy; she'd go home and spend the day in bed, she wasn't for this heavy drinking set. Michael she thought had been pleased with her, and although she'd been shameless with Mendova, well

Michael didn't seem to mind. Next time she'd definitely drink less.

Down stairs she wandered about through the now unfamiliar corridors, servants were everywhere, clearing up after the bacchanalian rumpus of the night before. There was no sign of Michael, or any other familiar face. She felt lost, the fuzziness and confusion increased, she felt distanced from yesterday as if it had never happened. Then she recognised the head of the household who directed her to the family dining room at the back of the house. Here she found Lady Jennifer Walmer sitting alone amongst the debris of a breakfast for at least ten guests. Jennifer was dressed in her house coat, and for the first time looked less than elegant. She looked rather as Rachel felt, hung over and exhausted.

"Good morning, Rachel my dear, a pretty hard night, but successful I think. Come and sit down and have some breakfast."

Rachel sat across the table from her hostess, "It's dreadfully late nearly eleven o clock, I would just like some coffee I think."

"Feeling a bit under the weather I expect."

"Yes, rather, I think I drank a bit too much Champagne."

"Would you like a little now, it might buck you up a bit, hair of the dog and all that?"

"No, no just some coffee, thank you." Rachel tried to focus on the breakfast table but she had difficulty doing so, the room swam, she felt nauseous again.

On returning from a hasty trip to the toilet, she sat once more. Jennifer was solicitous and kind; got some aspirin and suggested a little dry toast. Rachel began once more to feel better.

Lady Walmer chatted about the previous afternoon's meeting and re-iterated that the Duchess was most impressed with Rachel's contribution and ideas. Jennifer would ensure that the next meeting of the Charity Board would fall in with Rachel's diary. "We can't do without our Star", she took Rachel's hand and patted it.

There followed a silence. Rachel was nervous about her complete lack of recall of the latter stages of last night's party, eventually she plucked up courage;

"About last night, I know I drank far too much, I hope I didn't offend anyone?"

"Darling on the contrary you were a great hit, Bradley says we must have you every time we have important guests, the boys are off somewhere already, closing the deal, so everyone's delighted with the way things have gone." Jennifer refilled her coffee cup. "I know it's all a bit strange, and the entertainment shall we say, a little risqué, but Bradley always knows what these overseas chappies want." She took a drink from her cup. "Anyway you're a big girl now Rachel, we've got to look after the boys, don't you agree?"

"Yes, yes I suppose so. Anyway what's the plan, I've lost Michael."

"The men folk are wheeling and dealing my dear, they should be finished by lunchtime, why don't I get dressed and we can have a walk in the garden, it'll help us get rid of our hangovers. You stay here, I won't be a jiffy."

Despite the apparent normality, Rachel still felt badly disoriented; her mind remained cluttered and confused. Her hangover was the worst, by far, she'd ever experienced and there remained the physical nausea. There was still a dread of those things she could not remember; they haunted her from behind the veils of confusion and apparent amnesia.

Jennifer returned looking as if she'd had a complete makeover. She was made up, not a hair out of place.

"Come on Rachel, let's take a stroll, it'll clear our heads." In the sunshine of the late morning the garden enchanted, the formality was so perfect, yet nature had provided the magnificent contrasts that the Capability Brown blue print could hardly enhance.

"Your grounds are quite the most magnificent I think I've ever seen outside Kew, or national parks, how do you do it?"

"Bradley, my dear, as you get to know him, you'll appreciate he doesn't do anything by halves. All this costs a fortune of course, we have an army of staff, but it's not always been like this. When we first bought the place, these gardens were just an overgrown mess really, the original Brown designs were barely visible. I hate to think how much we've spent; it must be hundreds of thousands, just on the gardens."

"Jennifer.... I don't quite know how to put this, but I'm still confused about last night, I've never felt so dreadful, and worst of all I can't remember a thing."

"Rachel, my dear sweet thing, what is there to remember, just a rather wild party, that's all. You were much admired, and I understand that the deal will be done today, so whatever went on last night, it was worth it, I expect Michael will get a very handsome bonus that you'll be able to enjoy."

They stopped at the end of the rose trellis that extended a good quarter mile towards the small lake complete with its marble temple like gazebo.

"Come sit down." Jennifer commanded rather than invited. "Rachel you are a gloriously gifted young woman and an immense asset to your husband.... I was like you twenty years ago.... perhaps not as gifted in your musical realm, few people are." She put her hand gently over Rachel's, "Bradley was not unlike Michael too, he was in politics quite a bit, but his love was dealing and, if you like, influencing others. These men are very single minded and our job is to support them." She paused looking and remembering, seeking answers it seemed from the blue horizon. "I wasn't hard enough and it took me a long time to realise that Bradley is one in a million, he has drive and ambition, and there was simply no choice but to follow and support, even if sometimes I wasn't comfortable.... you know with all those men looking at me and pawing me as if I was some sort of man's toy."

"You mean Bradley let his men ....paw you.... wasn't he jealous?"

"Oh, what does it matter, yes he was jealous, he still is, though I'm long passed my prime. But that was the thrill really, daring him to see how far he'd let me go."

A blackbird's song piped the brilliant morning. Rachel took in the view, trying desperately to get this conversation in perspective.

"You must love Bradley very much."

"Yes, I suppose I do, but love is not always kind you know. My love for him is as much a fascination, delight, loathing.... I don't know.... never a dull moment. Some say we're pariahs; Bradley has never forgiven the Party for blackballing him. He's more powerful than most of them put together but he'll never get to the Lords, and that's a thing he'll never get over. For Bradley; to control is one thing, to be accepted quite another. Anyway I've loved him, he's been a bastard of course, men can be and sometimes I've been a bitch, but we're still together. We've been together over twenty years and in that time I've seen the things he's done. Good things, not everyone would see them as good things, but that's because most of them are jealous. Look at Deddington, outside the Royal palaces I don't suppose there are many equals, certainly very few that are lived in and not supported by The National Trust or whatever…. I'm not sure if I'm articulating myself well."

She looked at Rachel who still wondered what this was all about. Love, of course she loved Michael, but what did Michael expect? Was he going to turn into a manipulative money grabber like Bradley Walmer? Then again her father had been much the same, though as far as she knew he was just a straight forward philanderer. Straight forward, what a world she lived in, none of the men and women she knew not even her parents were…. well what was ordinary anyway? Jennifer had implied, alluded to, but had not been clear. Did she say Bradley was jealous but let his customers'….clients whatever, have sex with her. How could he? How could anyone? Then through the morning sunshine she saw Michael's face when he possessed her, his jealous rages and his grotesque fantasies. Tears blurred her vision as they slowly returned to the house. Rachel was as lost as it was possible to be, she tried to think about Becky and the need to practise, of Mozart and Igor Franek, how innocent all that seemed.

"God, I still feel dreadful, I really shouldn't do so much fizz in the future."

"Rachel, my dear, we have to keep going and I dare say you popped a pill or two, takes some getting used to, but next time you'll find it easier."

The memory of Sarah came flooding back, her caffeine tablets, could they have done this? "I thought caffeine would have been fine, a bit like the opposite of sleeping tablets that I sometimes use if I'm travelling, you know wake up or go to sleep tablets."

"Don't fret about it, my dear, they help us get along and a little speed never did anybody any harm."

'Speed', no one had mentioned 'speed', 'speed' was a drug she knew, amphetamines and other things, was she now a drug taker as well as a God knows what else? She had to be alone and frame her views before she saw Michael again. She had to have it out with him, what did he expect of her, what was going on? Lunch was served.

The men were absent, still out playing games or doing whatever international wheelers and dealers did. There was a chauffeur laid on to take Rachel back to London. The journey was tedious, and Rachel slept through most of the journey. On arriving home she went straight to the music studio and immersed herself in the Mozart for two pianos, her concert with Igor Franek was approaching fast, and although she was excited by the prospect, she was also apprehensive about her ability to live up to Franek's brilliance.

It was getting dark when she hauled her bag to the bedroom to unpack; her mind was at last beginning to clear and the events of the previous night, with a shock she remembered the lewd cabaret, the magnificent black male dancer. A sudden but irresistible surge of lust surged through her; she couldn't put the scenes out of her mind. She busied herself putting her things away, aware once more of the sensuous way Michael had chosen to dress her. She undressed and stood in the shower hoping the cascading water would rein back her desires, but they did not. She was uncontrollable, and rushed still wet to lie on her bed and there she relieved her almost unbearable desire.

In the sleep that followed there was no rest but constant dreams of unbelievable depravity. She awoke in the early morning disturbed as Michael slid into bed beside her, her troubled mind and aching body feigned a deep sleep, but Rachel remained lost and confused, troubled by the wildness of her sexuality, and the discovery that there was a world out there where the debauchery of Walmer's parties were routine happenings. It was a world where Michael was becoming at home, where she was being sucked in with an ever more consuming susceptibility. Alarmingly she did not know if she would be able to resist. She lay awake, aching to have Michael to herself, excited by the things she suspected had happened but she still could not be sure about. Despite herself she wanted to experience the excitement again, but next time to be there and to sense the full enjoyment.

As dawn broke early Michael stirred, he found Rachel awake and anxious to make love, which they did. Again Rachel dominated, devouring him until he was utterly spent. In the shower, he smiled to himself, she was his and she was all he ever wanted her to be. She would do anything he wanted, and he was sure he wanted a lot.

Rachel had a busy week ahead, a recital in Guildford on the Tuesday, a BBC recording on Wednesday, and she was due to leave for Saltsburg on Thursday. She was to practise and record on the Friday and the Concert for two pianos was to be on the Saturday.

Michael was aloof over breakfast, professing his disappointment that they would see so little of each other over the coming week. Neither mentioned the weekend, they were like strangers who shared a secret that neither would confess.

Michael went off to work with a brief kiss from Rachel, he muttered that he might be late; she closed the door locked in the vacuum of her own uncertainties. In the studio she found it difficult to concentrate. She played the works but almost remotely, it took the ghost of Eva to bring her back to the devouring demands of her trade. "Mozart, meine Liebe, can be played a sousand vays, make you vay ze best." She would try.

That afternoon she went to 'Hands' and relaxed in the wondrous comforts of Betty Grimshawe, they chatted as old friends as hairdressers and physiotherapists do.

"How's your husband dear, behaving himself is he?"

"Rather not talk about that if you don't mind Betty, I'm trying to get myself shipshape for Saltsburg, lot's to think about, none of it domestic."

"Well your wrists look to be fine, but the rest of you appears to have been in a wrestling match, that is if you don't mind me commenting on my patient's well being."

Rachel closed her eyes and the images of the night at the Walmers' came flooding back. Again there was an intensity and excitement that she found hard to suppress, and a simultaneous shock that made her shut her eyes so tight, so she could hide in the darkness of her shame. They were silent as Betty continued with her ministrations. Her skilled hands worked away the anxiety, and her hands and shoulders felt as if they'd been renewed by the energy of angel's wings.

Guildford was a shambles; she didn't know why, but it was by far and away the worst recital she had ever performed. She had failed entirely to get to the music, she had played mechanically, Eva would have turned in her grave. On the journey back to London she felt a dreadful panic. She was changed, from a musician who was a young and passionate woman, to a woman who was fast becoming an ordinary musician.

Somewhere she had lost her most precious gift, the gift of devotion to her music, that total absorption, that absolute commitment, the ability to sacrifice self awareness for her music. "Michael, oh Michael, what have we done? Have we sold our souls to the devil? Can't we be who we were, in love just for each other?"

The Chauffeur embarrassed by her loud wailing, turned and asked,

"Everything all right Miss?"

Rachel startled out of her misery replied, "Oh sorry, just tired, I'm fine." But she was not.

She arrived at the House at close to midnight, the hi-fi resonated through the hall, Michael was in the sitting room with Nicolai Mendova and Sarah, Sarah the procuress.

Rachel's heart stopped; at once she was furious and confused. Did they expect to carry on the party, the grossness of it made her want to vomit? Here in cold sobriety and in her own home she felt the weight of her upbringing, everything that she had been taught detached her from them; these interlopers, these dehumanizing flesh traders.

Michael, rose to greet her, he was drunk; "Hello my darling girl, I've brought your friends to see you, shall I pour you some champagne?"she stiffened under his sodden embrace.

"Oh, forgive me, I'm afraid I've had a difficult evening, it's been so nice to meet you Nicolai, but I'm so tired I've just got to go to bed." She turned and walked from the room escaping Michael's hopeless attempt to grab her. She went straight to the bedroom where she locked the door and sat petrified on their bed.

She hurriedly washed her face, took off her concert dress, and wrapped herself in her oldest house coat. Still there was only the noise of the music and the muted tones of the three revellers. Still Rachel was afraid to undress and go to bed; she paced the room not daring to drop her guard. The minutes passed like hours, and just as she was beginning to relax, she heard a tapping at her door. She paid no attention to it, she remained silent and frightened

The tapping grew more insistent. Rachel was not going to open the door.

"Rachel, it's Sarah, Michael asked me to fetch you down to say good bye to Nicolai, he's leaving in the morning."

Silence.

"Rachel, darling this is Michael, come down for five minutes sweetheart, just to see Nicolai, he's off in the morning, and he's been so good to us darling, it would be so bad mannered not to say good bye properly."

Silence.

"Rachel, I know you must be tired but, how about a little white pill, you seemed so much fun, come on down for a half hour or so, it'll help you unwind."

Rachel sat cuddling a pillow, afraid almost to breathe. If she made no noise they would go away. 'Please, please make them go away.' Exhaustion was now taking its toll but she was afraid to sleep. Where was the other bedroom door key?

"Rachel, its Sarah, here, I thought you'd like to see the photos of the party, I'll slide them under the door."

In the dim light Rachel saw the envelope slide under the door and into her consciousness, and she knew then, at that instant, that all could be lost or saved. She would not look at the photographs, no matter what they showed. She would try and sleep, they would not drag her where she did not want to go.

At last there was quiet, she crept from the bed and pulled the envelope from under the door and with shaking fingers she spread the contents on the bed. She could not make them out; she put on the bedside light. Rachel George-Johnson; harlot; filthy bitch, shocking, lascivious, disgusting, degraded, soiled, fouled, yet not raped.

She had been party to sex with strangers, with women, in a group; she had been party to the grossest indecency imaginable. Yet, yet there remained an excitement that she could not exorcise, despite her shame there remained within her a terrible lust that she would have to learn to repel.

She heard the taxi take Sarah and Nicolai, and she unlocked her door and waited for Michael, hoping despite her abject fatigue, that he was sober enough to fuck her to sleep.

Chapter 17

The flight to Saltsburg was miserable, Rachel felt exhausted after the dreadful night where'd she been made to face her demons. She was still low in confidence after her dreadful performance at Guildford, and on top of this she feared that she would not be able to support young Franek. Igor, the original musical geek, yet despite his curious looks and his stunted conversation there was a genius, a brilliance far beyond her own musical skill.

Max Luberoff sat as ever fidgeting at her side. Through the last month or so Rachel had seen little of Max, she had been alone without her guardians, Eva gone forever and she still felt the grief, but she'd missed Max too. Ever since Michael had assaulted Max in the house, Max had understandably avoided coming to see her. They now either met at M.I.L's London office or more often they had long telephone calls discussing her engagement calendar and programme development. She missed Max, and it was a comfort to have him at her side for this engagement. However nothing much escaped Max's attention.

"Darling," Max sipped his drink, "you have to tell Max what you've been up to. You are, how can I say – not how you were. A little bird tells me that you were awful in Guildford, though fortunately there were no real 'music' people in the audience. Darling you are never awful – tell Max what is my beautiful girl doing to make her awful?"

"Oh Max, Guildford was awful, but it was just an off night, I wasn't really into the programme." She turned to look at the crisp white sun lit clouds knowing that Max would not let it go.

"Max loves you, you know that darling, so don't tell me silly tales – this morning darling you look nearly awful – any man would love to take you, but I have never seen you so –" he hesitated, "tired, grey, worn out, and Max knows this is not from playing the piano."

"Max leave it alone, let's just say I've had a couple of off days, I'm fine though I'm a bit worried about keeping up the pace with wonder boy Igor."

"Max needs to know darling, that's what I'm for…. to look after you," his eyes rotated wildly, "Rachel if you fail, I fail. My last eight years have been devoted to building your career; I cannot let you put it all at risk. So…." He finished his drink and waved his glass at the stewardess for another. "You have to tell Max what is wrong." He held her hand gently, "look my darling you can talk to Max, Max knows about things, so trust me darling, if well,… if there's something personal like …. you know family…. husbands etcetera, etcetera, Max is OK to talk with."

"Max please leave it alone, I'm fine." Rachel detached her hand. The conversation moved to her coaching, nobody could ever understand how she missed Eva. She couldn't wait for the journey to end.

Igor Franek had not changed; he was still a charming gawky adolescent with his piercing eyes peering out from under his bushy eyebrows. He still stood flagstaff straight, and still greeted Rachel with his delightful innocence. After a light lunch they went to the concert house where the chamber orchestra was already set up, the maestro was a little known but apparently brilliant young Austrian conductor Rupert Nessler. Nessler was the antithesis of Franek, though only twenty five he was intensely stylish and Rachel's first impression was that of a young Simon Rattle. He was slender, with carefully styled hair, fine features and long elegant hands. He was in fact what everyone's idea of what a young maestro would be. Rachel was suspicious.

Nessler spoke accentless English, was courtesy itself and for once Rachel did not sense any predatory male threat; he was after all four years younger than her. In fact the whole concert was a testimony to youth. Rachel was the oldest musician on the platform. The Orchestra was made up of young musicians drawn from the European Youth Orchestra so that the average age of orchestra, soloists and conductor was less than twenty five. She and Igor parenthesized the group at twenty nine and eighteen.

Nessler was in command, he brought the orchestra to order, introduced the soloists, there was the usual polite applause. Igor, Rachel and Nessler, discussed briefly their part, choices and tempi, and then they settled to rehearsal.

Rachel found Nessler too pedantic, they never seemed to get into the first movement without Nessler constantly stopping and pointing out this and that to members of the Orchestra. After about the ninth interruption, Igor stood and gesticulating to the maestro;

"Maestro, please, let's just take it through, ….. all straight through, then you can ….we can see what we thought……please Rachel and me, we must get some …how you say …some feel …some give and take from the pianos.." He sat down and gave Rachel the most outrageous wink.

Nessler approached Rachel, "I feel we need to be absolutely clear about the tempi, and I'm not that comfortable with the strings, violas to be precise."

"Rupert, may I call you Rupert, I think Igor has a point if we go right through we'll all be able to get in touch, it'll be fine, I think the violas are fine." 'Pompous ass' she thought to herself.

Nessler duly obliged and they went straight through the concerto from top to bottom. The pianos absolutely fizzed. The magic had not deserted her, and working with a genius like Igor just carried her along, her tiredness lifted and she was back where she belonged, making music with all her heart and soul.

At the end the orchestra applauded not out of politeness but out of enthusiasm, even Nessler stopped preening, and was aware of how special these two pianists were. He had joined the spirit of the moment and the Orchestra had been a delight.

Igor beamed a smile and as soon as the hubbub died down, launched into the fugue for two pianos, Rachel joined in and they romped through it again to the delight of the young orchestra. At the end of this piece, Igor came round to Rachel took her hand and they bowed to the orchestra, generously he enjoined Nessler to the team hug and then they broke for coffee. Rachel felt the hubris of being home, back in the warmth of music and musicians. This concert had all the hall marks of something special, the miseries of Guildford faded from her mind. Nessler wanted to rehearse areas he felt they could improve, Igor protested there was no need, Rachel as the senior musician was reluctant to side with either, but in any case the sound engineers wanted to do some microphone balancing so they had to play the concerto some more. In fact Nessler had several good points, Igor was tending to run away with things, even from the second part, and was if anything too precise in the slower movement. Igor though was not a bit put out by Nessler's proposals and modified his performance without a second's thought. He could see other musical points of view with such speed it was breathtaking.

The orchestra was dismissed and Igor and Rachel went through the rest of the programme. Just as before, the chemistry between them was electric. The recording crew canned the sonata k448, and the fugue. The small body of guests in the great hall were mesmerized by the brilliance and the empathy of these two young people who had only played together for a matter of a few hours. Max Luberoff could hardly contain himself; he spent the rest of the afternoon with Franek senior and the host of recording executives and impresarios "striking my darling, while the iron is on!"

The hall was sold out, the unusual nature of the concert had seen to that, the first part was given over to the pieces for two pianos and after the interval they were to play the concerto. They kept the fugue for the encore.

Rachel could not help but be nervous, Igor on the other hand fooled around as if they were just going to play for each other as if the audience did not exist. As the time came for their entrance, Igor took both Rachel's hands in his; "Rachel, Mozart can be played a thousand ways, but our way will be of the best. Any way I will play for you, and you must play for me, zat way it will be fun." He bowed his formal little bow, he looked so young; Rachel could not help but kiss him on the cheek. "Let's do it."

The whole night went off without a hitch, the first part they played as if they'd been brought up together. Their sense of each other was uncanny, their performance almost flawless. The audience adored these two young geniuses who delivered a sparkling night that no one there was ever likely to forget. Not since Liverpool those light years ago did Rachel feel so moved, the crowd roared as Igor gave Rachel a huge hug at the end of the first half. It was simply stupendous.

The concerto went wonderfully too, Nessler and the orchestra were sensitive and responsive, Nessler even restrained Igor, reminding him with an elegant wave of his baton what they'd agreed that afternoon in rehearsal. For Rachel the fantasy was that she was part of it, saw it, felt it, understood it and in her way commanded it. At the end the three of them stood; Nessler at the centre. Igor and Rachel received their bouquets, Igor graceless and awkward, Rachel ravishing and graceful. It seemed that the applause would never end. They made six curtain calls, then Nessler in his imperious way signalled for calm and the audience subsided. Igor and Rachel took their places and they played the fugue. The hall went mad; the Austrians who are expected to be so disciplined shouted and shouted Encore! Encore! They stamped their feet and they clapped as if there were no tomorrow. A quick conference with Nessler and they played the last movement of the concerto again.

There was a huge party afterwards at the Bristol Hotel. Max announced at the press conference to the delight of both pianists that MIL and Igor's managers had come to an arrangement where they would be performing this concert programme 'in the footsteps of Mozart', certainly in Paris, Prague and Vienna. The Orchestral arrangements awaited confirmation, it was hoped that Nessler would be their maestro again but this remained unresolved as the dates, of course, were to be finalized. There were some final negotiations but agreement had been reached by Concordia and Sony to co-operate in the release of the live concert recording.

Rachel felt cleansed from her guilt, euphoric at finding her talent that she'd thought was lost, and delighted to be with Igor, whose adolescent charm and directness she found engaging. Max was at his fussy best, trying hard to resist the surfeit of champagne and an unmistakable attraction for Rupert Nessler. Rupert was not entirely averse to Max's charms. Rachel imagined that if Max continued to drink at his frenetic rate, it would not be long before he did something outrageous, Rupert became the most likely of targets. To Max's annoyance she squeezed between them;

"Max you must be a good boy and look after your client," she whispered conspiratorially

"Darling, you just fight off young Igor whose ardour knows no bounds," he whinnied, downing more wine. They jockeyed for position at dinner, Max becoming petulant in that he was kept at a distance from Rupert.

Rachel sat between Max and Igor, Max fidgeting as always, Igor restrained under the close supervision of his father Jan. After dinner where everyone including Max behaved well, there were more photo calls. Rachel and Igor were taken off to the piano bar where they sat cosily side by side on the piano stool.

"I shall be your lover!" Igor's statement pronounced with his stilted Germanic Silesian accent was clipped and matter of fact. Almost ridiculous, but not quite. Rachel humoured him as best she could, but knew in her heart of hearts that Igor's passion, eighteen or not, was going to be a problem. Igor sidled up to Rachel, "how can we make music so perfectly and not be lovers?" His bushy eyebrows raised comically above his coal black eyes, his smile, not ugly almost beguiling.

"That's what's perfect Igor, and that's what we shall keep perfect. You and me we're piano partners, put your passion into your music, there will be hundreds of girls out there who would die just to be seen with you. Me, I'm a complicated married lady." She touched his arm, teetering on the brink of saying something she would regret. She looked into the eyes that hid so much, past the pasty geekish smile; she almost felt his rampant ardour. "Igor you'll just have to respect me, and I'll be your friend and we'll keep our emotions for our music. Now we both need a good night's rest, more photo calls and press conference in the morning." She kissed him primly on the cheek and made her way to her room.

"One day, uggh; Rachel, one day. Good night I love you."

She didn't turn but walked resolutely to her empty bed. There her demons returned, her desires rose despite her efforts to sublimate them. The horrors of those photographs, the fear of the future, her desire for Michael all tumbled in upon her, as she eased herself into pleasure and sleep. Igor faded from her vision, Michael, her Michael she wanted him despite the persistent vision of Sarah that she could not exorcise.

Chapter 18

Max was absolutely beside himself with delight. Their journey back to London was pleasant and Rachel eventually arrived back at the Mews in the early evening.

The phone was ringing as she opened the door, it was Sally Nye who'd heard all the news from Saltsburg, "Sounds wonderful Rachel, congratulations, I hear you're going to tour next year with Franek, you've found your musical core or perhaps an extension of it."

"Maybe, it's certainly exciting, reminds me a bit of the Lyon Quartet, it's a very intimate form of music, I never thought I'd enjoy it so much. Igor is of course utterly unbelievably brilliant and he has a kind of drive that is.... I don't know.... exhilarating!"

"That's not what I hear; I gathered you led the concerto with terrific drive.... Tom Driver rang me and said it was the best thing to happen in Salzburg for twenty years, praise indeed my dear, anyway well done.... I must dash.... Be in touch."

And so it went on, phone calls from Concordia, a message from Cy Allman, a call from Jamo Jadesjo, who said he was jealous and who was this Nessler guy? They laughed and looked forward to their next meeting in Gothenburg. There were calls from the magazines, the broadcasting companies all requesting interviews, she turned them all over to MIL.

Michael barged in at seven-ish, he immediately picked her up and kissed her passionately, he smelled of Brandy, and vaguely of perfume. Still it was what she wanted and they tore the clothes from each other and lurched to the bedroom where they had wild sex. Rachel could not contain her passion; so much was pent up inside her.

Michael was commanding but at the same time compliant and it was one of those occasions when they gave to each other in equal measure, they fed on each other's desire.

"Have you looked at your photos, you little whore?"

"Oh yes, we've got to get rid of them, Michael just shut up and do what you're doing ....some more," she urged herself riding up and down forward and backward over his prone hips and manhood.

"Christ they are the most erotic things I've ever seen, Jesus Rachel, you could make more money as a porn queen than a pianist."

"Michael if you don't shut up, you're going to break the spell, now fuck me some more."

"My my, Mozart does make you randy."

When they had consumed each other they showered, dressed in their casuals and slipped round to the "Grenadier" for drinks and a meal.

Rachel was happy, released from tension, she loved Michael physically, he was like a drug she couldn't get enough of him. Even when he was at his most extreme she knew that despite her fear, she adored to be his. They talked about Saltsburg, he probed in his silly way about Igor, and sounded almost as if he wanted Rachel to have bedded the boy and reported back to him. But he looked so lovely, he was such a good looking man, and he was hers, and Rachel knew that nothing had really changed, she loved him unreservedly.

They talked about Michael's passed day or so, he readily admitted he'd been to the 'Gaslight' Club that afternoon, 'entertaining' clients from unlikely Middle East countries.

"Nearly drank too much my love, could have dampened my ardour." He laughed and ordered another pint of bitter, "what about you darling, what'll you have?"

"Another red wine, but that's the last."

They sat in silence watching the other drinkers and diners. There was an ease between them so complete that they both could sense the other's thoughts. Rachel knew she was his possession, despite all her independent principles, she knew she belonged to him.

Michael knew that at last she was his. They smiled knowingly at each other, "Come on," he said, "I think I want my evil way with you again."

Rachel sank her red wine in one draught, "Then we'd better get going."

They almost ran the short distance back to the house; there they left a trail of clothing through the hall up the stairs to the bedroom. It was as if they'd been apart for eternity rather than a little more than an hour since they'd last made love.

The wine took its effect on Rachel who happily slipped into their erotic games, Michael produced the cuff restraints, as Rachel lay helpless he rained erotic pleasures on her with his tongue, teasing her until she was almost demented. Then when she thought she could bear it no more Michael raised himself from her and stood at the end of the bed and looked down at her.

"Rachel you're the most sexy woman in the world, what men would pay to fuck you, they'd give the world."

He reached behind him and produced the photographs from the Walmer's party, and lay beside her once more, he showed them to her at the same time continuing his erotic treats.

Involuntarily Rachel bucked under his ministrations unable to shut out the stimulation of the reminders of that astonishing and erotic adventure at the Walmers. It was wrong, the shadow of what she'd done echoed like a chorus of ominous double basses, an ominous undertone to the symphony of their erotic bliss.

"Look, Rachel, look you're in heaven, Sarah said she'd never been to bed with anyone as exciting as you, he ran his tongue down her stomach, and Nicolai, well he thought you were worth half a billion."

"You bastard," Rachel was engulfed in the sensuality of it, and succumbed to a climax of volcanic proportions. But there was that undertone of regret and fear, not so much about what she'd been persuaded to do – however lewd or shocking – she knew she had fed the poison that she was driving her precious Michael to very dark places. Places of evil where there could only be hell on earth.

The following day was spent with Max in MIL where there was yet another press conference; Rachel was taken aback at the pace of things. This was the nearest she had become to being a celebrity, even in the muted world of Classical music.

Concordia had put forward a whole range of proposals that were due to be resolved by the month end. What all this meant was an extremely busy schedule on top of an already crowded diary. Max though was excited and delighted, at the rate of career enhancement, Rachel could be in MIL's top ten artists by year end. From a money standpoint Rachel could be assured of a life time's security with just three or four years' hard work.

Despite the fame and hubris of the moment Rachel was always conscious of Michael's ability to ignore what ever went on in her musical world. He treated each piece of news with a casual "Well done" or "Good show" and almost inevitably exhibited annoyance when Rachel had to be away giving a performance. She tried to involve him but he seldom engaged in conversations about her impending travel and work schedule. He still barged into the studio and interrupted her practice as if her piano playing was an incidental hobby. His own schedule with the Walmer bank was as busy as ever and he flitted from one obscure country to the next, so that once more they became ships passing in the night.

Rachel yearned to spend time together, but their liaisons when they had a moment together were almost always exclusively sexual and Michael became more and more distracted. The only common happening was the return of Michael's jealous fits, particularly when he had been drinking. Sadly this was more often the case than not. Michael ranted about Max and then Igor who had been much in her diary lately, and Cy Alman, whether he were involved with her work or not. This constant badgering had become very wearing; Rachel felt weary and began to find herself looking forward but at the same time dreading their infrequent times together at home. There was the same old passion but at the same time fear, fear of his ranting and sometimes brutal and cruel couplings. His beautiful face was often contorted with a jealous rage of imaginary infidelities, all this fed by the evidence of that fateful night at the Walmers. Rachel wanted to wash the slate clean but Michael's obsession seemed implacable.

There were times when Michael was his gentle kind and loving self; Jekyll or Hyde, Rachel never knew what to expect. Despite all the success she was lonely; she had not found a coach/mentor since Eva's demise.

When she arrived home, she was relieved if Michael was not there but at the same time disappointed. She spent hours in the studio with Becky working, practising and assimilating an ever widening repertoire. Her music was becoming her singular companion, there was solace and there was joy, there was contemplation and there was challenge. Music was the love she could trust, music demanded of her extraordinary commitment, a commitment she remained ready to deliver. The emotional roller coaster with Michael sometimes drained her and even in the most intimate moments, she felt her musical master urge her to save herself for the devotion that her muse must have.

She had changed, in just the last year she was barely recognizable as the young pretty talented also ran, she was emerging as a pianist of international renown. In herself she knew lay the enemy of her ambition; her susceptibility, her vulnerability to the man she still loved despite all the abuse and all the pain. There gaped inside her a yawning pit of sadness, a pit she longed to close and to heal. Her desire to see Michael as he once was, was insatiable. Her love remained unshakable despite the inevitable tragedy that she knew lay ahead.

Time raced by, each day, each week seemed more crowded than the one before. Igor Franek became a frequent visitor to London and they had nine engagements booked over the next twelve months in the series in 'Mozart's footsteps.' The format had been changed, now each of them played a solo sonata, then they played the double concerto, then the other would play a solo sonata and they would end with the duet. The format was sensational and they drew rave notices where ever they appeared. Igor was changing too, he was maturing musically and becoming more assured socially. He no longer looked gangly and awkward, at least not to Rachel. Nessler was not able to appear at many of the venues because of complications with the orchestral arrangements with the attached conductors. Despite this the magic remained.

In London they played with the Orchestra of the Age of Enlightenment with Roger Norrington, The concert was a smash; Norrington was as far as Rachel was concerned the most accomplished Maestro she'd ever worked with. He sat in the individual sonata rehearsals and was a wonderful commentator and coach; he was absolutely empathic and even had Igor eating out of his hand. The whole experience was a wonder and once more Rachel was astonished and thrilled to be part of such a superb musical event made special by the superlative talents of Norrington, Igor and the delightfully musical ensemble.

Rachel's only disappointment was that Sir Roger could not attend the after concert supper party at the Savoy hosted by the series sponsors. As usual there were VIP guests, Governors of the Orchestra, the leader, and assorted dignitaries all of whom were a delight. Igor and Rachel were given a warm and enthusiastic reception.

Igor for some reason was without the normally present father and watch dog, Jan Franek, he had been entrusted to the care of Max. The supper started with much syrupy complimenting by the sponsor who presented both Igor and Rachel with a watch of much worth. There was a discussion on Mozart's visit to London in 1764 and his meeting with J.S. Bach, Rachel's home territory, and she waxed poetically about her two heroes. Igor in the meantime distracted by his freedom consumed more than his fair share of wine, Max of course was already over the top and took little if any notice of the decline of the young Franek.

"Is she not the most beautiful of all musicians.?"

Franek was standing or rather swaying at the next table apparently proposing a toast. He held his glass filled indecently full.

"I tell you," he announced, " Rghhachel is most beeautifool musician and I love to play with her." There was a stony silence.

Rachel was appalled. Where was Max?

" Rghhachel I tell you, you are the most wanderfool....
Mozart he would love you like me...." he staggered, started
to sit then thought better of it, Rachel wanted to be
swallowed up; where the hell was Max?

"In London, you very fine people," continued the inebriated
Igor, " Mozart and Bach they are meeting here long ago,
maybe here in Savoy....now Rachel George-Johnson and Igor
Franek we meet, same thing.... we make music, I love this
music, I love herrr!" At which point he collapsed into his
chair.

There followed a smattering of embarrassed applause. At
that point there was a shuffling and Max re-appeared from
stage left, Igor seemed to have passed out.

The party broke up, the sponsor was very polite and quite
understood the strain of travel and the artistic
temperament. Igor had recovered to some extent, though
his English had quite deserted him and he mumbled in
Polish.

"Max how could you?" Rachel was furious, ""how could you
let Igor drink so much?"

"He was fine, earlier." Max, his eyes rolling in their frenetic
way shuffled uncertainly, like a small school boy found guilty
of smoking behind a shed.

"His father will go berserk if he learns what happened
tonight, have you any idea what would happen if we called
off the rest of the series?"

"Darling, it won't happen, no one will find out, this I promise."

"What are we to do with him? Poor silly boy."

 Igor looked pathetically about him, he had reverted in a moment to a little boy lost, just as she remembered him in Saltszburg.

 "Come on let's get the young man a coffee and then to bed, we have a conference with 'Gramophone' don't we in the morning – What time?"

"Ten o clock my dear, we shall be fine – tonight was another triumph darling – you are well and truly on your way."

"Max never mind all that, let's get Igor to bed." At that moment they heard him wretch, and saw Igor Franek's evening come to a very undignified end indeed. The management of the Savoy with impeccable courtesy cleaned up and provided a wheel chair to transport the unconscious prodigy to his bed chamber. Max and Rachel escorted the cortege as it was manoeuvred through the labyrinth that is the Savoy to Mr. Franek's suite. There the staff respectfully and tidily undressed the unconscious young man and put him to bed in his comical pyjamas. Rachel and Max waited nervously in the drawing room and left quietly to the less than melodic tones of Igor's snores.

Rachel made her weary way home to the empty house; Michael as usual was away in some country with an improbable name. She could not escape the exquisite sounds of Igor's playing, the way he drew her into the harmony, the magnetism of his musicianship that drew the most natural and the best from her. She felt a desire to hold the silly boy and feel the music in his bones.

In his suite at the Savoy, Igor snored in the deepest of alcoholic comas, but in his deepest dream the adolescent becoming man dreamed of the perfection that was Rachel, her music, her incredible ear, but above all her sensuality and femininity. He had known nothing like it, the heat of his infatuation boiled his sub conscious and imprinted an obsession that could sublimate even his love of Mozart.

Despite the omens, the press reception went well, Igor and Rachel sat each with their PR advisor fielding a variety of questions, most of them serious and musically focused. However towards the end of the conference a young female correspondent asked;

"Since Rachel and Igor show such remarkable musical empathy is there any romantic link between you two?"

The PR man with Rachel immediately dismissed the question. Igor went into an intimate conversation with his minder in his native language.

"Does Mr. Franek have a comment?" the young woman reporter insisted.

Again the PR people dismissed the question and the conference broke up.

In that evening's London paper, the headline read; 'Stars in their eyes,' the article went on quite sensibly but ended with;

 "Could it be that these superstars of the classical piano have more in common than just playing the piano? Such empathy was uncanny; clearly these two young musicians, despite their age difference, are soul mates with more than just music on their minds."

On the following day there was a piece in the gossip column about how Rachel and 'her entourage had escorted the paralytic Pole to his Savoy suite.'

Rachel had a call from her stepmother Lady Jacqui George, full of advice on how to respond.

"Just weather the storm it'll all go away in a day or two."

 Rachel was appalled, but the MIL people seemed sanguine about it all and Max merely smirked, "darling, it's all part of becoming a celebrity" he giggled, "You're such a luscious morsel my darling, your reputation could do with a little spicing up, good for sales."

Rachel came as close as ever she had, to slapping Max firmly across the face. She burst into tears. "Max you absolute bastard, have you any idea what Michael will make of this when he gets home?"

"Don't worry darling, it will all have died down by then, he need never know."

"That's just it Max, there is nothing to know, for God's sake all we did was take poor Igor to his room, and any way it's your fault, he should never have been allowed to drink so much. What will his father say?" The tears flowed once more. She collapsed into Max's arms.

"Darlink, my sweet girl, has Max been a beast? I'm sorry, I just assumed he could drink like anyone else, and then when I got back from a toilet call, there he was being ridiculous. He is a silly boy."

"Oh Max, that's just it, he's not a silly boy, he's a genius who needs our support to be one of the greats; he's never been outside Poland or the Russian Academy on his own, never mind drinking in the Savoy, what were you thinking of?"

"What has happened has happened, we must learn, I, Max Luberoff will write to Franek Senior and apologize for my lack of diligence, then everything will be alright."

"Max, I do hope so, I do hope so! Any way I must get ready to get up to the BBC for 'In Tune', please God, Sean Rafferty sticks to the script."

Sean Rafferty, as always the scholar and gentleman, was charm itself and Rachel enjoyed the Radio 3 live show. She chatted to Rafferty and played three contrasting pieces, Bach, Grieg and Bela Bartok. Everything she thought, as the chauffeur brought her back home, would be fine.

Rachel, despite the ease of the Rafferty interview, continued to be plagued by her fear that Michael would somehow find out about the mischievous press reports and have another of his jealous ravings. As the days went by, despite a busy schedule of practice and a recital, her mind could not escape what she felt were bound to be horrendous consequences. There was no one she could confide in except….except Jacqui George.

The night before Michael's return she arranged dinner with Jacqui who as before took her to her favourite Knightsbridge restaurant. Again the Krug flowed liberally. Rachel found great comfort in Jacqui's worldly attitudes and the nonchalant attitude to men and their moods.

"When he gets home tomorrow, Rachel, give him a welcome to remember, give him such a treat, he'll be reminded where heaven really is, in bed with you."

Rachel now relaxed by the Champagne easily drifted into the scenario of giving Michael all his favourite bedtime treats, but his contorted grimace of jealousy repeatedly interrupted her reverie.

"I hope you're right Jacqui, but.... can I tell you something in confidence? .. It's about Michael, he seems to be getting more and more jealous.... ever since he had those accidents he's just got worse and worse,...." she began to cry.

"Oh come on my dear, you can tell me everything, a problem shared is a problem eased...." she patted Rachel on her shoulder and handed her a napkin.

Rachel told her everything, about Josie Fellowes, about how Michael had almost strangled her during sex, how he'd become very excited as he'd fantasised about her infidelities, how he'd damaged her wrists and threatened her; all from her secret and darkened memory of Michael's excesses.

"When Michael was ill we saw a psychiatrist who asked me if I'd seen any change in his behaviour.... but I lied.... I said no.... I believed he'd get better and be my lovely Michael again, and sometimes he is."

"Have you talked to this Doctor again?"

"No, every time I think about doing something – anything, Michael seems his old self again, kind, gentle, passionate, the man I married."

Lady George blew a perfect smoke ring over the coffee table in the hotel drawing room, "A trick I learned at school .... ever thought of leaving him?"

"Yes, but only for the odd moment, you see I love him, I love him so much, it hurts." Rachel started to cry again.

"Jealousy is a terrible thing. Love is sometimes crazy, both are the product of each other, but jealousy can destroy your happiness and his. The world is full of battered wives who say they love their husbands; I don't think you ought to be one of them. Rachel for your own sake, go and see this doctor who ever he is and see if Michael can be helped, if not honey you have to think about disengaging." She drank more coffee. " You of all people have everything going for you, you can be a star in your own life, not just some five minute wonder but a wonderful talent who's already got an international reputation. No man is worth what you are going through, so fix it through the doctor or ship out."

Rachel listened, the words tumbled over her but already she was rejecting the advice, maybe.... maybe she would contact Dr. Lucas.

Chapter 19

Michael's return was not unusual in many aspects. He was tired - not surprising - he'd travelled from Georgia to Moscow to London that day. He seemed genuinely glad to be home and after a shower and coffee they made love with all the passion and gentleness that affection and weariness would predicate. They dined as usual at the Grenadier and Michael was sound asleep by ten o clock. Rachel lay at his side happy, happy that all her fears were unfounded that Michael was as he used to be and from now on all would be as it should be.

The weekend was unusual in that they were both at home with no engagements either social or professional. On Saturday they walked in Green Park, Michael napped in the afternoon, they dined, just the two of them that evening, in Beauchamp Place, and happily did not see a soul they knew.

On Sunday morning their blissful weekend came to an abrupt end with Sir Bradley Walmer summoning Michael to a meeting at the West End Offices. They kissed a breezy farewell and Michael avowed he'd be home by mid afternoon.

Rachel listened to the empty house and as soon as Michael closed the door behind him, she felt the chill of fear. All that was so lovely she knew for certain would be smashed to smithereens when Michael had spent time with Walmer, that evil man who conspired to turn Michael against her; the man so invidiously powerful, his presence was everywhere like a stinking poison.

She went down to the studio and Becky and tried as hard as she could to concentrate on the work that lay there in massive abundance. However, try as she might, she felt the sickness in her stomach of the terror that must come once Michael had been fed the worst of the press releases and stories that Walmer was bound to give to Michael. She wept in her frustration knowing that whatever the truth, whatever the goodness of her relationship with Igor, Michael would burn it up as fuel for his fantasising and consuming jealousy.

Not even JS could rescue her, the sickening fear gripped her, reducing her ability to think, or even look ahead at what to do next. The minutes passed like hours, the heaven of the last two days slipped away in a freezing mist of despair. Eventually she thought of contacting Michael's parents, and perhaps asking them over for tea, or Bertie, or even her mother. But really there was no one, no one who'd understand, because Michael would be sweetness and light until they were alone, and then – then the devil in him would rise up and consume him and devour their tenderness in the bile of his jealousy. She knew it as sure as night would follow day, yet she was powerless, absolutely vulnerable there was nowhere to run and hide, nowhere to shelter from the storm, nowhere where the terror would not find her.

It was four o' clock when her heart stopped as she heard the key in the door, she sat rigidly in the sitting room, staring at, but not seeing the Sunday papers. Michael looked at ease, he smiled, bent and kissed her gently on the top of her head.

"Lonely, darling? Sorry to have been so long."

She caught the whiff of scotch on his breath.

"Missed you of course, I can't think when we've had a whole weekend together." She went over and gently took the scotch decanter from him and nuzzled his neck.

"My, aren't you the one," he said pushing her softly, but surely to one side.

"Isn't it a little early for whisky!"

"Oh, come on dear, Mikey's been hard at work since this morning." He poured a very large scotch. "Why don't you join me?"

"Tea's fine for me, maybe a little later."

He sat and picked up the papers, "any reviews about my brilliant wife this week?" He spread open the arts section, where sure enough there was a very complimentary review of the Mozart concert of the Tuesday before.

"You and Ivan or whatever his name is seem to be a bit of a hit." His casual remark failed to hide the emerging malice in his voice. "What were the earlier reviews like?"

"Very good actually, Igor by the way, not Ivan, and he's a super talent and Roger Norrington was fabulous to work with, it really went well."

"So I see, when's your next outing with the super brat?"

"As always we're trying to fit everything in, you know, my diary and his, venues, orchestras, I'm very busy up to the Prom and then I'm off to Scandinavia with the Gothenburg, so probably in October."

Michael swallowed his scotch and reached for the bottle again.

"Michael, darling, please don't drink that it's not even five yet and you're taking me out for dinner – remember?" She felt herself shake as she spoke, but her hands shook as she felt the wave of his rage rise like an inevitable tide.

"Don't tell me how to drink, darling," 'Darling' he spat at her. "It must be hard for you to be away from darling Igor, the superstar, for a whole two months, you must miss him – eh?"

"It's work, you know that Michael, it's work; yes Igor is extraordinary and I'm very lucky to have been able to work with him – but its work – that's all."

"Oh, that's all is it, just work! Well since when does work entail taking your partner to bed?" He staggered to his jacket and pulled the neatly folded Wednesday edition scandal sheet and brandished it in front of her nose. "Work, my pretty one; taking Igor to bed ?"

" Darling, you know that it has been exaggerated, both Max and I helped poor Igor to bed after he drank too much at the reception," she appealed, already knowing that once Michael had started his rant there would be no going back, " please Michael don't be silly, you know there is no one in my life except you."

"No one, eh? What about all the musicians, bloody Max and all his queer friends, what about Cy Alman, and don't forget I was with you at the Walmer party and I've got the pictures to prove it." He staggered into the bedroom and emerged waving those dreadful pictures.

Rachel recoiled into a confused hopelessness, she shook with fear and the tears poured down her crumpled face.

"You know that you got me into that horrible situation at the Walmers 'I didn't know what I was doing, and all the rest is untrue. You know it's untrue." She launched herself into his arms. "You're the only one, the only one...." The tears poured down her face.

Then there was a violent snatching of her hair, her head jerked back and she stared into eyes that she did not know. Michael glared a venomous look that increased her fear to levels so far unknown. Her breathing stopped as she tumbled backwards as Michael dragged her from the sitting room, she felt a sharp pain as her shoulder collided with the door as Michael half carried, half dragged her to the bedroom.

"Michael, no, no don't do this." She felt the pain and the tears merge into an agony more profound than anything she had known. She watched from outside herself as Michael tore her clothes from her, invaded her without any emotion except a vengeful indulgence and the pain of his weight as her pinned her down with his knees, his elbows and his hands. The deed was vulgar, it was dirty, it was foul. All the pain meant little, but her heart broke, that it had come to this, as she knew it would. That was the worst part of the whole ghastly experience, she had known it would come to this, and yet she had done nothing to avoid it. She felt an insidious guilt that compounded the pain.

The storm when it cleared, was soon a distant memory even a second after, Michael was asleep. Rachel picked herself out of bed, rushed to the shower to scrub away the nightmare. Then she hurried to hide her torn clothing and any signs of the incident. Like a criminal she crept around the house erasing any remnant of Michael's rage.

Her wrists though hurt and she knew instantly that her fingers and hands were somehow incapacitated, they felt stiff and painful. A look in the mirror showed a welt rising on her lip and a bruise begin to form under her eye. Her breasts hurt, her legs and vagina all had visible signs of the savagery of Michael's attack.

She made up as best she could, dressed and talked to herself, she stood admiring her make-up job in front of the mirror, "welcome to the world of the battered wife," She sighed, and yet.... and yet.... was it her fault ? She loved him still, she knew now that he would get better, she knew now that he would get worse, the point was that it didn't matter, she loved him still, she could handle it.

Chapter 20

There was no doubt the following morning that her hands and wrists were badly bruised, her right arm particularly was bruised right down her forearm, with a very black bruise near the heel of her hand. Her left hand was less badly damaged. Her face wasn't so bad as she could hide most of the damage with rather heavier than usual make up.

Hastily she rang 'Hands' and got an appointment with Bettie for one o clock, Bettie's usual lunch hour. Rachel filled the morning reading her studies, tried to play but she could not. The middle fingers on her right hand particularly were very stiff and there was a sharp pain in her right elbow.

Clad in sun glasses and a long sleeve cashmere sweater despite the warm overcast day, she arrived early at 'Hands'. She had avoided Max's phone calls and also avoided looking at her diary. Rachel clung to the ordinariness of life. Last night was just a tantrum and everything was alright. She just had to get this hand better and all would return to normal. She shuffled the magazines, impatient to see Bettie who, as always, would make things better.

"Hello darling" greeted the jolly Physio, what brings you here so urgently, eh? Let's have a look dear."

Rachel saw Bettie's expression change," Look, I'll have to get Dr Bloom down to have a look dear, you know these injuries are serious don't yah. You poor mite, what have you been up to?"

With that she left Rachel who once more started to cry as the enormity of Michael's behaviour dawned on her. She felt lonely and bereft, lost with no idea what to do or where to go. Rachel George-Johnson, the upcoming international star was lonely, hurt and lost. Michael, would Michael change and make it all better? Something deep within her whispered 'Don't give up, don't give up' and her heart ached and she knew she wouldn't; come what may.

The remainder of the afternoon was spent, not with Bettie, but having her forearms and wrists scanned. There were no breaks, thanks to the strength and training, but the bruises were deep and there could well be injury to tendons and serious swelling within the wrist of her right hand. Rest was the imperative, no piano for at least ten days and physiotherapy every day, after two days complete rest. Dr Bloom also warned her that there could be residual damage, although they would have to wait and see.

Rachel had already decided that her injuries were the result of a fall, a fall forward down the stairs to the studio. She imagined the fall forward, her arms outstretched and the consequent injuries to her inner arms and wrists as she went head first down the stairs. It was already four thirty when Rachel emerged from the 'Hands' medical wing, sun glasses and long sleeves still her first defence against reality. She phoned Max, whose reaction was sympathetic but as always agitated. Agitated about postponing or cancelling engagements, anxious about a defined time for recovery and agitated about getting a full medical report for the insurer.

Rachel for her part played the whole thing off as an unfortunate but unavoidable accident. The more she lied the more real the fall scenario became. Both their main concern was the approaching Prom that was only five weeks away. Should they warn the producers and Jamo of the potential inability to perform? Max said he must, Rachel argued that she was absolutely sure that she would be fit and ready to play. Max countered that there would be a long break in her practice regime and this would almost certainly jeopardize her readiness and that she could not possibly know the prognosis.

Their telephone debate continued all the way home and at the end there seemed to be no real agreement, Rachel knew that in the last analysis MIL would have the final say. She let herself in with difficulty as her right wrist was bound and her hand supported on a rigid metal splint. She had hardly got in, when the phone went and Max telephoned once more,

" Darling, tomorrow we will meet with Dr Bloom and a medical advisor of ours, we want to be sure that everything is covered."

"Max is everything necessary? You know Bloom is the top man, he's already done all the scans and everything, I can't see what another so called expert can add, apart from that Max I shall be fine."

"Darling, I know you'll be fine, but be at 24 Harley Street at ten sharp, Bloom's private practice, I'll be there with our man Morrison. – sorry Rachel, but you must be there darling." With that he hung up.

Rachel caught sight of her face in the mirror, the bruise seemed more obvious, her lip fatter. The fear returned, not fear of Michael somehow she felt she'd be able to handle him, no, it was a fear that all she'd lived for was balanced on the edge of a dark void, her music and her marriage both teetered on the brink of disaster.

The uneasy evening crawled on; Rachel sat lonely in the sitting room watching the clock tick-tock, tick-tock, the leaden footed minutes dragged as she sat staring at her wounded hand and wondering, through the mists of impenetrable greyness, a vacuous never-never land, waiting for Michael. Waiting for what? More battering, more grinding sex, more what?

Michael returned close to eight, he'd been drinking. His spirits though seemed high. He expressed surprise at Rachel's injuries and commented with genuine concern that she ought not to practise so much. Apart from that incredibly glib comment he was charming, kind and considerate. Indeed Rachel felt warm and safe with him, and that elixir that is love's expectation, drugged her once more into a hubris that echoed all the things Rachel longed for.

As they lay quietly in bed she shared her day's experience relating how her fall has put her recital program into disarray.

"You must be more careful in future" muttered Michael as he stroked her head and slipped gently into a contented sleep.

Chapter 21

The doctors were charming and concerned; Bloom had already examined Rachel the previous day, his colleague, Morrison, a consultant surgeon from Stanmore Orthopaedic Centre seemed detached but competent. Max Luberoff was not allowed in the consulting room, but his nervous presence pervaded everywhere. Rachel herself felt the injury was already improved, though her right hand and wrist were still very sore.

Rachel was asked to respond to a variety of wrist movements and was interrogated about the precise nature and location of any discomfort. Bloom urged her to be as precise and objective as possible. Bloom himself had specialized in pianists' hands and wrists for years, his expertise was legendary and pianists from over the world flew to London to consult with him. Morrison likewise was a top man in his field, their objective was to give Rachel advice on treatment, and estimate as far as they could, how long Rachel would be unable to play. Max as her Manager had to make informed decisions as to whether to line up replacement artists, cover insurance and PR matters.

After some forty minutes Rachel was asked to wait with Max while both doctors conferred on the prognosis. Rachel sat with Max in the plush waiting room where the decorous and genteel nurse receptionist offered tea and biscuits in the best Harley Street manner.

Max fidgeted, "I'm dying for a cigarette darling," he paced the room, he muttered to himself; " I cannot understand, Rachel? " He coughed, "We know you did not fall down the stairs." He left the comment hanging in the air.

Rachel poured the tea with her left hand, and fiddled with a digestive biscuit. "I don't know what you mean Max, if I say I fell down the stairs, I fell down the stairs – alright." She felt the tears rise.

"My darling, Max is your mentor, Max is like your uncle, Max loves you, so please tell Max what he wants to know," He coughed again, "Max is not so stupid you know, and besides I have to look after you. " He snapped a biscuit, it flew from his fingers on to the floor and he immediately made a great fuss of clearing up the crumbs. " You know," he continued, his rear end visible above the coffee table, "You cannot fall down the stairs again." His head appeared, his eyes buzzing in concentric and agitated circles. "We understand each other, you know Max cares, but whatever you say I will believe if you want? But you cannot have an accident like this again."

Rachel pretended as best she could to misunderstand the clear message. Max knew or at least had a very good idea of what had happened. She stared into her teacup. Could she confide in Max? If not Max, then who?

The door opened and they were summoned into the consulting room where both Bloom and Morrison sat smiling. Bloom stood and waited for Max and Rachel to be seated. He introduced Morrison again, stressing how eminent he was in his field. He then spent a good ten minutes explaining both the anatomy and physiology of the elbow, arm and wrist; he launched into a lecture about the bones of the wrist, the transmission of movement to the fingers, the causes of repetitive strain syndrome, and the need for appropriate exercise and maintenance of healthy joints, particularly for Rachel. He described her as a subject who had been consistently using her hands from the age of five, and the consequences both good and bad. He went on so long that Rachel began to feel the whole thing was an academic chore for Bloom. She drifted away to the Mozart fugue and felt her fingers strain. This brought her back to the present with an unpleasant twinge of pain.

Morrison then took over the chair of the conversation; Max as usual gave an impression of nervous confusion. Both Manager and pianist wanted to get to the bit that mattered to them, 'How long must she rest and when could she get back to full practice and recitals?'

Eventually they affirmed that as far as the scans showed there had been significant bleeding in the carpel tunnel, but this now had stopped. The inflammation which manifested itself as a sprain would hopefully heal completely.

How long? That was another matter; with extensive physiotherapy perhaps three weeks, perhaps more. In Morrison's opinion it would be folly to start a busy programme in less than six weeks, Bloom concurred though when pressed said "yes' it's possible that Rachel will make better progress, even as much as three to four weeks might see her restored to fitness." They both emphasized that to get back to work too early would be folly, and that such impatience could do lasting damage.

At Rachel's insistence they debated the damage to both hands and squeezed agreement that she could start work with her left hand in perhaps four or five days.

Max and Rachel left the Harley Street rooms and walked briskly away in the London morning. Rachel almost running, trying to keep up with Max.

"Max, where are we going? Please slow down, Max what are we going to do?"

"We are going to have lunch, Max and his Rachel must decide what we are to do. Max always makes better decisions when he is happy in his stomach."

They hailed a cab and soon were sitting upstairs in Max's favourite Covent Garden restaurant.

"Today Rachel, I want none of this water nonsense; I want you and Max to put things on the table, we have to make maybe the most important decisions of Rachel George-Johnson ever; so Chambertin it will be, to wash down the truth." They sat and Max held her splinted right hand in his, " Darling you have in these hands maybe one of the most outstanding talents of your generation – you understand that don't you?"

Rachel looked away, again she wanted to cry, but somehow she could not, she still lived in her fantasy world where everything was alright, where Michael lived – a busy but loving partner who she loved so very much.

"Well" said Max, "What have you to tell Max?"

"Max for goodness sake, you know I don't want wine, not with lunch."

"Never mind the wine, how did you get hurt, Max needs to know, Max thinks he knows, the doctors also think they know, so please tell Max the truth."

"Max I've told you all there is to know, I fell down the stairs going down to the studio, stupid I know but I was lucky I could have broken my neck – for all you care." Her weak jest fell flat

"Rachel, darling, Max must tell you this – I do not want to upset you but you must know we are at a crisis.."

Rachel tried to interrupt, "No darling hear me out, we are at a crisis because your injuries were inflicted on you, they are not consistent with falling down the stairs," he waved his hand, "the doctors have told me these are pressure injuries perhaps you were restrained or tied up or something – bedroom games darling – but dangerous ones, and ones that hurt you are not what – how would you say – uggh pleasant, proper?"

The waiter had brought some tapas, Max drank enthusiastically, waiting to continue. Rachel could stand it no longer; she burst into tears and fled to the ladies' room. There she composed herself as best she could, but even here the mirror screamed the truth, the bruise under her eye looking more exaggerated than ever. She made up and returned to the table, this was after all none of Max's business and she would tell him so.

She sat and accepted Max's insistence that she take wine, it was lovely and spread like perfumed velvet over her tongue. She felt a little more composed.

"Max you have to understand that I fell down the stairs, and that's that, whatever you think is of no importance, and for that matter, not your business." She felt relieved she'd stood up for herself – at last.

"Darling," Max gushed, "Max understands you want to fall down the stairs – so that is fine with Max, but from there you are wrong, it is Max's business starting right now. MIL will have to have stand-ins available for all your engagements for the next six weeks. I cannot do otherwise, so if you miss the Prom, so be it; it will be sad but there will be other days – darling you are young yet."

"I shall be at the Prom; I can tell you Max there will be no doubt about this, you are not to engage a stand-in for the Prom, I do not want Jamo or the Gothenburg people to know anything of this." She swallowed more wine.

"We have no choice, all our contracts state what and when we must give notice if an artist is indisposed, we are absolutely obligated to give maximum notice, Max can do nothing about this; this must and will happen."

"Max you know I want to do the Prom, I'll be fit , you'll see, please, please don't tell anyone that I can't do it."

"Darling we have to notify every one of your possible indisposition and we have to produce a substitute option, and some have a right to engage their own; it's the law of the game, falling down the stairs is not allowed."

"Max, I will talk to Jamo; he'll want me to be his partner, you'll see." She gulped more wine, the feeling of panic spread through her in a hot torrent.

"Jamo may have some influence, but it will be the BBC who'll have the main say, but we'll try to make a deal that gives you four weeks to be absolutely fit, you'll have to be absolutely sure, I've told you many times you cannot, nobody can, afford the reputation of being unreliable.... this falling down the stairs.... it must not be allowed to happen again, remove the stairs, darling, leave him."

Rachel squeezed her eyes together but she could not stop the flood of tears, she sobbed uncontrollably; Max could not and didn't understand, anyway it wouldn't happen again, Michael would be kind, she would talk to him, it would be alright. Her sniveling stopped, she dried her eyes.

"The stairs will stay and I won't fall again, you have my word, you needn't worry. Oh God, Max I'm in such a state, look at me I'm a mess."

"Darling you never look a mess.... sad maybe, ... pathetic maybe.... but never a mess. Soon Rachel you are going to have to choose, you know this. Max is sad for you, but you will have to decide, unless the stairs somehow get mended. Rachel you have a wonderful talent, but that's only a start, if you want what I know you want, there is no room for falling down stairs. There may be no room for anything else; God knows half the world would die for a tiny piece of your talent. Don't throw it away for anything. Don't cut us off from what you have to offer the world. If you do, you will never forgive yourself, nor should you. Now Max has said enough let's eat."

Max ploughed into his lunch, eyes constantly rolling, observing all those around them, twitching nervously, pretending that everything was alright.

Rachel toyed with her food, drank more wine though she knew she was tipsy, 'right, I must get to grips with Michael, I will get fit and we shall be fine.' But there was shallowness in her deliberation; all she knew was that she loved Michael and that would never change.

At home she slept the afternoon away and felt terrible when she woke. Michael came home at seven and they dined at their favourite pub, the Grenadier. There she dwelt on the problems of her injury and talked at length of the need to be careful in the future. Michael expressed some sympathy though he seemed to be detached as if the whole episode had nothing to do with him. Rachel perhaps was so subtle he missed the point, the point being that when Michael was drunk his love making was selfish and bordering on extreme violence. Bordering on? No, he was violent, he hurt her and knew he was doing it. But afterwards he was always so gentle, not apologetic, but detached and kind.

What she could not deny was the beauty of him, the masculinity that she had seen in Cambridge, it was still there, he was quite the most attractive man she had ever known. She found that when they were together, sober and content, her infatuation was as rampant as it had been when they married.

Her heart still missed a beat when he came into the room. Even the horrors of his jealous fits, the brutality of his angry and possessive sex melted away as they sat together, a young couple still very much in love. She wanted him now, she wanted him often, tonight was no exception, tonight it would be good, it would be tender, voluptuous, consuming. This is what being in love was all about.

The days that followed were idyllic as Michael was home each evening and was nothing other than kindness and consideration, her days were frustrating, split between exercises for her left hand and trips back and forth to 'Hands'. Bettie had made a number of efforts to discuss 'the accident', but Rachel remained firmly detached, convinced herself that Michael would never hurt her ever again.

The news on the career front was good, her recovery was well under way and the doctors were pleased with progress. Max had done wonders with the client futures, the Prom was to be hers if she could report fit five days before the performance; a very eminent stand-in had agreed to stand by. Jamo Jadesjo had reinforced her confidence by ringing frequently to encourage her recovery and to chat about things musical.

Her splint was removed ten days after 'her accident' though she was still urged not to play. Despite the warnings Rachel could not resist some gentle JS, and her hand and arm felt well enough.

The rest had done her good, she went to see her mother who gushed over her and did not dream for one moment that her daughter lived in anywhere other than a perfect marital heaven. Over tea they'd chatted about this and that, Rachel heard herself boast of how well things were going, both career wise and at home. She extolled the virtues of Michael, brushing out any reference to the darker side of their relationship.

Rachel caught herself exaggerating tales of his working life, no reference here to the odious Walmers, no mention of the curiously debauched episodes that Michael so loved. Indeed it was as if Rachel was inventing her life anew. Describing what she knew she wanted and that she periodically experienced, but her secret remained locked away; denied to the outside world and even hidden from her.

Mummy had insisted on booking a logia box for the Prom and bringing along her lifelong chums , most of who were what Rachel considered to be the 'Blue rinse brigade' of matronly gawpers. Rachel was floored to learn that her mother had acquired a male admirer and that the she was 'dating a lovely man', recently retired from the Brigade of Guards. Rachel was flustered at the news, she'd never thought her mother, still an attractive woman, could possibly have another relationship after Daddy. Despite herself, she wondered if Mummy was having a physical relationship with her gallant Colonel.

Chapter 22

That night she had agreed to dine with Michael at the Savoy, it was 'business' and they should be home quite early, or so Michael had promised. Despite a slight apprehension, Rachel looked forward to an evening when she could be seen on the arm of her beloved Michael, he'd been so wonderful since the 'accident'.

Her disappointment was palpable when they were ushered into Monsieur Barre's suite, he looked strangely familiar, but that was not what caused her disappointment for there, standing in a gaggle were Sir Bradley, Lady Jennifer, and worst of all the decorous Sarah, draped around the Monsieur Barre.

"Enchanté`, Madame Johnson, it is wonderful to see you again." His lush French accent melted over her like overly sweet chocolate. Rachel stared back trying like mad to recall where she'd seen this handsome man before.

"Monsieur," she replied in her perfect French, " You have the advantage of me, forgive me but I cannot quite recall where we last met." – "Oh excuse me everyone, I still slip into French so easily." She snuggled Michael's arm under her own. She felt, or thought she felt, his arm go rigid, and like a bolt of lightening the fear of his loathing jealousy returned.

"Ah," sighed the Frenchman, "If I were as beautiful as you, you would not forget, but I will never. Rachel do you not remember the party on my little boat in Hvar all those years ago, is it five years already?"

A red flood of panic coursed through her, of course this was the French man she'd flirted with, that innocent silly night on their honeymoon, the night when Michael had first emerged as the raging jealous animal that still remained, hidden sometimes, but always there, menacing, but there.

Michael laughed and patted her bottom, "I'm glad you don't remember the charming Monsieur Barre darling, I remember you were quite taken at the time. Anyway in the strangest turn of events, Monsieur Barre, Alain, may we call you Alain?"

"Mais oui, but of course."

"Alain " Michael continued, "is the broker for some work we are doing in the Middle East, but that's too boring to go into now, we're just delighted to welcome Alain to London, and the beginning of a long and prosperous relationship."

"I'll drink to that." Sir Bradley lifted his glass, echoed by the assembly.

They dined sumptuously in the suite, the table was set by the terrace window overlooking the Thames; Rachel sat between Barre and Walmer, Michael between Sarah and Jennifer. The meal passed well enough and Rachel, on guard, refused more than two glasses of wine, which after the champagne was enough.

She watched detached, as the others drank copiously, she saw them change as they imbibed, each becoming more a caricature of themselves, more charming, jollier, more touchy-feely. The knees, the hands from either side encroached at any opportunity, she withdrew her hand or knee as quickly as she could, but there it was again, the odious Walmer, the charming Barre, on either side covering her hand or brushing her legs under the table.

As the meal went interminably on, Rachel became more and more anxious, avoiding the advances of her table companions and watching with defensive alarm to see what Michael observed and what his reactions were. Michael as far as she could see was engrossed in the ministrations of Sarah, who, as always, looked fabulously attractive.

After the waiters had cleared the table, liqueurs and more Champagne were offered, Rachel again declined. Sarah, teased her about being so demure and urged her to relax. There was something about Sarah that Rachel hated but found attractive at the same time.

She was without doubt one of the most beautiful women Rachel had ever met, it was almost impossible not to be fascinated by her sheer classical beauty that at the same time radiated sexiness. Her physical presence influenced the whole group; she dripped sensuality, it was impossible to escape it.

She hated the way Sarah always had Michael eating out of her hand, and she disliked most of all the way Sarah could attract her, the way she acquiesced to Sarah's will, like some female Svengali; Sarah commanded and Rachel obeyed, Rachel could do little other than yield. But tonight she knew that tomorrow was crucial, her meeting with the medical team and Max would prove decisive if she would or would not play the Prom.

This above everything detached her from the languid and sensuous group; this was the one thing in all the world that she wanted most, to play, to play her damned piano, it was more important than anything, even Michael?

As the group left the table to set off to more drink and heaven knew what, at Klingers Club, Rachel reached for her clutch bag and announced that she was unable to stay with them.

"I'm terribly sorry Alain, Sir Bradley, but I really have to go; I have a crucial medical in the morning and I simply can't turn up full of Champagne."

Sarah was alongside her crooking her arm in hers, "Darling we quite understand but we promise we won't be long and we have a special surprise just for you."

"Yes, yes," slobbered Walmer, "we won't be long, and I know you'll love our surprise, now we'll hear no more of it and we promise to get you home by midnight, before you turn into a pumpkin."

They all laughed and now Michael was at her side, and he and Sarah almost frog marched her down to the limo waiting at the hotel entrance. Rachel could do little but confirm her acquiescence, "I must be home by twelve, or I will turn into a pumpkin."

The Klingers Club was discreetly situated down a quiet alley off Tottenham Court Road. The entrance was barely visible, the light above the door hardly more than a candle. Inside though it was another world, a large lush entrance heavily carpeted, and furnished in heavy light oak, the place reeked of wealth and discretion; Rachel had certainly never heard of the place though Michael and Sir Bradley and Jennifer were greeted with familiarity, Sarah nodded to the reception manager. The familiarity of the nod, gave Rachel a nervous start, this was a place she felt where she ought not to be.

The first room was an octagonal atrium beautifully lit, at the centre there was the most wonderful and extravagant flower arrangement that took Rachel's breath away.

Around six sides of the octagon were doors leading to other rooms, all as far as she could see quite vast, she caught sight of a huge restaurant, then a bar, and then what appeared to be a library.

"My God, Michael this place is so opulent it's almost beyond belief."

"Believe me darling, to be a member here, you have to be worth a billion, and I mean a 'billion,' maybe dollars, but still a billion."

Their table was already ready, the Crystal already chilled, the table host all charm and unctuous attention. In the centre of the bar a piano trio played the most delicious jazz. Rachel was astonished to see Peter Crosier, the successor in waiting to Oscar Peterson.

"There" said Sir Bradley, "did we not tell you it would be worth coming."

Perhaps for the first time ever, Rachel could not help but smile at Walmer, " Yes you were right, just listen aren't they fabulous?"

From that moment on Rachel was immersed, absorbed in, lost in, the incredible mastery of Crosier and his colleagues. They were truly fabulous. The astonishing thing was that there were not more than twenty guests in the lounge to hear them.

After a set of thirty minutes Crosier approached the table, he was strikingly handsome, black, slim and tall. He greeted Rachel as if she were an old friend, after acknowledging the other guests with a charm and confidence that made Barre and Walmer look common.

He engrossed Rachel and entreated her to join her on the set to play some Tatum arrangements, "I'd be honoured if you would join us."

"The honour would be all mine, but unfortunately I've not been fit for several weeks, so I'm just not up to it." Rachel meant it out of both fear and respect for a man who she idolised, albeit till now, from afar.

Jennifer Walmer started to entreat her, and soon they all joined in pushing her forward. Crosier, stood and bade her stay. He went back to the band , and then announced in his relaxed cultured American accent that he was honoured to have Rachel George-Johnson as his guest, and despite her recent layoff she had consented to join him to play a work for which she was famous – "Ladies and gentlemen, our tribute to Art Tatum."

Covered in confusion and not knowing at all what to expect Rachel joined Crosier on the one piano stool, and he whispered, "Come in when you're ready, and off he went. His huge hands moved like butterflies across the keys. Rachel was mesmerised, she sat with her toes involuntarily tapping to the beat.

Then Crosier nudged her and stopped playing but the base and drums continued driving along the exquisite beat. Rachel started to play, at first tentatively then as the melodies flowed, with confidence. She looked up and Crosier was nowhere to be seen. Panic almost overtook her, but then from behind her she sensed him directing the rhythm section, then he was at her side again and they played four hands for what must have been five whole minutes and with the instinct so deep in both musicians they ended as if they had played together for years.

Her tears fell in floods; Walmer, Michael, Jennifer, Barre and Sarah stood round them clapping, ringed in smiles, the small audience were on their feet and advanced to the group.

It was then she recognised ex President Clinton, who was a guest of the Sultan of Brunei, she had no idea who the others were. They were all ecstatic with their praise both of Rachel and Crosier and that was a real thrill for Rachel. Michael hugged her, he was genuinely delighted, and as the now enlarged group settled for another drink, Crosier the complete professional went back to his colleagues for another set.

It was twelve o clock, Michael announced that he was taking Rachel home and everyone stood to bid their farewells; Walmer hearty in his polite handshake, Sarah took both her hands and looked directly into her eyes, " Rachel you are so lucky and so talented and yet so beautiful." Then she kissed Rachel squarely on the mouth. It seemed almost normal, no one seemed to notice the shudder that went down Rachel's spine.

In the taxi on the short ride home, Michael was as she wanted, attentive, affectionate with an obvious desire for her. When they got home they kissed once over the threshold,

"Let's go to bed," Rachel invited.

"Let's just have one brandy" replied Michael, "and then we'll go to bed and I'll make wild love to you."

"No, Michael, let's go to bed now, I want you – now!" her tone almost anguished.

"Come on, just one for the sake of your wonderful celebrity, I thought you were terrific, I was so proud." Michael clicked on the sitting room light and reached for two brandy balloons.

Rachel stood on the threshold, afraid to break the spell and afraid that it was about to be broken. Should she protest, should she have a brandy and humour him? Would he drink too much? How should she please him? She bore a mixture of fear and excitement, she was filled with desire and fear at once, in many ways the feeling was exquisite.

"It's been a wonderful evening, even if the doctors would have a fit if they knew I played for Crosier and Co., anyway I don't want to be too late darling because tomorrow is so important and I have to be at 'Hands' early. Come on, let's go to bed and I can make a fuss of you."

She purred, draping her arms round him, and licking him sensuously along his lips. Much to Rachel's relief Michael abandoned the brandy and returned her kiss, she could feel the urgency in him.

"Was it you who organised the Club tonight? It was such a lovely surprise, God what a sumptuous place, where else in the world would you get the world's best jazz combo playing to a private party?" She pulled him gently to the bedroom.

"Well my dear, it certainly wasn't me who organised it, I've never been past the door before, not many people have. It was your devoted admirer, my boss Sir Bradley, there are fewer than fifty London home members including the Royal Family, so you were greatly honoured, so was I for that matter – being asked to enter the hallowed portals is a privilege known to few, and it must mean that Monsieur Barre is very important indeed, anyway my sexy piano player, let's play each other."

And so they did, with delight and lust and laughter, Rachel went to sleep happier than she could remember.

Chapter 23

Max picked up a radiant Rachel on the dot of nine o'clock, and she was whisked to 'Hands' for scans on both wrists, hands and elbows. This took an hour and the data was electronically sent to Bloom's office. Rachel and Max arrived there on the hour at eleven to find the doctors pouring over her records and the scans.

Bloom in his pedantic way took ages to express his view that Rachel was fit and that he felt no lasting damage had been done.

Morrison explained the physiology and that what they were looking for was any sustained damage and bruising in the wrist and elbow. There was no sign on the scans but there might well be susceptibility to strain injury that needed to be guarded against.

Max's eyes rolled as he got more and more excited as all the news appeared to be good, Rachel could hardly wait to get back to Becky and to work. Her practice schedule had been drastically reduced though she had spent a great deal of time working her left hand that had been less damaged in the 'fall', than the right one. From now till the Prom only days away, it would be a minimum of six hours a day practice.   Morrison urged her to be careful and gradually to return to her full regime of practice and study.

They emerged from the Harley Street office, close to twelve thirty, Max as always wanted to celebrate the good news, with an expansive and alcoholic lunch.

"Darling, Max has good news for you, come we will have lunch together and we talk of the Prom and many other things."

"Max please let me go and practise; I don't want lunch, please darling Max let me go."

"Max will not let you go, did you not listen, my darling? Do not, Morrison repeated ... Do not.... leap into six hours a day of practice.... So it's lunch with Max." He hugged her, "come spend some time with Max, we have lots to talk about, about Mozart and your little Polish friend, America and a long tour including Chicago and much more... Max is going to be with you on the next part of your journey.... you will not believe what Max has to tell you."

So they piled into a cab and set off to Max's favourite watering hole off Berkeley Square, 'The Guinea'. Once seated on the rather uncomfortable velvet bench seat, Max was off, volubly rattling about Rachel's apparently assured future and unqualified star potential. The inevitable burgundy was presented, and Rachel had to admit to herself that the bouquet of strawberries was something that befitted this lovely day. Along with relief at her clean bill of health, the excitement of the 'Prom' and most of all the love of her lovely Michael, everything in her world smelt of strawberries, and was filled with light.

"Darling, I have heard from our American colleagues and we have to change lots of your engagements; after the Prom, no more chintzy village concerts, darling, no more little town church recitals, the world and its bigger stages are where you will belong. You will be Max's number one – you know Max loves you - So!" He swigged his burgundy with such an enthusiasm that the red wine splattered his white shirt. He brushed it with his hand making it much worse. Rachel reached across and tried to swab the stain with soda water but Max brushed her hand away. "Darling that is why I wear a bow tie – now you know Max's little secret" He cackled like some old crone.

For all his idiosyncrasies Rachel could not but hold Max in her highest affection, Michael she knew was jealous of him and called him the most vile names, but Max , gay or not, was like an uncle to her. He believed in her and never ever failed to give her all his enthusiastic support and she knew he worked like a dog on her behalf.

The lunch was delivered, Max waved his knife and fork , "Boston, Albany, Chicago, Cleveland, Columbus, St Paul and Washington DC, these are almost firm now, " His knife whistled passed Rachel's nose. "You will travel in the Spring, the repertoire I think will not be a problem – we will discuss in the next week," …. he sliced another huge slice of bloody beef, suspending it precariously from his fork, "but before, we have the Mozart two pianos this Winter, London, Paris, Leipzig, and Vienna."

"Oh Max, do you think they will really come off and who will I work with?" She was breathless with excitement, her food untouched.

"When did Max let you down, drink some wine, eat some food, you need to be strong."

He plunged another mountain of meat into his mouth, his eyes spun in their peculiar way – he shared her excitement, he loved her in his own peculiar way.

"You are so beautiful, men I know go crazy for you, but me, you know I just want to be your uncle.... you know me.... I am harmless .... yes, so please my darling, your career is mine also.... so no secrets.... no more falling down the stairs.... you follow?"

"I follow Max, you needn't worry, the stairs have been mended.... now what about repertoire?'

"Next week darling we will have a better idea, anyway I want you to be a good girl and not work too hard, it's only a short time to the Prom, so you have enough to do. But in broad terms we want you to mix recitals from Baroque to romantic and I think your concerts from Mozart through mainly the romantics. Maybe some premières but it depends, you know your strengths and the few weaknesses."

"Max steer me clear of Rachmaninoff, if you can, the concertos kill me. I'd like to do more Chopin, I'm really into his Second Piano Concerto so I'd like to do that in the States, somewhere big," she squealed and squeezed Max's arm.

They babbled on, each as excited as the other, Rachel uncharacteristically drank three glasses of Max's favourite burgundy, and was quite tipsy when she hailed a cab and headed home for some hi-jinks on Becky. She arrived home with her hubris fading as the effects of the wine translated into the beginning of a hangover. Nonetheless she was steadfast about her need to start practice without delay. When she opened the door she was alarmed at first to hear someone in the study, and after a tentative call was relieved to find that Michael was home searching rather tetchily through his desk drawers.

"Wonderful news darling" she threw her arms around him, "declared fit for the Prom." She tried to kiss him but he was preoccupied with his search.

"Christ, you've been drinking – you stink of booze."

"It was just that, Max and I, we had a lunch to discuss what's next."

Michael's face turned, blackening to his jealous rage, "You and that old Queen, what's he up to? Procuring some poncey musician for you is he?" She didn't see it coming but the back of his hand caught her across the left side of her face knocking her into the door.

Rachel ran into her studio and locked the door. She sat at her stool and wailed, as the tears poured from her. Her face did not matter, was it bruised? Who cared, why? Oh why? Michael, why? Why? You know I love you. She could just hear his thumping outside the soundproofed studio door. She lay her head down and drifted off into a miserable sniffling sleep.

She awoke some two hours later, reminding herself that lunchtime drinking was not for her, in fact drinking at any time was not for her. She was enormously thirsty and her head banged whether from the wine or the slap she knew not. She unlocked the studio door and listened, but there was no sound from the rest of the house. She went to the kitchen, quenched her insatiable thirst with what felt like a gallon of water and then went to the bathroom to examine her face in the mirror. It wasn't so bad, she'd cut the inside of her cheek, but there was no bruise, just a redness that she felt sure would clear in a day or two. Thus reassured and refreshed, she returned to Becky and started her practice that would consume her for the next weeks, till her great night arrived.

She had recovered ahead of schedule so that she had some two weeks to prepare. From that moment on she practised as she had never before, she was in the studio every morning by seven thirty and worked with short breaks till dinner time.

Michael as he always had done, completely ignored the incident in the study, and complained without due fuss that Becky was seeing more of Rachel than her husband. There were some wry comments about the sexuality of her piano. Otherwise they lived out those frenetic days leading to the Prom comfortably, their bed time couplings were infrequent and unremarkable. Rachel's days were filled with solitary practice, or publicity meetings, or phone calls to MIL and a million other people; so she seemed to have all too little time to perfect what many would consider already perfect..

Jamo and his band/orchestra had two consecutive nights at the Promenade Concerts, their first night consisted of Scandinavian works of Nielson and Berwald as well as the Violin Concerto of Sibelius and on the second evening they would celebrate the genius of Grieg., starting with the Holberg Suite for Strings then the Piano Concerto, and after the interval, Grieg's seldom performed Symphony.

Her rehearsal was to be on the morning of the performance at nine thirty and although her practice had gone well, Rachel could not help feel the nervous tension that grew as the date got nearer. Having been hassled by her mother to help with getting last minute tickets for the 'blue rinse brigade' she felt anxious and lonely. Lonely; in the sense that she wanted Michael to share in this, her greatest professional accomplishment. She had dreamed as a child and it had been a recurring dream throughout her life that one day, one day she would play at the Prom. Yet Michael stood steadfastly aloof, as if her musical world was akin to the housekeeping.

Whilst he was unable to ignore this world of hers he certainly did nothing to embrace it. It was like living with a relative who she loved, but who just tolerated her work, considered it an unnecessary diversion. Despite all that, Rachel's love and enthusiasm for her music never dimmed, it was a passion that was alive, palpable, it drove her rhythm of life and along with her love of Michael was the meter of her existence. Now that her dream was in touching distance, the Prom, and all the consequences, at last she would walk onto the concert platform and the world would be at her feet. Eva, oh how Eva would have loved this time, and the time was now.

As the taxi pulled into the pavement outside the Royal Albert Hall, it was a lovely English Summer morning with a bright blue sky. The stage door of the Royal Albert Hall is situated next to door 12, and for all the world, is very ordinary. Rachel paused outside, took a deep breath and entered the hallowed portals, in the steps of so many of the all time greats of every genre of music. At the reception desk the Stage Door Manager greeted her with a smile, came round the front of his booth, hand extended:

"Miss George, welcome to the Albert Hall, this way please." He led her through a glazed door down the steps and along the curving corridor. She was immediately struck by the drab concrete lined passage surreally lifted by the music of Grieg that enveloped her. "Mr Hughes, the BBC . Miss George." She was greeted by a man of about her age, he clasped a sheaf of papers in his hand and was festooned with wires and electronic devices including earphones draped around his neck.

"Welcome, I'm Robert," he smiled comfortably, his hand shake firm and dry, " Jamo is just finishing off the Holberg, let me show you around, he won't be long." He strode off in front of her, "This is your dressing room, he darted to the left, this is Dressing 2, Jamo is across the hall in the principal's and I'm afraid we commandeer the No1 spot for our production team, it's along here just next to stage entrance right."

She looked up the short ramp that led to the stage and saw Jamo, his neat frame silhouetted in the lights behind him, the backs of the orchestra strings in an uncanny unison of syncopation. Her heart hammered, as she stole a glimpse through the stage lights to the inimitable Albert Hall; huge, but so close, grand, but so intimate.

"Across here is the green room it has a piano for you to warm up if you like, not very grand I'm afraid, and next to the green room is the artists' bar; I expect your management will have fixed up all the social side, your dressing room is not very big I'm afraid."

Her dressing room was indeed rather Spartan, the crescent shaped room following the circular pattern of the Hall, had a shower, a tiny wardrobe, a toilet, sink and a few chairs, none of which looked particularly comfortable. There was a pile of messages from well wishers, much too big to go into now, as well as a lovely bouquet of flowers that had been unceremoniously dumped into a bucket like vase.

Robert Hughes looked at his note pad, "the BBC car will pick you up from your Belgravia home at six forty five, I believe there will be a reception in the Royal Garden Hotel after the concert. It will be hosted by MIL and the BBC. Guests will include the Swedish, Danish and Finnish Ambassadors. The car will take you there after you've had time to shower and change after the performance, I believe some of your personal guests will be coming down around the interval and we've made accommodation in the artists' bar which is across the hall."

"Thank you Robert, do call me Rachel." The music had come to an end, and there was a murmuring and the noise of the orchestra reforming on the platform.

"Ready, Rachel, let's go and meet Jamo and the band."

Jamo was arranging his scores when she walked up to him unnoticed, he looked up immediately his wide smile creased his face, friend meeting dear friend. He hugged her and immediately raised her hand and called for the orchestra to bid her welcome.

There were smiles all round, old friends nodding and tapping their bows.

"Ladies and gentlemen, one of our favourite soloists, and one of my dear friends; Rachel George –Johnson." More bow tapping.

The piano lid was being opened and the stool put in place, the members of the orchestra chatted quietly; for them – a routine, another tour, another concert, another soloist, except this was a BBC Prom; that made it special.

"I'm so delighted you are fit and we can make music again, especially here, in your Albert hall, last night was terrific, it was a fantastic audience."

"Jamo I can't believe we're here – at last, I'm scared stiff, I hope I don't let you down."

"Don't be a silly girl - how long since Liverpool? Wasn't that great, and tonight it will be even greater you'll see." The piano pusher left the platform, "Come on let's do some work."

Rachel took her place at the piano, adjusted her stool, the Orchestra went quiet, Jamo raised his baton and the rehearsal was off. It was horrible, Rachel was tentative, hesitant even. She just didn't seem to settle, her memory was confused, her fingers unresponsive. Rachel wanted to cry. They stopped, they started and stopped and started a hundred times and eventually they came to the end of their allotted time.

"Jamo, I'm sorry this is awful."

"Rachel, it was awful by your standards, but believe me, I've heard it a lot worse, and remember, tonight it will be different, you will shine like you always do, so I'm not worried."

She left the stage shaking like a leaf. She could not remember a time when she had played so badly. It was as if her Muse had left her entirely. She sat in her dressing room and clasped her hands, squeezed her eyelids shut, and searched for her musical being. Surely she would not crumble now; in front of the millions who would watch on television, all her friends and all who she so loved, all who had spent so much of themselves for her. She would not!

There was a tap at the door and Roberts asked if it was OK for her to do a tele-recorded interview with the BBC concert commentator. A rather aggravating young man as it turned out, and what should have been a pleasant discourse on the Grieg concerto, turned out a rather distracted monologue by the commentator to a thoroughly distracted Rachel.

Max appeared, his eyes rotating in their wild concentric way. He was clearly agitated but was trying desperately to be calm.

"Darling, it was a shaky rehearsal, that's good because you made all your bad notes go away this morning – not tonight. Tonight will be fine." They emerged into the sun light, she held back the tears.

"Please Max take me home and just don't talk about lunch or I will scream."

"What about tonight, everything is OK, you know cars, hair, dresses and all the things Max like to make sure about?"

"Yes Max, everything will be OK, I'm going to the hairdresser right now and then home to rest."   But she didn't, she went to the Jewish cemetery, where she sat and talked to Eva, at least she thought she did, and with hair undone she returned home with little time left to do anything except shower and lay out her clothes.

Michael was not at home, he was due to join Robbie and his mother, as one of the many supporters at the concert. She left a note, rather disconsolate that he wasn't there to see her off to the greatest musical adventure of her life. She didn't answer the hundred and one messages of goodwill and she was mildly alarmed that Michael had not been among the well wishers. Still it was time to go.

For whatever reason, she knew not, the time at Eva's grave had not cured her nervousness, but it had given her a feeling of serenity, a serenity that made her feel that whatever fortune threw at her she would take it. There was an inevitability about the next few hours that she could do nothing about; her future seemed in other hands.

The polite knock on the door at precisely six forty five did not surprise or alarm her, she gathered up her dress and bag, looked at herself in the mirror, then decided to revise her note for Michael "I love you" is all it said.

Jamo popped into her dressing room, "I'm looking forward to the concerto, it will be wonderful I'm sure", he smiled and pecked her on the cheek, "to work." And he marched off confidently, and Rachel was left alone as the thunderous applause engulfed the old hall and everything in it. Rachel shivered.

The strains of the Holberg suite permeated down to her loneliness, she worried about Michael's absence, she hadn't heard a word from him all day, even he must be aware of what a big day this was. She tried to concentrate on the opening of the concerto, she ambled into the green room and sat at the rather tacky upright piano and played a little JS, the time passed second by second, her nerves had subsided, the serenity taken over, she was numb, was it with fear?

There were quite a number of the orchestra hanging around waiting to take their place when the Holberg string suite was over. They smiled at her or just ignored her. She returned to her dressing room, edged between the flowers, felt her tummy cramp and went to her toilet. She sensed the change, the great swell of applause from within the hall. She scrambled to get ready, uncertainly adjusting her dress, and dabbing at her make-up.

"Five minutes," an anonymous tap on her door. "Ms George-Johnson."

"Fine" she replied, not feeling fine at all.

The applause died down, another tap on the door, it was Jamo. "They're a fabulous audience Rachel, they will love you."

Rachel felt like crying, she was bereft of confidence, of all her ordeals this seemed to dwarf them all. She took his hand, hers shaking now. He squeezed her hand firmly, "I believe in you." He pulled gently and led the short way to the stage entry ramp, they picked their way over the TV cables, passed the BBC producers unit and stood waiting for their prompt to go on. Rachel could hardly breathe. She heard the audience cheer as the piano lid was raised, and then the babble of the excited Promenaders.

Richard Hughes appeared, earphones clamped to his head, he pointed at them "Go, good luck."

A gentle prod in her back, she swallowed hard and walked between the orchestra with Jamo immediately behind her. As she stood by the piano before taking her seat, she saw for the first time what the Proms meant. There they were not six feet away, the Promenaders, in funny hats, dinner jackets, waving flags from Norway and lots of other countries, and their cheers raised the roof. They smiled right at her, she could have leant over and shaken hands with them. They were so happy; they loved music and by so doing loved her too.

She took her seat, adjusted her stool, looked up at Jamo, He smiled, nodded, her hands poised over the keys…. It was sublime, whatever the Promenaders wanted she gave them, she inhaled the atmosphere, the ecstasy of the moment permeated her whole being. It was as if she and the orchestra were one, the serenity morphed into an experience she had seldom experienced both out of herself as observer and inside herself completely absorbed as part of the musical moment.

And then it was over, she looked first at Jamo whose face was wreathed is smiles, and the leader, a such reserved gentleman, who looked at her and quite improperly blew a kiss to her .Then she turned to the Promenaders, she had never heard such a din, they stamped and cheered and roared and clapped. Her tears poured in torrents, 'Oh Eva, are you here?"

There were six curtain calls, stamping and thunderous applause, Rachel wanted it to go on forever, but TV schedules did not permit, and she was too soon back in her dressing room, composing herself, and clutching Jamo who was all tears as well.

There followed the inevitable visit from her mother and friends, Robbie and mother in law, and of course Max. Their euphoria was wonderfully elevating, but there was one thing missing, the one thing she wanted most of all; Michael, where was Michael? He had meant to be with his father Robbie, but Robbie expressed some anxiety that Michael had not turned up as expected.

"I expect something pretty dramatic must have turned up at work," he said distractedly amongst the hubbub. "Must be something pretty important to keep him away, I expect he'll turn up at the reception any way."

Anxiety gave way to a gnawing fear that something awful had happened to Michael again, surely not, where was he? She became obsessed by his absence, her eyes never leaving the doors, every time they opened or closed she jumped and started , but Michael didn't come. Her evening of bliss and delight was turning to disappointment and agony.

The post concert reception at the Royal Garden Hotel was a splendid affair jointly organized by MIL and the BBC, as Max explained, MIL paid and the BBC took the credit. The musical press was there in force, as were many friends from her world of music, from the Royal College, members of the Symphony Orchestra, a number of BBC officials, Impresarios and just a few lucky friends and family who were fortunate enough to get an invitation. There were several US people who were somehow connected with her future US tour as well as, and much to her delight, Igor Franec and his father with their retinue of record producers and PR men. However despite the glitz and the glamour the most important man for Rachel was not there; of Michael there was no sign.

The cameras flashed, there were announcements about her future that would have been so exciting, but they were not; she ached to see Michael to enjoin him to this glittering event, for him to be proud of her. For him to understand what this all meant to her, to share, just to share with Michael the very best she had to offer. He was not there and the emptiness hung in a black sadness that ached through her being. Despite all the praise, even the delight of Igor and sharing the plans for the two pianos tour, it was all rather flat.

Robbie was obviously concerned and volunteered several times to run off and phone Michael at home, at work and on his mobile, but each time he returned with a disconsolate shake of the head. The reception dragged on and it was past one in the morning when Robbie dropped her off at home, they went inside together but there was no one at home and of Michael there was no sign. Robbie and mother in law stayed for a coffee and then left reluctantly at close to two. Rachel made her way to bed exhausted, and cried herself to sleep. Where? Oh where was Michael?

She was awoken by the stumbling entry of her drunken husband at around four am.... She leaped out of bed and embraced him,

"Michael, Michael darling are you all right? Darling where have you been, we've all missed you."

"Where have I been? What's it to you? You've been playing your God damned piano while I've been working, that's where I've been."

She felt the rigidity in his arms, the physical rebuttal, the utter lack of tenderness. She stepped back,

"Robbie and your Mum missed you, but so did I, oh Michael you knew tonight was special, why didn't you come, you've ruined my night, it should have been the best night of my life and it's been ruined because you were not there." She started sobbing.

"Me not there, that's rich, all those bloody lecherous musical types, creepy Max, and those other bastards who all want to get you into bed.... and have done for all I know; me, you couldn't give a shit about me."

Rachel stood back, knowing full well that they were on the verge of catastrophic violence or she hoped, maybe she hoped, the last lap, the time when she could bring him home from his reckless jealousy and that devil that lived within him. Her hopes were soon dashed.

"Who brought you home eh? Some gallant musical creep I daresay. Did they fondle you in the back of the car? Did you let them touch you, could you resist them?" he was swaying as he moved for the bottle on the nightstand.

"Michael stop it, why do you torture yourself, you know I love you."

His fist exploded in her stomach, the pain was unbelievable, she collapsed on the bed, where she felt her nightdress being ripped off and her legs spread and he mounted her, his oaths foul and his physical strength overwhelming. She felt his elbow lean down on her throat, she could not breathe, she looked up at him, tears pouring as she began to drown under the weight of him.

She awoke as the London dawn peaked over Belgravia; his snoring was regular and sounded so content. She lay there silently, listening to Michael and trying desperately to sort out the confusion. Her ribs and stomach hurt, her throat felt as if she'd had a hot poker stuffed down it, and her head ached, and yet, and yet this man beside her was the man she ached for the night before, he was the man she'd married and yes, even now loved.

She raised herself gingerly and went to shower and clean up, in the mirror she saw the ugly bruise spanning her solar plexus and her first two ribs, her throat had a bruise but not so visible, her face was unmarked and her hands and arms seemed fine, It was good, nobody need find out, she would manage, Michael would get over this stage, she knew it in her heart she had nothing to fear, she would love him and it would be wonderful again, just like it used to be.

When Robbie rang she made excuses for him, 'he had been unavoidably detained at work' she said, 'he had been very upset to miss the celebrations.' She lied convincing herself that what she said was the truth. The violence she swept away and hid it in a very secret place that not even she visited.

She had a busy day ahead. Michael went off to work, pleading for once her forgiveness for what he described as our "Tiff of last night." Rachel pecked him on the cheek and wished him a good day at the office like a million other wives that morning. When the door closed behind him she walked with some discomfort down to the studio.

She had never realised before how much of her whole body she used when playing the piano, her stomach ached dreadfully, so much so that she stopped playing after about five minutes, she rolled up her blouse and was alarmed to see the ugly red and blue black bruise pulsating on her lower ribs and solar plexus. Her ribs stabbed short sharp arrows of vicious pain. What could she do?

Her throat too, was sore and now the bruise there was much more obvious than it had been in the light of the bathroom earlier. Panic seized her, she had an interview with 'The Listener' magazine later that morning and a further interview with some short piano work that evening on BBC 3. She fled to the bathroom once more and busied herself with a variety of make ups camouflaging the bruise on the throat; this she thought she could get away with, but could she play on the BBC "In Tune" programme later?

She draped a silk scarf around her neck and tried to rest her rib and waited for Max and all the paraphernalia of the press.

The bell rang and here was Max Luberoff who looked as though he had had a fierce night of alcoholic abandon, his hair was dishevelled, his tie a little more chaotic than usual and his eyes moved hardly at all in their bloodshot ponds.

"Darling, how is my darling this morning? The world is at your feet, Max will take you to where ever you want to go and may be further." He went to hug her but he felt her stiffen as the pain in her rib stabbed viciously home. "What, you will not hug Max, are you too grand now?"

"Max, come in and stop making a scene, I'm just a bit stiff that's all. Look at you Max you look like nothing on earth, what did you get up to last night – come on I'll make you a coffee."

They went to the sitting room; Rachel eased herself into a chair and could not help but wince with the pain. Max missed nothing.

The house keeper brought the coffee and biscuits, and Max looked hard at Rachel, "Rachel, Max thinks the stairs, you have fallen down again – no? Why are you wearing this ridiculous scarf, it is so warm today?"

She ignored him, "What time is 'the Listener' crew coming?"

Max stood up and came across to her and offered both his hands, "Come take my hands," Rachel gingerly put her hands in his and suddenly but gently Max pulled, the pain was unbearable, and Rachel uttered a cry and tears filled her eyes. Max sat her gently back into the chair. "Darling, please tell Max, this falling down the stairs will it ever stop?"

Max without further ado, postponed the interview till later in the day, contacted the BBC about the 'In Tune' programme and postponed that. He made several other calls and before she knew it Rachel was seated in yet another Wigmore Street consulting room. This time the young doctor was a pleasant, attractive and efficient lady of about forty. She was gentle and had x-rays of Rachel's tummy and ribs done in no time. She announced that Rachel had a cracked rib that would take about ten days to heal, as long as she had lots of rest and no physical exertion. She strapped Rachel up and bade her return in a week. Max flapped; the exhaustion of the night before banished by his natural concern for his 'Darling' client.

They got back to the house after noon. Rachel was disconsolate, she new Max was about to make her face the inevitable. She did not want to open up her secrets; she hoped that Max would not insist that she confessed her sins. There was an invisible and unbreakable barrier that locked out the world where Michael was involved. No matter what, it was no one's business but her own. If Michael was unfaithful – yes she knew he was -if Michael beat her – yes he did - if Michael loathed her music – yes he did - it was no one's business but her own.

She and only she knew that one day she would restore that idyllic love that had so engulfed them all those years ago. It was not Max or anyone else's business.

Chapter 24

Two weeks later, Rachel, despite her still sore ribs, prepared with Igor their 'two piano concert' in Paris. Igor was as brilliant as ever, and she felt he helped carry her through the programme with a musical affection that non musicians could never understand. She was modestly concerned that the hound-dog look of admiration that never left his face, and his constant pledges of undying love, were, nothing more than an adolescent prank.

During rehearsals, whilst Franek senior was present, Igor behaved in his staccato well mannered way, always smiling, his matted eyebrows twitching and making extravagant hand movements. When Franek senior was not in the room though he became surlier, she felt the chemistry of his desire thicken his diction, slow his hand movements and make him altogether more uncertain. Of course when he got to the piano he came alive and all his energies and his natural genius filled the room, it was here that Rachel could be at one with him. To be at one as she had never ever been before, it was without restraint, there was no holding back and the music rewarded them both. For Rachel this was perfection, this was music that tied their souls, it was beyond the physical, it was passionate and it was ecstatic.

Love? She loved the experience of making music with this sublime young talent, she loved the sheer exuberance of their playing together, and it was in a dimension that she had never lived before.

At once being perfect, but at the same time profoundly disturbing, she felt herself transmogrify his gorky image to one of affection and inevitably attraction; his huge grin, his wild though graceful hand movements, his lisping laugh, his animated eye brows, his gentle nervousness, his hesitant and hapless physical approaches.

Above all, she found his innocence irresistible. She felt an overpowering desire to take him in her arms and hold him and protect him from the world, a world where music was incidental, but where there were prowlers like Walmer, where money ruled, where there was daily violence, where passion could turn to poison in a trice.

This affection rolled over her, twisting her emotions and troubling her soul. Michael, what of Michael, she feared him but surely she loved him still. His great physicality, his gentleness and humour, the man who'd loved her like no other. In her confusion she still harked back to their early years, when they'd worked so hard and delighted in each other and devoured each other on those idyllic times between the frenetic building of their careers She remembered the sweet evils of the Walmers' parties, the hedonists who were ruthless but so glamorous.

Where oh where did she belong? She sat up late alone in her room, she had rung home but Michael was not there, she'd rung his cell phone but it was off. There was a knock at the door and there was Igor, hands thrust into his pockets, his eyes cast down, his fear and embarrassment palpable.

"Yes Igor, what is it."

"It isn't anything, but it is of course, my English is so.... so bad, Rachel I ...."

"Oh come in for goodness sake, don't stand in the corridor – where's your father?"

"Cghhee has gone to bed, he is sleeping now."

"And so should you be, we've got a long day tomorrow and I'm so looking forward to it."

"We will make music, and I will love you at the piano."

"You're so sweet Igor and I know what you mean, I love you too, we make the most glorious music, I can't help but love us as a pair at the two pianos. – but before we go any further you know I'm a married lady, ten years older than you, so love at the piano is all it will ever be – now be a good boy and go off to bed."

"I am not a boy," his voice was imploring, "I am a man and I love you in the piano, I love you as a man, Rachel you know I love you."

Tears filled his eyes and he tried to look away, but Rachel reached forward and gently rubbed his tears away with her thumbs, gently holding his sobbing face in her hands, and before she could think, she kissed him, kissed him on the mouth. She tasted him, as his overeager tongue pushed hers aside, despite herself, she relaxed and bade him be patient.

And so their passion grew and Rachel took him gently and sweetly to herself. She lay him down, undressed him easily, smoothed his chest, kissed his nipples, and nursed him so that his anxiety did not overtake them. The crescendo of their meeting was not for her, but she watched with pure joy as Igor, for perhaps the first time in his short life, life was complete. It was her gift to him, as close as they were in music, she was close now as close as two humans can be. He slept and when they came together again there was more harmony and Rachel let him take the lead and it was good.

She felt him slink away in the early hours, she knew he was racked with desire, but fear of his father, at least for now, would keep him in check. She lay there watching the grey dawn seep through her hotel window. Rachel was full of joy, of sorrow and fear all at once. Poor Igor, he was only a boy and yet she had seduced him, taken him to her bed and fed him with all her passion – should she be ashamed? The concert tonight, working together, would it be the same? Michael did she love him after all? Should she tell him? Would he understand? She shivered and caught a glimpse of his jealous snarl; she couldn't sleep so she got up and showered though the Parisian streets were hardly awake.

The rehearsal was at ten, she breakfasted with Maria, the MIL French representative. She was always at home in France and with the language. She relaxed as best she could, but the apprehension she felt of seeing Igor again made her fingers shake, her tummy turn, she had no idea how he would be.

At the same time she couldn't wait to see him, he was probably pounding the pavements with his Dad. She hoped fervently that Franek Senior had no idea of what went on last night.

She need not have worried, the rehearsal with the orchestra at the Salle Pleyel was a delight, their music making was as explosive and exciting as ever, perhaps more so. After the Orchestra packed up, they went through their encores, and broke at twelve thirty. Maria invited both the Franeks to lunch, and much to everyone's delight, Jan Franek excused himself. They dined at a Brasserie not far from the Concert Hall just off Place des Ternes, the day was warm, the sun shone and Paris was Paris, they sat at a table on the pavement; to passers by, the young man was observed as having lunch with two beautiful women, Rachel the younger, Maria perhaps in her middle thirties and full of Gallic charm and poise. Of course they talked of music, and the rest of the Mozart tour, the itineraries of Rachel and Igor as they were to go their separate ways. Igor was animated and happy, Maria made some light hearted quips about the two pianists being a partnership made in heaven. Rachel laughed and watched as Igor blushed a lurid pink.

Maria took her leave at around two thirty, leaving Rachel and Igor to stroll back to their hotel Rachel felt the excitement in her grow as their hands touched as they walked along, and then their hands were intertwined, searching, reaching for each other.. They separated as they reached the hotel lobby,

"I'm going to have a shower and then a nap, I'll see you at six," her voice was thick with nerves, her proposition, for that's what it was, hung in the air – out there at risk of language fog, and inexperience. Would he follow her? Her knees trembled, she hoped he wouldn't get his own key.

Igor was about to ask the concierge for his key, "Leave that Igor." Rachel almost blurted out, "I need to talk to you about a new score I'm studying."

They walked swiftly to the elevators, and thence to Rachel's suite. This time there was no gentleness, this time there was raw desire.   He was inexhaustible, and she eventually shooed him from her room at around four fifteen. After he had left, Rachel knew only one thing; she was happy, happier than perhaps she'd ever been.

The limousine picked up the party, Maria, Jan, Igor and Rachel and took them the short distance to the Rue du Faubourg Saint Honoré. There were already crowds outside and the paparazzi were gathered outside the artists' entrance, the concert was a sell-out, the buzz was unmistakable. Rachel wore a plain black gown with pearl necklace and ear rings and despite the severity of her dress she looked ravishing. Igor wore a traditional white tie though with a short jacket, somehow she thought he looked so much more mature than the boy she'd gone to bed with last night.

The concert was a smash by any standards, it exceeded even the Vienna concert and Rachel felt so exhilarated she felt she could burst. This man, this lover , this boy had once more transcended any musical experience she had ever experienced, they had come as close to perfection in musical terms as Rachel thought it was possible to go. Even Franek Senior gave her a great big hug, and much to Rachel's delight Max Luberoff had sneaked in unannounced to the concert.

The post concert party was a mix of a wild press conference and a gourmand's delight. Max was really at his most excited, bow tie askew and eyes racing their unending circuits. Igor's French, whilst not as good as Rachel's, was better than she had expected, it was indeed as good if not better than his English. She was astonished that despite their intimacy of the last few days and their trip to Vienna she hadn't taken this in, French being his accomplished third language. From now on she knew that there would be another bond, the bond of the beautiful language of France.

That night she waited, and then at two o'clock he came, and they made love with very few words, they slumbered and loved once more as the new dark day dawned. They both knew they must say good bye, at least for now. She shushed him, no need for words. Their tears melted together, afraid that their meeting in London would never ever happen, afraid that the perfection of their union would be snuffed out in an imperfect world. They bade farewell, and Igor crept off to his room, not looking forward one jot to running round Paris with his father.

Chapter 25

During the journey back to London Rachel felt an emptiness she had seldom if ever experienced. She was conscious of her journeying North whilst she knew that Igor was travelling South West, away from her, at every moment they were that many more miles apart. Max beside her babbled on about how things were going faster and better than he could have hoped.

"Darling, they'll be crying out for you, already I've had enquiries about extending your North American Tours, they want you in Toronto and they're considering putting you on the bill in Chicago, maybe with the great man himself."

Even thoughts of Barenboim failed to elicit a response from Rachel.

"What's the matter Liebe, are you not excited like Max?"

"I'm tired Max, just tired."

"I hope Max is wrong but I think I know why eh?"

"Because Max I am working so hard."

"I hope so; Max is thinking maybe you are mothering the young Polish gentleman." He giggled, "maybe you in love with his instrument." He cackled.

"Max I wish you wouldn't be so crude; you always reduce everything to the gutter, shut up and let me rest."

Rachel closed her eyes, she knew she had given herself away and Max as usual had seen straight through her. What of Michael, would he? Her mixed feeling jostled through her, fear, shame, love, confusion and misery. Why couldn't life be more simple? Why was Igor so young? Why had she not met him before? Did she love Michael? She tried to sleep.

Eventually she made it home and after unpacking went straight to the studio and her beloved Becky. There she tried her hardest to concentrate on the Schuman Concerto; try as she might her ears strained for the sound of the front door and Michael's return. This was impossible anyway through the soundproof studio door, but she kept on listening. Would she be able to face him? What would she feel when she saw him? Time passed.

It was not unusual for Michael to be late, nor was it unusual for him not to leave a note or telephone. There was nothing to do but wait. At seven thirty she rang his office, there was no reply; hesitantly she rang his mobile and it was switched off. She made coffee, had some biscuits and sat down watching invisible TV.

Ten o'clock, she was bone tired, nervous, exhausted in every way, should she stay up to welcome Michael home, she fell asleep in the sitting room.

She was awakened by a loud noise as Michael, Sarah and a man Rachel had never seen before made a chaotic entrance into the sitting room.

"What oh! My lovely piano player, waiting up for your hard working old man eh!"

Michael reached down and kissed her, his breath stale with God knows how much alcohol, he was very drunk. "Let me introduce you to Sami Tolba, he's an Egyptian colleague of mine; the delicious Sarah," he hiccupped, "you know." He leered at her. "Come on darling, where's the Brandy?" He lurched to the drinks cabinet, Sarah smiled with a hint of sympathy.

"Coffee, I'll make some coffee, by the way what's the time?"

"Quarter after three," mumbled the plump Egyptian, "maybe I better get back to my hotel."

"We'll have a coffee first and then we'll slip away, Sami and we'll leave these love birds to it." Sarah sounded bored; her smile was that of a woman who has to tread the mill one more time.

"No, no, let's have another brandy, it's bloody good stuff, come on old boy, come on Sarah, the night is young." Michael slumped into his chair, his body language belying his ambition for more night time frolics.

Rachel brought in the coffee, and true to her word Sarah shepherded her charge away, and she was left with Michael in his drunken state, lying, slumped dangerous as a wild animal. Would he sleep? Would he demand her body, or would he pick a fight? Rachel shook and held her arms about her, she closed her eyes, 'Please, please if you are up there, let him sleep.'

It was not to be.

"Well my little piano player how was your Polish geek? Fucking you yet, is he?"

"Michael it's too late for this, let's go to bed."

"Answer me you little bitch, are you screwing him like all those other musical whimps, come on show me how you make them happy." He dragged Rachel by her arm to the bedroom. There he held her by both arms against the wall, he began to slobber over her, suddenly Rachel could take it no more.

She fought with all her might, but she was no match for Michael's strength, then suddenly she blurted out, "All right Michael, he is screwing me, he screwed me all last night and this morning, and you know what, I loved it, I love him, so fuck you."

She was not sure what she felt first, was it the blow of his knee in her crotch, or the explosion of his fist in her face? He rained blows down on her, tearing at her clothes, she felt the blood rush down her nose, the sharp crack of her ribs, then she was on the floor, and she felt the crunching of his black brogue shoe into her chest and then nothing – nothing, it was over.

She woke, but could barely see, except the blood red inside of her eyelid, it hurt to try to open it. Her hands, she felt the destruction, the splinters, the throbbing as the blood tried to course its way through her battered limbs. Her side was stiff with daggers grating on her ribs, and worst of all she felt the nausea rise. She could not move. Then something moved beyond her and a gentle arm raised her slowly on what seemed to be a pillow.

"Mrs Johnson, Mrs Johnson" a gentle female voice, "can you hear me?"

With enormous effort Rachel opened one eye, she shut it almost immediately blinded by the brilliant white of the hospital intensive care ward. She was safe.

"I'll give you something to make you sleep, you're safe now, we'll look after you, your husband and your mother have been along, but no visitors today, sleep now."

The soft cloud of sleep, and time stopped once more. Again she woke, again they sent her back to sleep, and time stood still until she opened her eyes and smelt the flowers by her bed, and saw the tubes and paraphernalia of the clinic ward. Who was that? It was Robbie sitting ashen white, his head now so old cradled in his city clean hands. Other than Robbie there was just the nurse, who seeing Rachel awake, came over straight away, "Welcome back Rachel, I'll get you something to moisten your mouth and the doctor will be along right away."

Robbie awake now, took her wounded arm, in plaster from elbow to fingers. She noticed for the first time, straining to look to her right, that her other arm was set in plaster as well.

"My darling girl, I know it's true but tell me that it's not," tears welled in his eyes, "the police arrested Michael the day before yesterday, he's been charged with your attempted murder, my darling child what can I say. Tania is in denial of course- but damn it I knew things weren't right and I turned a blind eye, how can you ever forgive us, and Michael my lovely boy," he shuddered and tears poured down his kind face, he was heartbroken. Rachel wanted to hold him. To say, no it's my fault, but she couldn't speak.

Robbie got shakily to his feet, "You know I loved you as my daughter, I would have gladly died for you and for Michael, he had everything," his head shook and he began to weep again. "I must go, please forgive me." She saw him leave her line of vision and her heart ached for that lovely man, her father in law.

The nurses came in and helped rearrange her bed, check her drips and disconnect some of the complicated equipment surrounding her. Then the doctor came, a tall willowy man with large spectacles and black, greying hair, who looked sharp and efficient.

Rachel felt alive but little more, there was discomfort or pain everywhere. She was aware though and could hear and understand, but for some reason couldn't talk.

"May I call you Rachel? I'm Doctor Wilkin, Brian Wilkin and I'm the senior registrar here at the Portman Clinic. First, don't try and speak because we've wired your jaw."
His hand reached for her ankle, the left one, the other leg was plastered to her hip," I'm taking your pulse, you're so covered with plaster it's hard to find a site." He smiled reassuringly. He shone a light into her eye, "You've taken a very bad beating, I'm afraid, so it's going to be a long job, but you're a very fit young woman and you'll be fine. I want you to blink with your right eye to say yes, and blink twice to say no OK?"

She blinked once.

"Good, well I needn't catalogue all your injuries but they are extensive; both arms and hands, one broken femur, at least five broken ribs, broken jaw, hairline fracture of your skull and some damage to your spleen. It's going to take some time and it's going to take a lot of guts from you; I can help you if you let me and my colleagues. Understand?"

She blinked once.

"Patients have to be patient, first rule, second rule, call every time you need help, you're out of intensive care, but still with staff on watch twenty four hours a day, so press the buzzer every time you need anything from a bed pan to a drink OK?"

She blinked once.

"We'll put a pressure pad under your right elbow and we'll make sure you can press it easily OK?"

The nurse placed the buzzer just under her right elbow. "OK, now press."

She did and she heard the loud and reassuring buzz.

The enormity of her shattered body began to penetrate through the drugs, the excruciating pain, the agony of being unable to move, the surrender of herself to these unknown helpers. And so the hours and the days passed, so slowly, a second at a time. Visitors came and went, they cried, they tutted, they were just plain embarrassed. Each day she became a little clearer, each day she pieced together the catastrophe of Michael's jealousy, her own guilt, her own misery.

For the first time in years her father visited her, not just once, but on a daily basis. She could not stop him as each day he railed and ranted about Michael, her lovely Michael, now locked away, barred from seeing her. How she wanted to see him, to let him hold her like they used to be.

After three weeks her jaw was unwired and she was allowed to speak, though moving her jaw at all was very difficult. She suffered the indignities of the patient medical routine, the cranking up of her cradle, the massage of her tender behind, the enemas, the x-rays and scans, the interminable poking and prodding by an endless procession of medics.

Her mother came rarely, and when she did, she said little. She just sat there sobbing, hopelessly fiddling with her handkerchief. When she did speak it was about a world about which Rachel knew next to nothing. Rachel could do nothing other than fade into sleep every time mother came.

The only time she felt alive was when Max came, he gabbled on about the future, he referred to "this falling down the stairs" infrequently, " the diary my darling, the diary we must watch, I am telling these people that I want dates, and soon they will give me dates."

Hope raised its limp hand when Max came, but as the days dripped painfully by, she knew with ever increasing certainty that 'the diary of engagements' would never be full again.

As weeks went by and casts were removed, her strength returned but slowly, so slowly, there were more operations on her hands and arm, reconstructive surgery they called it. Now her plaster casts were replaced by dressings and braces, her fingers lay yellowed and with prehensile nails curving up like some old nicotine stained crone.

But still Max came, and still he prattled on about the future, the future that was not to be.

And still in those dimly lit nights she lay alone, her arms strangely suspended, the sounds of nurses clattering along the corridors, she thought of Michael and cried silently, and missed him as much as she missed Becky. She dreamt of Igor sitting at the other piano as she played without arms and hands, Igor played all the parts at once. Then as she received the bouquet, the flowers fell to the floor, she had nothing to hold them, no arms, no hands, and the audience cheered and clapped and laughed.

When Bertie Frobisher came, he was awkward and embarrassed. He held an extraordinary bunch of flowers in one hand and his attaché case in the other. He didn't seem to know what to do, whether to put down the flowers or his case. He eventually tipped his load onto a chair and approached Rachel and stalled at the bedside.

"Bertie darling you won't break me – any more than I'm already broken anyway, come and give me a kiss."

He pecked her on the cheek.

"How are you, Rachel…. look this is awful and we're all very sad about it …. what's the doctor say?"

"Well Bertie, except for my hands and my left arm things are so much better I hope to be let out of here in a week or two, so we're making progress. They've been wonderful really and everyone has been terrific, but they won't let me see Michael. How is he?"

Bertie looked down. "Look old girl, you know that Michael nearly killed you."

"Yes, but it was my fault Bertie, I cheated on him, I didn't mean to." she started to cry.

"Don't cry my dear, as you know the police wanted to prefer charges against him, but that's now been withdrawn, as I understand you've refused to swear a complaint or testify in any way. It's been very difficult for him. I know there's no excuse for what he did, but I believe he loved you, still does I dare say.... any way he's been fired again and Robbie has taken charge and had him sent for psychiatric treatment. I'm not sure what that will mean, but.... Rachel you shouldn't see him again, it wouldn't work, I don't pretend to understand it but that's it, I'm afraid."

"We just loved each other too much."

"What about the future, will you carry on playing?"

"They haven't told me yet, but I know I'll never play a recital again, who knows I may not be able to play at all. I'll be glad when they tell me, at least we'll stop all this pretence, dear old Max keeps coming to see me and talks a lot of tosh about my engagement diary."

There was a silence, Bertie shuffled in his bag,

"Look my dear, Robbie has settled a compensation package, he won't hear of anything else, it will make sure you'll be comfortable, you have the house and you can keep it or sell it, and you'll have all the medical support you need."

"I don't want a bloody settlement; I want Michael and me to be as we were."

Bertie coughed, he shuffled his feet, "Michael is offering to co-operate with your divorce action, and has promised the court he will not approach you again; he's the subject of an order, so he can't see you …. even if he wants to, honestly Rachel he's not well and everyone thinks you should make a clean break."

"Thank you Bertie, I'm tired, give my love to everyone."

Bertie shuffled out.

They unbound her right arm, and each day she underwent physiotherapy, but from the outset she knew her fingers were detached, paralysed and unresponsive, they didn't work and they would never work. You only had to look at them, her formerly beautiful hand was gnarled, the scars of surgery, red and ugly, the tendons prominent, the muscle wasted, they were wrecked in the true sense of the word. Her left hand was less damaged and as she walked out of the clinic seven weeks to the day after her admission, it was Max who was at her side.

"Come on Max, let's have some lunch, a big fat steak and some of your feisty wine, there's nothing for me to worry about, no diary, no practice and Max, will we be friends?"

Max stopped at the taxi's threshold, "mein Liebe, Max will always love you and somehow, we will make music again," his eyes rolled trying to dissipate the tears.

All Igor's letters were in French. He was so fluent that it was hard to recognise the diffident and unsure boy from these strident and beautifully scripted letters. He was only vaguely aware of Rachel's accident as he had been tremendously busy working across Europe, Israel, and the Russian Federation. He was aware of the postponement of the "In the steps of Mozart" series; he confessed his undying love for her over and over again.

The letters had been delivered via MIL and Max had cheerfully delivered the missives She read them over and over and as she did she felt the music in them, inaudible but alive. She knew Igor was an episode from the past, an impossible dream. They would never share music together again – that perfect music. Now the silence of the days slammed her shut in the prison without music. Music had been like blood in her veins, music that flowed through her hands; now useless and locked in their infirmity.

Sally Nye visited and encouraged Rachel to keep up the therapy and to come to the Royal College and perhaps become an associate. Rachel asked for time, but inside her there was only the blackness of grief, the grief that killed all enthusiasm. Sometimes when she slept she dreamed..... perhaps...perhaps she could see Michael again, and by some miracle play JS and stand before an adoring audience and inhale the joy that her music had created.

Daddy had made sure she had her pound of flesh, and in return he had lessened his demands for Michael to be prosecuted or at least publicly humiliated. No one assaulted the daughter or any other asset of Sir Lewis George without appropriate compensation. Sir Lewis saw everything in terms of dollars and cents, pounds and pennies, even his daughter's life and worth.

Inevitably Max's visits became fewer, and it was her stepmother Jacqui George who befriended her, she called regularly, took her out often when Rachel did not really want to go shopping or for supper. She cared for her in a manner that Rachel found superficial; she attended to Rachel's make up for example when Rachel could not have cared less.

Rachel grieved for Michael; she grieved for her music as she lived in an icy silence, a dark place where neither Jacqui nor anyone else could enter. Lady George though was tough, tough and generous, she knew grief, she knew how hard the world could be and so as the weeks and months went by she continued her visits, her jolly little dinners out, her jokes about men, and sometimes, she took her stepdaughter's hand and sat patiently by as Rachel wept or stared into the blackness of her depression.

Igor's letters now came directly to her, she had responded on a number of occasions. In her replies, she minimised her own misery, made light of her injuries and pretended that her rehabilitation was only months away. She encouraged Igor, and lived for news of him and his music. She listened to his every concert, every disc or radio broadcast. Her love for his music was a small light in her darkened world.

Her injuries did indeed get better, she could play the piano once again, nothing like before, but she could find solace in the simpler music she could handle. Her hands no longer could span ten notes, she could no longer fly up and down the keys, she could no longer play for more than a few minutes before her hands and arms felt utter exhaustion. She could listen though, and she read performances as perhaps others would read a story. Each pause, each note dwelt on or diminished was like a work or even a colour that whoever played made his own. Her own musical memory was as acute as ever, it was just the way to the keys was forever blocked by her useless hands and arms.

The arrival of Mr and Mrs Hugo Love was her first really happy day, Josie heavily pregnant with Hugo heavily shapeless as ever, but both of them so radiant in their happiness. Josie, the hopeless tramp of music school days now a woman in love, utterly fulfilled by the shapeless man and the life in her belly. How things had changed from that Christmas so long ago when Michael had abused Josie on that Christmas Eve. How the wheels had turned and how Michael had turned them. Amongst all the joy and sorrow, the joy and the tears Michael had been the angel and the beast and she had loved them both.

Her old life was for ever gone, the only connection was that Rachel still visited 'Hands' and Bettie still philosophised about life in general and men in particular. Bettie was a strength, a listener, a constant friend rather like a friendly pillow where Rachel could lay her head.

"Well my love," Bettie was working her wonders on Rachel's shoulders, "it must be nearly a year now since your accident, it's time you were out and about my girl."

"Out and about, where? I'm thinking about teaching again, but I don't know, my hands still aren't up to much, but I suppose I can teach. Sally wants me to work at the College on theory and interpretation but I think she's doing it just to help, I can't remember my tutors not illustrating their thoughts on the keyboard. But music is all I know, I'm a bit like a blind rifleman, lots of knowledge but no way to deliver – any way Bettie, I'm going to a very special concert next week, Igor Franek is playing at the Queen Elizabeth Hall, a fantastic programme of classic and modern, can't wait."

"That'll be lovely I'm sure, will you get to see your man then, will y'u."

"No Bettie, no good digging up old wounds, I'll just lap up the music, that'll do for me."

Chapter 26

Igor's programme was typically brave and very demanding. Rachel couldn't wait to hear him play. She had received a phone call from Igor's agent inviting her to the recital, but she had turned down the invitation on the grounds that she would be out of town. Her feelings were still confused, she still held herself responsible for the 'sin' of her adultery and the collapse of her world with Michael.

Igor the boy, Igor the pianist, had she loved one or both of them? All she knew now, a painful year on, was that she had lost everything; everything she had loved had been consigned to another world, a world she was excluded from – forever.

In the year that had passed since she limped from the clinic, she had hesitated on the brink of suicide. She had fondled the bottles of morphine she had secreted from the clinic. She had planned in the midst of her horrendous pain, and foregone those little white pills and the relief they would bring, to stay in hellish pain, saving for the day she could end it all. Night after night she had wept and stared into the silent misery without love and without music. She barely heard the light smaltzy encouragement of her step mother, even the visit of Josie and Hugo had been like a movie she had watched rather than taken part in. She was locked in her silent glass box, outside the world went on, whilst inside the emptiness was infinite.

Now, despite herself, she bought a ticket and would go like a thief in the night to Igor's recital. When the day came she spent the morning in the studio reading all the scores, picking out the themes and then strenuously analysing the moods and sounds of these masterpieces. At the end of several hours study she felt exhausted, but perhaps for the first time there was a glimmer of light. She knew what she wanted to hear, she knew what she wanted Igor to deliver. Not in all the works, but she could hear within herself the magic moments where Igor would stun the multitude. Then she knew that she was looking forward to hearing this boy, this lover, this genius and it would go some way to fulfilling her, go some way to making her alive again.

She dressed in a Burberry mackintosh, dark slacks and her hair covered in a plain black bandana, she wore no make-up and no jewellery. She agonized over what time to call the taxi as she didn't want to get to the Hall too early or too late. She feared, she knew not why, that she would be recognized. By whom she didn't know. She debated with herself whether to take scores with her and decided against it. She didn't answer the telephone all day lest she was discovered as a teller of lies. When she eventually set out as anonymously dressed as she could possibly be, her whole being shook with nerves. She wanted to be unseen, but at the same time she hoped she would be discovered and somehow meet Igor again.

The recital was a sell out. Igor's reputation was already highly regarded internationally. He was known to be an innovative and brave soloist with incomparable technique.

Tonight's programme was typical, very demanding and a mix of styles and composers that would tax even the greatest exponents.

Rachel took her seat about five minutes before the recital was to start; it was warm, she removed her coat and felt self conscious in her slacks and plain white blouse. Her neighbours were unremarkable and she contented herself in reading the programme that extolled the soloist and detailed his programme.

After what seemed an interminable delay Igor appeared looking surprisingly dapper in a white Tuxedo and black tie. The applause died and the Liszt rhapsody engulfed the Hall. From the first note it was electric, stunning, an old war horse of a piece given new life. It was magnificent, full of bravura, subtle contrasts and incredible precision. The Funeral March in the Beethoven, so measured, so solemn yet so beautiful. The Brahms waltzes by contrast magnificently ebullient and the Schumann absolutely dazzling.

Yet it was the encores that captured Rachel, first a Scarlatti sonata and then pure Franek; a Mozart theme from his music for two pianos, variations so stunning, so complex that they combined the musical jokes of their rehearsal in Saltsburg. There was no doubt he was speaking to her directly. It was a love song of musical genius, a musical reminiscence from one lover to another, and despite its intensely personal nature the audience stood and cheered and stamped, for the South Bank had seldom heard such passion and brilliance.

For Rachel, her heart burst with happiness, and when the music stopped it burst with agony. Igor had shown her what could have been, but was no more. She wiped away the tears and trouped out pulling on her coat against the crisp night air. She felt that she had seen all she wanted to, she received the grace of music and Igor had anointed her with the ultimate gift of musical love. There settled on her a peace she had not known for so long. Within herself, she didn't hear the man hail her, "Miss George is that you?"

She tumbled into her taxi and dwelt on that wonderful encore all the way home. When she got there the phone was ringing, but she didn't answer. She went to the studio and picked out Igor's melodies, and then she played a little simple prelude of JS. She closed the studio door, walked to her lonely bed, stopping to take the cognac bottle and those little white pills with her. Her eyes closed, Igor's music fading so sweetly as the light shone for the last time on her brilliant stage.

Chapter 27

In the national broadsheets two days later, the obituary of Rachel George-Johnson figured prominently. The Times spoke of a musical star crashing from the firmament; others compared her loss to that of Jacqueline Duprés so many years earlier. The BBC ran a programme of her recordings and that was interspersed with commentaries from Sally Nye, Max Luberoff and Jamo Jadesjo. Her funeral was held in St Martin's in the Field where many of her friends gathered and paid their most sombre but loving tributes, and so the curtain fell on what may have been the most glorious musical career of the century.

Michael Johnson read of his wife's death in his room at the Stacey Clinic. He had been committed to be detained "until the court could be assured that he was no longer a risk", and despite the influence of his father, the charges brought against him on two counts of assault and one of manslaughter still hung over him like the sword of Damocles. The charges were not related only to Rachel but to other crimes, all against ladies who frequented the darkness of his nights.

Little Emma, his baby sister, still visited him in his dreams, staring up from her watery grave; he counted the brown pots and the green pots till he slept, but then, so often he woke again crying and cursing that Rachel had been taken from him, for he had loved her like no other.

About the the Author.

Anthony James is a Welshman whose published works include:

"Smiles in Africa": A novel about white commercial domination in Nigeria in the seventies.

"My Boy" A memoir:- A story of an imperfect father coming to terms with the death of his imperfect son.

"The Poisoned Banquet" – A novel about a celebrity battered wife.

Under construction :"The Psychedelic Traveller" A collection of short stories from around the world.

Contact: **Anthony@anthony-james.net**

Web page: www.Anthony-james.net